Praise for Synithia Williams's Jackson Falls series

Scandalous Secrets

A *Publishers Weekly* Buzz Books 2020 Romance Selection!

An Amazon Best Romance Book of the Month!

A *Woman's World* Romance Book Club Selection!

"Fans of second chances, reconnecting friends, friends-to-lovers, and political romance stories will enjoy this book."

—*Harlequin Junkie*

Forbidden Promises

"The perfect escape. *Forbidden Promises* is a deeply felt, engrossing, soapy romance that manages to both luxuriate in its angst, while also interrogating something far more wide-reaching and universal than the admittedly sexy taboo appeal of its central conceit."

—*Entertainment Weekly*

"Emotions, relationships and business are tangled in this soap opera-esque tale, and readers will find themselves unable to look away from Williams' well-drawn and larger-than-life characters. It's impossible not to enjoy this entertaining glimpse into a world of wealth, political ambition and familial loyalties."

—*BookPage*

"A romance for readers looking for equal parts passion and family drama."

—*Kirkus Reviews*

"Fans of Elle Wright and Jamie Pope will be seduced by this charming and passionate family saga."

—*Booklist*

"Politics, passion, and family drama combine to make a deliciously soapy second-chance, brother's-best-friend romance. Readers of Alisha Rai's Forbidden Hearts series or Reese Ryan's *Engaging the Enemy* will be tantalized and surprised by the many twists and turns."

—*Library Journal*

Also by Synithia Williams

Forbidden Promises
The Promise of a Kiss
Scandalous Secrets

For additional books by Synithia Williams,
visit her website, www.synithiawilliams.com.

Look for Synithia Williams's new novel,
Foolish Hearts,
the next sexy and irresistible book in the Jackson Falls series
featuring the Robidoux family
available soon from HQN.

SYNITHIA WILLIAMS

Careless WHISPERS

ISBN-13: 978-1-335-41998-9

Careless Whispers

This edition published by arrangement with Harlequin Books S.A.

For questions and comments about the quality of this book, please contact us at CustomerService@Harlequin.com.

HQN
22 Adelaide St. West, 40th Floor
Toronto, Ontario M5H 4E3, Canada
www.Harlequin.com

Printed in Spain

Recycling programs
for this product may
not exist in your area.

To Eric and my boys.
I love you, even when you break a vase while I'm writing.

Careless
WHISPERS

CHAPTER ONE

ELAINA ROBIDOUX STEPPED into her sleeveless black sheath dress. She shimmied her hips as the cool material slid across her skin and she slipped the dress up. Reaching behind her, she struggled to grab the zipper before a larger hand pushed hers aside.

"I've got you, baby." Robert's deep voice flowed over her like the satin lining of her dress.

She'd promised herself she wouldn't let him see how happy she was they'd reunited. Wouldn't reveal how much she'd needed a win in the relationship department, but after the sexy night they'd just had, she couldn't stop herself from grinning over her shoulder. "You've got me?"

He zipped her dress and ran his hands up and down her arm. "You know it." He pulled her against his chest and kissed her neck. "Can't you stay longer?"

Elaina glanced at the unmade bed in their hotel room. If only she could stay. These moments with Robert were the one good thing in her life. Robert was the "one who got away." The guy she'd fallen in love with years ago when she was too young to appreciate a good guy over the allure of the bad boy. They'd debated books, movies and politics. He'd challenged her on everything without caring that she was a Robidoux and most people let her get away with being demanding. Before she knew it, she started anxiously sitting around waiting for him to call.

Then she'd gotten pregnant by the first guy who'd made her feel passion and soon after announced an engagement rather than besmirch her family's name. The pregnancy, and later the marriage, had both ended. The former in heartbreak, the latter way too late.

Robert had moved on, married and divorced, and was now frequently visiting Raleigh, North Carolina, which wasn't far from her home in Jackson Falls, to follow up on potential business deals. She didn't know the specifics of his business dealings. They hadn't reconnected based on business. Their reconnection had been almost coincidental. She'd learned he was divorced thanks to a nostalgia-fueled trip down a social media rabbit hole, then attended the conference he'd mentioned looking forward to, and they'd run into each other at the bar.

The coincidence had been the bar. She hadn't *known* he'd be there at that time, so her surprise had been genuine. His interest in reconnecting was as welcome as ice water in a desert after being so unhappy in relationships for so long. They'd started their affair that week and kept it going off and on for months.

After years of disappointments, she hadn't wanted to feel too much anticipation about their reunion. Robert traveled to Raleigh often, and Elaina came over whenever he was in town. Despite her efforts to keep things strictly physical, she was well and truly in a state of deep infatuation with Robert.

"I wish I could stay longer." Elaina eased her head to the side, giving Robert better access to her throat. "I'm expected home. Family stuff."

Her brother, Byron, had unsuccessfully run for the U.S. Senate but easily won the race for Jackson Falls mayor two years later. Her brother's political career combined with her dad's business connections meant multiple requirements for the family to show support at some event or another. Today it was a garden party to thank donors of Byron's political campaign. Elaina would have to break multiple North Carolina traffic laws to get home in time to shower and change. She hadn't brought anything with her when Robert called the evening before to let her know he was in Raleigh and wanted to see her. She'd put on a sexy dress, grabbed her purse and raced down the highway.

She would not think about how pathetic and lonely she would have accused anyone else of being for doing the same.

"Do you think you'll be able to come back tonight?" Robert's lips brushed across the sensitive spot on her neck. He was taller than her, with sandy skin, and green eyes that used to mesmerize her. Her dad once called Robert a pretty boy. An assessment she attributed to her dad's usual attempts to push her in the direction he'd preferred.

Once they'd reconnected, she'd begrudgingly admitted to herself that her dad may have been right. Robert's suits were expensive, his car pricey and his tastes high-end. All things he didn't mind letting people know about but Elaina was willing to overlook his arrogance, because he still didn't back down when they debated, and the sex was amazing.

"I wish, but this thing will go late, and I do need to be in the office on Monday." She regretfully pulled herself away from him and walked to the dresser. She picked up her diamond earrings. "You'll be back next week, right?"

Did she sound desperate? She hoped she didn't sound desperate. Elaina Robidoux didn't chase after a man.

Tell that to your gas light.

She pushed aside the reminder. Her gas light had come on when she was ten minutes away from the hotel. She'd ignored it in her haste to get to Robert, which meant she'd have to stop on her way home.

Robert cringed and rubbed his hands together. "I don't know."

She slipped an earring into her right ear. "Okay, the following weekend, then?"

Robert shrugged. "I'm not sure when I'll be back."

Elaina stilled. "Not sure." Her voice didn't betray any of her sudden paranoia. She turned her back to Robert as she slipped the other earring into her ear.

"The investors I thought I'd have for my business venture didn't pan out." He paused for a heartbeat. "I don't have a reason to keep coming back."

No reason? Her heart raced, and a cold sweat broke out over her skin. Elaina frowned as she lifted her multistrand gold necklace. "Oh, really?" she asked in a cool voice. She fastened her necklace and schooled her features to the bland expression she'd perfected before facing Robert again. "Does that mean the end of us?"

"It doesn't have to be," Robert said. His lips lifted into a nervous smile. "You know I want to keep this going."

"What are you proposing?" She crossed her arms and watched him while her pulse fluttered. She was being a romantic. Of course he wasn't proposing something serious, but a part of her, a foolish part, wished he'd ask her to move back to Atlanta with him. Not because she was in love with Robert, but to start her life over. To have hope she could get back what she'd lost when she'd been young, impulsive and ridiculously rebellious.

"I need seventy-five thousand dollars," Robert said.

Elaina blinked. Seventy-five what? "Excuse me?"

"Just to start out," he continued. He ran a hand over his dark, curly hair. "If things go well, I can pay you back in a year. Though you'll be a partner and might want to consider increasing your investment."

The request for money was so far from what she'd expected that it took several seconds for the audacity of the statement to filter through the confused fog in her brain. He was seriously asking her for money? "What exactly am I investing in? You haven't given specifics about your business."

Robert's eyes lit up. She recognized that look. Greed. He thought he had her on the hook. "I'm opening a beauty supply store."

"You can't be serious." Wasn't he in finance? At least, she'd thought he'd said finance. Admittedly they hadn't gotten deep into discussions of their work in between the hasty, tear-each-other's-clothes-off meetups they'd had.

"I'm serious. I know a guy who has a hookup on premium hair I can get at a discount. He's been selling it out of his car for now, but once I get a storefront, he'll start supplying me. I've got another friend who has a connection with hair care products and supplies. I just need the initial money to get started."

Elaina held up a hand, her brain spinning with what she'd just heard. "You need seventy-five thousand dollars to set up a beauty supply store with hair and supplies you're buying from bootleggers?"

"None of this is bootleg stuff. It's the real deal. They just get it." He waved a hand and shrugged. "Before it leaves the truck."

Elaina pressed her fingers to her temple. Tension radiated through her neck and jaw. She was getting a headache. "I thought you were in finance."

"I was before my divorce. She took everything, and I'm starting over. As much money as she used to spend on her hair—" he scoffed and shook his head "—this was a good way to make my money back."

Elaina dropped her hand and studied him, but there were

no signs this was a joke. No suppressed laughter or mischievous twinkle. His eyes were serious and eager. "Robert, I'm not giving you seventy-five thousand dollars to start a beauty supply store."

The excited gleam in his eye dimmed. He took a step back. "Why not?"

"Because I'm not interested in investing in a beauty supply store."

"I guess that means you don't want to see me again, either." He lifted his chin and threw out the words like a challenge.

Elaina's spine stiffened. "Is that what this was all about?" She pointed to the bed. "You hoped I would give you money?"

"That wasn't everything," he said quickly.

Despite her irritation, a spark of hope flared. "What was the other thing?"

"I've always wanted to sleep with you," he said without flinching.

The words were like a kick to the gut from a champion kickboxer. Hard, fast and lethal. Her stomach muscles clenched, and she swallowed hard. Disappointment weighed so heavily on her she wanted to sink to the floor. But she wasn't the type of person to sink. Not in situations like this.

She straightened her shoulders and returned his stare. "Well, at least we both got that out of our systems." She picked up her purse. "Goodbye, Robert."

He hurried across the room and blocked her exit. "Come on, now, Elaina. What did you think this was?"

"Not an attempt for you to get money from me," she said in a cool voice.

"I wasn't initially going to ask you for the money, but you've got it. Your family's company is always looking for investments. Why not invest in me?" he asked like a petulant child.

"Helping you sell hair that your friend has in his trunk isn't that appealing." She sidestepped him. "Don't call me again."

Robert's disbelieving laugh stopped her. "So you're dismissing me again."

She spun around toward him. "Dismissing you? You're the one who threw out the ultimatum. Give me money or go?"

He held up his hands and dared to look offended. "I don't know why you're acting surprised, Elaina. You didn't want to give me the time of day when we were younger because you were caught up with that thug your dad took in. Now, because he left you and married your sister, you think you can just call me up, sleep with me, and then we're going to be a couple. You're a coldhearted businesswoman. I knew I was just an itch you wanted to scratch. You knew I wasn't looking for anything serious after my divorce. I thought we could at least grow this into a business partnership."

She watched him with her practiced dismissive stare for several seconds. She needed those seconds to control her emotions. Needed those seconds to keep the pain blasting through her like a grenade from coming through in her voice.

"And I'm not looking to be your bank. Good luck with your beauty supply store." She walked out of the room without a backwards glance.

Her entire body shook with the effort to hold in the hurt, rage and embarrassment surging through her system. He had told her he didn't want anything serious after his divorce, yet she'd asked him to consider Raleigh as a place to restart. She'd come to his hotel room when he'd first visited. She'd ignored the infrequent mentions about searching for investors between pillow talk. All because she'd thought they'd pick up where they'd left off.

She'd watched too many rom-coms on cable. The old boyfriend comes back, love is rekindled, and everyone lives happily ever after. She knew not to believe in fairy tales.

"You're the oldest, Elaina. You have to be smarter. Never give more of yourself to anyone, because they'll try and take advantage of you."

Some mothers read bedtime stories to their daughters at night. Elaina's mother imparted advice on what it meant to be the oldest child and the responsibilities she'd one day have. Elaina had gotten some form of the same speech from her grandfather and her father. She was the one who'd one day take over Robidoux Tobacco, which later became Robidoux Holdings. She had to lead by example. She had to be smarter. She had to be stronger.

Elaina pressed the button on her key to unlock her Mercedes and slid behind the wheel. She turned on the air conditioning to combat the stuffy heat in the car. Her hands gripped the wheel until her knuckles hurt. Her gas light mocked her.

"I'm tired of being strong." She whispered the words. Too afraid to admit as much even to herself. Her cheek tickled and she swiped at the stupid tear that escaped her eye.

She took a shallow breath and shook her head. She didn't have time for a pity party. Her life was good. She owned her own business. She still stood to take over her family's businesses. She was healthy, rich and able. No one cared about her broken heart. Why should she?

"To hell with Robert," she said in a strong, confident voice before easing her car out of the parking space and searching for a gas station.

CHAPTER TWO

ELAINA PULLED UP at the Robidoux estate thirty minutes before the first guests were scheduled to arrive. The estate included a huge brick mansion with spiraling staircases and grand entrances fit for a king. On the ride back from Raleigh, she'd had enough time to get herself together and pack away all lingering hurt feelings about Robert and what they wouldn't be to the darkest corners of her mind. She got out of the car and tossed the keys to the one of the valets her father hired whenever they had parties.

"Thank you, Marvin," she said, nodding at the attendant.

"I'll take good care of it, Ms. Robidoux," Marvin said with a smile.

"You always do."

Elaina hurried to the front of the house and through the doors into the bustling interior. A quick glance around proved the staff had followed her directions. The right plants were in the right places, the furniture was polished to a high shine, and the doors were open to allow easy flow from the entryway through the downstairs sitting room out to the back garden.

"Your father is looking for you, Ms. Elaina."

Elaina's foot froze at the bottom of the curved staircase to the second floor. She turned and faced Sandra, the family's lead housekeeper. "Tell him I arrived thirty minutes ago and that I'm changing."

Sandra raised a brow. Most days Sandra wore khakis

and a wine-colored polo shirt, but today she wore a white button-up blouse and A-line black skirt. The typical uniform when the family hosted an event. Sandra's short dark hair had a few gray hairs and was tightly curled.

"That'll be hard to do when I told him ten minutes ago I haven't seen you," Sandra said with a tilt to her head. "I *can* tell him I missed when you came in and that you're in your room."

The corners of Elaina's mouth lifted in a small smile. Elaina would be forever grateful that Sandra was more like a cool aunt than just a member of their staff and often looked out for her. "Thank you, Sandra. I'll be down just as the first guests arrive."

"I'll be sure to handle things until you're ready. Take your time."

Elaina nodded, then rushed up the stairs. If only she could take her time. She'd love nothing more than to take a long shower and scrub off the regret of her last encounter with Robert. Instead, she only had time to jump in for a quick, cold washup of the important parts before hopping back out. Her hair was a mess, but messy buns were in, so she didn't bother to rework it. She reapplied her makeup, slid into the peach-colored sheath dress laid out on her bed—she really would have to thank Sandra for that later—slid on her mother's pearl necklace and matching earrings and was back downstairs just as the doorbell rang.

Sandra gave Elaina an approving smile before she opened the door. *Let the games begin.* Elaina took a deep breath and pasted on her practiced smile. Not too big to seem overly eager or friendly, not so small as to appear aloof and unwelcoming. She held out her hand and greeted the first of their guests.

After that, things became a whirlwind. Even though the party was unofficially for Byron's donors, she didn't expect her brother to show up until twenty minutes into the party.

Elaina fell easily into her role as hostess and greeter. She welcomed people and directed everyone outside, where the string quartet her sister, India, usually played with provided soft background music. White-linen-covered tables were set with green-and-blue flower arrangements that matched her brother's campaign colors. Corks popped as champagne flowed to make mimosas, and the caterers walked around the ever-expanding crowd to make sure everyone had their choice of appetizers. Elaina's eyes watched the tray carrying the drinks as they passed just out of her reach. If she was going to get through today, she'd need one, two or three.

Her dad arrived thirty minutes after Elaina greeted the first guests. His gaze immediately landed on her. She could feel his scrutiny from across the yard. She excused herself from the conversation with a council member and her husband and crossed the lawn to where her dad stood. She snagged a mimosa on her way there.

Grant's light brown eyes studied her as she neared. "Where have you been?" he asked in a suspicious tone. His salt-and-pepper hair had the crisp lines of a fresh haircut, and the dark blue blazer he paired with a white shirt and cream slacks perfectly fit his broad frame.

Elaina took a sip of her drink. The sweet orange juice mellowed out the dry champagne. Tension eased from her shoulders. Just what she needed to deal with her dad. "I've been here greeting our guests. The caterer is doing a great job. I haven't had to threaten anyone once."

Grant's stern expression didn't relax. "You know what I mean, Elaina. You ran out last night and show up today right before an important event."

"Don't worry, Daddy, my days of sneaking out are over." She looked away from him to smile and wave at one of the other councilwomen.

"Just because I didn't react when you stole my company—"

Elaina held up a finger. "Acquired, Daddy. I didn't steal anything. You were selling your share. I bought it."

Grant's eyes narrowed. People said she looked like her father, but that was only because Elaina's mom unfortunately wasn't around to be a part of the comparison. Her dad never failed to remind her how much she favored her mother in both personality and looks. That was one of the reasons Grant expected her to be both a charming socialite and a ruthless businesswoman, just as Virginia Robidoux had been.

Grant shifted his stance. His dark brows drew together. "Don't play with me, Elaina."

"I wouldn't dream of playing with you, Daddy. I only use the tactics you taught me. Now, smile, because Byron's coming over. He wouldn't want to see us fighting."

The argument in Grant's eyes drifted away. It would come back later. If Elaina had secretly purchased several shares of anyone else's business, he would praise her for it. Because Elaina had purchased *his* business, he'd carry a grudge all the way to the gates of heaven and beyond.

"You're a coldhearted businesswoman."

Elaina slightly shook her head as if to rid herself of the memory of Robert's words. She took another, longer sip from her glass. She just had to get through the afternoon.

"This party is great," Byron said as he reached them.

Her brother was a younger, fitter version of their father. He leaned in and kissed Elaina on the cheek before slapping their dad on the back. His wife, Zoe, was on his arm. Her natural hair was styled in an intricate twisted updo, and a butter-yellow sundress that complemented her dark brown skin skimmed her body. Years ago, Elaina never would have believed she'd like Zoe, much less be close to her. Elaina once believed Zoe was only going to hurt her younger brother. Later she understood their feelings were real and mutual. Now that she'd gotten to know Zoe, Elaina couldn't imagine Zoe ever hurting Byron or taking him for granted.

Nope, apparently, I'm the only one wanted for their money.

Elaina pushed the thought aside, leaned in and gave Zoe an air kiss over her cheek before finishing off her drink. "Only the best for the mayor."

"Your sister did a good job," Grant said. "She is good at party planning." He tossed out the phrase as if that were the only thing Elaina was good at.

Byron and Zoe exchanged a look. Elaina's hands tightened on the glass. "Good thing that MBA is paying off." Her lips stretched with a fake smile.

Grant glared at her. Byron chuckled and squeezed her hand. He was good at smoothing things over between her and Grant before they spun out of control. "You're great at everything you put your mind to. We all know that."

Elaina squeezed his hand back, then let go. She turned to Zoe with a genuine smile. "You look beautiful today, Zoe." Her voice warmed on the compliment. Zoe had dealt with the full brunt of Grant's criticism and helped Elaina secure the company from him. She was the one person outside of Byron who Elaina felt comfortable talking with.

Zoe gave Elaina a reassuring smile before she ran a hand across the front of her sundress. "I got it from Ashiya's consignment store. You know I'm still getting used to all of these fancy parties."

A caterer with a tray of drinks came by. Elaina quickly exchanged her empty glass for a new one and handed a second to Zoe. "Girl, stop. We both know Byron's life of politics isn't over after four years as mayor."

"I know," Zoe said with a mock whine. "But a woman can dream."

Byron slid his arm around Zoe's waist and pulled her close to his side. "I couldn't do it without you."

The love in her brother's eyes sent a pang of longing through Elaina. Less than four hours ago and she'd been held close. Kissed.

She sipped her drink. "Okay, lovebirds, stop it. Byron, go mingle. I'm going to check on the food."

She turned to walk away. She needed a better distraction. Her brother, happy and in love, was not it.

"Elaina." Grant's authoritative voice stopped her. "I invited Alex Tyson. I need you to be nice to him."

Elaina slowly spun on the heel of her shoe to glare at her father. "Why would you invite him?"

Alex Tyson had been a thorn in her side from the moment her father hired him three years ago. The man ignored everything she had to say, disregarded her directions and acted like an arrogant asshole. She'd tried to fire him only to have her dad hire him back. Since then she'd avoided his company and worked through liaisons whenever they needed to talk.

"Because he's the head of research and development. I'd like to keep him on and, of course, convince him to vote for your brother."

"I don't have to speak to him."

"Yes. You. Will." Grant enunciated each word. Scolding her the same way he'd done when she was a rebellious teenager. "Getting Alex to work for Robidoux Tobacco was good for us. You will not run him off, Elaina. It's time to play nice. Now, be a good hostess when you see him."

"I don't like him." After the day she'd had, she didn't want to deal with him.

"So? Do you know how many people your mother didn't like but she still found a way to work with? How do you think she'd feel to know you'd rather pout and be petty than continue to do what's best for the company?"

The well-played guilt trip had the desired effect. She had to be smarter, better, stronger. Elaina lifted her chin. "Fine." She took a long sip of her drink, and took a modicum of pleasure from the way her dad's eyes clouded with disappointment. Good, she wouldn't be the only one in a bad mood today.

She turned away and went in search of someone to talk to who wouldn't irritate her. Her gaze slid over her sister and her husband, Travis. Elaina's ex-husband. She didn't love Travis. Hadn't loved him when circumstances pushed them into a bad marriage. She was happy he'd found happiness with her sister, but a small stab of spite pierced her heart whenever she was around them. She was happy for her sister, but it would be difficult to pretend to be okay seeing her ex-husband and India together with Robert's words still fresh in her heart. Not the distraction she needed. Pivoting in the other direction, Elaina headed for the house.

Heat from the sun bore down on her back. She glanced around at the smiling faces at the party. Everyone was happy and having a good time. Things had moved into an easy flow. If she was subtle, she could escape right now. She needed a few minutes alone. A few minutes to not be "on" and pretend as if she hadn't been humiliated hours before.

She lifted her glass to her mouth only to discover it was empty. That was two. Her limit was four during public social engagements. Frowning, she placed the empty glass on a table on the patio as she made her way toward the house and grabbed a full glass from a passing waiter.

Elaina smiled and nodded when people spoke to her but kept moving in a straight line toward the house. The upstairs sitting room was just for family. She'd be able to get some quiet time there before coming down and seeking out *Alex Tyson* in order to be a good hostess.

She'd overheard some of the women in the company gush about how handsome Alex was. Elaina didn't see it. She supposed he could be considered cute. He was broad-shouldered with clear chestnut skin and piercing obsidian eyes. But when he worked, he wore those stupid glasses that connected in the front. She hated those glasses. Not just because they reminded her of her grandfather, but because he often looked at her as if she had the intelligence of an amoeba over the rim of those glasses. The man refused to debate with her. Instead he just stared at her as she made her point, said no, and walked away as if that were the end of the discussion. She hated the man.

The quiet upstairs was a welcome balm after the steady hum of conversation downstairs. She opened the door into the sitting room. The scent of Robidoux cigars hung in the air. Elaina breathed in deep, the smell of her family's claim to fortune working its magic and easing the tension out of her shoulders.

Her brows drew together. That wasn't just the lingering scent of a cigar. That was freshly lit cigar.

Elaina scanned the room and her eyes narrowed. Lying back on one of her family's leather sofas with a Robidoux Tobacco cigar in his hand was the person she'd come upstairs to avoid. She slammed the door and glared at her nemesis.

"What the hell are you doing in here, Alex?"

CHAPTER THREE

ALEX DID NOT want to be at the Robidoux family garden party. His original plan for Saturday afternoon was motorcycle shopping with his brother-in-law, Chris. Alex wasn't in the market for a bike, but that didn't mean he couldn't enjoy checking out the various models and imagining himself on one. After examining every type of motorcycle in the area, they would have met up with their other brother-in-law, Walter, at their favorite sports bar and grill for beers and bullshitting.

Instead he was here. Wearing a damn seersucker suit, holding a cigar he didn't want to smoke, and contemplating ways to leave the party as early as possible while simultaneously fulfilling the promise to his stepdad to cement a deal with the family. He was supposed to be long past the days of brokering deals at parties on his off hours. That was why he'd moved to Jackson Falls in the first place. Less stress and more time for "self-care," as his baby sister insisted. A term he would have sneered at before a heart attack at thirty-seven reminded him he wasn't immortal or superhuman.

If anyone other than Thomas, a man he thought of more as his dad than a stepdad, had asked him to come, he would have flat-out said no. His parents never asked anything of him. Had never expected anything from him except to get good grades and look out for his younger sisters. The fact that his parents asked for his help was both unexpected and something he couldn't deny.

Therefore, he suppressed his groan as Elaina "Evil Eyes" Robidoux shot visual daggers at him from the door. Having a run-in with her was exactly why he hadn't wanted to come. Elaina had given him a wide berth since she'd tried to fire him. Now their work relationship was civil, but not civil enough to make him look forward to entering the dragon's lair.

Grant had greeted him with a hearty handshake and a big smile. When Thomas called soon after he'd arrived, Grant escorted him to the upstairs sitting room to take the call. He'd shoved a cigar in his hand, told him to take his time, and left.

Just his luck that Elaina would catch him before he'd gotten his mind right and jumped back into the world of the rich and privileged.

Alex sat up slowly and took a deep fortifying breath. "I came up here to take a phone call. Grant said I would have more privacy."

"This is the family's room."

She said the words as if he were a toddler encroaching upon a forbidden space. He supposed Elaina did view him as an unruly child. "That's what he told me." He stood and put out the cigar in the crystal ashtray next to the leather sofa.

When he looked back at Elaina, her eyes narrowed. Alex's stomach did an unwelcome flip. He *hated* how much he was attracted to her. He'd rather be attracted to a man-eating succubus than Elaina. At least a succubus would take him out with a smile on his face. Elaina was not the type of woman to bring a smile to a man's face.

She was beautiful. Her thick, wavy dark hair looked so damn soft. God was the only person who knew how many times he'd considered the softness of her hair, her smooth terra-cotta skin, or her full lips, and even then he'd deny it on judgment day. Her chestnut-brown eyes were bright and sparked with intelligence when they weren't narrowed with skepticism or frozen over with disdain. Then there were her curves. The woman could make men stop in their tracks. He knew because he'd seen it happen. Full breasts, trim waist and rounded hips. He'd wanted to taste her luscious lips the second he'd seen her. Until she'd opened her mouth and told him all the reasons Robidoux Holdings didn't need him.

He wasn't sure why Elaina disliked him so much. Despite the rumors that he wanted the CEO position, he didn't, and had made that very clear to Grant. A part of him was glad she openly despised him. Knowing he had absolutely zero chance with her made ignoring the way his body automatically reacted to her easier.

"There are other places you could have gone. Why did he let you up here?"

Alex wasn't in the mood to argue. He also avoided being alone with her for too long to prevent any evidence of his crush from showing. If Elaina got a hint that he was attracted to her, she'd have his balls skinned and mounted on her wall like a trophy in no time.

"Ask him, Elaina," he said in the blasé tone he used with her. "Your father invited me. I decided to come. I won't be bothering you anymore." He walked toward the door.

Elaina grunted softly. "I guess today's the day I run men off." The words were muttered under her breath.

Alex stopped at the door. Her hand shook as she brought her drink to her lips.

He frowned at the unusual display of a chink in her armor. Her words hadn't been for him to hear, and he had no reason to find out what was wrong, but the slight slump of her shoulders tugged at an empathetic soft spot he hadn't realized he possessed. "Are you okay?"

Her head whipped in his direction. Her eyes widened, and her arched brows drew together. "Of course I'm okay. Go down to the party and enjoy the free food."

The coarseness of her words bristled. His hand tightened on the doorknob. He was ready to leave without another word, until the light glinted off the sheen of tears in her eyes. She looked away quickly and went further into the room.

Unsettled, Alex stared at her profile against the window. Elaina was a force to be reckoned with. If he made any reference to her tears, he might end up with his jugular ripped out. He didn't have a clue what to say to lift her spirits. The two of them weren't friends or cordial colleagues. Yet that newly discovered empathy wouldn't let him leave without saying something.

"You did a great job on the party."

She frowned at him. "What?"

"The party. I know you did most of the planning. From what I can tell, you did a great job."

Her chin lifted. "It's not that hard."

"Still, I know your dad appreciates it."

She sipped her drink. "Doubtful."

"He does. But even if you don't believe it, then know that I appreciate it."

"Why would you appreciate it?" she asked suspiciously.

He thought about her earlier comment. "I like free food," he said with a smile. Her mouth fell open. He'd at least succeeded in surprising her and taking away the sad look in her eyes. Alex hurried out the door before she could think of a snarky reply.

He made his way downstairs to join the party. As much as he wanted to know more about what was going on with

Elaina, he wasn't there to make her feel better. He'd accepted the invitation and come to the party for one reason: to help his parents.

When Alex's mom suddenly declared winters in New York were too cold for her and decided to move south, he'd supported his parents' decision. When his younger sisters and their husbands moved two years later, he hadn't realized how much he'd miss having his family around until they'd all left him in New York.

Well, that and until he was in the hospital recovering from a heart attack alone. None of his colleagues at Global Consulting had shown up. Neither had Dahlia, the woman he'd been sleeping with for a year. Nor had any of the various people he'd mingled with at dinner parties and conferences. He'd gotten cards and a few flowers, but though he'd believed he didn't need expressions of love or affection, only receiving cards after nearly dying created a craving for the one thing he'd once shunned.

Not long after, he'd started searching for positions in North Carolina before accepting the position as head of research and development for Robidoux Holdings.

Thomas had taken moving to North Carolina better than anyone expected. He'd decided to become a farmer, of all things, purchased a failing hemp farm, and slowly worked to increase production. Once Alex accepted the job with Robidoux Holdings, Thomas had been on him to find a way to get the Robidoux family to take an interest in buying hemp from him.

Alex was good at networking, schmoozing, closed-door dealing. Whatever people wanted to call it. He was a scientist and researcher who'd learned quickly that it took money—and lots of it—to fund new research and even more to turn discoveries into actual products or services. He turned his ability to convince those with money to fund a project into a lucrative career. Granted, the career almost killed him, but quitting and moving to Jackson Falls hadn't erased those skills.

He grabbed a cocktail shrimp from a passing waiter and channeled the charm that once funneled millions of dollars into new projects. He scanned the crowd for Grant. He spotted his boss across the lawn, talking to a few people.

Alex made his way in Grant's direction. His heart rate picked up with every step he took. Anxiety sent sweat down his back. He took a long, slow breath. This was why he'd left the fast-paced world of New York. He'd literally made himself sick trying to deal with the pressure and demands of his previous job.

This is different. You're just casually talking. Nothing depends on this.

"Alex," Grant said with a huge smile as Alex approached. "Come on over and meet my youngest daughter and her husband."

Alex smiled and nodded at the young woman who reminded him of Elaina, if Elaina ever erased the scowl on her face, and the tall, slim man standing next to her.

"India, Travis, this is Alex Tyson, head of research and development. Alex, this is my baby girl, India, and her husband, Travis Strickland."

Alex held out his hand and shook theirs. "Pleasure to meet you. I've heard a lot about you, India."

"All good I hope," she said with a teasing smile.

"Nothing but good things. Your father is proud to have an accomplished violinist in the family." He focused on Travis. "And your reputation as a defense attorney precedes you."

"You ever need a good defense, let me know," Travis replied casually.

Alex held up a hand. "I hope to never need that type of service."

Grant pressed a hand to Alex's shoulder. "So do I. I wouldn't want to risk losing our top researcher to anything. Alex is researching ways Robidoux Holdings can expand into other areas. That and keeping Robidoux Tobacco alive."

India's brows rose. "That sounds like a big responsibility. What are you looking at now?"

He couldn't have wished for a better opening. "One way is by processing and using hemp," Alex said. "Even though sales in cigars remain strong, tobacco sales overall are declining. Now that hemp has been approved as crop in the state, there are multiple uses that could be beneficial to us. From fabrics and textiles to body care and food."

Travis's lips pursed, and he nodded. "Really? I had no idea you could do all of that."

"It's true. That's one of the reasons my stepfather invested in a hemp farm when he moved south five years ago. He saw the benefits."

Grant faced Alex fully. Interest lit his eyes. "I didn't know you had connections with a hemp farmer. We'll have to talk more about that later."

"I'd be more than happy to do so," Alex said. A rush of satisfaction blew through him. Bringing up his stepfather's interests had been easier than he'd expected. Even though it was a small victory, the familiar high of getting the first bite from a potential donor infused his blood. He'd run himself ragged to feel the surge of adrenaline from winning.

He'd planted the seed. Now he just had to continue to water it, but not now. He couldn't come off as too eager or interested. His stepdad wanted to sell his first full crop to Robidoux Holdings, but Alex still wasn't completely sure the company was ready to expand in that direction. For now, putting the possibility on Grant's radar was enough. "I didn't come here to talk shop, though. I'd like to walk around and introduce myself to some of the people here."

A wide smile came across Grant's face. "Let me introduce you to my son, Byron. You know he's the mayor of Jackson Falls?" Pride oozed from Grant's voice.

Alex tilted his head to the side as if contemplating the question. "You may have mentioned it once or twice."

India laughed. "Or a thousand times. Go on, Daddy. Travis and I will mingle."

Grant introduced Alex to Byron and his wife, Zoe, before taking him around to meet other members of the Robidoux family, local politicians, and entrepreneurs. Alex smiled, nodded, and engaged in idle chitchat. He'd forgotten how tiring networking could be.

At some point, Elaina rejoined the party. She kept distance between them. He wasn't sure if it was on purpose or because she was busy. He'd never seen someone do so much during a party, or maybe he hadn't noticed before. He hadn't been very observant before his heart attack. She was everywhere. One minute talking to the musicians, the next giving directions to the caterers or mingling with guests. When someone dropped a glass, she oversaw the clearing of guests out of the way so the waitstaff could come in and clean the area.

Not once did he see her sit down. He thought about the sheen of tears in her eyes earlier and the sadness that hung over her. None of that was apparent as she took care of everything. If he hadn't seen it for himself, he wouldn't have believed she was distressed and doubted anyone at the party knew.

He shouldn't care, but when she was alone, inspecting the area being cleaned, Alex walked over.

"Do you need anything?" he asked.

She jerked her head up and frowned at him. "Pardon?"

"You've been running around all day. Do you need anything? Something to eat, a drink, time to sit down?" He hadn't seen her eat anything all afternoon. "Let me get you something to eat."

"I'm fine," she said in a clipped voice.

Heat prickled up his cheeks. He was foolish for asking. Alex lifted and lowered his chin in a stiff nod. So much for trying to be nice to Elaina. She looked at him as if he'd grown a green head, and the sight of the green head irritated rather than alarmed her.

"I'll leave you alone, then." He turned and walked away.

"Alex," she called.

He looked over his shoulder and raised a brow.

Elaina shifted as if uncomfortable before holding her head high. "Thank you."

He had to clench his teeth to stop his jaw from dropping. Never once had Elaina thanked him for anything. She looked so damn beautiful and regal. Always cool and unbothered. What would she look like if she let her guard down? How would he react if her fathomless brown eyes softened when they looked at him?

He nodded, cleared his throat and walked away before he did something he'd regret later. Elaina Robidoux was exactly the type of high-intensity woman he needed to avoid. He'd moved south to relax and recuperate, not fall into the same traps that once brought him to the brink. Still, he glanced back once more and caught her eye as she watched him walk away. Try as he might, he couldn't stop the brief fantasy of what it would be like to have Elaina focus on him with desire in her eyes instead of disdain.

CHAPTER FOUR

ELAINA'S PHONE VIBRATED in her hand Monday morning as she entered Robidoux Holdings. She glanced at the text message icon at the top of the screen. Robert's name flashed quickly before the icon disappeared. Her steps faltered, and she stopped. Someone bumped into her. Her head shot up as one of the interns from marketing held up her hands.

"I'm sorry, Ms. Robidoux," the young woman said quickly. Her eyes were wide.

Elaina suppressed a sigh. She wasn't going to eat the girl for bumping into her. "I stopped in the middle of the lobby. You're fine."

The intern blinked, then nodded before rushing toward the elevators with the rest of the morning crowd milling through the spacious lobby. Since the family had branched into areas outside of tobacco, their original headquarters also served as the home office for some of their other businesses. Elaina was more at home at Robidoux Holdings than she was at the family's estate. Her office on the top floor was the same one her mother used to occupy. The same office where Elaina would sit in a corner and draw or do homework while her mom directed employees, brokered deals over the phone or dropped new ideas on her dad.

She should wait to read Robert's text until she was safely behind her office doors. She'd already made a fool of herself nearly tripping over her feet just because he'd texted.

A small, irrational part of her brain wanted to see what he had to say immediately. Was his text an apology, or just another attempt to ask her for money?

She opened the text before she had the chance to change her mind.

Thinking of you. *eggplant emoji*

Elaina frowned at the screen. Was he serious? After asking her for money and basically saying they were done if she didn't, he had the nerve to text her something like this?

Her fingers flew over the screen with her quick reply. I thought we were through.

She hit Send and immediately regretted the words. She should have taken time to consider her reply. *I thought we were through"* gave the implication that she'd be okay if he thought otherwise. They most definitely were through. She was not going back. Though she wouldn't mind watching him grovel.

A picture of Robert on his knees begging for her forgiveness went through her mind. Maybe he realized he'd been hasty. Maybe he realized she had cared. Maybe he realized she wasn't the coldhearted businesswoman he'd accused her of being. Her phone buzzed.

My bad. Sent to wrong person.

She was the world's biggest fool.

Her cheeks heated and her heart caved in on itself. If he'd sent that to the wrong person then there was someone else he was thinking of. Someone else he felt comfortable sending eggplant emojis to. Not once had they talked about being exclusive. Still, the idea of him with someone else already proved how wrong she'd been to believe in the second-chance-romance-with-Robert fantasy.

"Damn it, Elaina, you're supposed to be better than this," she muttered to herself. She closed her eyes and took a slow, deep breath. The humiliation and pain from the weekend plowed through her. She took both emotions and wrapped them up into a tight ball of anger.

She threw her phone into her bag and marched to the elevators. No one said anything to her on the ride to the upper floors. Many avoided her gaze. She couldn't muster up enough energy to care. She didn't want to talk to anyone. If she did, she might take out her anger on them, and no one deserved the brunt of this anger. No one but Robert.

She stomped into the outer waiting area of her office, then froze. Alex Tyson sat on the couch, chatting happily with her administrative assistant, Terry. They both stopped mid-laugh to face her. Terry's happy expression slowly melted into an it's-gonna-be-one-of-those-days look. She quickly stood and walked over to the table with the coffee maker.

"Good morning, Ms. Robidoux," Terry said. "Looks like a two-tea morning, huh?"

Terry knew Elaina as well as anyone. The woman had worked for Elaina ever since she'd taken over an executive position at Robidoux Tobacco.

"Make that three, Terry, thank you." She raised her chin and glared at Alex.

He stood and straightened to his full height. He wore a light blue button-up shirt and gray slacks with those stupid grandfather glasses around his neck. Unlike Terry's, the smile on his face hadn't disappeared at the first sight of her bad mood and still lingered around his lips. His lips weren't exactly full, but they were smooth, and his mouth was perfectly shaped. She jerked her eyes away from his smirk to his dark eyes.

"I'm canceling our nine o'clock meeting," Elaina said sharply.

She wasn't in the mood to deal with Alex this morning. He'd been relatively nice to her during the garden party on Saturday, but the more she considered it the more she'd attributed his actions to wanting to get on her good side before their early-morning meeting rather than him caring about her feelings. He'd been bugging her to consider taking his plan for turning tobacco into a biofuel from research into consumer testing. Elaina admitted they were probably ready to move forward, but he still hadn't answered all the questions she'd had. Instead, he'd told her everything she needed to know was in the proposals he'd sent her. As if she had time to read every word in his fifty-page document.

Her words got rid of the lingering smile. Good.

"No, you're not," he said matter-of-factly.

Elaina's eyes narrowed. "Yes. I. Am." She turned to Terry. "I'll be in my office. Please clear my morning schedule."

Terry's brows drew together. "You have the directors' meeting at ten thirty."

A headache started behind Elaina's eyes. "Then postpone it until three."

"That's when you're meeting with your father," Terry countered.

Elaina ground her teeth. She needed a minute. Several minutes to get herself together. The humiliation of knowing that Robert not only wanted her for her money, but had quickly moved on—more than likely he'd been sleeping with someone else the entire time—made her shake with fury. She needed a drink, or to hit something. Anything to dull the pain.

"Fine, push it back thirty minutes." She reached out her hand and accepted the cup of tea Terry brought over. Elaina went to her office door.

"Hold up." Alex's voice cracked. "We aren't done."

She sighed and looked at him over her shoulder. "Yes. We are."

She entered her office, went inside and slammed the door behind her. She locked it for good measure. Once in the privacy of her own space, she let her shoulders slump. She dropped her purse to the floor and went to her desk. She'd deal with Alex later. She'd deal with everyone later. She couldn't deal with making decisions when she was this... irritated.

Opening her bottom desk drawer, she reached inside but came back with nothing. With another sigh, Elaina shoved the drawer closed. She'd stopped bringing mini bottles to work months ago. Part of her "don't make alcohol your best friend" initiative. She brought the cup to her lips and took a long sip of the tea. It was hot and scalded her throat on the way down. Good. She'd rather focus on real pain than the pointless pain caused by a broken heart.

ALEX STARED AT Elaina's closed office door. What the hell was that about? He'd delayed scheduling this meeting with her for weeks. Worked through others to answer her questions in order to avoid dealing with her "sparkling" personality. After the last round of questions and excuses she'd sent, he'd finally accepted they needed a face-to-face meeting. He'd waited patiently for a half hour to open on her schedule, and she canceled and slammed the door in his face.

"It's one of those mornings," Terry said apologetically. "She'll be fine after she's gotten some caffeine."

"Is she always like this?" He pointed to her door.

Terry walked back to her desk and shrugged. "She's under a lot of stress. Mr. Robidoux is pressing her harder than usual."

"That's no excuse to be rude. How can you stand working for her?"

"She's not that bad," Terry argued. "She's really a great boss. She's thoughtful and doesn't give me hard time when I have to leave early because of my kids. She always remembers my birthday and that I'll be in a horrible mood around the anniversary of my mother's passing. She's secretly a nice person."

Terry's admissions surprised him. He would have expected Elaina to be heartless. Regardless of how she was with Terry, that didn't take away from the way she treated him and some of the other directors in the company. "She's spoiled, rude and narcissistic."

"I'm not going to let you talk about her like that," Terry said defensively. "I'll reschedule your meeting."

Alex clenched his jaw. He should go back to his office, wait for Terry to reschedule, and bring up his points in the directors' meeting in a few hours. That was the direction least likely to increase his blood pressure. Still, he couldn't afford to wait another two to six weeks, knowing Elaina, for the meeting to get rescheduled. Their product was ready to go into testing, and she was the only person who could sign off. Sure, he could go around her and ask Grant, but one day Grant would retire, and he'd be left dealing with Elaina. Therefore, he followed he chain of command.

He strode directly to her door and knocked three times. Terry gasped and stood. "What are you doing?"

He glanced at her. "Getting my meeting." He knocked again.

Terry rushed over. "She's not going to like this. Alex, just let me reschedule."

"No, we had a meeting scheduled. She canceled on a whim because the queen doesn't want to be bothered. Well, I'm not a subject, and she can't ignore her job." He knocked harder than the first two times.

The door swung open. Elaina's eyes were like ice daggers. "What are you doing?" she damn near snarled.

"We have a meeting," he replied in a calm, even voice.

"I told you it was canceled." She spoke the words slowly as if he wouldn't understand their meaning otherwise.

He understood her meaning just fine. She expected him to comply and submit to her whims. She picked the wrong day. "You can't ignore me, Elaina. My proposal sat on your desk for six months. Just because you want to play power politics doesn't mean you can't do your job."

Her eyes widened and she lifted her chin. Her dark eyes sparked fire. If she wasn't directing her evil eyes his way, he'd marvel at how damn attractive she was when she stood her ground.

She pointed to her chest. "I do my job." She pointed a finger at his chest. "Your job is to listen to my direction."

He took a step forward until her finger pressed into his chest. "My job is to research new products and bring them forward for further development and testing. You've stopped me on every product I've brought up."

She poked his chest harder. "You haven't answered my questions. It's not my fault you're incompetent."

He stepped back, the imprint of her finger lingering. "Incompetent? If anyone is incompetent it's you."

She blinked several times. Her mouth opened and closed before she scoffed. "I know you didn't just say that."

"I said that and will say a lot more. You got this job because your family owns the company. Instead of appreciating what you have, you spend your time playing empress and treating your employees like your subjects. You don't like to make decisions, don't like to listen to reason, and would rather stifle progress than have someone disagree with you."

Elaina's glare was frigid as she took a step closer to him. "And you think just because you came from some fancy overpriced consulting firm that we're supposed to take you at your word. Well, your research may be good, but when I ask questions they aren't to be ignored. You still haven't given me the possible downsides to mixing with ethanol."

He slid closer. "It's on page thirty-two," he said between clenched teeth. "Take the time to read the document I sent you."

Her chin lifted higher. "I haven't seen the potential profits."

"Page nineteen."

Her eyes narrowed. "Nor have you gotten with distribution on supply needs."

He leaned in until he could see the light reflected in the brown depths of her eyes. "Page forty-five." He shook his head and snorted. "Exactly what I thought. You didn't bother to read the proposal. You're just asking questions you already know the answer to just to delay my projects and screw me over. I can't believe you've been in your position for as long as you have."

Her head snapped back. Uncertainty flashed briefly across her face before her cool mask slid back into place and she crossed her arms under her breasts. "You don't have to believe it. I've been here since I was a girl, and I'll be here long after you."

"Not at this rate."

"Exactly at this rate." She smirked. "You're fired, Alex. Pack your stuff and get out of my building."

Alex's hands balled into fists. He would never hurt a woman, but the idea of shaking some sense into Elaina sometimes crossed his mind. He didn't have time for this. He'd moved here to have less stress. If he worked with Elaina Robidoux, his life would be nothing but stress. The woman would give him another heart attack.

"Fine," he said.

"Not fine." Grant Robidoux's voice cut through the thick tension.

Elaina's eyes widened and she shifted to the right. Alex spun around. The look on Grant's face sent cold tendrils of dread through his midsection. He thought back on the stuff he'd said to Elaina. The last time they'd argued, and she'd fired him, Grant had given him back his job and promised to deal with Elaina. This time Alex didn't believe Grant would go to bat for him, after the insults he'd thrown. He didn't care. He couldn't work with her.

"I'll have my stuff out of the office this afternoon," Alex said.

"You are not quitting," Grant said.

Alex nodded. He couldn't keep going in circles with Elaina. "It's for the best."

Grant shook his head. "That's not what's best for the company, but this is." He looked at Elaina with a hard, re-signed gaze. "Elaina, you're fired."

CHAPTER FIVE

FIRED. *FIRED. FIRED!*

The word reverberated through Elaina's head with each determined step she took down Main Street toward her cousin Ashiya's consignment shop, Piece Together. She couldn't believe her father had fired her. At first she'd laughed. He'd threatened to fire her before, but she was his daughter. The oldest child. The one they'd groomed to take over from the moment she could talk.

Once she realized he was serious, she'd argued. He couldn't fire her. She was overseeing the acquisition of other projects. She was the person handling the transition from Robidoux Tobacco to Robidoux Holdings. She was heading a strategic planning meeting with the other directors later that day.

"Someone else can handle that."

Her father had spoken the words with calm resistance. Then she'd gotten angry. How could he possibly say someone else could handle things when her entire life had been nothing but accepting the things she had to be responsible for as the eldest child? She'd yelled, cursed, maybe even thrown something. All completely out of character, which was why her father watching her entire rant as if she were a five-year-old having a tantrum in the middle of the grocery store checkout line over candy had only infuriated her more.

He'd asked her to leave, then called security when she

refused. Terry cried as Sam, the head of security and a person she'd spoken to every day at work for years, led her out of her family's business. People gawked or pretended not to stare as she left, stone-faced and back straight. He wanted her out. She'd get out.

Now she had to talk to Ashiya. She couldn't go back to the Robidoux estate. Was she even welcome anymore? The answer was immediate. Grant would let her stay, but at what cost? He'd love nothing more than to convince her to stop being *unreasonable*, do what she was supposed to do, behave, and she could have her job back.

Hell. No.

Elaina was done doing what was required. All the promises of one day running Robidoux Tobacco and all their holding companies were broken. She was getting nothing. She was cast out.

Her hands balled into fists. Her nails bit into her palms. She wanted to dig them into Alex Tyson's smug face. Well, not smug. He'd first appeared shocked, then remorseful after Grant fired her. She didn't have to guess what he really thought. He viewed her as just as much of a spoiled screwup as her dad did.

Her shoulders slumped. She was so tired. She needed someplace to go. And a drink.

Elaina pushed through the door of Piece Together. Her shoulders straightened as soon as the eyes of the workers swung her way. She wanted to break down and cry, but she'd never show the world that.

"Is she in the back?" Elaina asked the woman behind the counter. Lindsey, she believed her name was.

"Yes, but—"

"Good. Thank you." Elaina headed to the back office without waiting to hear whatever Lindsey had to say. If

Ashiya was in a meeting, then she'd apologize later. Right now, her cousin had a lead on what Elaina needed.

Elaina knocked on the office door. "Yes," Ashiya's voice said from the other side.

Elaina opened the door and froze. India sat in the chair across from Ashiya' s desk. They both were smiling. Elaina didn't miss how the edges of their smiles stiffened like concrete when they spotted her.

"Elaina? What's up?" Ashiya asked. Her cousin wore a bow neck green shirt that brought out the green in her hazel eyes. Her short hair was curled and styled to perfection.

Her gaze slid to India. She'd hoped to keep the problems between her and her dad away from her siblings for at least a few hours. Longer than that wasn't an option. Elaina loved her baby sister, but their relationship hadn't been the closest before India married Travis. Now Elaina had to work hard to make India feel comfortable to avoid the brief flashes of pity in her sister's gaze whenever she thought Elaina was on the verge of an emotional breakdown. The effort was exhausting.

Elaina focused on Ashiya. "Do you still have that apartment for rent?"

Ashiya blinked. "What apartment?"

Elaina tamped down the irritation that tightened her shoulders. "In the building you own with Aunt Liz. You mentioned needing a tenant. Is it still available?" Elaina fought to keep her voice cool and even, but at the back of her mind, she heard the hint of desperation.

Understanding blossomed in Ashiya's eyes. "Oh. No, I just rented it this morning."

Shit! Could nothing go right for her today? Now where was she going to go?

"Why are you asking about an apartment?" India's curly

natural hair was pulled up in a knot at the top of her head. She wore her favorite white peasant-style blouse and slim-fitting jeans.

"I'm moving out of the estate." Elaina pressed a hand to her pounding temple. She couldn't go home. Could not face looking at her father and hearing a lecture on responsibility and duty.

"Really? Why?" India sounded like Elaina was incapable of living on her own.

"Do I need a reason?" Elaina snapped.

Guilt flashed in her sister's eyes. Elaina immediately wanted to kick herself. Deflect and attack. That was her automatic response. India didn't need that.

"I apologize," Elaina said. "I need a place. Daddy fired me this morning. I'd prefer not to stay with him."

India jumped to her feet. "What? He can't do that."

Her sister's immediate defense almost made the tears threatening to spill come forward. India was always the fighter in the family. The one with the most heart, who wasn't willing to fit into the perfect mold their parents had for them. It was why she'd pursued her dream of being a professional violinist. Why she'd fought to marry the man she loved despite the awkwardness of the situation.

"He can, and he did," Elaina said. She ran a hand through the straight strands of her hair. "I was there, and it wasn't pretty."

India came over and took Elaina's hand in hers. She pulled Elaina into the room. Elaina couldn't muster up the energy to fight. "Talk."

Elaina sank into the chair next to India. She looked first at Ashiya and saw sympathy in her cousin's gaze, then back at India, who looked ready to fight. Buoyed by their support, she told the story of what happened.

As the words came out, she couldn't ignore her part in the blowup with Alex. The flinches and quick glances between India and Ashiya proved they thought the same. By the time she finished, she was still angry about being fired, but she couldn't blame Alex for everything.

"I deserve my job," Elaina said.

India nodded slowly. "I agree. You've always wanted to run Robidoux Tobacco." Her sister's words were carefully spoken as if she were tap dancing around what she wanted to say.

"Did you really not read any of his proposal?" Ashiya, blunt as usual, asked.

"I was going to get around to it," Elaina said defensively. Though honestly, she wasn't. Alex was a threat. He'd been a threat to her position from the moment he'd stared at her with those unwavering, all-seeing eyes. He looked at her as if he saw how thin her barriers were. How hard she tried to prove she deserved her position.

Ashiya raised a brow and her hands but didn't talk. She leaned back in her chair.

"That's beside the point now," Elaina said briskly. "I can't go home. I need a place to stay and I need it tonight."

India snapped her fingers. "I've got it."

Elaina shifted uncomfortably. Her emotions too raw, her nerves too on edge to allow her to relax. "Got what?"

"Travis was just talking about a client who's moving to Hong Kong for a year. He asked about anyone needing a sublet. You can have it." Excitement filled India's voice.

Elaina wasn't so enthusiastic. "Stay in someone's house?"

"If the person is paying Travis, I'm pretty sure the home is up to your high standards," India said with a grin. "Besides, I agree. You don't need to go home tonight. Let this blow over and we'll figure out how to get your job back."

If she even wanted it back. That thought sent a shiver of nervousness through her. Did she need to go back? She'd purchased the hemp manufacturing facility right under her dad's nose. She had Zoe handling the update of the building and machinery. Maybe this was what she needed to dedicate more time to making her new purchase a success.

"Do you think Travis will help me?" She hadn't been the best wife to him and had been an even worse ex-wife. Even now they barely spoke to each other.

"Of course he will. If he even thought of saying no, he'd do it for me."

Elaina's spine stiffened. "I know he would."

The my-pitiful-sister look came into India's eyes. Shit! She'd let her emotions show through. She wasn't supposed to be jealous of what her sister had. She was supportive. She was okay.

"Let's call him," she said quickly before India would change her mind.

TRAVIS CAME THROUGH. Elaina wasn't surprised—Travis had always been true to his word. Honorable in a way that often surprised her. After a few phone calls, Elaina was signing paperwork and picking up the keys to a four-bedroom craftsman-style home on the east side of town.

Elaina clutched the keys in her left hand and shook Travis's with her right. "Thank you for working this out."

He lifted a shoulder as if finding the perfect home for his ex-wife at the last minute was something he did every day. "You're actually doing me a favor. When Michael left his keys with me to handle things, I thought I'd have to spend the next year checking on his house once a week. I know you'll keep it in good hands."

Michael was a heart surgeon at Jackson Falls Hospital

who'd decided to work with another prominent surgeon in Hong Kong on a new procedure. That's what she'd gathered from Travis. His effort to save the hearts of millions already had one success with her. Her heart wouldn't have been able to bear going back to the estate today.

India slid up to Travis's side. "If Elaina is staying there, the house will be in better shape than he left it."

Travis wrapped an arm around India's waist and brought her to his side. The movement was effortless and easy. More intimate than a kiss because it showed how comfortable they were with each other. A pang went through Elaina's chest, and she missed Robert for a heartbeat.

She shoved thoughts of her screwed-up love life aside and focused on the right now. She didn't have to go home. She didn't have to face her dad. "It wouldn't be on brand for me if I didn't make his home better." She clutched the keys tighter. "I'm going to get settled in."

"I'll come with you," India said. "I can help you move your stuff from the estate."

She wasn't about to face her dad tonight. "I'll send for my stuff."

"Then at least let me come with you to buy groceries or something."

Elaina shook her head. "I appreciate your efforts to domesticate me, but we both know I'll order food. I'm tired and it's been a long day. I'd prefer to sit and think about my next steps." Luckily the house was furnished so she could move in with no problems tonight.

India's brows drew together. "Are you sure? I'm happy to come over and spend some time with you." She glanced up at Travis. "You don't mind, do you?"

Travis shook his head and smiled at India as if she scattered the stars in the sky. "You know I don't. Go have fun."

Elaina did not want to be babysat. She didn't want company. "I'm good, India. Seriously, I want to be alone."

India looked as if she were going to argue, but Travis gently nudged her. India sighed and nodded. She came over and held out her arms.

Suppressing a sigh, Elaina gave her sister a quick hug. India smelled like flowers, and her arms squeezed her as if she wanted to protect her from harm. The longing to have someone hold her and tell her things would work out was overwhelming. Elaina's eyes burned. Her breathing stuttered. She pulled back quickly and flipped her hair over her shoulders. Everything was piling up and she needed time to compose herself.

"Thank you for your help. I'll call you later this week." She turned and hurried out of Travis's office before her sister tried to hug her again.

Elaina drove the short distance from Travis's office to her new neighborhood. She pulled up to the gate house at the entrance to the subdivision. Even though she'd gotten the code to punch in to access the gated community, she wanted the guard to be familiar with her. The guard, a middle-aged white man with curious eyes and a wide grin, came out and greeted her.

She glanced at the name tag on his shirt before speaking. "Hello, Gary, I'm Elaina Robidoux."

Gary grinned and nodded. "I know who you are, Ms. Robidoux. Not only did Dr. Bodine tell me you were coming, but so did Mr. Strickland. Did they give you the code to the gate?"

She nodded. "I have it, thank you."

"I'm glad you'll be staying here. My son works for Robidoux Holdings in the accounting department. My cousin works in production, and my dad and I even took some summer work in your fields when I was a kid. I appreciate everything your family has done for this area."

Elaina's smile froze. Gary had dozens of ties to her family's company. It wouldn't be long before his son told him about Elaina getting fired. His excitement at having Elaina passing through his gate would twist into pity and disappointment. Would she ever escape the weight of responsibility that came with being a Robidoux?

"Thank you, Gary," Elaina said in the clear, professional voice she'd heard her mom use a dozen times when speaking with clients. "I appreciate your support. Have a great afternoon."

He tipped his hat. "You too, Ms. Robidoux."

"Please, call me Elaina." With a wave, she went through the gate.

She didn't pay attention to the manicured lawns and beautifully designed houses. She thought about how long it would take for the word to get out about what happened to her. How hard she'd have to work to overcome the image of the disgraced Robidoux child. She'd have to work faster at getting the hemp manufacturing facility repaired and up and going. She needed to find a public relations person and craft a statement about her business. She'll also need to follow up leads on potential suppliers, so she could be sure she had a supply when she opened.

She pulled up in front of her new home and quickly got out of the car. Everything she needed to do ran through her mind. Tonight, she would focus on hiring people to get her belongings from the estate and determine what she needed from the house. She could hear India telling her to take time and relax, but if she stopped and took her time, she'd end up thinking about what happened. How everything she'd worked and sacrificed for was snatched away in an instant.

The house was clean and welcoming, but it was quiet. Too quiet. She'd grown accustomed to the background sounds at the estate. Talking to Sandra in the kitchen. Overhearing her dad and his fiancée, Patricia, in the halls. She was well and truly alone now. She had never been alone before. Her hands shook, and tears burned again.

"No. No crying." Elaina slid her phone out of her purse and called the one person she didn't mind letting her guard down with. It rang twice before her sister-in-law answered.

"What's up?" Zoe asked.

"Grab your purse. I need to go out."

CHAPTER SIX

ALEX CLUTCHED THE side of his brother-in-law's new Slingshot three-wheeled motorcycle as they sped around a curve. The red and black, half-car, half-motorcycle had side by side seats and could go from zero to sixty miles-per-hour in five seconds. When Chris asked him to go out for drinks after his horrible day, Alex readily agreed. Chris easily maneuvered the vehicle around the curves through the outer edges of the county. Trees and houses blurred by. Alex closed his eyes and held his head back. He let the rush of adrenaline wash through him. Sucking in a deep lungful of air, he tried to let go of the shitty feeling he'd had ever since Grant fired Elaina.

It's not your fault. You didn't make him fire her.

No, but he had let his emotions get the better of him. He wasn't doing that anymore. He'd prevented Elaina from getting under his skin for eighteen months. He knew how she was. He could have waited for the meeting to be rescheduled instead of blowing up and letting every thought in his head come through.

And you'd still be in the same holding pattern.

He regretted her losing her job, but he didn't regret what he'd said. She'd tied his hands from the moment he'd come through the doors of Robidoux Tobacco. What he said needed to be said. The way he said it, though—maybe he could have worked on that.

Chris swung the roadster into the parking lot for S&E

Bar and Grill. It was a new spot on the edge of town that was popular with the thirty-and-up crowd and had a club vibe on the weekends. S&E was their hangout spot and the perfect place to grab a drink to wash away the taste of guilt in his mouth.

"What do you think?" Chris asked as he unhooked his seat belt.

Alex nodded and admired the touch display, audio system and leather seats. "It's nice."

Chris's eyes widened. "Nice? It's more than nice. Pam made me give up the racing bike, but she didn't say I couldn't go for the three-wheeled bike."

Alex unbuckled his seat belt. "If she ever rides with you in this thing, she may make you give it up."

Chris waved a hand. "Nah, this is our compromise. Plus, your sister loves it."

Alex had to unfold his legs and push up out of the vehicle. As much fun as he'd had riding in the low-to-the-ground vehicle, his knees and back were happy to no longer be folded up into the passenger seat. He raised his hands over his head and stretched.

"Just be careful, man. I don't think Pam can handle another accident."

The smile on Chris's face melted away. "I hear you. I can't handle one either."

The previous summer, a car had swerved into Chris's lane, knocking him from his motorcycle and nearly breaking his neck along with his arm and leg. The recovery had been long and brutal. Even though Chris had fought to keep his bike, Alex's sister hadn't budged.

"I'll be careful," Chris said.

Alex nodded and followed Chris into the restaurant. The place was crowded for a Monday night, mostly due to the Monday night back-to-work specials. R & B music played in the background beneath the sounds of multiple conversations. They found seats at the end of the bar. Chris ordered a cola and Alex got the same with a shot of rum.

"You drink, I listen," Chris said after they got their drinks.

"Nothing much to say except it was a bad day." Alex was here to forget his problems, not relive the scene with Elaina. Still, he wanted to talk about what happened with someone else. Just to find out if he was in the wrong.

"Is the boss still giving you shit?" Chris asked.

Alex sipped his drink. "She was, but I don't have to worry about that anymore."

"Why not?"

"Her dad fired her." Alex's voice was grim.

Chris's eyes grew wide. He brought the side of his fist to his mouth. "Are you kidding me? Why?"

Alex sighed and rubbed the bridge of his nose. "Because of me."

"You got her fired? Damn, bruh, I knew you didn't like her, but I didn't think you'd go that far."

"I wasn't trying to go that far. I didn't want her fired. I just wanted her to hear my proposal and give me the go-ahead to start testing. She refused to hear me out, I got angry, and there you have it."

Concern clouded Chris's gaze. "You got angry? You aren't about to have a repeat of what happened before, are you?"

Alex shook his head. "No." Though he couldn't meet Chris's eyes. Any hint of Alex getting stressed or angry and the family was ready to call the nearest cardiologist.

"You talk about me and a wreck? Your sister couldn't handle it if her older brother had another damn heart attack."

Alex rubbed his chest. The phantom memory of the tightness in his chest echoed. Thankfully, Alex's heart attack hadn't been massive. He could almost laugh at how foolish he'd been when a colleague casually suggested he go to the hospital when he'd complained of chest pain, and he'd said he was too young to have a heart attack. He'd pushed aside the chest pains as signs of his acid reflux. One bypass surgery later, he knew he was not too young for the universe to remind him of his own mortality.

"Can we move along from putting me back in the hospital? I'm good," Alex said. "The job at Robidoux Holdings isn't putting nearly as much pressure on me as I had before. My paycheck isn't determined by how many clients I keep happy and how many hours I can bill to a project. Elaina and I didn't see eye to eye, but I knew how to work around her."

"Now she's fired." Chris snapped his fingers. "Does this mean you get her job?"

Alex slammed down his glass and shook his head. "Hell no. I'm not trying to sign up to be anyone's CEO. I'm good where I'm at."

"But if you were CEO, then you'd be able to help Thomas get the supplier contract with Robidoux Holdings."

"I think I'm good on that already," Alex said. "I dropped the hint this weekend at the garden party. Grant's interested in Robidoux Holdings going into hemp production. I would have brought it up this week, but I think I need to let this situation with Elaina die down before I approach him about Thomas's interest."

"Don't wait too long," Chris said. "Thomas needs some income to make the place profitable."

Alex chuckled and sipped his drink. "I still can't believe my mom and Thomas moved here with the hopes of making money off hemp."

His parents wouldn't be in financial trouble if the farm failed. They'd owned a profitable storage unit business back home, which they'd sold for good money before moving to North Carolina. That didn't mean they wanted to grow hemp without finding a use for it.

"There is money to be made," Chris said. "Thomas just came in after the industry already got going. He can't expect to see the same results as people who've lived here forever and already knew what to expect."

"I won't wait too long. I'll talk to Grant next week."

Laughter came from the other side of the bar. Alex and Chris both glanced in that direction. Alex froze. What the hell was Elaina Robidoux doing in this bar? His bar? This was the last place he would expect to find her, but there she was. Still wearing the cream-colored silk shirt and tan pants she'd had on earlier. She sat with another woman he recognized as her sister-in-law, Zoe. Wineglasses sat on their table, and Elaina's face was bright with humor as she listened to Zoe talk.

Alex's breath caught in his chest. He'd never seen Elaina smile so big, much less laugh. And to see that, today of all days, made time stop for a second.

Chris followed Alex's gaze over to Elaina and Zoe, before turning back to Alex with confusion in his eyes. "What?"

Alex blinked, then shook his head. "That's her. Over there in the booth."

"Oh shit, for real?" Chris looked over his shoulder. "Do you want to leave?"

Leaving was probably smart. He was certain that if Elaina saw him, the smile on her face would disappear. She'd found something to bring her joy after the hellish morning, and a part of him didn't want to ruin her evening. But guilt made him stand. His intention hadn't been to get her fired. His apology might not mean anything, and she had no obligation to accept it or even hear him out, but he had to say something.

"Give me a second. Then we can go."

He crossed the room to Elaina's table. Her laughter created a funny sensation in his chest. He liked the sound of it. Light and choppy, almost as if she weren't used to laughing as much. Zoe must be a miracle worker. He wondered what type of miracles he'd have to perform to ever get her to smile at him like that.

She looked up as he neared. Her laughter dwindled off. The smile on her face melted away. The room seemed darker.

"I just can't escape you, huh," she said with a rise of one brow.

Alex stopped at her table. "I was going to say the same thing about you."

Zoe looked from Elaina to Alex and back again. Elaina sighed and pointed at him. "This is Alex Tyson. Alex, this is my sister-in-law, Zoe Hammond."

Zoe's eyes widened. "Oh, we met at the party. I'm just surprised you stopped by our table." She sounded slightly impressed.

"I'm not afraid to get what's coming to me." Alex looked to Elaina. "Can we talk for a second?"

Elaina let out a heavy sigh. Her fingertips turned the stem of the wineglass so that it rotated on the tabletop. "Coming to gloat about getting me fired."

Alex's spine stiffened. "That was never my intention."

Elaina picked up the wineglass and took a long sip. Zoe's lips pressed together. She gave Elaina a stern look.

Elaina rolled her eyes and shrugged. "Fine, we'll talk."

Zoe slid out of the booth. "I'll give you both a second." She patted Elaina on the shoulder. "Play nice."

Alex took her seat after she walked away. Elaina put down the wineglass and sat up straight. Her eyes met his. "Okay, talk."

"I want to apologize. I was angry and upset earlier. I said some things I shouldn't have. I never would have said it if I'd known what would have happened."

She crossed her arms primly on the table. "But you meant it. The things you said. It's not as if you take back your thoughts."

"No, but—"

She waved a hand. "No buts. You got what you needed to off your chest. Don't go back and apologize for saying what you think. Most people don't have the guts to get that far."

"What I said got you fired."

"What you said gave my dad the excuse to do what he's threatened me with for years." She lifted the glass and took another long sip. "You were the catalyst, but you didn't light the match."

He didn't know what to say to that. "I'm sorry."

"Don't be. Besides…" She drummed the manicured tips of her fingers on the table and pursed her lips. After a second she let out a breath and said in a rush, "You weren't exactly wrong."

Alex fell back against his seat. "Excuse me?"

She took a deep breath and shifted in her seat. "You heard me. I won't be repeating myself."

He wasn't about to argue with her on this, or gloat. He was curious, though. "What brought you to this conclusion?"

She glanced over at the bar, where Zoe watched them. "People have reminded me today that I can be stubborn and difficult at times."

The corner of his mouth twitched. "That's an understatement."

Her eyes narrowed, but there wasn't any censure behind them. "I have to be difficult. Being easy and soft wouldn't have gotten me anywhere in my family's world."

"Why were you so difficult with me?"

She met his eyes. She looked as if she were about to say something, then shook her head. She lifted her glass and finished the wine. "Doesn't matter because you don't have to worry about me now."

"What are you going to do?" He did care about where she landed.

She lifted her chin and smiled. "Don't worry about me, Alex. I'm a big girl. I can land on my feet." She slid out of the booth and stood.

Alex got up as well. He wanted to keep her there longer. Talk to her about how she planned to stay on her feet. She really couldn't be okay with what happened. How was she not angry at him and trying to use his balls as the bull's-eye on the dartboard on the wall? He recognized the signs of ignoring bad things. He'd been her a few years ago. "If you need anything…"

"I'll be sure to find whatever I need." She held out her hand. "Thank you for the apology. I wish you well."

He reached out and took her hand. Her hands were clammy. Her fingers trembled. Alex gave her hand a comforting squeeze. "Elaina…"

She pulled away quickly and squeezed her hand into a fist, which she pressed into her midsection. "Goodbye, Alex. Have a nice life."

She spun quickly, wobbled a bit, then strode to Zoe. Zoe stood and slid her arm through Elaina's. Alex watched as the two of them left. At least she had someone with her tonight. The idea of never seeing her again didn't sit right with him, though. She'd been the bane of his existence for nearly three years, but now the thought of never seeing Elaina Robidoux again left a gap he'd never expected.

CHAPTER SEVEN

THE FOLLOWING WEEK, Alex was no closer to having the plan approved to take the biofuel into testing. The fallout of Elaina's firing sent the company into a tailspin. Grant reallocated Elaina's work to some of the other directors in the company, but Alex received a majority of the larger projects. He'd been asked to oversee the placement of the company's high-end cigars in several popular cigar lounges on the West Coast, and also tasked with coming up with ways to help retailers meet new regulations for product placement. Both Elaina's key projects.

"Alex, have you had the chance to go over the projected revenues if we supply biofuel to the federal government?"

Alex looked across the small conference table in his office at Randy Clark, one of the members of the research and development team. He was younger than Alex, with his dark hair cut in a trendy style, and clothes perfectly tailored to his slim frame.

Alex's weekly Friday morning meeting with his team of three other research and development managers not only helped him stay in the loop but also provided an opportunity to reflect on the work completed during the week. Something he used to report to Elaina every Monday whether she wanted it or not.

"I'm sorry, Randy, but I haven't had the chance to look it over," Alex said. He tried to sound apologetic. He'd completely forgotten to review the information. With everything in limbo and work shifting until Elaina's vacant position was filled, he didn't have much time to double- and triple-check his employees' work. For the first time, he believed Elaina truly might not have had time to review the extensive progress reports he'd sent her. "Why don't you give the group an update on what you found out?"

"Okay." Randy sounded as if Alex's recommendation was anything but okay. He cut his eyes to Rebecca sitting next to him.

Rebecca's full lips pressed together and she'd pulled on her long microbraids which were in a ponytail. Her dark eyes darted to Charlene, who studied the pen in her hand as if it were fascinating.

Alex didn't need a translator to understand the silent exchange. He'd heard just how much his reply sounded like the excuses Elaina used to throw his way. He wondered if Elaina missed her work. If she'd landed on her feet. How things had played out between her and her father. It wasn't the first time he'd thought about her since Grant fired her.

Alex pulled the edges of his glasses until the magnet holding the lenses together gave and refastened them around his neck. He sat straight in his chair and eyed his team. "Why don't you tell me what you're really thinking."

He didn't bother pretending he hadn't noticed the look. The three shared another glance. He saw the nonverbal debate of who would speak up first. He wasn't surprised when Rebecca turned his way.

"I'm just going to say it. Is it true that you're getting Elaina's job and are on your way out of research and development?"

Alex leaned back in his chair. He drummed his fingers on the table and studied his team. He'd expected irritation because he hadn't reviewed anything they'd put on his desk this week. Or having to explain why he hadn't focused their eagerness to launch the new biofuel in time for a federal government contract to Grant. Even for them to hint around for the details of Elaina's firing. He hadn't expected this.

"Where did you hear that?" he asked carefully. He tried not to overreact with his team. Part of the stress from his previous job was the way the firm's CEO would blow up and turn every simple challenge into a level ten disaster. He'd spent most days wondering what bomb would fall that they'd have to recover from next. The idea that he'd take Elaina's job was preposterous—he didn't want the job and had made that clear. But he didn't want his team to feel as if they couldn't come to him with their questions.

"Everyone is saying it," Charlene chimed in. "That's the reason Grant hired you in the first place. To possibly take over one day."

"I am not taking Elaina's job." He met each of their eyes as he spoke. "I've been asked to help with some other projects, just like the rest of the directors. I need you all to bear with me as we wait for the dust to settle."

They exchanged skeptical looks. Rebecca spoke up again. "You don't want her job? What if it's offered to you?"

"I'm happy doing what I'm doing. Now can we please stop talking about me getting jobs I have no intention of going after and focus on the remaining items on our agenda?"

They nodded, and they finished going through all the various items left to discuss. Alex remained calm and outwardly focused, when internally he fought a battle. Was that really what everyone thought? Worse than that, did people think he'd intentionally gotten Elaina fired just so he could advance at the company? He needed to talk with Grant and find out how long this limbo situation would last.

His meeting ended thirty minutes later, and just as his team walked out, Grant strolled in, all cool confidence and I-own-this swagger.

"Do you have a second." It wasn't a question. Grant crossed the room and pulled out the chair across from Alex's desk.

Alex didn't have the time. He needed to review the proposals on his desk, but catching Grant for a conversation was even harder now that Elaina was gone. He might as well use this opportunity to get a few things straight with Grant. "I've got a second. Plus, I want to talk to you."

Grant sat, crossing one ankle over the opposite knee. "About what?"

"A few things, but at the top of the list is the situation with Elaina."

Grant's eyes sharpened. "What situation? She's gone. You shouldn't have any roadblocks now."

"That's the thing. I didn't want her gone. Elaina and I had a tense working relationship at times, but I respect her. There are some aspects to these projects that she is more familiar with. I wonder if getting her back would help move things along."

Grant waved his hand dismissively. "There is no coming back. Elaina is no longer a part of this company."

Grant's curt rejection of Elaina's return surprised him. A part of him assumed Elaina would eventually be back. She and Grant disagreed on some things, but there was no doubt Grant was proud of his daughter and frequently talked about the legacy she would one day take over.

"With all due respect, she is your daughter and was expected to take over as CEO of the company. Do you really want to let her go so easily?"

For a second Grant looked unsure, before his face hardened. "She knew the consequences of her actions."

Grant's voice was firm, but his eyes held a glimmer of doubt. Alex would bet Grant hadn't expected things to go this far. The man was used to winning. He'd fired Elaina, which meant he couldn't ask her to come back. Maybe he thought Elaina would beg for her job back. Alex didn't need a degree in psychology to recognize Elaina's personality type wasn't the one to beg.

"Have you spoken with her?" he asked.

"Elaina moved out of her office here and out of the family's estate. If she wants to talk to me, she'll come to me," Grant said gruffly.

Alex blinked, taken aback. He hadn't expected Elaina to move out of her family home. Clearly the rift went deeper than her problems here at work.

"Which is why I'm here. I want you to step in as interim head of Robidoux Tobacco."

Alex barely stopped his jaw from dropping. Grant couldn't be serious. There was no way he wanted to step into Elaina's shoes. Not only because he had no desire to play whatever game Elaina and Grant had going on, but because he hadn't moved here to take on another high-stress role.

"Sir, I appreciate the offer—"

"Don't give me any buts." Grant's hand sliced through the air. "This is just temporary. I need to handle the loose ends with Robidoux Holdings. Until then, I can't focus on Robidoux Tobacco as I'd like. I know I can count on you to make the right moves and decisions here until a permanent head is brought in. I've asked the lead directors at my other holding companies to do the same."

"I really don't think—"

"You have free rein to hire whomever you need to assist you in the meantime," Grant continued in a cajoling tone. "My goal is to have the position filled within the next two months." He uncrossed his legs and leaned forward, his eyes serious as they met Alex's. "Please, Alex, you'd be doing me a big favor."

Alex suppressed a groan. He didn't want the position for two weeks, much less two months, but he'd also never heard Grant say please to anyone. "Two months? That's it?"

Grant placed a broad hand over his heart. "I'm already vetting potential people. I won't even get in the way of you pushing the biofuel product into testing. You're right, we've got to find other uses for tobacco if we want to keep this part of the business going. Use this as your opportunity to take us in a new direction."

He knew Grant was only trying to sweeten the deal. The disappointed faces of his team after he admitted he hadn't reviewed their work flashed through his mind. They'd worked on various projects for several months that got nowhere. He'd just told them he didn't want Elaina's position, but now was the perfect time to get their projects moving before a new CEO came in and potentially held them up. Besides that, if he were in charge, he controlled the stress levels. No dancing to the beat of someone else's drum.

Alex let out a deep breath, then nodded. "I'll do it."

Grant grinned and rubbed his hands together. "Great. I've already let HR know about the change. They'll get you set up. Elaina used to keep up with our connections with the local business, civic and social organizations. I'll send you a list of our community involvement and the clubs you'll need to join in the meantime. Elaina's assistant can help get you set up."

"Organizations?"

"Just to help you play the part until things are settled."
Grant stood and strode to the door. "Thank you, Alex.
This is a tremendous load off my mind." He snapped his
fingers. "Oh, you said you had a few things you wanted to
talk to me about."

He shook his head. His mind fought to catch up with
the realization that his agreement came with the responsibility of joining local organizations. What the hell had he
signed up for? He was ready to take back his words when
it hit him that control of Robidoux Tobacco gave him the
opportunity to include his stepfather's farm as one of their
hemp suppliers if they explored the possibilities of hemp
manufacturing.

"It can wait."

Grant nodded. "Good."

Grant turned and walked out. Alex rocked back in his
chair and stared at the smooth ceiling. He'd have to tell
Rebecca she was right. Apparently, he was being set up to
take over after Elaina's downfall.

CHAPTER EIGHT

"WE'RE GOING TO need more money if you want to resume production in six months."

Elaina's fingers tightened on the fountain pen in her hand. She took a slow breath and eyed Zoe across the table from her. Muted sunlight filtered through the dirty windows of the upstairs conference room of the hemp manufacturing facility she'd purchased from her father. The metal chairs they sat in made her butt hurt after an hour of going over, in extreme detail, all of the renovations required and employees needed to get the place up to code and running.

When she'd purchased the place, the time needed to restore it to its former glory hadn't been an issue. Though she'd always wanted to take over her family's business, making the facility a success was part of a long-term goal to build her own wealth apart from her family's fortune. Her time had run out.

"How much money?" She kept her voice calm and even, though her heart punched against her rib cage. She had money, but she'd put most of it into buying the place. She couldn't go to her father for help. She no longer had a salary. The cold edges of anxiety scratched the back of her neck. She shifted her shoulders.

Don't panic. You can do this.

Zoe's neat brows drew together. "The plan was to take eighteen months to renovate the facility. That was with the expectation of being able to book the contractors we need in advance and give them a realistic window for completion. You're taking a year off that timeframe and trying to crunch it all into less than half that time. Anyone you find to help you is either going to be a con artist or good enough to charge extra in order to meet your deadlines."

Elaina ran her tongue over her dry lower lip. She tapped the pen against her fingers. She couldn't pay overpriced contractors. "Could we do it in a year instead of eighteen months?"

Zoe sighed and glanced at the screen on her laptop. "We could, but it's going to be difficult. Why do you want to rush things? I know losing your job—"

"Getting fired by my father. Let's not sugarcoat it. We both know what happened," Elaina said.

Zoe held up her hands. "Fine. But still, why rush? Now you have the time to fully devote to getting this place up and running without a problem."

"I need a win," she admitted. Before, taking her time to gradually rebuild gave her more opportunity to coax investors. Now she had no source of income, and her dad would be expecting her to fail and come crawling back for her job. She refused to do either.

"I get it. I want this place to open and be successful just as much as you do, but you don't want to rush things."

Elaina appreciated Zoe's partnership in this and knew she was just as invested in the facility as Elaina. Although Zoe had made peace with Grant's involvement in separating her and Byron back in college, she still fought to reduce Grant's influence on their personal lives.

"We don't have time to be patient," Elaina said. "Finding investors is easier if I'm still working at Robidoux Holdings and have my dad's backing. Now it's just me and I've been fired. I thought I'd have a steady stream of investors to supplement the money I put into this giving me time to update the machinery and building. I'd have to shut down production for a short time but not for the entire renovation. Without that I need a lot of money up front to at least replace the machinery as soon as possible. If I can't do that, I don't know if I can keep the facility open. I promised no layoffs. Not to mention paying you."

Zoe looked at the numbers on the screen and sighed. "Then I suggest you look for investors."

Elaina straightened her shoulders. "I can do this."

Zoe didn't look convinced, but she didn't argue. "Maybe you can start by asking Robert. Isn't he in finance?"

Elaina blinked. Heat filled her face. She hadn't told Zoe about the disaster that was Robert. At the party, she hadn't wanted to discuss the still fresh humiliation. After she'd been fired, they'd gone out and Zoe had done a great job distracting Elaina by making her laugh.

"What? You don't want to ask him?" Zoe asked. "I thought you two were getting serious."

Elaina felt even more like a fool. She held back on telling anyone about Robert because she'd been afraid she'd jinx things. Just as she'd begun to believe in them and finally revealed their relationship with Zoe, they'd broken up.

Elaina took in Zoe's hopeful expression and couldn't bring herself to admit the truth. "I broke things off with him."

Zoe's head jerked back. "Why? You were really into him."

Elaina glanced away and lifted a shoulder. "I was really into the sex. That's different. I'm not ready for anything more and I've got other things to worry about."

"Was he cool with that?"

More than cool. She pushed that sad truth aside. "He understood my reasons. It was good while it lasted, but we both knew this was just a temporary reconnection. Everyone doesn't get the second chance that you and Byron had."

Zoe smiled, but there was something else in her eyes. Elaina's stomach churned. She was so sick of everyone looking at her like the poor pitiful spinster. She would get this company together and she would build her own empire. She didn't need her family's company or a man to be happy. She would create her own happiness.

"We've met long enough, and I need to get back home to start thinking of next steps. Will you continue to look into potential suppliers?"

"I've already got one in mind," Zoe said. "Though you may not be interested."

"Why not? I need hemp if this is going to work."

Zoe ran her fingers over the keys of the laptop. "Well, I found out Alex Tyson's stepfather owns a hemp farm. He's looking to supply someone."

Elaina frowned. "Alex?"

"Yeah." Zoe shook her head. "Don't worry about it. I'll look into other areas."

Elaina wanted to hate Alex. Their argument was the reason she'd been fired, but even she had to admit she'd contributed to things getting out of hand. India, Ashiya and Zoe had properly schooled her on the part she'd played in her bad relationship with Alex. Grant had seized the opportunity to remind her that he still had influence over her life.

Plus, she couldn't stop thinking about the way he'd tried to apologize. If he'd gloated, she would happily proclaim him the biggest jackass in America. There hadn't been a single glimmer of satisfaction in his eyes. He'd looked genuinely upset. And damn if that didn't piss her off. She didn't want to *like* him.

"I don't have the luxury of being picky right now," Elaina said in a no-nonsense voice. "We'll check his place out. If his stepfather has a good production, then why not? I don't have to deal with Alex to work with his stepfather."

Zoe's eyes widened, but she nodded. "Okay, I'll look into it and set up something."

Elaina nodded. "Good."

They packed up their things and walked out of the conference room together. On the way out, Elaina spoke to the plant supervisor and some of the employees she'd kept on to handle maintenance of the equipment she did plan to keep. They were so afraid she was going to shut the place down permanently. She had no intentions of doing that, but their worried expressions added the same amount of responsibility she'd felt whenever she'd seen the employees at Robidoux Holdings look at her. Her success meant their success. She couldn't forget their well-being.

Her mind drifted back to Alex. He'd only wanted to help and make things better. Even though Grant brought him in to take over if she didn't perform to his satisfaction, Elaina hadn't seen any evidence of Alex intentionally trying to get rid of her. Her lips pressed together. Shit. She had been the bigger problem in their bad working relationship.

You're planning to give his father money by buying his product. That's apology enough.

Feeling moderately satisfied, Elaina said goodbye to Zoe, who was sticking behind to give the plant manager an update on their meeting. As she slid into the seat of her car, she connected her Bluetooth to her phone and turned on her favorite motivational podcast to listen to on the ride home. She needed motivation right now, but instead of focusing on the words, her mind kept going back to Alex. The regret in his eyes. The warmth that had spread through her midsection when he'd apologized that had nothing to do with the wine she'd consumed. She hoped to never see him again while also wondering if their paths would cross if she made his stepfather an offer he couldn't refuse.

THE LAST THING Elaina expected to deal with after realizing she'd need a lot more money to get her new facility renovated was to find her father's sleek black car parked in the driveway. Her lips curved up in a smirk. It had taken just two weeks for him to realize what a mistake he'd made. She understood that while vacant positions could be refilled, replacing a stellar employee was damn near impossible. Served him right. She'd handled so many big and small projects that couldn't easily be passed along. She might actually enjoy watching him beg for her to return.

Elaina parked in the garage. She took her time gathering her purse before getting out of the car. Barry, her dad's driver, was already out and opened the back door. Elaina crossed her arms and watched her father get out of the car with her practiced bland expression. She'd gloat after he asked her to return. If he got any indication she was enjoying this, he'd change his mind.

He must have come straight from the office. He was dressed in one of his dark blue suits. She could only imagine the impending disaster that had him leaving the office to come straight to her.

"I expected you sooner," she said in a slightly smug voice. So much for hiding her real feelings. She rarely got to have one up on her father.

Grant raised a thick brow. "Then I guess you got Lilah's call."

Elaina blinked. Before she could ask for clarification, Lilah bounded out of the back seat. Lilah's braids swung as she rushed forward to Elaina. A huge smile creased her young face. Elaina couldn't help but open her arms and accept her niece's hug.

"Aunt Elaina!" Lilah's arms wrapped around Elaina.

Despite her confusion, Elaina squeezed Lilah back. "What are you doing here?"

Lilah leaned back and met her gaze. "You haven't called me about the debutante ball at the country club. You promised you'd help me get ready for it."

Elaina closed her eyes for a second. She had forgotten about that. All she'd cared about was taking a break from her family. She hadn't gone back home, and after explaining things to both India and Byron, she'd focused completely on what she needed to do next career-wise.

"You are still going to help me, aren't you?" There was a tremor of panic in Lilah's voice.

Elaina placed a hand on Lilah's shoulder. "Of course I'm still going to help you. I've just been busy."

"But the information session for participants is tomorrow. You haven't called or come by to say anything. Mom thought you might be too busy to still help out."

Elaina squeezed Lilah's shoulder. "One thing I don't do is break promises. I'll be there. Do you need me to pick you up from archery practice?"

Lilah's eyes brightened. "Will you? I don't think Mom will mind. Then we can strategize in the car on the way there."

"Strategize about what?"

"How I'm going to be the best." Lilah's smile was cunning. The confidence in her voice made Elaina proud.

When Zoe had shown up in their lives with the kid

Byron agreed to say was his, she hadn't expected to fall for Lilah as quickly. The young girl had been so awed and appreciative of Byron, and so eager to learn and be a part of their family, Elaina had taken one look at her and decided to step in and help her. Otherwise, Grant would use Lilah's eagerness to be a part of their family to commit her to obligations too heavy for the young girl.

It was the same way she would have protected her own child, if things had worked out differently.

"Then I'll pick you up directly from practice, and we'll go to the information session. Don't worry about a thing."

Lilah grinned, leaned up, and kissed Elaina's cheek. "You're the best."

Warmth spread through her chest. Elaina doubted she had what it took to be a good mother, but she damn sure loved being an awesome aunt. "I got a new perfume sampler yesterday. Go in and pick one you want."

"I know this is just an excuse for you and Grandpa to talk, but I'll take it," Lilah said. Her grin slowly drifted away, her face pensive. "Maybe you two can make up."

If only she had Lilah's optimism. There were too many years of disappointments and regrets between Elaina and her dad to make this an easy reconciliation.

Elaina held up her keys with the house key separated from the rest. "The perfume is in my room on my dresser. The master bedroom shouldn't be hard to find." It was Lilah's first time there. The first time anyone from her family had been there since she moved in.

Lilah sighed, but took the keys and went to the house. Elaina turned back to her father, who'd watched her exchange with Lilah. She crossed her arms and met his smug stare.

"You didn't have to use Lilah as an excuse to talk to me," she said.

Grant walked toward her. "Not going to invite me in?"

"Why should I?"

"So I can check out where my daughter is living," he said evenly. "I need to make sure this place is decent."

"Don't worry, Daddy, the house has passed all inspections and is up to par."

The edges of his smile stiffened. "How about because I'm your father and you can't just keep me out here in the driveway?"

"Why not?" she asked innocently. "You've decided to kick me out of the business I've been promised since I was a girl, so I can keep you out of my house."

His eyes narrowed. "You aren't ready to admit you were wrong."

"Only when you are," she said evenly. "How are things going at the office?" She raised a brow. She didn't care if he'd had to use Lilah to speak to her. She knew things couldn't be going well without her. Why else would he try so hard to come up with an excuse to visit her?

He rubbed his hands together and leaned back on his heels. The picture of relaxation. A cobra before it struck. "Things are good. In fact, that's one of the reasons I want to talk to you."

Unease twisted her midsection. Could things really be fine without her? "Oh, really?"

"I want you to hear it from me first. I've appointed Alex as the new CEO. He started today."

Elaina's lips parted. She was momentarily stunned. He'd given Alex her job. She hadn't even been gone a month and he'd already replaced her. Fury slithered and pulsed through her veins like a thousand angry snakes.

Elaina suppressed the emotions. That's what he wanted. Further proof his daughter was emotional and incompetent.

"You've got what you wanted. That is why you hired him." Her voice was tight. Her body tense.

"I'd hoped I wouldn't have to get rid of you," Grant said. He almost sounded sincere.

Elaina sucked in a breath. She'd always wondered if her dad hired Alex to slide into her spot if she didn't do what he wanted. Wondered, but refused to believe. She'd viewed Alex as more of a vague threat. Like when they were little and her mom threatened to take back their Christmas presents if they didn't stop fighting with each other, but they knew she never would.

Dad is not Mom.

Grant watched her closely. She could just imagine him waiting for her to break down or throw a fit. Instead, she lifted her chin and straightened her shoulders. "Good luck with that. I'll get Lilah and send her back out." Elaina turned on her heel toward the door.

"Elaina, I had to. It was for your own good."

She heard the barest hint of regret in his voice. Elaina paused. She wanted too much to cling to that regret. To turn around, have him open his arms, hug her, and tell her they could work things out. When was the last time he'd hugged her? Besides for a picture or other social event. When was the last time he'd held her tight, told her things would be okay, just comforted her?

Not since before she started rebelling against him. Before she realized his suggestions and advice were always more about furthering the family's goals and less about the best interests of his children. Her dad loved her, she knew that, but his love was conditional.

She faced him again. "The last time you told me, that

was the day before I walked down the aisle and married Travis," Elaina said in a cold voice. She'd never forget the way her father basically told her to marry Travis or lose any chance at taking over the company. Silly her for believing he wouldn't find another reason to snatch the company from her. "Like then, this was a decision to benefit you and not me, Daddy." She glanced at him over her shoulder. "I think we're old enough now to admit you've never had my best interests at heart."

The pain that flashed across his face was almost enough to make her feel guilty. Almost. Once again, years of fighting him only to ultimately be forced back into whatever perfect box he wanted her to fit into hampered any remorse. He'd punch back. Grant didn't mind showing when she landed a blow, but she could never knock him out.

The fight between her and her father was never-ending and exhausting. She forced her shoulders to remain rigid, her chin to stay up, and clenched her teeth as she turned away. She blinked rapidly to stop the tears burning her eyes when her back faced him. She took quick, efficient steps to the front door before he could return his own parting comment. She was too fragile right now. She was afraid she'd shatter, and she couldn't afford to shatter in front of her father.

CHAPTER NINE

ELAINA SMILED AS she watched Lilah and the other kids participating in the Jackson Falls debutante ball huddle together as they waited for their paperwork and assignments. Even though she had a thousand things going wrong in her personal and professional life, she was glad she'd agreed to take the time to help Lilah with this.

She glanced around the room and caught the eye of Lauren Holmes, the director of fundraising and events for the country club. Elaina smiled and inclined her head. Lauren excused herself from the group of parents she was with and crossed the room.

"Elaina, hello. I'm so glad you're sponsoring Lilah," Lauren said.

"Ever since I mentioned the ball to Lilah, she's been eager to participate," Elaina said. "Since I brought it up, I figured I'd step in and sponsor her instead of putting it onto Byron or Zoe."

Lauren's thin face morphed into a fake sympathetic smile. "That's nice since you have so much extra time on your hands now."

Elaina froze. Lauren's stab had come quickly and unexpectedly. She'd let her guard down and Lauren slit her to the quick without a blink. She watched as Lauren's eyes sharpened with anticipation. Her eagerness to get a reaction out of Elaina was about as obvious as the excitement of the teens.

"Actually," Elaina said slowly in order to keep her emotions under control, "I've been busy working on a new venture, but Lilah was looking forward to this, and I couldn't tell her no."

Both of Lauren's overly arched brows rose. "A new venture? Well, good for you. It's not easy to bounce back after losing a job. I admire you for finding a little project to occupy your time." Lauren spoke as if she were a child who'd just learned to ride a bike without training wheels.

Elaina suppressed the urge to sigh and roll her eyes. Lauren wanted to get a rise out of her, but Elaina had sparred with people way more cunning than Lauren would ever be. If Lauren thought her thinly veiled pettiness was enough to make Elaina react, she was sadly mistaken.

Elaina tilted her head to the side. "I've purchased a manufacturing facility and am currently in the middle of renovations before reopening in a few months. I can understand how you might view that as a *little* project, considering you have no experience working for larger corporations."

She took immense satisfaction in watching Lauren's lips thin. She wasn't in the mood to sit there and participate in Lauren's tepid verbal sparring match. She'd expected having to save face after getting fired from her family's company, but she hadn't expected how quickly word would spread or how enthusiastically someone like Lauren, a person she'd volunteered with on numerous occasions, would relish in her downfall.

Does everyone really hate me that much?

The thought formed a depressing shadow over her previously sunny day. She'd looked forward to this afternoon with Lilah and didn't want to slide into a bad mood.

"If you'll excuse me," she said before Lauren could think of an adequate response and crossed the room to Lilah. "Hey, I'm going into the bar area to make a phone call. Come get me when you're done."

Lilah beamed and nodded. "Okay, Auntie. I'll be there in a minute."

Elaina wrapped the warmth of Lilah's smile around her bruised feelings before leaving the room. Many of the other adults in the room watched her. Some huddled together, whispering to each other. Were they talking about her? How she'd crashed and burned? Were they all secretly gloating about her firing the same way Lauren had?

Shaking away the thoughts, Elaina raised her head and strode out of the room with confidence. She went straight from the meeting room to the restaurant and bar. She wanted a drink.

Not when you're driving Lilah.

Something else, then. She took a seat at the end of the bar and ordered a seltzer water with lime. Her eyes scanned the restaurant while she waited and collided with a pair of intense dark eyes. Her brows drew together. What the hell was Alex doing here?

She looked away quickly, hoping he'd get the hint that she didn't want to be bothered. Even though he'd been nice to her the last time they'd seen each other, that didn't mean they could be friends. Sure, Alex outside of the office was nice enough. He'd seemed so much more relaxed and normal away from work and without those glasses. Then there were his eyes. She'd never really noticed how dark his eyes were before.

Her drink arrived at the same time a tall figure stood next to her. She knew it was Alex without looking. How in the world could she *sense* him?

"We need to talk." His voice was cool, commanding.

A shiver tickled her spine. Elaina frowned and shifted her shoulders. What the hell? She wasn't supposed to shiver at the sound of Alex's voice.

She turned in her seat and gave him what she hoped was a bored stare. "About what?"

His broad shoulders were stiff, his lips tightly pressed together. Those deep, dark eyes of his focused solely on her. Elaina suppressed the urge to shift in her seat. She hated when he looked at her like that. Like he could see through her bullshit.

"Your offer." He spoke the words as if she should have a clue as to what he meant.

"What offer?" she said.

His head tilted to the side. "You know exactly what offer. Look, Elaina, I know you're upset about what happened. I had no idea your dad would do that, or that he'd give me your job, but that doesn't give you the right to go after my family. My stepdad has put everything he had into that farm."

Her spine stiffened. She held up a hand. "Hold up. I don't know what you're talking about. If this is your way of gloating for getting my job, then you're not very good at gloating."

"Are you denying the offer you made for my dad to supply hemp to your facility?"

She was two seconds from cursing him out. Then she remembered what Zoe had mentioned. Zoe must have approached Alex's stepfather. He must have read the understanding on her features because his jaw clenched.

"If you hurt them—"

Her temper snapped. "I don't care enough about you to hurt them," she said with a flip of her wrist. "Even if I did,

I wouldn't use him or anyone else in your family to get back at you. I know this thing my dad's pulling is all his idea and his way of hurting me. Unlike my father, I don't use other people as pawns in my game."

She stood abruptly, forcing him to stumble back. She didn't care if Lilah wasn't finished. It was time to go. Elaina couldn't stay in here another minute. The sly looks and snide comments. The laughter about her getting fired. Now the accusations that she'd go after someone she didn't even know for revenge. She wasn't her dad and didn't want to be.

She turned and walked away with her head held high even though she wanted to rush out. The sound of Alex's footsteps followed her out of the restaurant and into the hall.

"Elaina, stop."

She spun on her heel and pointed at him. Her breath caught in her throat when her fingertip landed in the middle of his chest. His surprisingly firm chest. He'd moved quickly to catch up to her. She tipped her head back to meet his dark, direct gaze. Only a few inches separated them. The scent of his cologne, sharp and peppery, was kind of nice.

She dropped her hand and stepped back quickly. "What? Are you ready to accuse me of plotting to blackmail a sister or cousin next?"

Alex sighed and slid back. "My stepdad told me he was going to meet with you about supplying hemp to your new company."

He spoke the words as if that were enough of an explanation. The heat of her anger made her blood simmer. "So you assumed I was so consumed with rage that I'd plot to dash your stepfather's hopes by promising him a phony business deal. I knew you thought I was a terrible boss, but I didn't know you considered me as a good candidate for an evil villain." She turned to march away.

Alex reached out and took her elbow in his hands. "I'm sorry, but I had to be sure."

Elaina pulled out of his grasp. She resisted the urge to rub her elbow. Not because he'd hurt her, but because his touch lingered and permeated her arm. "I only recently found about your stepfather. My sister-in-law, Zoe, is making the connections with potential suppliers. She's setting up the meetings. Not me."

He studied her for a few more seconds, then nodded. "I'm sorry."

She scoffed at the hollowness of his apology. "I can't believe this. You still don't truly believe me?"

"Elaina, I don't know what to believe. I've tried and failed to understand you for more than two years."

The corners of her lips lifted. She hadn't given Alex many opportunities to get to know her. "Fine. I'll give you that." She met his gaze. "Look, I wouldn't try to work with your stepfather just to get back at you. Honestly, I need to make this company successful. Playing around with suppliers isn't going to help me at all. I can't afford to have another failure." She took a step toward him. "Please, tell your stepfather that I'm serious. Please ask him to give me a chance."

His eyes widened. "Wow."

Elaina drew back. "Wow what?"

"I've never heard you say please before."

The astonishment in his voice stunned her. Then she laughed at the absurdity of it all. At Lauren's smug satisfaction and Alex's belief that she would go after his family. Apparently, she was viewed as an evil villain. Too bad she didn't have the heart to truly be as evil as they assumed.

"I am capable of saying please," she said. "I just don't have to often."

A smile crinkled his face, softening his dark eyes and bringing a light to his face that poked a soft spot in her chest. He looked at her as if he appreciated her plea for a chance. The hesitant trust in his eyes made her want him to believe she wasn't the spiteful, inconsiderate, coldhearted bitch most people took her for.

Elaina's breath caught. What was she thinking? This was Alex. She hated Alex. He hated her. She shouldn't care what he thought.

"I've never made you laugh before," he said in a deep, satisfied voice. "I like your laugh. A lot."

The soft spot in her chest was bordering on squishy. She wasn't a squishy-feeling-type person. Even more unsettling were the areas much lower heating up just because Alex said he liked her laugh.

Elaina cleared her throat and broke eye contact. "I'm here with my niece. I should go to get her."

"I'll tell him to give you a chance," Alex said. "I'm sorry for accusing you."

The relief that went through her was palpable. She needed a win. Even one from her nemesis with eyes that made her feel both self-conscious and seen.

She raised her gaze back up to his. "Thank you."

They stared for the span of several heartbeats.

"Aunt Elaina, I'm ready." Lilah's voice broke the moment.

Alex blinked and took another step back. "I won't keep you." The corner of his mouth lifted. "Have a good night, Elaina."

"You too, Alex," she said briskly. She held out her hand. His warm hand clasped hers. A shot of electricity shot up her arm, tightened her nipples, and swirled through her sex. *Oh no! That is not supposed to be happening.* She pulled her hand away quickly and turned.

With fast steps she met Lilah, wrapped an arm around her niece's shoulders and headed toward the door.

"Who was that?" Lilah asked, her voice full of teenage curiosity as she looked over her shoulder.

"No one," Elaina said quickly. "Just an old coworker."

"Well, he's still looking at you like the guys in movies look at the woman they want."

Elaina snorted. "Stop being romantic, Lilah. He doesn't want me any more than I want him."

"If you say so," Lilah said with an eye roll before pulling away to go out the door.

Don't look. Don't look. Don't look.

Elaina looked over her shoulder. Alex stood where she'd left him. Watching her with those damn eyes. Elaina's face burned as she spun and rushed out the door. Four glasses of wine tonight. That's the only way she'd forget the smoldering look in Alex Tyson's hypnotizing eyes.

CHAPTER TEN

"OKAY, SO WHO'S the guy?"

Elaina eyed Zoe sitting in the passenger seat of her car. A question about a guy was the last thing she'd expected. They were on the way to meet with Alex's stepfather and determine if his hemp farm would be a good one to supply their facility. They'd gone over the details they wanted to cover and the game plan for making him feel confident they'd be ready when his harvest came in. She hadn't told Zoe about Alex's accusation that she was toying with his family for revenge. No need to get her sister-in-law worked up over that.

"What guy?" Elaina asked, genuinely confused.

"I don't typically like to bring up gossip, especially gossip out of the mouth of a teenager, but Lilah can't stop talking about you making googly eyes at a man last night after the pageant meeting."

Elaina sniffed. "I do not make googly eyes."

Zoe grinned. "According to my daughter, both you and this unnamed man were making googly eyes, and I quote, *'just like they do in the movies.'*"

Elaina rolled her eyes and flicked her wrist dismissively. "Lilah is being overly dramatic."

Zoe shifted and sat up straighter. "So there was a man?"

Heat prickled up Elaina's neck and cheeks. "I was talking to a guy last night. No big deal. There were no googly eyes involved."

There had been unexpected tingles and the inability to stop herself from taking one last look at him over her shoulder. Then there were the thoughts. Thoughts she'd tried to suppress but kept coming back. Did Alex really think she was that terrible? Why did she want him to think better of her? She'd spent two-plus years treating him as her nemesis. She shouldn't care, but the idea of Alex thinking she'd try to hurt his family had her stomach in knots. She should hate him.

"Okay, what the hell is going on?" Zoe said. "You're over there frowning and chewing on your lip. You never chew on your lip. Who is this guy? Is he the reason you broke things off with Robert?"

Elaina flinched. She could happily go the rest of her life and never hear Robert's name again. "No. It's not like that."

"Then what is it like?"

Zoe's gaze didn't waver from Elaina. She could ignore her sister-in-law, or she could just answer honestly. The thought of baring her ridiculous feelings for Alex, feelings she hadn't translated or explored, was scary. Too scary after her feelings typically led her to make the wrong decisions.

"There were no googly eyes. I didn't realize how much people at the country club would relish me being knocked from my pedestal. It was a rough night, and Lilah caught me talking to another person who believes there are horns hidden by my hair."

"Who was it?" Zoe's voice became defensive. Her willingness to fight for Elaina when so few people did was one of the reasons Elaina trusted Zoe more than anyone.

"I saw Alex Tyson."

"Say what?" Zoe shook her head. "So much for listening to Lilah. So, what did he say?"

"He thought today's meeting was my attempt at revenge on his stepfather. I told him I didn't even know this was his stepfather when you approached him."

"I didn't think we'd even have to deal with Alex." Zoe drummed her fingers on her thigh. "I can't believe he'd think that."

"I convinced him that I'm not so much of a conniving bitch that I'd take out any anger at him on his family. I know this situation is because of my father and not him."

"He believed you?"

The uncertainty in Zoe's voice didn't make Elaina feel any better. Zoe needed them to find suppliers as much as Elaina did. If Alex convinced his stepfather to go somewhere else, that made opening and producing on time difficult.

"We're having the meeting today, aren't we?"

"We are. I just hope he hasn't taken his concerns to his stepfather. Either way, we've got this," Zoe said, her voice filled with optimism. She crossed her fingers.

"We need this," Elaina said. She did. She needed the facility to open to prove to her dad she could be successful without him or the damn company he'd dangled in front of her like a morsel of food before a starving puppy.

They arrived a few minutes later. Elaina was familiar with the house and the land. When she was younger, the Rawls family used to live there. They also farmed tobacco but hadn't been as successful as her family. Mr. Rawls's children all wanted to get out of Jackson Falls. He'd sold the place, and Elaina had heard about the man from New York who'd moved down to make a fortune growing and selling hemp. She never would have guessed that man to be Alex's stepfather.

"The house is in good shape," Zoe said. "Byron mentioned it suffered some damage after the previous owners moved out."

Elaina nodded and turned off the car's engine. "The winds and rain left over from a hurricane messed up the roof and flooded the fields. I'm not surprised the house was salvageable, but the fields? Can they really produce what we need?"

"I guess we'll find out." Zoe unbuckled her seat belt and opened the car door.

Elaina did the same, and they both walked toward the front of the house. The exterior of the two-story home was finished in soft yellow siding. Blue shutters framed the windows, and a wrap-around porch with white Adirondack rocking chairs completed the overall welcoming feeling to the place.

Elaina gave Zoe a quick nod, sent up a prayer that this would work out, and rang the doorbell. The door swung open and Elaina's stomach flipped.

"Alex?" she said, surprised. "What are you doing here?"

"I promised Dad that I'd help him during this process," Alex said as if she should have expected him.

In hindsight, maybe she should have. He had accused her of trying to sabotage his stepfather's dream. If the tables were turned, and she liked her soon-to-be-stepmother, she would do the same.

"Of course," Elaina said in a tight voice. "You remember Zoe?" She indicated her sister-in-law.

"I do. Zoe, it's good to see you again." The smile he gave Zoe was wide and friendly.

Elaina tried not to think about the alleged "googly eyes" she and Alex supposedly made at each other the day before.

He hadn't bothered to smile when seeing her. Obviously, she'd been the only person feeling anything yesterday. Good. She was here on business. To find a supplier for her company and convince Alex that she wasn't a conniving, spiteful bitch.

Alex stepped back. "Come on in. My parents are waiting in the living room."

Elaina and Zoe followed him into the house. The home was just as warm and welcoming on the inside as it was on the outside. They entered the dining room, and the two people sitting at the table stood. The woman was clearly Alex's mom, Brenda. She had the same tall stature as him, curvy where he was hard, with a heart-shaped face and the same dark, penetrating eyes. Thomas was shorter and broader than Alex, with closely cropped dark hair that was thinning at the top, a big smile and a strong handshake. Elaina immediately felt comfortable around them. Something that didn't typically happen.

After the introductions, they sat around the dining room table. Thomas pushed over a plate with chocolate chip and oatmeal raisin cookies. "I made some refreshments."

Elaina blinked in surprise. "You made these yourself?" She couldn't imagine him in the kitchen baking cookies.

Alex spoke up before Thomas. "Dad is a whiz in the kitchen. When he's not out in the fields, he's whipping up something to eat."

Elaina picked up an oatmeal raisin cookie and took a bite. "This is delicious. You could have been a baker."

Thomas's smiled sheepishly and shook his head. "I love cooking for my family, but I couldn't imagine cooking for strangers all day. I don't have the patience."

Brenda poured everyone a glass of sweet tea and then clasped her hands on the table. She smiled first at Zoe, then at Elaina, before her eyes sharpened. "So, tell us why we should trust you with our harvest."

Elaina immediately knew where Alex got his stare and direct nature from. Her stomach clenched. She had a second of doubt. What if she couldn't make good on her promises? What if she didn't open in time, or her sales didn't meet the projected demands?

"You can't control the future. Control the now."

Calmed by the words her mom always spoke to keep Elaina from spiraling into a panic, Elaina took a deep breath and met the eyes across the table.

"Because I want to succeed more than anyone you'll come across. My facility is new, but it has my tenacity behind it. I'm willing to work with you to make sure we're both ready to meet the needs in this ever-changing industry. That, and I'm willing to pay top dollar if what you produce is good."

Brenda lifted her chin, then looked to her husband. She nodded, and Thomas inclined his head. The words were unspoken, but Elaina knew she'd at least gotten past their first test enough that they would hear what else she had to say.

Thomas sat back in his chair. "Tell me about your facility."

Elaina and Zoe spent the next several minutes going over their plans. Not only the logistics of square footage and equipment updates, but also the products they would manufacture, and potential buyers. Buyers weren't set in stone, and she still had to secure more investors, but she had to believe she would.

Alex didn't speak up. He watched her and Zoe the entire time, but let his parents dictate the questions. She felt as if he could read her inner doubts and concerns. That only made her want to work harder. She wouldn't let him believe she couldn't deliver. She was more than the entitled executive he'd accused her of being.

By the time they finished, Thomas looked eager and Brenda seemed satisfied, while Alex remained quiet and aloof.

"Can we have a few days to consider?" Thomas asked.

Elaina would have preferred a yes on the spot, but knew no one liked to appear overly anxious in business. "Of course, but I would like to have an answer sooner rather than later. I'm looking for several suppliers and prefer to use local ones. I'd hate to have to look elsewhere."

Thomas nodded. "Fair enough. Now that the business part is over, we can relax. Elaina, Zoe, I'd love for you to stay for dinner."

Zoe shook her head. "I'd like to, but I've got to pick my daughter up from school."

Thomas looked to Elaina. "What about you?"

"I'm riding with Zoe," Elaina said.

"That's no problem. Alex can take you home after dinner," Thomas said easily.

Brenda's eyes lit up. "That's a great idea. We'd like to get to know you more if we're going into business together."

Elaina wanted to say no. She dared to glance at Alex. His jaw was tight, but he didn't speak up for or against. He was probably praying for her to decline. If it wasn't Alex but another potential business partner, she'd agree. She'd stick things out and try to build a relationship with them. She couldn't let him scare her off.

Elaina smiled back at Brenda and Thomas. "If Alex doesn't mind, I'd love to."

CHAPTER ELEVEN

ALEX LEFT ELAINA talking with his dad in the dining room about his oatmeal raisin cookie recipe and followed his mom into the kitchen.

"Why did you invite her to dinner?" he whispered as soon as they crossed the threshold. Voices traveled in the house, and he didn't want Elaina or Thomas to overhear.

"What? Why are you surprised? You know we've always invited partners to join us for dinner."

Alex couldn't argue with that. When he was growing up, it wasn't unusual for his parents' potential and current business partners to join them for dinner. They both insisted social interaction was one of the best ways to figure out if you should trust someone in business. Anyone could be pleasant in a conference room, but put them around people in the service industry, kids, or out of their element, and their true nature tended to come out.

"We don't even know if we're going to supply her company," Alex replied. "Don't you think it's premature to have her over for dinner?"

"She seems to want to work with us just as much as we want to work with her," his mom countered. "We can't be sure that she's the right person unless we get to know her better."

"But Mom—"

Brenda held up a hand. "Look, I understand that you two

didn't get along together at work, but this isn't Robidoux Holdings. We're on even ground here."

"It's more than that, Mom. She—" He didn't want to admit that he'd been the reason she'd gotten fired. Elaina might not hold a grudge against him, but he still felt bad and knew his parents would, too. Not only that, but Elaina was complicated. She could be ruthless and cold one minute and clever and charming the next. She infuriated and fascinated him. He'd thought he'd felt something flowing between them the night before, and it was too soon after that to have her so close up in his personal space.

"She's not very personable," he said weakly.

Brenda scoffed and rolled her eyes. "She seems nice enough." She opened the oven, and the rich aroma of the chicken and potatoes his dad had put in earlier filled the kitchen.

"Well, she's not always nice. She's a good businesswoman, but she may come across as cold."

Brenda put on the oven mitts and pulled out the pan with the chicken. "I'll be sure to keep that in mind." She put the pan on the cooling rack.

They left the kitchen. Elaina's and his dad's voices came from the living room. He and his mom followed. Alex stopped short at the threshold, and his jaw fell open. Laughter greeted them as Elaina and Thomas stood in front of the couch. Thomas's new reflex bow was in her hands.

"Oh, Lord, you've pulled out the bow," his mom said. "Elaina did not come here to hear you talk about bow hunting."

"Actually, I noticed and asked him about it," Elaina said eagerly. "My niece is on her school's archery team. I've learned a little from her and picked up a bow and arrow for practice a few times. It's a fun sport."

Thomas tapped his bow proudly. "Elaina was telling me about the time she practiced with her niece's bow and accidentally put a hole in the window of her pool house."

Elaina held up her free hand. "I've gotten much better since then."

"I've got the bull's-eye set up out back," Thomas said. "We've got a few more minutes to wait on dinner. Want to shoot a few?"

Elaina tested the string. "There's way too much weight on this one. What's this set at, forty pounds?"

Brenda waved her hands and took the bow out of Elaina's hands. "It is, but I've got one, too. It's set at twenty pounds. You can shoot with mine."

Alex stood dumbfounded. His mom couldn't be serious. Thomas, he could see. Once his dad got a new hobby, he was all in for months. He'd thought his mom was just indulging him, but from the excitement in her eyes, she was just as eager to show off their new bows to Elaina as Thomas was.

Elaina grinned. "Perfect."

"I'll go get it. It's in the bedroom. Give me just a second." Brenda hurried down the hall.

Thomas took the bow from Elaina. "I'll check the targets out back."

"Dad," Alex cut in. He pointed to the kitchen. "Dinner is ready. Mom just took out the chicken."

Thomas waved him off. "It's got to cool for a few minutes. This won't take long." He turned and strode out the door.

Alex looked at the paths his mom and dad had taken, then back at Elaina. "You don't have to do this."

Elaina raised a brow. "What's the problem, Alex? Afraid

I'll put an arrow through your heart?" Her voice was even and calm, but he saw the spark of humor in her eye.

A feeling he didn't want to identify pierced his heart. If he didn't stop thinking he saw more in Elaina's eyes than was really there, he'd be in jeopardy of being hit by another type of arrow.

"You wouldn't ruin a business deal like that," he said.

Her lip quirked up into a small smile. He remembered the huge smile she'd had on her face the night he'd seen her in the bar with Zoe. That and her light laugh that seemed to come more naturally today than it had then. What would it take to hear her laugh like that again?

"You're right about that," she said. "Can you shoot?"

He waved his hand side to side. "A little, but I'm not as into it as my parents."

Her brows drew together slightly. She looked as if she were going to ask something, but then her face cleared. "Well, you can watch."

"And I'll be sure to stand clear so that my heart doesn't go the way of your pool house window."

Her small smile returned. "Glad to know you're ready to protect your heart from me."

He went to the door, and she followed. Alex opened the door, then pushed open the screen door for her to go out before him. "I don't know. Sometimes I wonder what you'd do if I put my heart in your hands."

She froze and glanced over her shoulder at him. A spark of energy shot between them. He hadn't meant to say that, but strangely, he didn't want to take back the words, either. Not after seeing the flash of interest in her eye. He was attracted to Elaina. Heaven knew flirting with her was about as smart as trying to pet an angry cat. He was more likely to get scratched than cuddled, but just the thought of a soft reply from her was enough to make him try.

"Got it!" His mom's excited announcement as she came into the entryway snapped him back to sanity.

Elaina blinked and looked away. She smiled over her shoulder at his mom. "Then let's have some fun."

ALEX DID HAVE FUN. More fun than he'd expected. The Elaina he'd worked with was nowhere to be found. She wasn't cold, dismissive or arrogant during the impromptu archery time or the subsequent dinner. Instead she'd been warm, interested and appreciative of the attention his parents gave her. At first, she'd seemed surprised by Thomas's genuine excitement about her interest and their encouragement of her pretty bad shots. So much so, he'd think she hadn't grown up with the constant reaffirmation of her talents he assumed came with a life of wealth and privilege.

Elaina held out her hand to his mom before leaving for the evening. "I really enjoyed dinner. Thank you for the invitation."

His mom waved Elaina's hand away and held out her arms. "We don't do handshakes around here. I'm a hugger."

Elaina stiffened, eyes wide, and stepped back. "I… I'm not."

Everyone stood still. He saw the surprise on his mom's face. No one typically turned away her hugs.

"But I'll make an exception this one time," Elaina said a heartbeat later.

His mom smiled. "Are you sure?" Alex knew she wouldn't force it.

Elaina nodded stiffly. "Of course." Elaina stepped forward, and Alex witnessed the most awkward hug he'd ever seen. He was about to tell his mom that was enough when the edges of Elaina's lips lifted before she turned her head to lightly rest on his mother's shoulder. When she pulled back, she pushed her hair behind her ear as if embarrassed. "Thanks again."

His mom patted her shoulder. "Come back any time."

"Thank you," Alex said once they were in his car.

Elaina stopped scrolling through her cell phone to look at him. "For what?"

"For…" What was he supposed to say? Thank you for being nice to my parents? He remembered the hurt look in her eye when he'd accused her of only trying to go into business with them to get back at him. He didn't want her to think he still believed she was trying to hurt his family.

"For giving Thomas a chance," he said. "When he and my mom moved down here to turn a tobacco farm into a hemp farm, I worried they wouldn't be able to make it. If this works out, then they'll both be happy."

"What he's done to increase production shows he knows what he's doing," Elaina said, looking back at her phone.

Alex chuckled. "That's the thing. He didn't know what he was doing. My parents left on a whim. Dad wanted to be a farmer, and my mom had dreams of the summers she spent with family down south."

"Then the fact that he's done so well without prior knowledge of farming only proves he's the right person to supply my facility."

"I can't argue with that. They've got a knack for business, and what they don't know, they're willing to learn. That's the one thing I appreciate about my parents. They're never afraid to step out of their comfort zone."

Elaina dropped her phone in her lap and looked at him. Alex glanced over. She had a frown on her face.

"What?" he asked.

"You keep saying your parents," she said carefully.

"I do?"

"But Thomas isn't your dad. He's your stepfather."

Understanding dawned, and he nodded. "He is, but my mom married him when I was ten years old. He raised me."

"Is your father… I mean…what about your real…" She sighed and shook her head. "I'm sounding terrible, aren't I?"

Alex laughed and shrugged. "No, you don't. My biological father lives in Seattle. His name is Warren."

"Do you have a relationship with him?" Elaina asked in a matter-of-fact voice.

Alex nodded and thought about his relationship with Warren. His biological dad was more like a favorite uncle than a father to him. "I see him every few years. We call each other on birthdays and major holidays. He paid for my undergraduate degree and bought me my first car."

"So you do have a relationship with him?" she asked sounding confused.

"I do."

"Then why do you call Thomas and your mother your parents?"

"Because Thomas was in the house with me every day. Warren paid child support, remembered to send a card for my birthday even if he didn't call, and asked about my grades when he did call. Thomas, Dad, was there the first time my heart was broken. He planned all my birthday parties and made the birthday cake. He helped me get my learner's permit and driver's license and moved me into my college dorm. He may technically be my stepdad, but I don't see him that way. He's my dad. He and my mom are my parents."

Elaina glanced out of the window. "Hmm."

Alex waited thirty seconds for a response. When she kept quiet, he had to ask. "Okay, what's the *hmm* for?"

"It's just… I couldn't imagine thinking of my father's fiancée as my mother. Sure, they've been together for years and she lives at the estate, but even when they get married, she's going to be my stepmother. That's it."

"They recently got engaged. I guess it's hard when you're older."

"I've known her since I was twelve," Elaina said. "She was my mom's friend and the lead chef in our house growing up. She took care of my mom when she got sick. She started sleeping with my dad before my mom died of cancer."

Alex gripped the steering wheel. He'd walked right into that. Elaina stated everything in a cool, unemotional voice as if she were reciting multiplication tables. If he hadn't seen her soak up his parents' warmth and affection earlier, he'd assume she didn't feel anything. That she was okay with the situation. Now, he heard the forced detachment in her voice. Noticed the way her hands tightened around her cell phone.

"I had no idea."

"A lot of people outside of the family don't know," she said evenly. "She's been around so long that I couldn't imagine my dad without her. He's happy in a way that I can't even remember him being when Mom was alive. Not since I was very little, anyway. While I don't begrudge anyone's happiness…"

"It doesn't make that any easier to accept." Alex couldn't imagine seeing his mom or dad move on with someone else, much less with a person they'd had an affair with. He didn't remember his mom and Warren's divorce because they'd split when he was two. All he'd known was that Warren helped when he could. Then his mom met Thomas, who absolutely adored her. He hadn't realized how lucky he'd been.

Elaina's lips lifted in a humorless smile. "My mom knew what was going on. She told him to move on when she couldn't give him everything he needed. She told me that women in our position couldn't afford to be jealous or possessive. That our role was to be the foundation that held everyone up. We had to be strong. We couldn't afford weakness, and loving a man so much that you were upset by his every move made you weak to his whims."

"Damn, that's fucked up."

Elaina's head whipped around toward him. "Excuse me?"

He cringed. He hadn't meant for the words to come out that way. "Sorry. I shouldn't have said that."

"But you did, so you might as well tell me why." Her death stare from the office was back.

Alex lifted a shoulder. He searched for words that were less likely to make her angrier, then decided to just say what he meant. "I mean, she was sick, and she gave your dad a pass. I guess I get that, but to tell you that you should do the same, or not care about having to do the same whenever you got married…that's a heavy burden to put on a child. Heavy and unfair. Wouldn't she want you to have better than she did?"

Elaina looked out the window again. He'd upset her. All the work his parents had done to get in good with Elaina, and he'd managed to ruin it in the span of a car ride.

"It didn't seem unfair to me," she murmured. "My mom was my everything. All I ever wanted was to grow up and be just like her. So much so that I made decisions I shouldn't have made." She clenched her hands into fists. When she looked back at him, the death stare was replaced by a look of understanding. "It was some bullshit and a heavy burden. Thank you for…giving me the space to say that." She turned back to the window.

They didn't talk for the rest of the ride. Alex was stunned into silence after she'd thanked him. Had no one given her the space to vent her frustrations before? What type of decisions had she made based on that logic? He wouldn't make excuses for her, but he understood her cold aloofness with people a little better now. He was in no way a hopeless romantic, but he had grown up in a loving household and knew that if he ever married, he wanted to marry someone he loved and respected, who felt the same for him.

After he pulled into her driveway, he got out to walk her to the door, even though Elaina rolled her eyes and said that chivalry was dead and unnecessary. Though he'd glimpsed the slight lift of her lips when she'd turned away. He didn't have to walk her to the door, but something in him wanted to show her a little more consideration. After what she'd admitted, maybe he'd been wrong for assuming Elaina's life of wealth and privilege had come with praise, caring and love.

She opened her door, turned off the alarm at the keypad, then faced him. "See, I am capable of letting myself in the house."

Alex smiled in the face of her clipped words. "I know you're more than capable. Heaven help any burglar who tried to break into your place."

"Only the most hardened burglars dare cross my path," she said with a trace of humor in her voice.

Alex held out his hand. "Don't worry. I won't try to hug you."

Elaina glanced at his hand. Her brows drew together.

"You know, besides my niece, Lilah, your mom was the first person to hug me in years."

Alex dropped his hand. Stunned again. "You can't be serious?" She had a brother, a sister, he assumed a lover. Someone had to have hugged her.

"I've gotten shoulder pats and squeezes. The occasional arm around the shoulder." She let out a self-deprecating chuckle. "When you're a coldhearted bitch, you don't tend to put off the hug-me vibe."

"You're not a coldhearted bitch," he said automatically. He hadn't penetrated her wall of armor, but he saw it for what it was now. Protection for someone who'd been told love was a liability instead of an asset.

She raised a brow. Alex lifted a shoulder. "Okay, you're cold and I have seen you be…"

"Bitchy?" she said with a half smile.

"Hard-nosed," he compromised. "But that's also what makes you fierce and fantastic. You're bad as hell, and I like it."

She watched him with her calm, impassive expression. Calm except for her eyes. They were bright, and surprised, and he'd dare say happy. Before he knew it, Elaina took two steps forward. His body responded before his brain. His arms opened, and in the next second Elaina was pressed against him. She held herself stiffly, but the warmth of her curves cushioned him. He turned his head to breathe in the scent of her hair and was surprised that he detected a hint of strawberries. He never would have expected that sweet fragrance on Elaina, but he also now couldn't imagine anything else. Her chest expanded. Then her breath released in a slow exhale, her body softening by a fraction. The need to lower his head to her neck and place a soft kiss there was a rough pull on his instincts. He wanted to follow the scent of strawberries to see if her skin also carried the fragrance. Would she taste as decadent?

Elaina lifted her head. Their eyes locked, and for several moments he couldn't breathe. Something hot and potent flared in her eyes before they dropped to his lips. She ran her tongue over her full lower lip, blinked, then pulled back quickly.

"Good night, Alex," she said in a soft, husky voice.

Alex shoved his hands into the pockets of his pants to avoid pulling her back into his arms. Crush her mouth with his. Add fuel to the spark he'd seen in her eye.

"Good night, Elaina." He turned away and hurried down the stairs before he did just that. Elaina Robidoux was a woman who wouldn't appreciate him coming on strong. And with that quick hug, he knew one thing for sure. He wanted Elaina to explore the vibe going between the two of them. He wanted to make her smile, give her a reason to feel comforted, taste the sweetness of her lips. Which was why he had to leave before he said something he'd later regret.

CHAPTER TWELVE

DARK SUNGLASSES MODERATELY helped the dull ache in Elaina's head as she walked up the stairs of City Hall to visit her brother. She was still waiting on the ibuprofen she'd taken to kick in. She hated hangovers and had gotten good at gauging how many glasses of wine she could handle and still avoid feeling the effects the next day.

Damn Alex and that ridiculously comforting hug the night before. She'd been shaken by how silly she'd been for initiating the hug but also by how much she'd liked it. Liked being held in his embrace. The welcoming warmth of his family triggered such a feeling of longing after finishing off one bottle of red wine she'd opened a second bottle and relived the events of the day.

Now she had a headache and her limbs felt like dead weight from a fitful sleep filled with dreams of hugging him, kissing him, *sleeping* with him. She'd have to do something about this. The last time she'd felt this way, she'd gotten involved with Robert, and before that, her ex-husband, Travis. Too many times, hormones and fantasies led her to bad decisions. She was zero for two. She wasn't ready to make Alex Tyson terrible relationship mistake number three.

She slid her shades to the top of her head as she entered the warm interior of City Hall. Her heels clicked on the marble floor as she crossed the lobby toward the metal detectors. Everyone knew she was the mayor's sister and would have easily let her go through without being checked, but Elaina never took advantage of that. She preferred being treated like everyone else.

She smiled and spoke with the two security guards as her purse went through the detectors, waved at the front desk receptionist as she crossed to the elevators up to the third floor where Byron's office was located, and even carried on a superficial but pleasant conversation about the weather finally cooling a bit with the woman riding up with her who got off on the second floor.

She was sure anyone who saw her wouldn't be able to tell that her head hurt, and her eyes felt like sandpaper despite the drops she'd used earlier that day. Byron's receptionist notified her brother she was there, and a few minutes later, she entered his spacious office.

Byron stood and met her halfway across the room. "What brings you down to City Hall?" He stopped in front of her and narrowed his eyes. "Are you okay?"

Elaina took a step back. "Of course, I am. Why do you ask?"

"You look tired." He continued to study her face.

"Gee, thanks, Byron. It's great to see you, too."

He had the decency to look apologetic. "My bad. I wasn't trying to call you out, but you do look tired. Your eyes are a little red."

He pointed to the couch next to the window overlooking downtown. Elaina walked over and took a seat. "I didn't sleep well." After a fourth of the second bottle, she'd fallen into a fitful sleep on the couch. She'd finally woken in an uncomfortable position early that morning.

"Shit, I hate this. I told Dad he never should have fired you." Byron sank onto the couch next to her. The sleeves of his light blue shirt were rolled up, and his tie was off. One glance at the hook across the room and she saw it next to the jacket of his suit.

"I didn't come here to talk about Dad." She breathed a sigh of relief that he assumed her bad night was about their father.

"We need to talk about Dad," Byron said. "You are a part of this family and he can't just toss you out like that. All your life has been focused on taking over Robidoux Tobacco and Robidoux Holdings. You deserve better."

Her brother's strong defense warmed her heart. She was closer to Byron than anyone else in her family. He idolized their dad almost as much as Elaina had idolized their mother. It had taken Byron a little longer to admit their parents weren't perfect and didn't always do the right thing in the name of protecting their kids. Yet even before that realization, he'd taken up for Elaina and trusted her advice.

Elaina reached over and patted his hand. "It's okay, Byron. This fight is between me and Daddy, and it's been a long time coming. I agree with everything you said, but I've known for a while that I needed to step out and build my own legacy. He's dangled taking away Robidoux Holdings from me enough for me to take the threat seriously."

"That doesn't mean I have to like it. He won't even talk about you with me or India. He just changes the subject and moves on. At dinner, he tries to pretend as if you not being there is normal, even though I've caught him looking at your seat, which he refuses to let anyone else sit in."

Elaina raised a brow. "You're kidding?"

Byron shook his head. "I'm not. He misses you, though he'll never admit it. Even Patricia said he's gone too far. She always asks if we've talked to you when he's around and says she can't wait for Grant to come to his senses again and give you your job back."

Elaina leaned back. "I find that surprising. I didn't think Patricia liked me." She and her dad's fiancée had a congenial relationship, but they weren't close and never would be. Elaina accepted her as the woman her mother chose for her dad to be with, but despite that, she couldn't accept Patricia as anything close to a mother, friend or confidant.

"Patricia likes us because Dad loves us," Elaina said. "Not liking us isn't an option."

Byron shrugged. "She's trying to be a mother to us."

Elaina rolled her eyes. "She can try all she wants. We've accepted her as Dad's future wife. She can be happy with that." Still, Elaina appreciated Patricia standing up to Grant about firing her. Must be the lingering effects of being around Alex's loving family. Now she was seeing affection where there had never been any.

"I agree with you, but this one time, Patricia is right. Dad should give you your job back."

Elaina held up a hand. "I don't even know if I want it back. I'm focusing on my own future now, which is why I'm here. I need your old campaign office." She brought the conversation to her reason for coming down here in the first place.

Byron blinked and frowned. "My campaign office? For what?"

"I want to make it the location for my new company. I'm meeting with potential clients and suppliers, and I need an address to give them that isn't just a PO box. You're not using the space, and I know you own it. Let me use it."

If she had a physical office, she wouldn't have to meet suppliers at their homes. She wouldn't ask them about their hobbies. She wouldn't have fun with them and stay for dinner. She wouldn't be wrapped up in an embrace that made her feel safe, secure, loved. She wouldn't long to be pulled back into that embrace.

"Love makes you weak. Never be the weaker person in a relationship." Her mom's words echoed in her mind.

"Is this temporary or permanent?" Byron's question pushed her mom's old advice out of her head.

"Temporary until Zoe and I get the facility remodeled. We'll have plenty of meeting space then. Once I turn a profit and can purchase other businesses, then I'll look at a permanent spot for my new holding company." The idea had hit her after the second glass of wine and fiftieth time reliving the strength of Alex's body against hers.

Byron nodded. "You know I'll help you in any way that I can, but I still can't imagine you not being a part of Robidoux Holdings."

Neither can I.

The thought was like a searing hot poker through the chest. As much as she knew that she needed to build her own legacy, that she couldn't rely on her father, or submit to his demands that she meet his standards anymore, she also loved that company. Robidoux Tobacco and Robidoux Holdings had been in her blood from the moment she'd gone in the fields with her grandfather and he'd shown her how they grew tobacco, to the times she'd sat in her mother's office to listen as she talked to clients, and the day she'd agreed to marry the guy whom she didn't love just to avoid a scandal and protect the family name.

She'd sacrificed so much for that company. She couldn't say she regretted the choices she'd made, because she'd always believed it would lead her to the top one day. Walking away from everything felt like ripping out a part of herself.

Elaina stood before Byron would see that hurt in her

expression. "We both have to get used to this new reality. I'm excited about my future. I hope you can be excited for me, too."

Byron stood. He studied her for long seconds before letting out a deep breath and nodding. She knew he didn't believe her completely, but in true Robidoux fashion, he accepted her excuse instead of diving too deep in her emotions. "I am excited for you. You're my sister, and I know you'll succeed at whatever you put your mind to. That or you'll outmaneuver the competition."

Elaina's lips lifted. The pride in his voice sent a rush of emotion through her. She almost leaned in to hug Byron, but held back. If she hugged him, the tears burning the backs of her eyes would spill. She didn't want anyone, not even her closest relative, to see how fragile she was right now.

"Then hand over those keys so I can go out and conquer the world."

LATER THAT WEEK, Elaina had Byron's old campaign office reworked to serve her new business's needs. Zoe now had an actual office to call potential partners and suppliers from, along with a desk for a receptionist, when they were able to afford one. Most importantly, they had a conference room for future meetings.

The idea of not having dinner with Alex's family again gave her a tug of regret she couldn't shake. She thought about him way too much. Thankfully, she had debutante ball preparations at the country club.

Despite her annoyance after Lauren's snide remark and the embarrassment of knowing people were probably delighting in her firing, she wouldn't let Lilah down. Which was how she found herself in a room full of volunteers who'd agreed to help design the stage decorations to match the theme of this year's ball. The most help with setup Elaina had ever provided was sending a check to cover the costs, but Lilah seemed excited about the idea of her aunt putting her fashionable stamp on the event.

There was a knock on the door just as they were getting settled to start. Elaina looked toward the door and froze. Alex stood there in a pair of tan slacks and a dark gray button-up shirt, looking like he'd stepped right out of one of her runaway fantasies.

"Sorry I'm late. I just found out I've been put on this committee." He glanced around the room. His eyes met hers and widened slightly before he nodded. "I guess I shouldn't have told them I'm good with a hammer."

There was a murmur of laughter through the other volunteers before he was waved in.

"You're not late," Elaina said. She'd been told she was the head of the decorating committee. "We were just getting started."

"Good." Alex came further into the room.

The group sat in a circle around the room. Alex took the seat across from Elaina. He sat with perfect posture and rested the ankle of one foot on the opposite knee.

Elaina shifted in her seat and cleared her throat. "Okay, let's get to the point. The theme of this year's debutante ball is 'Reach for the Stars.'" There were more chuckles and a few groans. It wasn't as if the members of the club put a lot of thought into original themes. "I understand your disdain, but let's not forget the kids are excited, and it's one of our biggest fundraisers for the youth center."

"Wasn't last year's theme 'To the Moon and Beyond'?" Sade Sawyer asked. She was seated to Alex's left, and her eyes had lit up when he'd entered the room.

Elaina almost smiled. "It was. The good thing is we could probably use some of the items from last year."

"We just have to switch some things up," Sade said.

Sade smiled at Alex as if she'd given some brilliant insight. Alex returned her smile. Elaina's stomach felt funny. She cleared her throat and forced her attention to her notes.

"Exactly," Elaina said. "Why don't we focus on ways to enhance this year's theme."

They spent the next few minutes talking about ways they could make the ball more exciting. Sade scooted her chair closer to Alex to show him pictures on her phone from the previous year. Alex didn't pull away and returned Sade's smiles with his own.

There was no good reason Alex shouldn't follow up on Sade's flirting. Sade was a great woman. She owned several insurance franchises. She was pretty, kindhearted and funny. Elaina had even tried to hook her up with Byron several years before. But with every inch that shrank between them, each little laugh and extended eye contact, Elaina's irritation grew. Both with their blatant flirting and with her ever-tightening stomach. The thought of Sade and Alex hooking up shouldn't bother her so much.

Sade laughed again and placed her hand on Alex's knee. Elaina's fingers tightened around the papers she held. She stood quickly. "I think we're done here. We can talk more next week."

Sade's brows drew together. "Are you sure?"

Elaina nodded. "We've been here an hour. I'll go downstairs to take inventory of what we have left from last year. I'll have the inventory complete and ready for our next meeting."

The rest of the group nodded and stood. Most seemed ready to end the meeting. Elaina turned her back on Alex and Sade. She walked over to one of the tables and slid her phone into her purse. She searched the papers in her messenger bag for the inventory list from last year.

Alex walked over to stand beside her. "I'll help you with the inventory."

She turned to face him. He leaned one arm on the table. The muscles bunched beneath the fabric of his shirt. She remembered how strong they'd felt around her. Heat filled her cheeks. "I don't need help."

He shrugged, and his unwavering gaze never left her face. "I'd still like to help. I got here late. It's the least I could do."

Elaina looked over to where Sade watched them. If she insisted, Alex would walk out, and Sade would slide up next to him. They'd get a drink or go to dinner. That would lead to another date, and then they'd be dating. Elaina would have to watch them make googly eyes at each other at every planning meeting between now and the debutante ball.

"Fine," she said quickly. "It'll go faster."

Alex nodded, and the edges of his full lips lifted in a smile. Elaina's heart stuttered. She had the urge to return his smile. She turned and headed toward the door before the memories of being in his arms reflected in her eyes.

CHAPTER THIRTEEN

ELAINA'S HEART POUNDED as she led Alex down the stairs to
the basement storage room. She chastised herself for feeling nervous when the only thing they were going to do was
take a quick inventory. Yet anticipation hung in the air like
a cloud of tobacco smoke. She wasn't big on pretending to
be stupid. She'd accepted his offer of help so he wouldn't
go off with Sade.

She unlocked the door to the storage room using the key
she'd gotten from the head of maintenance. She left the key
in the door and held it for Alex to come through. He placed
his hand on the door, and Elaina went in.

"There is a stopper on the floor. Use it. Otherwise we'll
be stuck—" The door clicked shut. Elaina spun around. She
looked from the closed door to Alex and back. He raised a
brow as if waiting for her to finish.

"We'll be stuck down here."

His eyes widened. "What?"

"The door only unlocks from the outside. Everyone
keeps saying we'll fix it, but since this room is only used
for storage, it never moves to the top of the list."

"You're kidding." Alex turned and tried the lock. The
door didn't budge.

"I wish I were. At least once a year someone gets locked
in this room."

He continued to rattle the lock. He looked at her over

his shoulder again. "If someone's locked in once a year, I don't understand why they don't make a point to move it up the list?"

"Because some people get locked in on purpose. Many a clandestine affair has sparked after someone was 'accidentally' locked in the basement storage."

Alex raised a brow. "But…"

She saw the question in his eyes. She held up her hands and waved them quickly. "No. I told you about the stopper. I didn't know you would let the door go."

She had tried to tell him. She'd held the door for him to hold just like she would for anyone else. It wasn't her fault he'd let it go before she finished talking.

"My bad."

"I'll just call maintenance and have them come let us out." She reached for her back pocket, but nothing was there. She closed her eyes and groaned. "Shit. I left my cell phone upstairs." She'd put it in her purse when she'd gotten the inventory. "Do you have yours?"

"I do." He reached into his pocket and pulled out his cell. He frowned at the phone. "It doesn't have a signal."

"You're kidding me?" She walked over and pulled his cell phone out of his hand. Nope, no bars. "This is ridiculous."

"Don't worry. Someone will realize we came down here and will come check. You'll be rid of me soon enough."

"It's not like I want to be rid of you," she snapped.

Alex's brows rose. "You don't?"

A smile hovered around the edges of his mouth. Her cheeks prickled with heat. Damn him for looking at her like that. As if he knew she couldn't stop thinking about one damn quick hug that happened over a week ago.

She sniffed and lifted her chin. "I just don't want to be trapped down here. I don't like to feel trapped."

Her voice tightened on the last part. Alex looked at her with those searching eyes. She hadn't meant to let some of the frustration she felt about her life in general creep through with a few words. Alex saw too much of her.

She turned away and glanced around the room. "We might as well do the inventory while we wait. I doubt we'll be down here long. Enough people saw us come down here, plus Lilah will look for me when she's done rehearsing. Someone will come get us soon."

She went over to the boxes marked Debutante Ball along with some of the pieces of the decorations used to stage the main ballroom for the event. Alex followed her over. He stood close enough that her body hummed with awareness.

He surveyed the boxes. "Where do you want to start?"

Elaina pointed to the farthest box away. "You let me know how many stage pieces are over there, and I'll check these boxes. I'm pretty sure we won't need much for this year's ball."

He nodded and started counting the pieces. Elaina opened one of the plastic tubs and pulled out the sheet of paper on top. It was a list of all the items in the box. "Well, I'm glad someone listened to my suggestion," she muttered.

Last year she'd recommended they include a list of items in each box to make planning the next year easier. That meant this year's inventory wouldn't take long at all. They'd be done before anyone came to open the door.

"How long have you helped with the ball?" Alex asked.

Elaina looked up and considered his question. "Almost all my life."

His eyes widened. "Really?"

She nodded. "My mom was on the planning committee

for the debutante ball and my dad was heavily involved in the management of the club when I was younger. We would spend almost every weekend here, especially in the summer. There was always something going on." She smiled as she thought back on those days watching her parents play tennis, taking swimming and golf lessons, and attending all the various events at the country club. "I would help my mom plan and put things together. By the time I was old enough to enter the debutante ball, I knew the running of the thing backward and forward."

"I didn't realize you were so heavily involved here," Alex said.

She shook her head. "We weren't as involved after my mom died. After that, my dad kept the membership but dropped his additional duties. It wasn't the same without Mom. Byron, India and I also limited our time here."

"I can imagine it was pretty hard. You seem to really admire your mother."

Elaina looked back at the list, but in her mind, she saw her mom doing the same thing the year of Elaina's debutante ball. "I did admire her. I believed and trusted everything she said. I would fight my dad on everything, but all he had to do was convince my mom and she would say the same thing and I'd agree. I used to think he was the most manipulative person in the family, but in hindsight I realize she had more influence."

"My mom definitely has more influence over my dad," Alex said. "He lives by the motto 'Happy Wife, Happy Life.'"

"I can see that. They're so happy with each other. My parents weren't like that."

"Your dad still talks about your mom, you know? I always assumed they were deeply in love."

SYNITHIA WILLIAMS   119

Elaina checked the items in the box against the list in her hand. "They were in the early days. I still remember when they were crazy about each other, but eventually things became more about the business, the family and growing our influence. That eventually killed some of the romance. I spent too much time trying to live up to that standard." She glanced around the room. "Sometimes I wonder if I'm still trying... Will I ever escape the pressure?"

"You have."

"Because I was fired?" she asked with a twist of her lips.

"Before that. You are nothing if not independent. I watched you clash with your dad and often you were right. I can tell you're proud of your family and your company, but I never saw you as willingly trying to be someone your dad thought you should be."

If only that were true. "It took one disastrous marriage to stop trying," she said softly.

"What?"

Elaina met his eye over her shoulder and shook her head. She didn't want to get into the reasons for her marriage with Travis. Not with Alex. He finally seemed to see her as more than a calculating businesswoman. How could he understand the reasons she'd agreed to marry a man she didn't love?

"Never mind," she said. "Thank you for coming down here to help and volunteering. I know you were told to be here."

Alex chuckled and walked back over to the box next to her. "I didn't realize being active at the country club was a part of the job description."

"It usually isn't. We recently lost the person who helped last year. You were promoted at an opportune time."

"Tonight wasn't too bad," he said.

"I suspect not." She watched him for a few seconds as he read over the list in the box he'd opened. "Sade was very friendly. I was surprised you chose to help me instead of going off with her."

He didn't look up from the paper. "I wasn't interested in going off with her."

"I couldn't tell."

"Was there a reason you paid so much attention to my interaction with Sade?" This time he did look up and nailed her with that I-can-see-through-your-bullshit stare.

Elaina glanced away quickly. "I just noticed, that's all. She's a nice person. I even tried hooking her up with Byron once. You could do worse."

"Why would I want to do worse?"

She lifted a shoulder. "Sometimes worse is more fun."

"In what way?" he asked.

"The person you know you shouldn't be with always holds the bigger appeal," she stated matter-of-factly. "It's the entire off-limits aspect that makes everything much more addictive."

"Are you speaking from experience?"

She turned to face him, her heart pounding again and a dozen warning bells going off in her head. She should shut down the flirting, but the look in Alex's eyes said he was willing to go with her down this path. "I've got some experience with wanting the wrong man."

"But that's all in your past now." He took a half step closer.

She shook her head. She'd never been good at not going for what she wanted. Her ego needed stroking, and Alex with his quiet understanding and empathy had shown her more care than anyone had in a long while. She'd be smarter this time. This was just to quell her curiosity. People said there was a thin line between love and hate. Maybe all their bickering had just been leading to this.

"Not quite," she said, choosing her next words carefully. She pretended to check the list in her box. "I find myself thinking about someone who I once despised. I miss clashing with him daily. I enjoy the verbal sparring. Not to mention he recently wrapped his arms around me, and for some reason I can't get that out of my head." She glanced at him. "He's stronger than I imagined. His embrace is comforting in a way I didn't realize I'd like. It makes me want more even though I know I shouldn't."

Alex stilled next to her. "What are you going to do about this ill-advised craving?"

"It kind of depends on him," she said. "I think he's interested, but I can't be sure. And you know I could never offer myself to a man who didn't want me." She said the last part with a slight shrug though her heart imitated a hummingbird against her ribs, and a mixture of excitement and adrenaline flowed with each beat.

Alex slid closer, closing the distance between them, and filling her senses with him. He pulled the paper out of her hands. "What if he wants you, too?"

His deep voice slid over her like warm satin. Elaina's nipples tightened as heat flooded her sex. She faced him and met his dark eyes. "Then I'm in trouble, because I'm no good at saying no to the things I want but shouldn't have."

Alex watched her for several heartbeats. The pulse beat quickly at the base of his neck. A question hovered in his eye. Was she being genuine, or was she playing with him? She wasn't about to back down now. Not after she'd worked up the courage to acknowledge the attraction humming between them.

Before he could let common sense kill the moment she

lifted on her toes and brushed her lips across his. "Tell me, Alex, am I in trouble?"

Alex's strong arm wrapped around her waist. He pulled her carefully against his body as if she were precious. Emotion squeezed her chest while a jolt of desire rushed through her. She never could resist a man willing to accept her challenge.

His penetrating stare didn't waver as he lowered his head. Anticipation coiled through her with each tantalizing second. Their lips finally met in a tentative kiss. His lips were soft but firm, and when he gently nipped her lower lip, Elaina trembled and opened to him. Alex's arms tightened around her, pressing her aching breasts against his firm chest. Her arms slid across his wide shoulders.

Alex was a damn good kisser. He didn't kiss her as if he wanted to devour her on the spot, nor was there any hesitance. Alex held her, kissed her, as if he cared. As if he'd been waiting for this and now didn't want to rush the experience.

The sound of voices on the other side of the door registered through the haze in Elaina's mind. She pulled back quickly, her breath racing and her chest heaving. "Come to my place tonight," she said without thinking.

There was no time to reconsider. The key turned and she sidestepped him completely.

The door to the basement opened. The maintenance guy, George, walked in. "Ms. Elaina, you down here?"

"Right here, George." Elaina's voice was calm and steady. This wasn't her first time almost getting caught kissing someone she wasn't supposed to.

"Good. Your niece was getting worried when she found your phone." He eyed Alex. "Everything okay?"

"Everything is fine," she said with a wave of her hand.

"No need for a fuss. Alex wasn't aware the door would automatically lock if he didn't put the doorstop in the way." She walked at a brisk clip toward George. "We did get the inventory complete while we waited. Though we weren't down here too long. I'll go up and get Lilah."

George nodded. "Good. I'm glad I got down here quickly."

Elaina didn't turn back to Alex as she put the doorstop in place and followed George out. She'd put the ball in his court. It was reckless and stupid, but she wasn't known for always making the best decisions. Her blood pulsed, and her swollen clit screamed for attention. Maybe it was just hormones. She needed to wipe away the bad memories of her last sexual encounter. Either way, she hoped Alex was just as reckless as she was and would come to her house that night.

CHAPTER FOURTEEN

ALEX COULD COUNT the number of dumb decisions he'd made on one hand. Not surprisingly, a few of those bad decisions involved a woman. Now he was about to add another to the list.

He parked in her driveway and stared at the house. Despite the reasons to stay away from Elaina—their joint connections, their cantankerous working relationship, the ice-cold wall around her heart—he wouldn't turn on his car and drive away. Women like Elaina were his catnip. Her fierce competitiveness, the way she refused to back down, and her drive to succeed all got to him. Plus, he just plain wanted to taste her lips, run his hands over the lushness of her curves and figure out all her intimate wishes.

Maybe his dick was the biggest peddler in this decision. He hadn't had consistent sex since his long-term lover broke things off with him while he was in the hospital recovering from his heart attack, and the few hookups he'd had since moving to Jackson Falls had satisfied an immediate need but were underwhelming. *Underwhelming* was not a word he'd associate with Elaina.

He got out of the car and walked to the front door. After taking a deep breath, he rang the bell. A few seconds later, Elaina opened the door. She wore a pair of slim-fit gray joggers that hugged her hips and ass and a fitted lavender V-neck T-shirt. She'd pulled her hair back into a ponytail with two loose tendrils framing her face. They stood there for several tense moments. Staring and unsure.

"I wondered if you'd actually show up," she finally said. Even though she'd spoken in her typical cool, confident tone, relief was in her eyes.

"Wondered or worried I wouldn't?" he asked.

"Never worried." She lifted the wine tumbler in her hand. "Have a drink with me."

She turned and went into the house without waiting for his reply. Alex followed her inside and closed the door behind him. Her place had an open floor plan. The kitchen, dining space and living space all connected to each other. The inside was tastefully decorated with interesting art pieces, neutral wall colors and stylish but comfortable-looking furniture.

"Nice place," he said.

"It's okay." They went into the kitchen, and Elaina walked to the fridge. "I don't like open floor plans."

"Why not? Isn't that what everyone on those home improvement shows wants?"

Elaina pulled a bottle of wine out of the fridge. The edges of her full lips lifted. "You watch home improvement shows?"

Alex pulled out a stool at the bar that separated the kitchen from the living area and sat facing her. "My sister and mom love them. One is always on television at my parents' place. I get caught up watching them, too, and start to think I want a fixer-upper."

Elaina chuckled, and the warm sound made his skin prickle. "You can keep that. Move-in ready is what I needed. That's one of the reasons I took this place." She pulled the stopper out of the bottle. "Open floor plans mean anyone who enters your space has the ability to see too much. What I'm watching on television or the dishes I left in the sink are open for comment. I don't like giving anyone that much access to my space."

She met his gaze, then looked away quickly. Elaina didn't give anyone access to her inner self. He could see why the idea of an open floor plan wouldn't be her first choice. She hid her emotions and inner thoughts. There was no place to hide here.

She took another wine tumbler out of the cabinet. "Anyway, the house works. Do you drink wine? It's all I've got. I don't keep hard liquor in the house anymore. Back at the estate, we kept a stocked liquor cabinet. I'm still getting settled in over here."

If he didn't know better, he'd say she was rambling. His brows drew together. Could she possibly be nervous? Maybe he'd read the relief in her eyes incorrectly. Maybe she'd hoped he wouldn't come and was having second thoughts. He'd admit he was wrong to assume she'd play games with his family. Elaina was more direct than that. Playing games with him wasn't completely out of the question, though.

Alex walked up behind her. He placed a hand on her hip. She stilled. He didn't press against her even though the soft heat of her body and the lingering scent of her perfume urged him to pull her into his embrace.

"Why did you invite me here, Elaina?"

Her breasts rose and fell with her short breaths. She poured a healthy amount of wine into both tumblers. "I enjoyed our kiss earlier. I thought you enjoyed it, too."

Her voice was nonchalant, but the pulse at the base of her throat fluttered, and a slight tremor went through her body. She was either nervous or unsure. Alex applied a slight amount of pressure to her hip to get her to face him.

She quickly put the lids on the tumblers before turning. She held them up between them.

She met his eyes, then looked down quickly. The hesitancy in her gaze unnerved him. Alex stepped back. No matter how much he wanted Elaina, he wanted her to be just as willing to open the same can of recklessness he was.

"Why did you invite me here?" He spoke the words slowly, deliberately.

She pushed one of the tumblers toward him. Alex took it and set it on the counter beside her. His gaze didn't waver from her face. Elaina took a sip of her wine. Her shoulders relaxed and she finally looked at him.

"Are you trying to make sure I haven't changed my mind?" she asked. "I understand. I invited you here because I enjoyed our kiss and I'd like to kiss you again. In fact, I'm open to us having sex tonight. If you're willing."

He blinked and his head jerked back. She took another sip of her wine. The unsureness in her gaze slowly drifted away. He wasn't doing this if she needed a drink to get through the night. Alex took the tumbler out of her hands and put it on the counter. When she protested, he shook his head and took her hands in his.

"Part of the question was to make sure you haven't changed your mind. I did enjoy that kiss earlier, and I sure as hell would like to kiss you again." He slipped his fingers through hers and tugged her closer. "But I want to know, why me? Why now?"

Her fingers flexed and held his hands tighter. Her gaze dropped to his lips, and a small line formed between her brows as she frowned slightly. "Because you were nice to me when you could have gloated. You hugged me when you didn't have to. And you've never backed down from me."

When her eyes met his again, they were calm and confident. "That and I couldn't let you leave with Sade."

The flippant final admission made him laugh. "So you *were* jealous."

"I was never good at sharing," she said arrogantly. "You're mine while we do this. Promise me."

The fierceness in her voice made him squeeze her hand tighter. Had someone hurt her? Maybe recently. To hell with whatever fool toyed with Elaina's emotions. He wouldn't make the same mistake. "I'm not good at sharing either."

She lifted her chin and smiled softly. "Good. Do you want that drink now?"

He released one of her hands and took her chin between his fingers. Slowly he lowered his head until his lips brushed hers. "I didn't come here for a drink, Elaina."

A tremble went through her, and Alex wrapped his arm around her waist and crushed her against him. He hadn't gotten exactly what he'd wanted from his question. Maybe it was foolish to think Elaina would admit she cared about him a little or felt something more than sexual attraction. But as her lips softened beneath his, he let foolish fantasies drift away. If being kind was one of the reasons she wanted him, then he'd take it, because kindness toward her was something he could continue to do.

Elaina rubbed against him. There was no room for hesitancy or time for him to think about the meaning of the promises they'd made. His tongue brushed across her lower lip, and she sighed softly. Elaina's arms wrapped around his shoulders, and her breasts pressed against his chest.

Desire shot through him like a rocket to the moon. He was about to be lost. All he wanted was more of her. More of the sweet taste of her lips. More of the decadent crush of her breasts against his chest. More of those soft sighs she made between kisses. If he didn't slow down, he'd throw her on the counter, rip off those pants and fuck her senseless.

Alex's mouth left hers, and she whimpered. He squeezed his eyes shut as his dick pushed against the front of his slacks. He trailed kisses across her cheek and down the side of her neck. Her fingers clutched his shoulders, and he flicked his tongue across the hollow of her neck. Elaina moaned a low yes, and he was quickly losing the battle to take things slow.

His hand slid inside the front of her shirt. Her skin was warm and soft against his fingertips. Her stomach clenched and unclenched as he caressed her. His hand lifted to cup her full breast. The bra was in the way. He wanted skin on skin. He went around back and awkwardly worked at the hooks of her bra.

She smiled against his lips. "I've got it." She reached around and worked magic because the clasps came free.

So what if he wasn't a bra whisperer? The damn thing was open, and he could finally fill his hands with her full breasts. She moaned as he kneaded gently. Massaging and caressing before his fingers gently pinched the hard tips.

Elaina's hips gyrated. Her breathing became more frantic. "My bedroom is down the hall," she panted.

Not yet. If he took her there now, he'd lose all self-control. He made a noise of acknowledgment, then lifted her shirt. She raised her arms, and he pulled the shirt over her head. He tossed it across the kitchen. Her bra followed quickly. She placed her hands on the counter behind them, thrusting her breasts forward. The tight chocolate tips called him. He cupped them in his hand and wrapped his lips around one nipple.

"God yes," she moaned, and she gripped the back of his head with one hand.

Alex's free hand slipped into the waistband of her pants. No underwear. His fingers brushed across the smooth skin of her sex. She was so damn wet and slick. He almost came in his pants right then.

Alex's head lifted, and he gently bit the edge of her ear. "I can't wait to taste you, Elaina."

Her entire body shook. "Taste me, Alex."

She was driving him crazy. His fingers slid between her slick lower lips. They brushed across her swollen clit. Her legs opened, and he pushed one long finger deep inside her. He pumped steadily while his thumb rubbed across her clit.

"That feels amazing," Elaina moaned.

He gazed at her through lowered lids. Her eyes were shut tight, her head thrown back, her lips full and open. "You're amazing," he whispered in her ear. "You're so fucking amazing."

Her hands gripped his arms. She clenched around his fingers. "Alex." His name was a plea on her lips. "Oh my God, I can't hold on."

She trembled against him. He stilled his hand. "Can I see you this weekend?"

Her eyes popped open. "What?" she said between breaths. "You're asking that now?"

He didn't want this to be a one-night stand. He didn't want her to shut down again once they were done. He didn't want to just take his pleasure and walk away. He slid his finger slowly in and out of her. She pushed her hips forward. "This weekend. Dinner." His voice trembled. "You and me."

His thumb ran a slow circle across her clit. Her body bucked. She bit her lip and nodded.

Alex kissed her softly. His fingers continued to play between her legs. "Say it, Elaina. Tell me you want to see me again. Tell me you want this again."

"Yes. Hell yes. Please, Alex."

The *please* took him over. He shoved her pants down, lifted her onto the counter, spread her legs wide and ran his tongue across her sweet center.

ELAINA WAS GOING to die from pleasure, and she didn't give a damn. In some surreal corner of her mind, she comprehended what was happening. That she was on the kitchen counter with Alex Tyson, of all people, between her legs. That she'd agreed to an actual date when she'd only wanted one, maybe two, impersonal hookups. She might rethink her choices tomorrow, but when his lips closed around her clit, her hand shot out and knocked over the tumbler of wine as she reached for the back of his head.

Her orgasm came quick, hard and fast. Stealing her breath away and making her heart stutter. By the time she came back to reality, he'd stood and pulled her against his chest. His heart beat almost as quickly as hers. She placed her hands on his waist and tried to calm down.

"Fuck," she said, half dazed while gulping in air.

Alex's chest vibrated with his soft chuckle. "You're welcome."

She was too sated to snap back at his cocky tone of voice. "Are you ready to go to my room now?" They hadn't even had sex, but she knew one or two times might not be enough.

He shook his head. "Not yet. Let's chill for a minute, okay?"

She frowned. His erection was prominent against the front of his pants. He wanted to have sex. "Your body is saying *right now*." She tugged on the waistband of his pants.

He placed a hand over hers and shook his head. "I just

want to take care of you first." He helped her off the counter. "And I need a minute to calm down."

"Afraid you won't last long?" she teased.

"I don't need you holding that over my head for the rest of my life," he said with a half smile. He cupped the back of her neck and pulled her against his chest.

The warmth and strength of his embrace were too much to resist when her body still hummed with pleasure. She kind of liked being taken care of.

"Just for a few minutes. Then we'll go to my bedroom." She rested her head on his shoulder. Her body felt weightless. Light and content. Between the two glasses of wine she'd had before he'd arrived and an amazing orgasm, she could go to sleep now if she let herself.

"I'm cool with that." Alex kissed her forehead.

They settled on the couch. She fit against his side as if she belonged there always. Alex turned the television to an old movie. She floated in contentment like she never had before. A dangerous place when she didn't want to get attached, but Alex smelled divine, and he held her as if he cared just a little.

"I can't believe you didn't toss me over your shoulder and haul me to the bedroom after what you just did," she said softly. "Most guys go straight for sex afterwards."

"I'm not most guys," he said.

She glanced up at him. "Just know, I'm not usually a cuddler." She wouldn't have expected him to be so touchy-feely. She typically wanted space after sex. She didn't want to lie in someone's arms and pretend as if things were more than they were. That only caused confusion. Confusion and embarrassment later when she realized letting her guard down had only given space for someone to hurt her.

"Neither am I," he replied, still watching the television.

"Then why are you holding me?" She tried to sound haughty, but her contented yawn at the end undermined her efforts.

He looked down at her. The corner of his mouth lifted in a knowing smile. "Why are you letting me hold you?"

Good question. They should have gone straight into sex after. She should have insisted on setting the tone for this relationship. No, this hookup. She didn't want to start thinking foolish things again. She wasn't about to let Alex step in and finish what Robert started. She tried to sit up he held her closer.

"Just a few minutes more, Elaina," he said, kissing the top of her head.

She held herself still, then finally relaxed against him. She'd only cuddle for a little while longer. There was no harm in briefly savoring this feeling. Only she'd know if she took a few precious seconds to pretend as if he really liked her and this could be something more than a quick hookup. Just this one time. She could be happy for just a moment, she thought, as her eyes drifted closed and Alex's lips brushed her forehead one more time.

CHAPTER FIFTEEN

ALEX COULDN'T FOCUS on a damn thing the next day at work, which of course made it the perfect day for disaster to strike. He glanced at the time in the lower left corner of his laptop screen. Six twenty-nine. So much for getting out of the office before six. Why did things always have to blow up on a Friday afternoon?

The trouble started with a fire at one of Robidoux Holdings' plastics manufacturing facilities. Thank God no one was hurt, but that didn't stop all hell from breaking loose. Their public relations department tried to reassure their investors and control the message to the media while Alex and the other directors of the plastics group worked to figure out losses and what would need to be rebuilt.

I'm not supposed to be in charge of this stuff.

It wasn't the first time the thought came to his mind. Whenever he thought about who was supposed to handle this, the person who could handle this without breaking a sweat, he got frustrated for a myriad of reasons. Elaina would have gotten to the bottom of the fire in no time, crafted the media response, and had investors as calm as sleeping babies before they realized there had even been a problem. Instead, Alex, the impromptu and unqualified interim CEO, was in charge.

Thoughts of how Elaina could handle this mess also brought memories of the night before. The slick sweetness of her against his fingertips. How fucking unbelievable her kisses were. The way she'd fallen asleep in his arms afterward.

She'd curled against him like a cat on the couch, and he'd had a moment of chivalry that convinced him to let her sleep instead of waking her. She hadn't stirred as he'd put her to bed, so he'd locked her door and left. He'd wanted Elaina, but he hadn't wanted the unsureness in her eyes. For a second he thought she was going to admit she'd invited him over because she liked him. Then she'd hidden behind a sheer curtain of flippancy. Instead of calling her on it, he'd kissed her, touched her, tasted her. She'd dropped the curtain, and he caught a glimpse of the uninhibited Elaina. He wanted to see more of that Elaina, one of the reasons he'd asked her for a separate date.

His dick stiffened at the memory, and Alex shifted in his seat. He opened his emails and tried to focus on work. That was the other thing that made getting through today harder. Thoughts of Elaina were never far away. If he survived this day, he'd get out of the office and figure out something spectacular for the date he'd asked Elaina on.

An email popped up on his screen from Grant. The subject line was, I need you to attend this.

Alex opened the email. His irritation grew with each word. Grant wanted him to represent Robidoux Holdings at a luncheon with shareholders the next day.

Alex immediately closed the email, shot up from his seat and marched out of his office. He took the elevator one floor up. He hadn't moved into Elaina's office in the executive suite. This position was only temporary, and he stayed in his previous office as a reminder to himself and Grant. Alex had been in a high-stress position once and he'd suffered a heart attack. He wasn't about to put himself back into a similar position.

He nodded at Grant's receptionist. "Is he still in there?"

"You just caught him," she said. "Go right in. He's getting ready to leave for the day."

Alex knocked twice, then strode into the office. Grant looked up from his cell phone and raised a brow. "Alex, what are you doing here?"

"I need to talk to you about that last email."

Grant nodded. "Yes, the luncheon with the stockholders. I know you can handle it."

"That's the thing, Grant, I shouldn't be handling it."

Grant frowned and slid his cell phone into the inner pocket of his suit jacket. "I don't understand. You're running things."

Alex took a deep breath. He pushed back his frustration and tried to talk calmly. "I'm the interim CEO. I'm not the right person to soothe investors after the day we've had."

Grant's face cleared. "You are exactly the right person," he said confidently. "You're the only person who can get them to calm down."

"Until just a few weeks ago, I oversaw research and development. Now I'm serving in an interim capacity. They need to be reassured by the actual owner of the company." If Grant wasn't going to bring Elaina back, he needed to at least handle things with the shareholders.

"I can't," Grant said, waving a hand. "I've got other things that have come up."

Alex's brows drew together. "What could possibly be more important?"

"That's none of your business," Grant said sternly. He walked around his desk and toward the door.

Alex shifted to the right to block Grant's progress. "It is my business when you're sending me into the lion's den without a clue of what to say or how to handle things."

Grant eyed him up and down. He leaned back on his

heels and slid his hands into his pants pockets. "I wouldn't have asked you to go or given you this job if I didn't think you could do it. Now quit acting like a child. Stop complaining and do the job I'm paying you to do."

Alex straightened his shoulders. "I'm not complaining. I'm pointing out that despite your trust in me, the company's investors don't know me. If Elaina were here, she'd—"

"Elaina isn't here." Grant's voice cracked like a whip.

"That's part of the problem," Alex said, not at all cowed by the edge in Grant's voice. The man had made a mistake firing his daughter, and he needed to be called on it.

"She made her choice."

"You didn't give her much choice. Call her. Work this out. She can help a lot more than I can."

Grant's eyes narrowed as he studied Alex. "Since when did you become a fan of hers?" He sounded confused.

Alex had come to appreciate what Elaina did in the weeks since taking over for her. While he wouldn't excuse the way she'd deliberately tried to block his actions, he also saw the hard work she'd done on the various other subsidiaries. Hell, he still couldn't get to some of the items his team needed and was holding out on naming someone interim because this CEO position was supposed to be temporary.

"Acknowledging someone's strengths doesn't make you a fan," he said. "I'm smart enough to recognize when I'm not the right person for a situation."

"Elaina had the chance to be here. Despite her strengths, my daughter has other weaknesses. She hasn't met a glass a wine she wasn't friends with, and when she's feeling vulnerable, she attaches herself to the wrong man. When things turn to shit, it spirals over into her professional life."

Alex was momentarily speechless. The words hit too close to home. "That's not true."

"Every word of it is true," Grant said irritably. "Why do you think she was so angry and unreasonable the day I fired her? It was just another meltdown after she ended another relationship with someone I told her long ago she should stay away from. I love Elaina, but until she gets her shit together, she's not welcome back at this company."

Alex's jaw clenched. He wanted to argue further, but Grant didn't beat around the bush or try to spare feelings with his opinions. There had to be a kernel of truth in what he said. If that were the case, what did that mean about anything that happened between him and Elaina? Was he just another guy she was attaching herself to while feeling vulnerable over being fired?

Grant placed a hand on Alex's shoulder. "Go to the lunch tomorrow. Smooth things over. It's not as hard as you think. Just smile. Tell them what happened and how the fire isn't going to affect production. I know you don't want this job permanently, and I'll work to fill it, but until that time, you're the face of the company. Stop living in that downstairs office trying to pretend as if nothing has changed. It's time for Robidoux Holdings to look to the future. You're a part of that future whether you like it or not."

The words effectively denied Alex's request to get out of the luncheon. He didn't like it, but Grant was right. He was in charge until a permanent CEO was hired. He had to sit in this chair and accept the hard decisions regardless of how he felt. As for whatever was going on between him and Elaina, he didn't want to think that he was just a rebound after a recently bad relationship.

"You're mine while we're doing this."

He'd suspected someone had hurt her recently. He'd figure out what Elaina's end game was with inviting him over during their date this weekend.

CHAPTER SIXTEEN

ELAINA SPENT ALL day Friday in a weird funk. She could barely focus on the proposals she put together for potential investors, overlooked typos on a presentation that Zoe thankfully caught, and nearly snapped when her favorite barista at the coffee house added whipped cream to her frappé after Elaina told her not to. Thankfully, she hadn't snapped, and she'd given herself a mental shake. She'd known the cause of her mood even if she didn't want to admit it.

Alex had tucked her into bed and walked out of the house. She'd been tired, sexually sated, and comforted in his arms. She'd woken up wet, aching and hoping to finish what they'd started only to discover he'd left. Now she didn't know where they stood, and she was not the type of person to be happy unsettled.

Top all of that off with the news of a fire at one of the Robidoux Holdings manufacturing facilities and she was surprised she'd even made it through the day. She'd thought of a multitude of things that needed to happen, then realized she wasn't there to offer any advice. Nor was her advice wanted. Talk about infuriating.

She'd considered telling disappearing Alex to kiss her ass when he'd texted that morning to confirm they were still going out on Saturday. She hadn't because he deserved to hear in person that getting her off and disappearing wasn't acceptable.

Which was the only reason she decided to go to his place that evening. He owed her an explanation before she decided whether to go out with him that weekend. If he was playing around with her, then he could kiss a date with her goodbye. She marched up the stairs to his home and pressed the doorbell.

Alex opened the door and stared at her on his doorstep. "What are you doing here?" No irritation, only confusion in his voice.

She raised a brow and eyed him from top to bottom. He was obviously in for the night and wore a pair of basketball shorts with a gray T-shirt. He looked casually sexy, and her mind went back to the way he'd kissed, touched and tasted her the night before. Desire prickled across her skin. She crossed her arms, irritated by how quickly her body responded.

"Why are you wearing those ridiculous glasses?" she said.

Alex cocked his head to the side. He unhooked them and placed them around his neck. "Because I was working, and they help." He sounded unbothered by her question.

His blasé tone made her face heat. He watched her with those unflinching dark eyes as if waiting for her to say something else. She glanced away quickly. Showing up unexpectedly was foolish, but pride wouldn't let her turn and walk away. She met his eyes and lifted her chin. "Aren't you going to invite me in?"

He stepped back and let her in without a reply. Elaina crossed the threshold and blatantly studied the inside of his place. He lived in one of the renovated older homes closer to downtown. From the entryway she could only get a glimpse of hardwood floors, neutral wall colors and sparse furniture. A true bachelor pad.

He closed the door and faced her. "What's going on?"

She spun around and faced him. "Why did you leave last night?"

He crossed his arms over his chest and leaned on the door. "You fell asleep."

Her eyes dropped to his arms and the way the muscles bunched beneath his dark skin. Her fingers flexed with the need to reach out and touch. She was getting distracted. Her eyes jumped back to his. "And," she snapped, "you couldn't wake me up?"

He lazily shrugged one broad shoulder. "I didn't want to take advantage of you."

The corner of her mouth lifted. His consideration for her even after what happened between them created a soft glow around her cynical heart. "Even though I asked you to take advantage of me."

Alex pushed away from the door and stepped close to her. The scent of his cologne tickled her senses, reminded her of the comfort she'd received in his arms the night before, made her want to snuggle with him again and breathe in deep. "I can't help it. I care about you."

Elaina sucked in a breath. His eyes widened as if the words surprised him as much as they'd surprised her. She turned away quickly before he could see her reaction in her eyes. The way that foolish, romantic part of her wanted to come out and play. She went further into his place. She needed time to think about how to respond to what he'd said. He wasn't supposed to care about her. Her heart wasn't supposed to flip because he'd said that.

The coffee table in his living area was covered with various files and a laptop. One glance revealed the files were about the facility that had caught fire. "I suppose you're getting ready for a meeting with the stakeholders."

"I was," he said evenly.

Her lips pressed together. How could he be so calm and unaffected? He didn't seem the least bit put out about them not finishing what they started the night before. A whisper of doubt floated in her head.

She crossed her arms over her chest and glared at him like she would have back when they worked together and she viewed him as the enemy. "I guess you got what you wanted all along. You've got my position and can do whatever you want."

Alex slowly crossed the room to stand in front of her, his dark eyes unwavering. "I never wanted your position. You know that and Grant knows that. But I will do what Grant asks me to in the meantime."

"Until he makes you the permanent head of the company?"

He slid closer, bringing his heat and a mountain of temptation with him. "Until he finds a permanent CEO or does what he should do and brings you back. That's what I told him today."

She wanted to believe him. As she stared into his eyes and saw the same unbiased honesty she'd always seen reflected in his eyes, she realized she did believe him. She believed he cared about her. Believed he wanted to be on her side. The compulsion to rely on that was almost a physical ache. Even when she'd been married, she hadn't felt like she was part of a team.

"I don't want you to care about me, Alex," she blurted out.

He smiled as if he expected nothing less from her. "What do you want from me, Elaina?"

For you to be legit. To be able to really count on you. To feel free to fall for you.

Each one of those thoughts was more terrifying than the other. His eyes softened as if he could read her wishes. He always saw too much.

Elaina lifted her chin. "I want you to fuck me."

That threw him. His eyes widened and he leaned back. Good. He needed the reminder. She needed the reminder. They wanted each other, but that was all this was. Strictly physical.

"Elaina…"

She grabbed the front of his basketball shorts and pulled hard. She didn't want to have a heart-to-heart. Not now. Not when her heart was soft and yearning after his simple admission.

She lifted on her toes and pressed her lips against his. His body was rigid as tension flowed through his muscles. He lifted his head. Reason tried to clear the fog of desire in his eyes. Elaina grinned and knew this was a fight she could win. She slid her hand into his shorts and wrapped her fingers around the hardening length of his erection.

Alex's eyes narrowed before he grabbed her and pulled her in close. His mouth crushed hers. The softness of his lips giving way to the hard heat of his desire. The low moan that rumbled through him was like fuel to the fire in her veins. He kissed her with the same urgent craving that had plagued her from the moment she'd woken up alone.

She wrapped one leg around his. The rough friction of the hair on his legs against the smooth skin of her legs, which were bare beneath the hem of her skirt, sent shivers through her body. His fingers worked at the buttons of her blouse, and then tugged so hard buttons popped and scattered on the floor. She leaned back and sucked in a breath, her eyes wide and surprised. He'd actually ripped her shirt off her. No one had ever been that hungry for her before. The smug gleam in his eyes made her breasts ache. They both grinned and she forgot about the damn shirt.

She pushed his shorts to his feet. His shirt was thrown. Her bra followed. He took her breasts in his hand and lowered himself to take the tip of one in his mouth. The warmth of his mouth was more delicious than any wine she'd ever tasted. Elaina sucked in a breath and clasped the back of his head. His fingers dug into her back and pulled her closer.

She tugged on the short, soft curls of his hair hard, lifting his head. He met her eyes, and the wicked grin on his face made her want to shout to the world that he was hers. Instead, she pushed him down onto the couch. Her legs wrapped around him as she straddled his waist. She kissed his lips, cheek and neck.

Her teeth nipped his ear. "It's my turn to taste you."

His hand tightened on her thigh. Slowly she looked over his muscled chest. A long scar marred the dark skin between his pecs. Elaina's eyes jumped to his.

The corner of his mouth lifted in a self-deprecating grin. "Heart attack."

She scanned his face and body as the words registered but still didn't want to settle as truth in her brain. "But you're too young."

He shook his head. "Tell that to the artery that was blocked."

He kept his voice light as if having a heart attack wasn't that big a deal. Elaina ran her fingers over the scar. The raised skin was smooth to the touch in the midst of the bristly hairs on his chest. Alex watched her as she studied it. She tried to imagine him in the hospital. The grip of a heart attack and the subsequent surgery must have hurt.

The entire ordeal must have been scary. Being faced with your own mortality at such a young age. Tightness wound around her chest. He tried to take care of her, but who was taking care of him?

"I'm sorry," she whispered.

He cupped her cheek with his hand. His thumb brushed her skin with such tenderness her eyes burned. "Don't be. The heart attack made me move here to be closer to family and slow down. Moving here led me to Robidoux Holdings. Robidoux Holdings led me to you."

The tightness in her chest squeezed a little bit tighter. She kissed him, and this time it was slow and deep. She pushed aside the feelings trying to weaken her. Focused on desire flowing through her veins like a raging river. If she didn't she'd be in too deep, too fast. She kissed her way from his mouth, neck, across the scar on his chest, to his ripped abdomen, until she settled on her knees between his legs.

Elaina watched him through her lashes as she took him in her mouth. She didn't rush and savored the taste of his skin, the ragged breaths causing his stomach to cave in, the soft moans of pleasure rumbling through his chest. She pulled back when she thought he was coming close and gave even more whenever she saw clarity coming to his eyes. She wanted him like this. To forget all the reasons they shouldn't be doing this. He'd made her forget, given her an orgasm and left.

His fingers dug into her hair. "You've got to stop." Instead of stopping, her hands worked in sync with her mouth. Her tongue played with the underside of him until he went rigid and he came.

She sat back, satisfaction and a fair amount of pride coursing through her as she watched him lie back on the couch. His breathing heavy, eyes closed, and body more relaxed than she'd ever seen. He didn't open his eyes as she stood and walked to the bathroom to clean herself up.

When she came back, his eyes were open, but he hadn't moved. She stood over him and cocked her head to the side. "I'm going now."

He sat up and wrapped his hand around her wrist. "What?"

She let out a small laugh. "I mean, that's what you did to me."

He tugged until she fell onto his lap. "I fucked up. Let me fix it."

She put a finger to the corner of her mouth as if considering. "What do you have in mind?"

"My bedroom. Multiple orgasms."

Just the thought made her sex clench. "I'll be okay with one good one."

"Deal."

He stood with her still in his arms. Elaina gasped and wrapped an arm around his shoulders. Alex took her to his bedroom with long, determined strides. They landed on the bed, and his mouth immediately covered hers. His hands performed magic between her legs, sliding over her swollen sex and driving her crazy while his lips, teeth and tongue brought her nipples to hardened tips.

She panted and clawed at his back and shoulders as he brought her to the brink again. She pushed him over onto his back. Her hand went between his legs. Thank heaven he was hard. If she came tonight, she did not want it to be without him deep inside her. "Condoms?"

"Nightstand."

Elaina reached over and found the box. She briefly noted the box was unopened and wondered when the last time he'd had sex, but when his hand squeezed her ass, she put that thought aside for another day. She grabbed one, covered him, then straddled his waist. With one hand on his chest, she used the other to guide him to her opening and lowered slowly.

Alex gripped her hips. "Damn, Elaina," he ground out.

Damn was right. She wanted to close her eyes and indulge in every hard inch of him stretching her. But this wasn't about savoring. This wasn't about emotions. She needed this. Not him. She worked her hips hard and fast. Closing her eyes, she focused not on the man beneath her, the way he looked at her with promise, or the way his arms comforted her. She needed an orgasm. A rebound. That's all this was. She just needed the release.

His warm hand cupped her cheek. Her eyes popped open. He watched her, but not just with the lust that had been there before. Something else mingled with the desire. Some unknown emotion that made her heart leap. His thumb brushed across her lower lip.

She grabbed his hand, brought it to her breast, and squeezed her thighs around him. The carnal heat returned to his gaze. Elaina closed her eyes to break whatever spell he'd put on her. She lowered her hand to where their bodies joined and ran her fingers over her swollen clit. Alex pinched her nipple and she crashed.

"Yes! That!" she cried out.

Her orgasm was strong and long. Alex's hips moved quick and fast beneath her, extending it. Had he come? She wasn't sure, but eventually he groaned and fell back. She collapsed on his chest. His arms wrapped around her.

She should move. But the steady rhythm of his heartbeat hypnotized her. His breathing evened out as his hand ran up and down her back. They lay there for several minutes before she finally made herself pull away.

He went to the bathroom, and she got out of bed. The stress of the day was gone. She could go home and be fine. She went to the living room to find her clothes.

Alex came behind her and wrapped his arms around her. "Don't go."

The soft plea in his voice made her want to stay. So much so that she knew she couldn't. She turned in his arms. "You promised me a date tomorrow." She cupped his cheek and kissed him softly. "I'll see you then."

She saw the argument in his eyes, but thankfully he nodded. He helped her dress, gave her a T-shirt since her blouse was torn, and then walked her to her car. She kissed him quickly and fought the urge to linger and get one more taste of him before pulling away. She slipped behind the wheel and left before emotions convinced her she should follow him back inside to spend the night in his arms.

CHAPTER SEVENTEEN

ALEX PICKED ELAINA up promptly at eight on Saturday. He took one look at her and hoped he hadn't miscalculated on where he'd chosen to go for their first official date. Elaina was stunning in a blush colored, spaghetti strap, sheath dress that hugged her full curves and sky-high gold heels that made him remember what it felt like having her shapely legs wrapped around his waist.

She glanced at him and raised a brow. "I'm guessing I'm overdressed."

Alex had opted for a pair of jeans and dark blue button-up shirt. "I've been in a suit and tie all day. I opted for casual."

She pointed over her shoulder. "Do I need to change?"

"Only if you feel the need to. My plan was for us to check out blues night at S&E Bar and Grille."

"What made you choose that place? I would have expected white tablecloths and valet parking." She didn't sound disappointed by his choice. He hoped that was a good sign for the rest of the night.

Alex shook his head. "I'm not trying to impress you."

She crossed her arms. "Obviously not." Though her words were short, there was a glint of humor in her eye.

Alex closed the distance between them. For a second, he'd thought she would stay with him the night before. He'd been disappointed when she left, but again, he knew pressuring Elaina into anything would get him the opposite reaction.

She lifted her chin as he came close. He figured every guy Elaina went out with tried to impress her, but what was the point of trying to impress a woman who had everything she wanted and could buy anything she desired? He opted for the truth instead.

He put his hands on her forearms. "That was the first place I heard you laugh. You seem comfortable there, and I heard the blues acts are good. I'd hoped to hear you laugh some more. I like your laugh."

Her shoulders relaxed slightly. The corners of her lips twitched as if she were fighting back a smile. She pulled away. "Fine. I'll get my purse."

Alex grinned as he watched her cross the room to pick up a small black purse on the couch. She might not like letting things show, but he liked watching her slowly warm up to him.

He held out his arm for her when she came back to him. "Then let's go."

She rolled her eyes, but the smile she'd held back previously burst free. "You're so ridiculous."

"You know you like it," he teased.

She shook her head and chuckled. Alex felt as if he'd found gold at the end of the rainbow. They walked arm in arm to the car. She stared out the window as they drove. Despite her slight warming earlier, she held her body stiff as if she were nervous.

He reached over and took one of her hands in his. When she glanced at him, he squeezed her hand and smiled. She let out a deep breath and relaxed. Even better, she didn't pull away for the rest of the car ride.

They arrived at the bar, and Alex got out to open the door

for her. Once inside, they settled in the VIP section he'd called and reserved for them the day before. In the small bar, it wasn't much except for a couch and short rectangular table with their choice of one bottle of alcohol, but they were close to the stage.

The waitress came over and asked what bottle they'd prefer. Alex deferred to Elaina. "What would you like to drink?"

"Chardonnay, please," Elaina said firmly. She clasped her hands together in her lap.

The waitress nodded. "You've got it." She walked away.

Alex turned on the couch and studied Elaina. She avoided eye contact and glanced around the bar. He tapped her shoulder. "Are you okay?"

She unclasped her hands and ran them over her lap. When she met his gaze, the glint of humor from when they'd left her place was gone. "How did the meeting with the shareholders go today?"

Her chin was lifted again. She was trying to deflect. From what, he didn't know. Alex rested his arm along the back of the couch. "I really didn't come here to talk about work."

"Why not? Is it hard for you to talk to me about how you're handling my old job? Come on, Alex, we're both adults. Maybe I can offer you some tips."

The meeting had been grueling and long, but he'd gotten through it as Grant suspected he would. The shareholders were pacified, the repairs for the facility were underway, and they were making plans to help any affected employees. But he wasn't going to let her bring up Robidoux Holdings as a barrier between them.

Alex took a long breath. "I thought we weren't going to do this."

"Do what?"

"Play games." He took a lock of her hair between his fingers. The thick strands fell in loose waves to her shoulders. The night before her hair had been soft against his palm as he'd clenched the back of her head. Later he'd noticed the smell of strawberries as her locks framed her face when she'd stared down at him. His body heated with the memories.

He met her eyes and tugged lightly on her hair. Heat flashed in her gaze, and her breathing picked up. "Last night and the night before didn't have anything to do with my job at Robidoux Holdings or the feud between you and your dad. Tonight isn't about that either. I'm here because I'd like to get to know you better."

Her gaze didn't waver from his. "Everyone knows me. I'm the coldhearted, practical daughter of Grant Robidoux with the screwed-up personal life."

Resentment crept into her voice. There was no teasing glint in her eye, no self-deprecating smile. She believed that. Alex let his fingers trail from her hair. "That's not all that you are."

She pressed her lips together. He thought about what Grant said. About Elaina having her own problems and making bad decisions. Maybe he was just another bad decision she was making.

"You don't know that," she said in a rush. "Just because we had two good nights doesn't change a thing."

"Who says I want you to change?"

She let out a brittle laugh. "I appreciate you for saying that, but you've seen me on my down days. I'm not the picture of perfection."

The waitress came with their bottle of wine with the

cork removed. She nodded at them, then walked off. Elaina leaned forward and poured two glasses.

"Who says I want perfection?" He took the drink she offered.

"Everyone wants perfection," she said, sounding irritated. She took a sip of her drink. "The perfect job, the perfect relationship, the perfect life."

"I learned the hard way not to strive for perfection." He tapped his chest. Her eyes dropped to where he touched his shirt over the scar. "Now I focus on what makes me happy instead of trying to meet everyone's demands."

Some of the fight left her eyes. Her lips lifted, and her smile was no less beautiful despite the sadness at its edges. "You sound like the supportive boyfriend on some romantic comedy. Follow your dreams and be yourself."

He chuckled and took a sip of his wine. "And what's wrong with that advice?"

"It's optimistic and unrealistic. People say be yourself, but if you ever say what you really want to say or do what you really want to do, then you open yourself up to criticism and censure. It's easier to do what's expected until you have enough power to be a version of yourself that's still acceptable." She stared into her wineglass. "Even then it's a challenge. Open up too much and someone will take advantage of you."

He placed a finger beneath her chin so she'd look at him. "I don't want to take advantage of you," he said honestly.

She stared into his eyes for several long seconds. "I'm surprised by how much I want to believe that." Her words were spoken softly, yet he still heard the longing in her tone.

Alex brushed her hair aside, then trailed a finger down her cheek. "Give me some time to prove it to you."

Elaina shivered slightly under his touch. The band came

up on the stage. The sound of them warming up filled the room. Patrons clapped and cheered. The entire time, Elaina never looked away from him. He didn't try to hide his feelings. Through all the battles they'd had at work, he'd still found her intriguing, and he'd crushed on her while also challenging her. He couldn't promise forever, but he could promise to show her that he was sincere.

Her chin lifted and lowered. The corner of her lip tilted up in that sly smile of hers that drove him crazy. "I'll give you a few days."

The teasing note in her voice made something in his chest squeeze. He had a feeling a few days wouldn't be enough. When it came to a woman like Elaina Robidoux, he was willing to take what he could get.

"Whoo, oh yeah!"

Elaina's eyes widened as she watched Alex get completely into the music. She placed a hand over her mouth to stifle her laugh. He sat next to her, hands clapping to the beat, head bobbing to the music. He wasn't the only one. The rest of the people in the now-crowded bar also clapped, sang and shouted out to the music.

He glanced at her and grinned. "What?"

She shook her head and dropped her hand. "Nothing. I'm just enjoying watching you enjoy the show."

"I love music," he said with a shrug. He stopped clapping and settled back.

Elaina hadn't wanted to embarrass him. She couldn't remember the last time she'd watched someone enjoy themselves so much. When was the last time she'd relaxed and enjoyed herself? She'd gone to concerts in high school and the early years of college, but when she married Travis and took on the role of trying to be the head of her family's company, concerts with upbeat music and audience interaction were exchanged for orchestra or opera tickets, lectures, and light jazz during a gala.

She was relaxed and happy in a way she hadn't felt in a long time.

Elaina sat forward and clapped her hands to the music. When the guy on the microphone gave another great line about the hard times he was having with his woman, she cheered with the crowd. "Alright now!"

She glanced back at Alex. His brows were up, and his broad smile came back. He sat forward. Elaina let her shoulders relax and spine loosen, and swayed to the music. No inhibitions, no worries about how she might look, no thoughts on her image or expectations. The feeling was intoxicating. She wanted more.

Elaina grabbed Alex's hand and pulled him toward the dance floor. She thought his eyes might pop out of his head, but he got up and followed her. She would have pegged him as a guy who didn't dance, but he twirled her and pulled her against him. She bumped against his hard chest and let out a delighted laugh.

"I'm a terrible dancer," she admitted.

"So am I, but who cares?" he said back.

The dance floor was so crowded, not being able to dance didn't matter. They could only do a simple two-step to the beat of the music. As soon as they got into a rhythm, the song ended and the band switched to a slower ballad. Elaina turned to go to their seat, but Alex pulled her closer. His arms encircled her waist, wrapping her in the steady comfort of his embrace. Being held by him was another form of intoxication.

She wrapped her arms around his neck. "Thank you for a fun night."

She tried to think of a better date and came up with nothing. She hadn't had many dates. Her relationship with Travis had been hormone-fueled hookups followed by an "uh-oh" pregnancy and a marriage of convenience. They hadn't dated before or after their wedding day. She'd done the basic dinner and coffee dates when she'd tried to get back out there, and those had fallen flat.

Then there'd been Robert. She'd thought her time with him had been romantic, but looking back, they hadn't dated either. They'd met at hotels, texted and video-chatted. She'd been so convinced he was her second chance romance that she'd settled. Funny how the guy she once declared her nemesis was the first person to take her on an enjoyable date.

"Is the night over?"

She lifted a shoulder. "I've been known to ruin a good thing, so I'm thanking you in advance in case that happens."

His brows drew together. "Don't do that."

"Do what?"

"Assume the night will end badly or that you'll do something to ruin things."

Years of doing just that were hard to undo. She didn't want to admit to him that she did tend to mess things up. Her life, her marriage, her career. The moment she let her guard down, things went wrong. Alex was good at coaxing her shields down.

He looked at her as if he believed she wasn't her own worst enemy. That's why she locked up any rebuttals. She liked pretending to be the woman he saw instead of the woman she knew she was.

"You're right. Tonight has been great. I'm thinking it can only get better." She pressed her hips forward. The thickness between his legs brushed against her. "Your place or mine?"

He lowered his head and kissed her softly. The brush of his lips was so teasing and tantalizing, she stopped moving to the music and lifted on her toes to deepen the kiss. Alex pulled back. His breathing picked up.

"Are you playing hard to get?" she teased.

"What would you say about taking things slow?" he asked carefully.

Elaina pulled her head back to get a better look into his eyes. "I think we're a little past the take-things-slow mark."

His chuckle vibrated through his chest. "Not necessarily. Before I moved here, my life felt like a never-ending roller coaster. My job, my relationships, everything was always rushed and high-intensity."

She liked the sound of that. "High-intensity is a good thing." She could definitely appreciate the idea of a few fast and quick orgasms in her future.

Alex lightly squeezed her hips. "Settle down. High-intensity can be good, but it can be too much. I was doing too much and it didn't turn out well."

Elaina eyed him closely. "Not well how? Like drugs or something?" Unfortunately, she'd come across too many people who thought living the fast life meant feeling as high as they tried to fly.

He lifted a hand and tapped his chest. Embarrassment burned her cheeks. The scar, the heart attack. "Oh."

He nodded slowly. "After the heart attack, I realized I needed to slow down."

She ran one hand across the back of his head. She liked the feel of the soft waves of his hair. "So you moved south to live the charmed life?"

"I wouldn't have moved so close to my family if I imagined a charmed life," he said with a rumbling laugh that made her toes curl. "I love them, but my sisters like to remind me I'm the older brother and therefore am there to cater to their needs."

The affection in his voice and love in his eyes as he talked about his sisters proved he was teasing. She understood his reasons but couldn't imagine moving to another state to be closer to her family. She'd never left and had been envious of the way India packed her things and left for five years to tour with the Transatlantic Orchestra. Elaina had never had the courage to give everything up the way India had. She'd always believed that if she stayed, she'd get everything she wanted.

"I guess taking things slow also refers to relationships?" she asked.

He shrugged. "Now I'm trying to avoid getting in over my head."

Elaina glanced away. "And sleeping with me would be in over your head? I don't know if I should be flattered or insulted."

He squeezed her hips again, and she met his eye. "Two months ago, you hated me. Now we're here. I don't want to hurt you, Elaina, and I'm not really interested in getting hurt. Besides that, you're starting a new company. Your dad is pushing me to fill your very big shoes even though I don't want to, and my dad is looking to go into business with you. I think we should take our time to figure out what this is."

"Damn, you're so grown-up and responsible," she said with an incredulous laugh.

Honestly, the prospect frightened her. It was one thing to have a quick affair with Alex. They'd both get some pleasure out of it. There was little chance of emotions or anything deeper happening. Little chance he'd one day look at her with the same disappointment and dissatisfaction she'd seen on too many other faces.

"Look, Alex, that's sweet and noble and all, but I'm not looking for anything serious or long-term."

He lowered his head and kissed her again. His tongue slid across her lower lip. Flames erupted in her veins. He deepened the kiss and she leaned into him. The heat of his body, the strength of his embrace, and the sweetness of his kiss scrambled her thoughts. All she could do was feel, want, enjoy.

Damn. He made a good point with a kiss. She wanted Alex. So what if they slowed down and got to know each other a little bit? She was a Robidoux, which made her a master of not revealing too much about herself. She could play this game for a little longer. Maybe even give herself enough time to make him comfortable with his dad going into business with her.

Like you're really thinking of that now.

Alex pulled away. His lips brushed her cheek before they rested against the shell of her ear. "I promise you the extra time will be worth it."

A shiver went across her skin. Elaina turned her head and kissed his neck. She was going down the wrong path. She was letting emotions guide her. She was going to regret this later, but right now she didn't want to let him go. She pulled his head lower and whispered, "I'm holding you to that."

CHAPTER EIGHTEEN

IN THE TWO weeks since Alex had taken Elaina out, they'd barely had time to see each other, which put his "let's get to know each other plan" into new territory. She spent most of her days traveling and having meetings to raise capital for her new manufacturing facility while he was busy keeping investors and employees calm after the multiple shakeups with the company.

He'd taken to texting her during the day. He asked how her day was going or sent silly pictures like the smiley face in his coffee or the two ducks and a goose near a pond with the caption "duck, duck, goose." He called her every night to check in.

To his astonishment, Elaina participated. He'd expected her to be too tired, too busy or too jaded to follow up. Instead, the texting and talking seemed to be working better than trying to see her. She seemed to want to talk about her day as much as he needed to. He listened as she complained about her hotels when she traveled, or what she'd had for dinner while meeting with potential investors, and the interesting things she'd seen on her trip.

He talked to her about the projects with his team, his mom's newfound love of a drama on Netflix, and sudden fascination with K-pop music. They never talked in detail about their work, nor did they get in deep about where their relationship was going, but he still found himself looking forward to talking to her.

Alex pulled out his cell phone as he entered the grocery store after another grueling day in the office with no news of a permanent CEO in his inbox. Elaina was out of town wooing investors, so he planned to grab something quick for dinner while reviewing the distribution plans for the new biofuel.

He grinned after noticing a new text from Elaina.

Should be back this afternoon.

He'd asked her earlier when she expected to be back in town. He wanted to take things slow and get to know her, but he wasn't a saint. He wanted her in his arms again. He wasn't ready to get in over his head, but that hadn't stopped the ever-present fantasies or the dreams about their one time together. The softness of her lips, the slick heat of her wrapped around him, or how good she'd felt in his arms on the dance floor.

His cell phone rang, and his mom's picture came on the screen. Alex immediately pushed aside thoughts of sex with Elaina before answering. "Hey, Mom, what's up?"

"What are you doing for dinner tonight?" she asked with anticipation.

Alex's eyes scanned the grocery store until they landed on the deli to the right. "I'm picking up a rotisserie chicken and a salad from the deli now."

"No, sir. Your dad found a new Bolognese recipe, and he's trying it out today. Your sisters are coming, too. Get over here now."

As much as Alex had looked forward to going home, reviewing the biofuels plans he'd pushed for, and calling Elaina for another conversation, he knew he couldn't use that as an excuse with his mom.

Didn't mean he couldn't try. "I've had a long day and wouldn't be good company."

"I don't care. A long day is the perfect reason to get over here," his mom replied in a matter-of-fact tone of voice. "Now grab a box of wine and bring it with you."

"And a cake," his dad added in the background.

"And a cake," his mom echoed. "See you in a bit." She ended the call before he could argue further.

Well, Bolognese sounded a lot better than deli chicken. He'd go to his parents for dinner, then call Elaina. He rounded the corner to the deli and bakery. Elaina stood in front of the display case filled with multiple dessert options. He froze when he saw her, then smiled. He didn't care that she hadn't called him as soon as she got back in town. That wasn't her style. He was just glad to see her.

He strolled over next to her. "See anything worth buying?"

She spun and faced him. "Alex, what are you doing here?" She sounded surprised and slightly flustered.

He pointed toward the deli. "I came for chicken, but my mom called and insisted I come try my dad's new sauce. So I'm picking up a cake and wine instead." He raised a brow. "What are you doing here?"

"I just got back in town, and after the day I had, all I want is something smothered in chocolate." She turned back to the display case. "Their chocolate ganache cake is delicious."

"Rough time in Wilmington?"

"I would prefer rough. Getting fired by your father doesn't exactly instill trust in potential investors."

As the person her father promoted after firing her, he didn't know what to say to that. They staunchly avoided talk about work, especially work related to Robidoux Holdings. He took a closer look. Dark circles were barely visible beneath her eyes, but they were there. Her ponytail was loosened, and her clothes were wrinkled. Probably from the car ride on the way back.

"Come to dinner with me."

She shook her head. "I can't intrude. Besides, I just got here, I'm tired, and I look a mess."

"You look fine."

She raised a brow. "I spilled coffee on my shirt. I look terrible."

His gaze dropped, and he noticed the brown stain on her cream-colored shirt. "You look like you've had a long day and need to relax. My mom loves to take care of me and my sisters after a long day. Plus, if she finds out I saw you here and left you alone to eat nothing but an entire chocolate ganache cake, she'll curse me out."

Her lips twisted, and her eyes narrowed, but humor sparked in their brown depths. "Curse you out, huh?"

"I swear." He reached out, took her hand in his and squeezed. "Come on. I'll get the cake, we'll choose some wine, and if anything, you'll get a few embarrassing stories about my childhood while enjoying a good meal."

He expected her to pull away, but she didn't. Her hand squeezed his back, and her full lips lifted in a small smile. "Embarrassing stories about you?" she said eagerly. "Sign me up."

ELAINA COVERED HER mouth as she laughed out loud around the dinner table at the Tyson home. Alex hadn't lied when he said his mother would provide her with embarrassing stories about his childhood. As she told the tales of Alex's escapades as a quiet kid with a voracious curiosity whose what-if questions often led to various mishaps, Elaina couldn't suppress her laughter.

She'd been hesitant about coming. Her day had been awful. Another closed door and failure to believe in her abilities to bring the hemp facility back from the brink, just because she was no longer with Robidoux Holdings. Suddenly everything she'd done in her professional life didn't count for anything.

She'd planned to spend the night lost in chocolate and a bottle of red wine. More wine than cake. She'd considered calling Alex to let him know she was back. The idea of being wrapped in his arms after a shit day held almost as much appeal as the chocolate and wine idea, but she'd stopped herself. She wasn't supposed to be relying on him. Even if he called her to ask about her day or sent text messages to check in. Unlike Robert, who only texted about wanting to "hit it" again and ask what color panties she wore—nostalgia had really played a mind trick on her when it came to Robert.

Then Alex appeared as if she'd wished him up, and despite never going to someone's house looking like something the cat dragged in, there she was. Sitting at the table with his warm and welcoming family and laughing so hard she was afraid she'd snort the horrible box wine he'd insisted was a favorite of everyone in his family.

"I think that's enough for tonight, Mom," Alex said with a grin. "You've embarrassed me enough tonight. Don't you think it's Pam's turn?"

Pam shook her head. "Oh no, don't try to turn this conversation my way. I was a perfect angel."

His mom snorted. "Not hardly. You were a terror. I didn't think we'd survive the teenage years. I got a call from the principal every day for four years."

"That's because he didn't appreciate my creativity," Pam replied.

Alex leaned over to Elaina. "I knew that would get her off me," he whispered close to her ear.

A shiver went through Elaina's body. His lips were so close, of course she'd want him to kiss her. Her body heated as she pictured his lips brushing her ear, gently biting it the way he had on the dance floor. She placed her hand on his thigh and squeezed.

"You're good at distractions, huh," she teased. His thigh stiffened beneath her hand. The rest of the family continued talking about their old exploits and for the moment weren't paying attention to her and Alex.

He kept his voice low. "I think you're the one working the distraction angle right now."

"Please rejoin the conversation." She smiled and slid her hand up his thigh until her fingertips brushed the growing erection between his legs.

His eyes were like molten chocolate as they stared into hers. "You're enjoying yourself right now, aren't you? You like driving me crazy."

She knew he was joking, but the words struck her. She had put extra pressure on him and made his life miserable while they worked together. She tended to do that with a lot of people in her life. For the first time, she realized how similar she was to her father. The need to press people's buttons, see how far you could push before they broke. She'd done that with Alex and continued to do that. She no longer wanted to play games with him.

"What are you two whispering about over there?" Thomas's voice interrupted.

The entire table went silent and stared at Elaina and Alex. Elaina snatched her hand back to her lap. His sisters giggled, and his brothers-in-law all grinned. Elaina's face flamed, and embarrassment swept through her.

There was a crash from the children's side of the table.

Red Kool-Aid spilled all over the floor and was quickly followed by a wail. The accident effectively snatched everyone's attention and ended the inquisition and the dinner.

Elaina avoided Alex's eyes as she helped Pam and her husband, Chris, clear the dishes while his other sister, Stephanie, and her husband cleaned up after the kids. His mom pushed her out of the kitchen when she asked about washing the dishes.

"With a family this big, things go in the dishwasher," Brenda said. "Besides, I can handle it. You're a guest. Go enjoy yourself."

Elaina nodded and turned to leave, then faced her again. "Thank you for your hospitality. I'd like to apologize if I disrespected you in any way or behaved inappropriately."

Her brows drew together. "What are you talking about? You were fine."

Heat filled her cheeks. "Still, for a second I thought…" That it would be a good idea to feel up Alex beneath the table. No, she couldn't say that. "I just wanted to say that."

His mom's eyes widened, and then she grinned and laughed. Her arms spread, and she pulled Elaina into a hug. "No apology needed. One day I'll tell you about all of the not-quite-appropriate things Thomas and I got into when we were dating," she said in a conspiratorial tone. When she pulled back, her smile slowly faded. "Alex had a rough time before he moved here. He's trying to pace himself, and I respect that, but a little push in the right direction doesn't hurt."

The right direction? Elaina was far from the right direction for him. He was her rebound relationship. The self-confidence booster to help get her bearings back after the disaster that was Robert and losing her job. If his mom and family were getting ideas there was more between them, so would he, and once again she'd be making his life miserable.

"Thanks again." She smiled and then turned to leave. The rest of the family had spread to various locations around the house. Elaina went to the family room where Alex, his dad and Pam were. A home renovation show was on television. She smiled as she listened to Alex and Thomas talk about how they'd handle the renovation of the house.

She wanted to stay and see what the appeal was of renovating a fixer-upper. But staying meant getting closer. Opening herself up to the love they so easily gave. Being hurt when things ended and she had to go back to the chill of her own family.

She lifted a hand. "Dinner was great," she said over the buzz of conversation. They stopped talking and looked her way. "I've got to get home. It's been a long day."

A chorus of disappointed responses came from everyone. Her chest tightened, knowing they weren't eager to get rid of her. Alex stood and crossed the room. His eyes searched her face. Maybe he saw the exhaustion there or the fight she was having with herself, because he nodded and smiled reassuringly.

"I'll walk you out."

After a round of goodbyes and more hugs than she'd had in years, she followed him out. He walked quietly beside her to the car. The sun had set hours ago. The sky was so dark on the outskirts of town. Nothing but the porch light illuminated their way. She looked up at the sky. The moon was just a sliver in the sky, the stars sparkling sequins across black velvet.

"I used to sneak out of the house when I was a teenager and go to this spot on our estate," she found herself saying. "It was near one of the creeks and quiet. I could look up at the sky and let all of my worries and cares go away."

Alex looked up, too. "I've never been one to stargaze. It

was hard to see the stars in the city. That and I was always running from one place to the next." He looked back at her.

"They're beautiful, but they also reminded me to take a breath, think rationally, don't feel so overwhelmed. Whatever I was facing, I could handle, because my problem was so small compared to all the problems of the universe." She took a deep breath of the cool night air. "The last time I went out there, I was pregnant and wasn't sure what to do."

Alex sucked in a breath. "I didn't know you had—"

"I don't," she cut him off. The pain of that memory spread through her chest. She looked back at Alex. "I'm sorry if I've made your life miserable. I tend to do that."

His jaw set. "Elaina, you haven't made my life miserable."

She raised a brow. "Do you not remember the day I made you rework a report five times?"

He closed his eyes, then chuckled. "Okay, you have pissed me off." He opened his eyes. "But every one of your comments and demands was right. You hold people to a high standard. There's nothing wrong with that."

"I was raised never to apologize for going after what I wanted. Somehow I also never got what I wanted."

He slid his hand in hers and squeezed. "Talk to me."

She wanted to talk to him. To tell him everything and not just snippets of what turned her into the person he thought would intentionally destroy his family's life. When honestly, if she hadn't have gotten to know his family and had blamed him for the fight between her and her dad, she might have intentionally hurt his father's business. Because all things were fair when it came to winning.

"This dating thing we're doing. Don't get in too deep with me, okay?" she said.

"What do you mean?"

"No talk of love or forever. We're becoming friends and that's fine, but that's it. Friends with benefits, but nothing else." She met his eyes. She knew ending things with him would be best, but she was selfish. She still wanted to experience the glow of the hope in his eyes, be wrapped up in the acceptance and comfort of his family, pretend she could be happy. But life didn't work out that way. She'd rather warn him to hold back than let him go.

He watched her for several seconds. That long, steady stare that could see so far into her. For a second she wished he'd say no and tell her he was already in too deep to look back. Then he nodded. "I know where we stand, Elaina. I think we both need this right now."

She swallowed the seed of disappointment at his words and straightened her shoulders. "Good. I couldn't have you falling in love," she said with forced haughtiness. "That would be messy and complicated."

The corners of his mouth lifted. "Maybe it would be."

"I've got to go." She turned to open the car door. Alex didn't release her hand. He turned her and pulled her into his arms. She didn't hesitate or pull back. She willingly went into his embrace and accepted his kiss.

"What are you doing tomorrow?" he whispered against her lips.

She had a million things to do to make up for the disappointing investor meeting. She and Zoe were meeting with another potential investor. It was someone she'd worked with for years while at Robidoux Holdings, so she had a good feeling about that.

Still, she shook her head. "Nothing after six."

"Do you want to do nothing?"

With him looking at her as if he couldn't wait to spend more time in her company even if she had plans, she'd cancel them. "You've got something better to do?"

He nodded and kissed her again. "Call me tomorrow and find out."

CHAPTER NINETEEN

"I'M SORRY, ELAINA, but you're too much of a risk. Once you get things up and going, please give me a call. Maybe I'll reconsider then."

Elaina held herself stiffly in her seat. She didn't look away from Emanuel Kent, even when she felt Zoe's gaze shift to her. She'd decided to treat Emanuel to lunch when he'd seemed interested in investing in her business. Now, as they sat in the Jackson Falls Country Club and completed their meal, she wanted to know why he'd wasted her time if he wasn't ready to invest.

"I can understand your hesitancy at investing in a new company, but to say I'm a risk is going a bit far." She kept her voice even. Inside she raged. Another setback. Another blow. "We've worked together in some capacity for years. You know my work ethic."

She'd in fact negotiated a partnership between Robidoux Holdings and Emanuel's commercial investment firm three years before. A partnership that had benefited both of them. He was well aware of her capabilities, which was why she'd felt confident he'd be willing to invest in her facility.

"I do know about your work ethic, Elaina, but if you remember the negotiation of our last deal, I can't go into business with a competitor of Robidoux Holdings."

Elaina clasped her hands in her lap and sat up straight. It was do that or clench them into fists. "I'm not a competitor." The idea of getting into hemp manufacturing was in its infancy at Robidoux Holdings when her dad fired her.

Emanuel shifted and tugged on this tie. "When I met with Grant last week, he mentioned plans to expand into hemp manufacturing."

"Plans to do so and actually doing so aren't the same thing, Emanuel." She smiled and infused her voice with warmth to take out the bite. "We both know you could be behind on this by the time a company as large as Robidoux Holdings makes a move."

He nodded. "I'm aware, but that doesn't change my mind. It's business, and right now I'm not in a position to rock the boat." He glanced at his watch. "If you'll excuse me, I've got another appointment."

Elaina nodded and held out her hand. "Thank you for taking the time to meet with me today." She wanted to squeeze his hand hard enough to break the bones but shook it with a firm but non-bone-crushing grip.

He didn't let go when she would have pulled back. She met his gaze and saw true regret in his eyes. "I know this is a setback, but you'll overcome it. As you said, we've worked together for years. I look forward to seeing what you build."

Elaina gave him a tight smile, then slid her hand away. Emanuel shook Zoe's hand before walking off. Elaina's hand trembled as she reached for her glass and took a sip of water. She wanted to scream.

"Did that mean what I think it means?" Zoe asked a few seconds later.

Elaina rubbed her temples as her uphill battle became steeper and a dull ache formed behind her eyes. "If you think it means that my dad may be behind our difficulty finding investors, then you'd be right."

Zoe let out a long breath and shook her head. "I can't

believe he'd do that." She held up a finger. "On the other hand, I'm surprised and disappointed in myself for not realizing he would."

"For once I thought he'd let me step out on my own. I should have known he wouldn't make this easy."

Grant never made anything easy. Anger burned in her midsection. It was one thing to fire her, but a whole other level of petty to undermine her.

"Why fire you only to make things harder when you're trying to start over?" Zoe asked.

Elaina took a deep breath and focused her thoughts. As much as she wanted to rush out of there, go straight to the estate, and tell her dad exactly which bridge he should jump off, doing that would feed into his plans. He wanted her to panic and rush back to him.

She put her glass on the table. The trembling in her hand was gone as she'd gotten her emotions under control. "Because he's trying to teach me a lesson. He wants me to come back to work for him, but it has to be on his terms."

"What are you going to do?"

She had no clue. Keep fighting was one, but she'd have to look outside of her circle for investors. "I made the mistake of going to people I've worked with in the past. I can't do that because they're in too deep with my dad's company." She glanced at Zoe. "We'll have to get creative with the people we approach."

Zoe sighed. "Creative but also quick. The repairs and updates are moving along, but if you want to keep your tight schedule, then you'll have to find more capital."

"I'll dig into my own investments and savings if I have to. I put money aside to cover this."

"I know you did, Elaina, but the work that needs to happen isn't cheap. If things don't work out, you'll be in bad shape."

"They will work out." She lifted her chin. "I can't fail." She'd worked hard and sacrificed to get the respect and position she had. She would not become the failure Grant expected her to be without his backing. Her mom had raised her better than that.

Zoe leaned forward. "Don't put too much pressure on yourself. It's okay to take things slow and figure things out."

"What's that supposed to mean?"

"For the first time, you don't have to live up to your family's expectations. You don't have to live your life based on what Grant thinks is right. Maybe getting fired was a blessing in disguise."

Elaina held up a hand. "Please don't give me some stop and smell the roses, self-care speech," she said in a tired voice. She couldn't afford to believe in fairy tales or being told she needed to use this time to regroup. She needed to use this time to get better. To come out stronger and smarter. Anything less was like giving up.

Zoe cocked her head and straightened her shoulders. "I am going to give you the speech," she said, using the same don't-test-me voice she used when Lilah got sassy. "You push yourself too hard. You're so busy trying not to live the way your dad wants you to, when in reality you're still living your life to please him."

"What I'm doing has nothing to do with making him happy. I want him to see that I can survive without his help."

"But you're living just like him. Sacrificing yourself to prove you're worthy."

Elaina picked up the bill, which the server had brought

over earlier. "Well, it's nice to discover how you really feel about me." She hastily signed the receipt.

Zoe placed a hand on Elaina's forearm. "I care about you. That's why I'm telling you this."

"If you care about me, then you'll continue to help me instead of telling me to lower my standards. I want this business to succeed, not just to show my dad that I'm more than capable of running another business, but also because the people who work there deserve better. He ignored a perfectly good purchase years ago and nearly let the business go into the ground. They suffered because he didn't care enough to fully put Robidoux Holdings behind their growth. I'm not giving up now. I won't be another Robidoux to disappoint them." She tossed the bill on the table and slid her chair back.

Zoe stood quickly. "Don't be mad at me. Listen, I'm only trying to help. I don't want you to end up hurt."

"How is this going to hurt me?" She frowned, confused. Succeeding would only make everything better.

"If things don't go as planned, I'm worried you'll take it personally when it's just business."

The concern in Zoe's face melted some of Elaina's frustration. She softened her tone when she spoke again. "I don't take anything personally. Look, I do appreciate you. Thank you for caring, but I'll be okay."

Zoe held her gaze for several seconds before nodding. "Are we still on for next weekend? You promised Lilah you'd help her find a pageant dress, and she can't wait."

Elaina smiled. "Yes. There's no way I'm giving up a chance to shop with my girl."

"Good. But be warned, she's got dozens of pictures saved on her phone and at least that many stores she wants to visit."

Elaina laughed. At least she had one good thing to look forward to. "I can hang. Tell Lilah I'll pick you both up early next Saturday. We can get breakfast to fuel up before the shopping marathon."

"She'll like that." Zoe snapped her fingers. "Oh, and will we see you at India's performance tomorrow night?"

They walked toward the door. Elaina's steps slowed. India had a quarterly performance with a string quartet at the museum of art. Elaina had missed the one the previous quarter and planned to miss this quarter. Hanging out with her family was hard enough with India and the rest of them trying not to look at her with pity. Since she'd gotten fired, she knew the looks would only be worse.

"I'm not sure."

Zoe pursed her lips and pointed a finger. "Oh no. You're coming. We all want to see you. Byron especially. You've got to come. No excuses."

When they were in the parking lot, Elaina stopped Zoe before they parted for their cars. She hesitated a second before saying in a rush, "Fine, I'll come, but don't tell Byron."

Zoe frowned. "Tell him what?"

"About Dad pressuring investors to not do business with me. I don't want him to step in the middle of this."

Asking Zoe to keep a secret from Byron was a big favor, but if Byron got involved, it would only complicate things further between her and her dad. She and her siblings had their own challenging relationship with Grant. Byron and India had worked through theirs for the most part. This current fight was between Elaina and Grant, and she needed to figure it out herself.

Zoe opened her mouth, closed it, then took a deep breath. "I won't say anything."

CHAPTER TWENTY

ALEX HADN'T SUCCUMBED to Chris's peer pressure and purchased his own motorcycle, but he didn't say no when his brother-in-law took him to test drive a few. He had a lot on his mind, so when Chris called him earlier that day and told him about a show at one of the local dealerships, he'd found a way to leave the office early for a few minutes to clear his mind.

They spent the afternoon looking at various types of bikes, test driving one of the three-wheelers, and doing nothing but talking about speed, horsepower and finishes. Afterwards, they ended up at the bar for happy hour and continued the talk over hot wings and beer.

"I forgot how much I missed doing this," Alex said, leaning back in the seat and looking around at the bar. The place wasn't overly crowded for a weekday afternoon. The after-five crowd would soon fill the space.

"Doing what?"

"Leaving work and spending an afternoon doing something not related to angry investors, employees who act more like children than adults, and weekly reports."

Chris chuckled. "Employees acting like children?"

"Worse." Alex turned in his seat and pointed at Chris with his beer bottle. "Do you know that I literally had to sit down with two department directors because one was mad about something the other said at a conference a month ago?"

Chris frowned. "What was said? Was it harassment or a threat?"

Alex shook his head. "No. One asked the other why they'd chosen to sit somewhere else in the room, and when that employee responded that he wanted to sit there, the other guy took it to mean he didn't like being a part of the group."

Chris blinked slowly. "Seriously?"

"Seriously, man." Alex shook his head and took a sip of his beer. "It's been a sore spot since they returned, and it eventually erupted because they haven't been talking and their teams are suffering. I felt like a middle school principal dealing with two adolescents."

Chris raised a brow. "Are you sure that's all that happened? You know some people get pretty comfortable at conferences. Maybe the seat situation was part of a secret lovers' spat."

Alex eyed Chris. "You should be a novelist. You're always coming up with elaborate stories and schemes."

"That's because I understand human nature. Believe me, there's more to that story than one didn't sit next to the other."

Alex rubbed his temple. "Just keep me out of it."

Chris slapped a hand on his shoulder. "That's why you get paid the big bucks, bruh. You can't get out of it."

Alex groaned and finished his beer. He wouldn't have another. He'd promised Elaina something better to do after she got off work. His plan was to pick her up and take her to the new coffee and dessert bar downtown. He would still have work to catch up on before picking her up. There would be emails to read and respond to along with potential phone calls and reports to review when he got home. The reminder sent tension through his shoulders and made his heart rate increase. He rubbed his temples as he felt the start of headache.

"Alex, bruh, if the job is stressing you out, then maybe you should quit. You didn't sign up to be the CEO. You signed up to concentrate more on research and development."

"I know."

"And you can find a job somewhere else with a less jacked-up environment. You don't have to stay there."

He rubbed harder. "I know."

"In fact, my place is looking for someone. I can put in a good word for you. You know I love my job, and for the most part, my coworkers aren't having off-hours drama they're bringing in."

"I know."

Chris threw up his hands. "Okay, well, if you know all of this, then why aren't you leaving?"

Alex dropped his hands and stared at the television over the bar. "Because…"

Because he didn't want to leave a mess for Elaina when she came back. Why he kept thinking she'd be back when both she and her father refused to give in was proof of his stupidity. He didn't owe the Robidoux family enough to be the referee in their family drama. Still, as he watched her try with the manufacturing facility, he knew she could do it, but Elaina's aspirations had always been bigger than running one facility. She could build her own empire, but the way she blatantly avoided talking to him about his job, he knew a part of her still wanted the empire she'd been groomed to take over.

"Because what?" Chris asked.

"Because I like the challenge. I hadn't realized how much I missed that, too."

Concern flashed across Chris's features. "I get it, but don't drive yourself as hard as you did before."

Alex ran a hand across his chest. "I won't."

"Alright, but don't think I'm letting up. You go and give yourself another heart attack and your sister is going to kill me."

Alex laughed. "Why is she going to kill you?"

"She's worried about you, too. She thinks you're stressing and getting in over your head. She wants you to take a break."

Alex's head drew back. "Wait a second." His eyes widened, and suddenly things made sense. "Is that why you called me today and dragged me out of the office?"

"Hey, man, I really did want to go to the bike show."

Alex shook his head. "Unbelievable. They can't help but stay up in my business."

"You knew that when you moved down here to be around everyone. Your sisters are plotting ways to make you take it easy. After you brought Elaina to dinner, they're even more worried."

"Why? I thought they liked her?" he asked, shocked.

Chris shrugged as if he didn't want any part of Alex's frustration. "Look, I'm not saying they don't. They're just worried. She reminds them of Sheila."

Alex groaned and rubbed his temples. He could go the rest of his life without hearing that name. "She's not like Sheila."

Chris's brow shot up. "I see you're delusional about other things besides coworkers sleeping together. She's exactly like Sheila." Chris slapped the bar with the words.

Alex waved his hand back and forth across his neck. "She's not. Besides, she's not as self-destructive."

Sheila had fed right into his previous life. Work hard,

play hard, ruthlessly climb to the top. They were like fire and gasoline when they were together. They hadn't been in love, but he had thought she'd cared about him. Until she didn't show up at the hospital after his heart attack, and later broke things off with him because, as she said, *"You had a heart attack, Alex? It's like dating an old man. I'm not ready to date an old man."*

"I won't lecture you on who you sleep with," Chris said. "It's none of my business, but I will tell you what everyone else is saying."

"It doesn't matter. Elaina and I are just figuring things out. Nothing serious."

"If it's not serious, don't bring her around the family," Chris said matter-of-factly. "What they don't see and know about, they can't worry about."

Alex wanted to immediately argue but held back the words. Chris was right. Bringing a woman around his family meant there was something serious there. The first time she'd come was legit and related to work. This time had nothing to do with her helping his dad. She'd looked tired after a long day and he'd wanted to make her night better.

Alex pinched the bridge of his nose. "Shit."

"Exactly," Chris said. "Elaina is cool and all. That little footsy game or whatever you two played at dinner last night was cute, but she's not the type of woman you bring home. Have your fun. Keep it between you two. Make a clean break before things get serious."

Alex nodded. "I hear you."

Chris dropped the subject, and they moved on to other topics before leaving. His brother-in-law's words stuck with him for the remainder of the night. *"She's not the type of woman you bring home."* Hadn't he seen the same qualities in Elaina that had driven him wild a few years ago?

The same things that attracted him to her were also the things he'd vowed to keep out of his life. Yet here he was, asking her to take things slow and bringing her to family dinners. She'd been the one to remind him to take a step back and remember what they were doing. Well, he would from now on. He'd remember they couldn't be anything more than what they were.

CHAPTER TWENTY-ONE

ELAINA MIGHT HAVE agreed with Alex to take things slow, but after the disappointing meeting with Emanuel, she needed to let off steam. Taking things slow and spending the night talking were not the way she intended to decompress.

She met Alex at the door wearing nothing but a red lace bra and panty set with a matching silk robe. The flowers in his hand fell to his feet. She grinned as he scrambled to pick them up.

"I was going to take you out for dessert," he said, eyeing her from head to toe.

"We can have dessert here." She reached out and pulled him into the house by his shirt.

He crossed the threshold and wrapped her in an embrace. His body was cool from the early evening air against her hot skin. He covered her mouth in a searing kiss, and she tugged his shirt out of the waistband of his pants.

Thankfully he didn't ask questions or try to slow her down. She didn't want to slow down. She didn't want to think about him bringing flowers or the plans to take her on another date. Thinking led to yearning, and yearning led to her believing in happy endings. Sex, their relationship was just about sex.

His hand squeezed her ass, and she forgot about everything but having Alex in her arms. She jerked on the front of his pants and eagerly wrapped her fingers around his grow-

ing erection. Alex's low groan echoed through the entryway. It didn't take long before he was thick, long and ready.
She pulled out the condom she'd slipped into the cup of her
bra. Alex's eyes flashed with excitement. She grinned and
tore open the packaging. In a flash she had him covered.

Alex lifted her with efficiency and placed her on the
entryway table. The flowers hit the floor as he slid into her
with one quick thrust of his hips. Elaina groaned, tension
seeped out of her, and a feeling of rightness settled into
her. This was what she wanted. What she needed. Alex, his
body, his kiss, his touch, pushed aside everything wrong in
her day. Their mouths came back together in a desperate
kiss. Alex trailed hot kisses across her cheek and finally
stopped when his lips brushed the sensitive spot at the corner of her neck. Her nails dug into the taut muscles of his
ass and urged him on.

The table creaked and swayed with their frantic move-
ments. Their moans and heavy breaths echoed in the entryway. Alex held on to her as if he needed this just as much
as she did. Elaina came hard and fast. Her body trembled
and clenched around him. Alex let out a shuddering breath
and followed her over.

Eventually, Alex carried her into the living room, where
he put her on the couch before shuffling to the bathroom.
His pants were still wrapped around his ankles. It was
amazing he hadn't dropped her. When he came back, his
pants were tossed to the side and she straddled his waist.
He leaned back and ran his hands up and down her back.
The stress of the day was gone.

"Thank you," she murmured into his neck.

"You're very welcome," he said, sounding slightly smug.
She didn't care. He'd done a damn good job. A com-

fortable silence fell for several minutes. Alex shifted and groaned.

"What's wrong? Am I too heavy?"

Alex grinned and gripped her waist. "Not at all."

She sat up and looked at his handsome face. He smiled at her, and her heart squeezed. She was feeling things that had nothing to do with desire. "I'll get us something to drink. I also have cake. So, you can have the dessert you planned."

She slid off his lap, reached her hands above her head and stretched. Alex watched her with his unreadable expression. His steady stare almost made her consider covering up.

"Do you like what you see?"

"More than you'll ever know." Sincerity rang in his words.

Heat spread through her cheeks. She cleared her throat and raised her chin. "Good. My body isn't supermodel perfect, but it's mine and I love it. Make any suggestions on ways to improve or negative comments and this is over."

He placed one hand over his heart. "Believe me, I have no suggestions."

Smart man. Elaina went into the kitchen, and he followed her. She pulled a bottle of water out of the fridge and stood at the kitchen table. He walked up behind her and slid his arm around her waist.

"What are you doing tomorrow night?"

She didn't pull away, but she was able to stop herself from being too needy and leaning back into his embrace. Elaina thought about the promise she'd made to Zoe and sighed. "My sister has a performance at the museum of art. She asked me to come."

"You sound like you don't want to go."

She lifted a shoulder and took a sip of the water. "Not particularly."

Alex spread his hand across her stomach. "Why not?"

Elaina tilted her head to the side to let Alex brush his lips there. "I appreciate music, but when it comes to being around my family, things are a little awkward right now."

"Because of the firing?"

"That among other things." She thought about how hard she'd have to pretend to be happy to keep everyone from asking over and over if she was okay. How India and Travis would try not to be too lovey-dovey in front of her for fear she'd shatter and break. No matter how much she said she was okay with their relationship—which she was—everyone still treated the situation as if she couldn't handle things. Granted, her earlier reactions kind of played into that, but she'd tried to be better.

"Then why go?"

Elaina turned in his embrace. "Because Zoe asked me to. Plus, Byron will be there, and I haven't seen him in a while." She tried to smile and seem optimistic. "It'll be fun."

He didn't look convinced. "You don't sound like you believe that."

"I've figured out how to be around my family and pretend like everything is okay. No one looks too deeply anyway. I'll be fine."

His eyes became thoughtful as he watched her. Until Alex, no one looked too deeply. Why did he always see through her bullshit? "The good thing is, I may come across some new investors tomorrow. It's worth going."

"What about the music? I thought you had an appreciation for the arts," he said with a teasing tilt to his lip. "I mean, you really got into the blues performance the other night. You even danced."

Elaina rolled her eyes but smiled. She was thankful he changed the subject instead of probing further into her complicated relationship with her family. "I promise you there will be no dancing tomorrow. I appreciate the people who perform the arts, if not always the result. A night of chamber music isn't exactly titillating."

"Are there any creative hobbies you're hiding from me?"

Elaina chuckled. "Not hardly. Mom gave up on piano lessons after I kept skipping them, art was my least favorite class in school, and I sing like a cat in heat. I'm far from creative."

Alex placed his hands on her hips and pulled her closer. "I don't know. You've found some pretty creative ways to make my eyes roll to the back of my head."

Elaina couldn't hold back a laugh. Alex said some of the silliest things. She liked that about him. "Unfortunately, I won't be performing those acts for a crowd."

"I wouldn't want you to do that for a crowd." His expression turned reflective. "Sometimes I think I only want you doing that for me. With me."

Her heart jumped. The words sent an emotion so powerful and scary through her that she didn't want to acknowledge it. But hope was something difficult to kill once it took root. She was not supposed to be hoping for something more or believing in the promise of happy endings anymore.

Alex's hands slipped away from her, and he took a step back. "I'm sorry."

"For what?" She twisted the top of the water bottle in her hand.

"For making this more than what it is," he said. "You

were straight up from the start. I've reminded myself to be clear about what we're doing."

"But?" she asked cautiously.

"But I'm having a hard time remembering to keep my emotions out of this."

There went that damn hope sprouting and blossoming like weeds again. She took a sip of her water bottle to stop a smile from spreading across her face. She lifted her chin and glanced away. "I don't know why. I'm not exactly love-able."

He took her chin in his hand and lowered it. Their eyes met. His were unwavering. Deep, dark, and determined to let her see that he wasn't toying with her. "That's where you're wrong. You're exactly my kind of poison. I've never been attracted to the soft and sweet."

He dropped his hand and went to the fridge. Elaina watched as he pulled out another bottle of water. Her pulse rushed through her veins. Her hand clenched the water bottle. Elaina bit the corner of her lip.

"Did you still want to go out?" she asked. The night was early. She didn't want him to leave.

"Actually, I have some work I need to do. I need to go over some emails and reports I missed when I left work early today."

She swallowed back the disappointment. "I have some things to catch up on, too."

He leaned back against the fridge and watched her with those steady eyes. "My laptop is in the car."

She pursed her lips then said in a nonchalant voice to hide how much she wasn't ready to watch him go. "You can bring it in and work here."

The corners of his sexy mouth lifted. "Are you asking me to stay?"

Elaina's disappointment dwindled away. She wanted him to stay longer. Giving him the option to work there was easier than admitting just how much she didn't want him to leave. Even though the knowing look in his penetrating gaze said he was on to her. "I mean, you might as well. As long as you don't wear those ridiculous glasses."

He raised a brow. "There you go talking about my glasses again. What's wrong with them?"

"I hate them even if they're kind of sexy, on you."

He grinned. "Good thing I have them in the car."

CHAPTER TWENTY-TWO

ELAINA ARRIVED AT the art museum and went straight to the bar. She ordered a glass of wine, and instantly the anxiety coursing through her eased. She took a fortifying sip, savoring the rich notes of the wine and sighed.

You'll survive the night of happy couples.

With that reassuring thought, she turned away from the bar and scanned the crowd for her family members. They stood close to the performance area. The quarterly chamber music performance was one of the art museum's most popular events. India started playing there shortly after she'd returned to town after touring with the Transatlantic Orchestra. Even though she worked as the assistant director for the Tri-City Orchestra, she was able to participate in the performances at the museum when the schedule didn't conflict with the orchestra.

Elaina watched her sister and the rest of her family. Travis's hand rested on India's lower back. His eyes lit with a type of love and admiration she'd never seen when they were together. India's enthusiasm about playing was evident in the excited way she spoke and the sparkle in her eye. Elaina's gaze shifted from them to Byron and Zoe. Byron laughed at something Zoe said and wrapped an arm around her shoulder to pull her close. Zoe pressed her hand to his chest and grinned up at him. The love between them was as bright and open as the love between India and Travis.

Tightness filled Elaina's chest. She gripped the glass in her hand and took another sip. She loved her family. She'd fight anyone who dared try to hurt either India or Byron, and honestly, she'd do the same for Zoe and Travis, because they were her family, too. But damn if it didn't hurt to be the odd person out.

Their easy and carefree conversation would die away as soon as she walked up. India would slide away from Travis as if she didn't want to hurt poor Elaina by showing just how happy she was with Travis. Byron would watch her for any signs that she was going to lose it and break down in tears.

Elaina rolled her eyes. She would forever regret acting the damn fool the day she'd discovered India and Travis were in love. She'd had a right to be surprised and upset, but her uncharacteristic outburst had left the entire family on edge.

No matter how many times she said she wasn't in love with Travis and wanted India and him to be happy, they didn't believe her. Now she had to try even harder to act indifferent when around them, which in turn only made things worse. Byron read her better than anyone, but he read her response wrong, and she was pretty sure he'd shared his suspicions with Zoe and maybe even India.

With another deep breath and sip of her wine, she took a step toward her family. Tonight was a three-glass night. No, she had to drive home. One glass here, two more when she got home.

Zoe looked up, and although she wasn't close, Elaina could tell she'd said, "There's Elaina." The rest of the group turned her way. The smiles on their faces dimmed, and the loose body language stiffened. Her stomach clenched. Was she really that difficult to be around?

A man stepped in her way. Elaina froze. Frowning, she prepared to curtly tell the person to get out of her way, but when she looked up, her eyes met Alex's. She hated the thrill of joy that shot through her at seeing him, which made her words come out sharp.

"What are you doing here?"

One to never respond to her sharp tongue, he only slid his hands in the pockets of his black dress slacks and lifted his shoulders. The dark jacket and wine-colored shirt he wore hugged his wide shoulders perfectly. Those ridiculous glasses were around his neck. Memories of the night before came to her mind. He'd worn those glasses while they'd worked, and she'd told him to keep them on after climbing onto his lap for another round. She pressed her lips together to stop her smile, but the way his lips turned up meant he knew what she was thinking. She never should have told him she thought they made him look sexy.

"I can't enjoy music at the museum?" he asked easily.

"I didn't invite you," she said. She'd told him about it, and secretly in her heart of hearts she'd hoped he'd ask to come, but when he didn't, she wouldn't dare ask the question out loud.

"I know you didn't. I decided to come anyway. If you don't want me to bother you, I can sit with someone else." He pointed across the room. "I see Sade. I'll go talk to her." He took a step to the side.

Elaina's arm shot out, and she grabbed his with her free hand. "No, you're not." Her voice was calm and matter-of-fact.

He raised a brow. "Why not?"

She lifted her chin. "You know you're mine." Her insides were jelly despite the bold way she'd made the statement. This was going far beyond the we're-just-having-fun boundaries they'd set.

"Am I?"

She slid forward. Her grip on his arm loosened, and she slid her hand up to gently squeeze his bicep. "Tell me you're not." She poked the tip of her tongue out of the side of her mouth and eased forward just enough for her breasts to brush his chest.

Heat flared in Alex's eyes. "You know I am." His voice was low and rough.

Elaina's nipples tightened. Triumph flared in her chest. His hand rested on her hip, holding her close when she would have pulled away. "And you know that you're mine." The possession in his voice made her want to jerk away and deny the thrill going down her spine.

Two people stopped in her periphery before she could reply. Annoyance flared in her chest at the interruption and in Alex's eyes at the same. They both turned to see who'd approached them. Byron stood there with Travis, both of them stiff and wary as they glanced between her and Alex. Byron looked as if he were ready to snatch Alex away for daring to touch his sister. Surprisingly, Travis also looked as if he were ready to step in if need be.

Elaina turned to them and cocked a brow. "Please don't tell me you two came over to protect my virtue? It would be cute if it weren't so patronizing."

Byron's gaze slid from Elaina to Alex. His eyes widened before he looked back at Elaina. "Alex Tyson? What's going on?"

Travis shifted his weight from foot to foot. "We just wanted to make sure someone wasn't harassing you."

Elaina let out a dry laugh and glanced back at Alex. "Observe my two saviors, Alex. Honestly, I expected more from my brother and brother-in-law. Apparently they have hidden Victorian senses of honor. Don't worry, their bark is worse than their bite."

Byron narrowed his eyes. "Elaina, stop."

"You apologize." She straightened her shoulders. "I invited Alex here. And you two rush up on him like he's some villain." She hadn't technically invited him, but she wasn't surprised that he'd come there to be with her after realizing the night would be hard for her.

Alex relaxed and held out his hand to Byron. "Hello, Byron. It's good to see you again."

Byron nodded and shook his hand. Alex turned to Travis and did the same. Travis's shrewd glance went from her to Alex during their handshake.

"How long has this been going on?" Byron asked. He sounded so much like Grant that Elaina almost told him to mind his own business.

"I think the show is starting," she said instead. "Is there room for both of us where you're sitting, or should we find another place to sit?"

"There's room," Travis said.

Elaina smiled. Good. She turned to Alex. "Let's go."

Alex held out his arm, and she slid hers through his. She took another sip of her wine, and her smile widened. Things were looking up tonight.

"I THOUGHT YOU hated him," Zoe said the second she got Elaina alone after the performance.

Elaina glanced around the mingling crowd. The chamber music performance had been a success. Now everyone walked through the museum enjoying hors d'oeuvres and cocktails. India was busy being swarmed by all her admiring music fans. Travis hovered close enough to step in if someone got aggressive but far enough away to not intrude. It was unlikely someone would get too handsy at this event, but Elaina appreciated that he looked out for India. Sometimes her sister forgot that being a local celebrity on top of a member of the Robidoux family could potentially put her in the sights of nefarious people.

Elaina focused her attention back on Zoe. "What's this, divide and conquer? I see Byron's pulled Alex to the side. You know the let's-protect-my-sister's-virtue vibe isn't cute."

Zoe tilted her head to the side. "He's not just trying to protect you. He doesn't know Alex. All he knows is you hate him, he got you fired, and he's in your old job. Grant talks about Alex as if he's an addition to the family, which means Byron wants to know what's up. He thinks Alex is trying to get close to you just to grab something from the family."

The thought was laughable. Alex was more straight-forward than that. "Something like what?"

"Oh, I don't know. Maybe steal away the company."

The idea was so ludicrous that Elaina laughed out loud. "You can't be serious?"

Zoe nodded. "I'm very serious. I'm surprised you haven't had the same thought."

Elaina looked across the room to where Alex and Byron stood at the bar, ordering drinks. She shook her head. "He's not interested in a takeover."

"How can you be sure? You looked up his reputation. He was ruthless in his previous positions. Even you said he was trying to push you out and take over."

Elaina waved a hand. "I was being paranoid. Believe me, I know this firing thing was my dad." She also believed Alex wasn't trying to live his life the way he had before. She saw the scar on his chest and the way his family worried over him. He really wasn't interested in a hostile takeover.

"Then how did you start up?" Zoe asked.

"Because I wanted to," Elaina said. "Everything is fine. Believe me."

"But we're going into business with his dad." Zoe said the words as if Elaina sleeping with Alex was breaking some law.

"I'm well aware of that," Elaina said.

Zoe's brows drew together. She stepped forward and lowered her voice. "Don't tell me this is just to secure that."

The words hit Elaina like a fast-moving car. She took a step back. Alex had thought the same thing, but hearing the words from Zoe were worse. "I'm going to walk away now before you say that again and make this worse."

Elaina turned and did just that. Her stomach churned. Anger and pain blended. How could Zoe think she'd sleep with Alex just to get his father's business?

Why wouldn't she? You married Travis to secure getting your family's business.

Elaina sighed and rubbed her temple. She needed a moment. Maybe several moments. The mistakes of her past would always cloud everyone's judgment of her. She didn't know what she could say or do to make anyone see her differently.

If everyone thought she was like that, maybe it was because she really was that way. Had she really agreed to this thing with Alex because deep down she wanted to win? She searched her soul and tried to find any hint of motivation for being with Alex just to ensure she had a supply for her new facility. She went through all their interactions and was dead honest with herself. Everything had been sincere. Sure, she recognized the benefits of having him on her side, but that hadn't been what drove her. Unfortunately, being honest with herself meant admitting that she liked him more than she should.

She found herself in the local artist section of the museum. One of Travis's paintings was displayed there. Since his elopement with India, he'd started painting again. He used to do that a lot when they were younger. Back when she'd overheard a girl from his old neighborhood talk about how good he was in bed, and she'd been curious and bold enough to find out for herself.

She didn't regret approaching Travis back then. They'd been young and impulsive, and he'd been her little rebellion and excitement. The boy her dad was so proud of saving from poverty and called his second son. The boy her mom had considered a nuisance. Her mom kept telling her boys like Travis were no good and not the type of guy a girl got serious about. She'd ordered Elaina to stay away from him. Elaina had never been good at being told what she couldn't have. If her mom said her dad could sleep with Patricia, then Elaina believed she could sleep with Travis.

Who would have guessed it would have gone on way too long and too far?

As if she'd conjured him up, Travis came and stood next to her. Elaina's lips lifted in a bittersweet smile. "Coming to check on me?"

Travis nodded toward his artwork. "Coming to hear your critiques on my painting."

Elaina studied the landscape. "I don't recognize it?"

"It's in Asheville near the Biltmore Estate." There was a happy note in his voice, as if the memory of being there brought him pleasure.

"It's nice. I have no critiques." She turned to him. "Did India send you over here to make sure I'm good?"

He rubbed his jaw. "She's signing a few autographs."

"And even though you can't stand to be away from her when she's surrounded like this, you came over to ask what I thought of a painting?" she asked in a dubious voice.

Travis raised a shoulder and met her eye. "I did."

She held his stare for a few seconds. No judgment or reproach was reflected in his gaze. "I'm good, Travis. I promise."

He glanced back to where Alex was crossing the room toward them. He looked back at her. "Be careful, Elaina. Remember what happened the last time you taunted your dad with the forbidden man."

Elaina's body stiffened as she prepared to once again defend her relationship with Alex. "I know what I'm doing."

"That's what I'm afraid of. People can get hurt."

"I don't want to hurt him." She watched Alex. He was getting closer but not close enough to overhear. "He makes me happy."

Travis blinked several times. It was true. His hugs, their conversations, the way he challenged her and called her on her bullshit. She enjoyed every second they were together. Not the way she'd enjoyed being with Travis when she was young and exploring her sexuality, nor the way she'd been infatuated with Robert and the idea of starting over. While she was admitting things to herself, she'd admit she'd enjoyed sparring with him in the office. Pushing him to do and be more than he was because she'd seen that he could.

Travis nodded. "Then I'll ask everyone to stand down."

She let out a relieved breath. That was the one good thing about Travis. He was always willing to help her. "Please do."

Alex reached them. He handed her a cup. Elaina took a sip and tried not to frown that it was just cola. This entire night called for more than the one drink she'd limited herself to.

"Are you ready to go?" he asked. Concern was in his gaze, and he slid his hand in hers and squeezed.

Elaina smiled and squeezed back. "Yes."

He pulled her close and wrapped an arm around her shoulders. "Good."

Elaina circled her arm around his waist. The warmth of his body eased the chill in hers. Elaina gave Travis a tight smile. "Good night, Travis, and thank you."

"For what?" Travis asked.

"For always being kind to me even when I don't deserve it."

Travis nodded. "Good night, Elaina."

She leaned in closer to Alex and turned away. She saw the questions in Alex's eyes. She'd save the answers for another time. He would want to know more about her relationship with her ex-husband who was now her brother-in-law. If they were serious about each other, he'd deserve an explanation. Until now she hadn't wanted things to be serious between them. The need to tell him everything was strong enough for her to realize that what she'd wanted out of this relationship with Alex and what it was becoming were two different things.

Outside, Alex walked her to her car. "Do you want me to come over tonight?" he asked.

Elaina lifted up on her toes and brushed her lips across his. She had a lot to think about. She wanted him to come over more than anything, but it was time for another honest conversation with herself.

"Not tonight. I'll call you tomorrow."

He looked as if he wanted to argue. "But—"

She kissed him again. "I promise. Tomorrow."

He sighed and nodded. Elaina got into her car and drove home. She was falling for Alex, and that wasn't good for anyone.

CHAPTER TWENTY-THREE

ALEX HAD JUST gotten out of a tedious meeting with the operations division when his cell phone rang. It was Grant's administrative assistant.

"Alex, Mr. Robidoux wants to have lunch with you. He's already made reservations at the country club. He'll be waiting for you there."

Alex looked at his watch. He wanted to go back and prep for his one-thirty meeting. Instead he now had to entertain Grant? It wasn't as if he could refuse. "I'm in Leesville. I may be a few minutes late."

"He understands."

Alex ended the call and drove to the country club. Even though he wanted to believe this meeting was about updates and plans for the company, Alex had a better idea of what this was about. He'd gone out with Elaina last night, and her family reacted as if she'd shown up with a villain. To her siblings he probably was the villain. The guy who'd gotten her fired. He could imagine this was Grant's turn to inform him to stay away from Elaina.

He'd expected that conversation from Byron when he'd asked Alex to join him at the bar. Instead, Byron stated he wouldn't get in Elaina's business because she'd kill him but warned Alex to be careful with his sister.

"I've seen the softness beneath the strength and ruthlessness. I'm always careful with Elaina."

Byron had seemed satisfied with that answer and turned the topic to other things. Though Alex believed he'd satisfied Byron for the time being, he saw the love and protectiveness he had for his sister. Alex felt the same way about his sisters. Byron could and would hurt him if Alex hurt Elaina.

Travis was another story. He wasn't sure why he'd eyed him up. It was obvious the man was in love with India. The two barely left each other's side and were always touching as if they feared the other would slip away. Yet he still had concern in his eyes when he watched Elaina. Elaina obviously felt something for Travis. Something Alex knew he had to ask about even if he didn't want the answer.

He arrived at the country club five minutes after noon and luckily found a parking space close to the clubhouse. Inside, the hostess took him to a secluded table sectioned away from the other diners. Grant sat alone, staring out the window, slowly drumming his fingers on the white tablecloth.

Suppressing a sigh for what he was about to endure, Alex thanked the hostess and sat. "I'm sorry for being late."

Grant waved his hand as if it were nothing. "I knew you had the meeting in Leesville. It's fine."

"Was there anything particular you wanted to discuss?" Alex asked. He'd rather get to the threatening sooner rather than later.

"Yes. Have you talked to your stepfather about supplying to Robidoux Holdings?" Grant asked.

Alex sat back, stunned. He hadn't expected that. "Well… no."

"Why not?" Grant asked as if Alex was supposed to have convinced his dad weeks ago when in fact they'd never discussed it except for a the brief talk at the garden party weeks ago.

"I wasn't sure if Robidoux Holdings was still moving forward with hemp manufacturing. There have been no other discussions, and with the recent fire and the loss of our CEO, I thought focusing on keeping things stable was the best option. Besides, the one manufacturing facility we had was sold."

Grant's hand tightened into a fist on the table. The one facility they'd had was the one Elaina had purchased right under Grant's nose. Back then he'd admired Elaina's guts for snatching away a company asset without her dad realizing what she was up to.

"Minor setback," Grant said. "We are going into the production business. I'm currently eyeing a replacement facility now."

"I wasn't aware of that." Further proof that he wasn't really considered a permanent replacement in Grant's eyes. The consideration of another acquisition should have come across his desk.

Grant plowed ahead without acknowledging leaving Alex out of business plans. "Talk to your stepfather. Get him on board to be our supplier."

"With all due respect, he's already agreed to supply Elaina. My dad met with her multiple times, and he's impressed with what she has to offer." The dinner he'd taken her to wasn't a business meeting, but still.

"She has nothing to offer but promises she can't keep."

Alex frowned. "I don't understand. She's working hard to get the facility back up and running. She's already made improvements."

"Her improvements are about to stop," Grant said.

The certainty in Grant's voice made Alex's skin crawl. "How do you know that?"

"She can't find investors. Elaina is doing this with her own capital. While she can sustain covering the expenses for a few more months, eventually her money is going to run out. Then she'll be behind and look even worse to the few investors who believed in her. It's best your dad look for other more stable sources."

Alex shifted as unease grew in his midsection. His dad didn't have backup plans to sell his hemp. If things fell through with Elaina, he'd have to sell quickly and probably at a lower cost somewhere else. "Trouble with investors? I haven't heard that."

Grant's brows rose. "Why would you hear about what's going on with Elaina's new business venture?"

And just like that, Alex walked into Grant's trap. He had no doubt Grant knew he was seeing Elaina and wanted Alex to bring it up. He probably expected Alex to be reluctant to say anything. Alex wasn't in the mood for playing games. "We've already agreed to work with her. It wouldn't be right to back out now."

"It would be in your father's best interests. People have expressed their concerns to me about her."

"Oh really?" Alex couldn't keep the sarcasm out of his voice.

"Of course people have asked me if she's a sound investment, and I have to be honest. She'd been shirking her duties at Robidoux Holdings for a while and becoming increasingly erratic. That's why I had to let her go. Combine that with the financial insecurity she's starting her business with and I couldn't ease their concerns without damaging my reputation."

Understanding dawned. Alex leaned back in his chair. "You're undermining her efforts."

Grant didn't appear the least bit fazed by the disillusionment in Alex's voice. "I'm looking out for people who trust me and my word. If you don't want to ruin your father's efforts just as they're getting started, then you'll convince him to supply us instead of her. I'd hate to see his first successful crop since he moved to North Carolina be wasted at Elaina's fledgling facility, or worse, never get purchased, and then he'll have to scramble to find another buyer. One who by then will offer him a lower price."

The way Grant said the words sounded to Alex like more threat than concern. "She's your daughter."

Grant nodded. "And I love her, but I also know her. Don't be fooled. Elaina is just as ruthless as me. Keep that in mind as you two attend concerts together."

Alex pushed his chair back and stood. "I just realized I have a lunch meeting elsewhere."

Grant smiled. "That's fine. I've said what I needed to say."

ALEX WENT TO Elaina's home later that evening. He wasn't sure what he was going to say to her, if anything. She'd repeatedly told him her firing was between her and her dad, and he'd known there was tension between the two. Still, he hadn't expected Grant to be so determined to control Elaina.

He didn't want to be in the middle of their argument. He had to either leave his position at Robidoux Holdings or break things off with her. If his dad found out about Grant's offer, he'd insist on going with the larger company. If Elaina found out, she'd assume he'd been toying with her the entire time only to back out on the deal. He decided to tell her up front about what Grant said and offered.

Elaina opened the door and smiled at him. She wore a pair of dark leggings and a loose sweater. Her hair wasn't in its usual perfect bob but instead framed her face in wavy curls. Despite her smile, she seemed tense and tired.

"Is everything okay?" he asked.

"I took the day off. I needed to think about some things." She stepped back so he could come inside.

"Things like what?" He slid off his suit jacket. Elaina took it from him and hung it on the hook by the door.

"Everything," she said with a sigh. "Come on."

He followed her through the house out back. It was the first time she'd taken him into the backyard. A fire pit sat in the back corner of the fenced-in yard. There a bottle of red wine sat on a table. Marshmallows, graham crackers and chocolate rested next to that with two long metal skewers.

"I was in the mood for s'mores tonight. I hope you like them."

She sat in one of the large chairs. Alex slid into the one next to her. "I've never had them."

She frowned. "No stargazing and no s'mores. You're really making me rethink your childhood."

Alex chuckled. "I had a great childhood. S'mores are camping food. My parents love being farmers now, but they were not let's-go-outside-and-camp people when we were kids. They still don't camp now."

She laughed. "Well, then I'll have to show you."

She put marshmallows on the ends of two skewers and they held them over the fire. Alex's caught fire. Elaina laughed, quickly brought it up and blew out the flame. His marshmallow was blackened.

"I need another one," he said.

She shook her head. "No. The best ones are the crusty ones. I promise."

She slid his blackened marshmallow between two graham crackers and a piece of chocolate, then did the same with hers. She watched him anxiously as they took a bite.

"Well, what do you think?" she asked.

Alex slowly chewed. The sweetness of the marshmallow and melted chocolate blended well with the graham cracker. The smoky flavor from the fire brought it all together. "I think I like it. I may have to make another one."

"Of course. No one can eat just one s'more," she said with mock seriousness.

They shared a smile before she looked away. She pulled her feet up into the chair and nibbled on the s'more. Her gaze didn't leave the flames. A line formed between her brows.

Alex put his skewer on the table. "Elaina, are you sure you're okay?"

She nodded and watched the flames. "I'm thinking of how much I want to tell you."

"About what?"

"About me. My past. My future."

"Your future?" He had a moment of panic. Was she leaving or doing something different?

"I didn't want to go to my sister's performance," she said.

"I picked up on that," he replied evenly. He hadn't pushed for more information from her because pushing Elaina would only make her back away. He wanted to know more about her. He wanted her to trust him. He didn't think there were a lot of people she counted on in her life, and he wanted to be someone she could count on, because despite all the reasons not to, he cared about her.

"I was so happy when you showed up. Everyone thinks I

don't want to be around India and Travis because I'm jealous or still in love with him."

"Are you?" He didn't believe she was, but he could have been wrong.

"I am jealous." She met his gaze. "But not because of what people think. India and Travis love each other. They've always been better suited. If I had taken a step back, I would have realized my dad knew that too when he pushed me to marry Travis."

"Pushed you?"

She took a long breath. "Travis and I started as a fling, but I got pregnant. My dad said I'd embarrassed the family enough by having an open sexual relationship with the boy he'd decided to mentor. My parents were just starting to go bigger than Robidoux Tobacco when mom died. He wanted to fulfill her dream of starting our holding company and wanted to look like a family business. We couldn't do that if I was sleeping with the help and having a baby. My dad said I either married Travis or gave up my plans to run the business. That it was what my mom would have wanted."

Alex sat there stunned. He knew from their talks that her parents put a lot of pressure on her. Pressure to succeed was one thing. Being told to marry someone to save the family was something else. "I don't know what to say."

"There isn't much to say to that," she said with a sad smile. "I originally said no. I'd met someone else. I thought I was falling in love. My pregnancy came at the worst time, but I wanted my legacy more. So I chose Travis." There wasn't any regret in her voice. He didn't say anything to that. He couldn't judge the decisions she'd made being young, pregnant, and told by her family that not obeying would result in her losing the only life she'd ever known. A few seconds later she continued.

"I…lost the baby." Her voice tightened. She cleared her throat and stared in the fire. "Even so, getting a divorce so soon after the marriage would have looked worse. We hadn't announced that I was pregnant. So we stayed together. Travis tried to be a good husband. I could have tried to be a good wife, but I was angry. Every time he smiled at me, I felt trapped and cheated."

Alex reached over and took her hand in his. Her voice remained tight and even, but he saw the pain in her eyes. There was nothing he could say or do that could take away the hurt from a forced marriage and later miscarriage. The best he could do was listen and let her know he offered her support without judgment.

She squeezed his hand. "By the time I realized I wanted to try and scrape some happiness from our marriage, he'd given up. Then we were strangers living together."

"Do you love him?" He didn't think so, but he didn't want to assume.

The frown on her face cleared. She met his gaze. "No," she said confidently. "I thought I could try, but there was too much between us. Travis was always good to me. If anything, he tried hard to take care of me. I appreciated that, and I'll appreciate that about him. What we felt wasn't something that would've stood the test of time."

"Is it because he's married to your sister that you don't want to be around?"

She shook her head. "It's the way everyone looks at me." Frustration crept into her voice. She pulled her hand away. "They act as if I'll break if they show they're happy. The *poor Elaina* looks are killing me. I have to try harder to show that I'm okay, and that seems to only make things worse."

"Are you happy?" he asked.

She stared into the fire for several long seconds, then lifted her lips in a half smile. "I'm happy when I'm with you. Even though I'm afraid to trust that."

Alex carefully put another marshmallow on his skewer. He had to be careful because inside, his heart was doing a backflip. It was the closest Elaina had come to admitting to her feelings. Trust was a two-way street. She'd shared with him. He felt the need to do the same.

"Back before the heart attack, I thought I had the best life. There wasn't a challenge at work I couldn't overcome. I worked hard and played just as hard. My life was nothing but travel, drinking, and outmaneuvering everyone else. I thought that was a sign of success. It wasn't until I was in the hospital and maybe two people of the crowd I belonged to visited me. Those two looked uncomfortable and ready to get the obligatory visit over with. Sitting in a hospital bed and then spending six weeks in recovery is a long time to reflect on your life."

"No one was there to help during your recovery?" She sounded surprised.

He lifted a shoulder. "My family had already moved to Jackson Falls. I didn't tell them until after the bypass surgery. Pam and my parents came up immediately once I told them. But they couldn't stay long, and I didn't want to admit that I needed help. I hired an in-home nurse and increased my housekeeping schedule, but it's pretty sobering to realize after everything I'd done and achieved that I was alone."

Sobering and sad.

"That's why you moved here and took the job heading research and development?"

"It is," he said. "I wanted to be closer to my family. I

wanted a job that would challenge me without requiring as much from me."

"Instead you get my dad and me," she said sardonically.

"I could manage. Besides, you haven't been all bad."

She chuckled and put another marshmallow on her skewer. "You're telling me to step back and reflect on my life, huh."

"I'm telling you to figure out what makes you happy, and to remind you of who'll be there for you when you can't be there for yourself."

"I'd like to start with being happy with you." She held up a finger before he could reply. "But, this isn't a request for happily-ever-after. I'm not asking for marriage, two kids and a dog. I'm just suggesting moving our arrangement from a friends-with-benefits status to an exclusively dating scenario. No pressure or promises about tomorrow."

Alex did not stop the pleasure her words brought from breaking through. He stood and reached for her hand. She took his, and he tugged until she was pressed against his chest. He wrapped his arms around her and kissed her neck. She hugged him tight, and right then he knew two things. He never wanted to let her go, and there was no way he would let Grant destroy his daughter.

Kissing her ear, he whispered, "You really want to do this?"

She nodded. "Please don't lie to me. That's all I ask. You can get mad, you can tell me when I'm being a bitch, you can remind me this was all my idea if it goes to hell, but don't lie. All my life I've dealt with people doing what they think is right for me while only saying what they wanted me to hear."

He met her eyes and knew he would do anything in his power to keep her happy. "I promise."

CHAPTER TWENTY-FOUR

EARLY SATURDAY MORNING, Elaina picked up Zoe, Lilah and India to hunt for the perfect dress for the debutante ball. Their cousin Ashiya was supposed to tag along for the day trip to the specialty boutiques in Charlotte, but she'd canceled after getting sick with a stomach bug. Lilah hooked her phone to Bluetooth in Elaina's car and got her mom and aunties up to speed on the hottest music of the day. They laughed as Lilah rolled her eyes when Zoe and Elaina countered one of her favorite songs with a song they used to love when they were her age.

It was the first time Elaina could remember being that at ease with her family in a long time. She and India had a similar day once. They'd gone out for a girls' day with manicures and pedicures. Elaina had hoped that was the start of their relationship getting closer. Then, later that same day, all hell broke loose when Travis was hurt, and Elaina discovered India was in love with him.

Elaina glanced over at India sitting next to her in the dressing room. Zoe and Lilah were behind the closed doors trying on the next option while India sipped sparkling cider and Elaina champagne. India insisted on drinking the cider so Lilah wouldn't feel left out.

"I'm sorry about what I said," Elaina blurted out.

India frowned at her. "When?"

"That day Travis was in the hospital. My reaction was in bad taste."

India's eyes were wide for a second before she took a deep breath. "Honestly, I deserved it. I should have told you about me and Travis from the start. Especially when I realized how deep our feelings were. I'm just glad that all is forgiven." Her brows drew together. "Right?"

Elaina thought back on that time. She'd been angry and felt betrayed at first, but quickly realized Travis and India loved each other. Things worked out the way they were supposed to. She nodded. "Right."

India's face relaxed before her eyes narrowed. "And now you're seeing Alex? That's…good?"

Elaina chuckled. "It is good."

"Are you sure? I mean, you're okay, right? This isn't about Daddy or the job or anything?"

Elaina's immediate urge was to roll her eyes and tell India not to be ridiculous. She suppressed it. The concern in India's eyes was real and came from a good place. If she wanted more days like today, then she had to also work on making their relationship better. "It's not."

"Even on his part?" India asked skeptically. "He was kind of an asshole. Byron told me everything he dug up on Alex confirmed he was known to be intense and rude when he worked in New York."

"I know, but he's not that person anymore. I trust him." She meant it, surprisingly. Especially after everything that had happened. Alex was open and up front with her. He didn't hide behind a mask. She couldn't imagine him going behind her back or deliberately trying to ruin her life.

"Okay, ladies." Zoe's voice came from behind the dressing room door. "I think we've got a winner."

Elaina and India sat forward. "Then come out and show us," Elaina said.

The door opened, and Lilah drifted out looking like a princess. The white dress had capped sleeves and a silver bodice covered in rhinestones. The skirt floated out like a sparkling cloud around her. For a second, Elaina thought to a picture of their mother at her first debutante ball in a similar dress.

"One day your daughter will wear this dress," her mom had said when she'd helped Elaina put on her dress for her first debutante ball. *"My dress was ruined by punch. We'll be sure to preserve yours. I always wanted my first girl to wear that dress."*

Elaina had donated her dress years ago after realizing she didn't want children. Pregnancy had trapped her in marriage. If she and Travis had had a child, she would have done everything in her power to make that child happy. But fate had chosen to break that bond between them. Things wouldn't have worked out as they did. Now, watching Lilah, she wondered what it would be like if she had a daughter. For the first time in months, her heart ached with the guilt of wondering if the only reason she didn't have a daughter was that she'd been so miserable.

"Aunt Elaina, don't cry. Is it that bad?" Lilah asked, looking horrified. She glanced down at the dress and back up.

Elaina shook her head. "No, you're beautiful. I've got something in my eye." Elaina blinked several times and waved a hand. Her cheeks burned with embarrassment. She was being sentimental. "This is definitely the right dress."

Lilah's face cleared, and she beamed. "If you say it's the right one, then I know it is. No one has better taste than you."

Zoe snorted and placed her hands on her hips. "Don't I get some credit for pointing it out?"

Lilah reached over and hugged Zoe. "Yes, Mom. Thank you."

Zoe grinned and kissed Lilah's forehead. "Alright, let's get it."

They purchased the dress and went to a nearby Italian restaurant for a late lunch. She pulled herself out of the weird mood she'd sunk into at the dress shop and enjoyed the company of her family. Still, the remorse that hung over her whenever she thought about the reason she'd married Travis hovered just over her head. She tried hard not to let her conflicted inner feelings show.

Things worked out the way they were supposed to. She definitely didn't want to have kids. Not having a kid had been beneficial for everyone involved. Why was she in her feelings?

Elaina excused herself to go to the bathroom. She checked her expression in the mirror. Her hands were steady, but inside she felt knocked off balance. She needed a drink to calm her nerves. She almost reached for her purse, but nothing was there. Alcohol wasn't going to be a crutch anymore.

She took a deep breath. Lunch was almost over, and she wouldn't have to be "on" anymore. She just had to get through the rest of the afternoon, and then she could go home and deal with her old insecurities without an audience.

Lilah came in the bathroom as Elaina was leaving. "Mom and Auntie India are waiting at the front door."

Elaina smiled and nodded. "I'll wait with them."

Lilah hugged her quickly. "Thank you for such a fun day."

Elaina hugged her back. A rush of emotion she wasn't used to warmed her. "You're welcome. I… You know I love you, right?" Elaina stumbled over the words. She didn't use them often.

Lilah beamed. "I love you, too."

Lilah's open affection helped soothe Elaina's mixed-up thoughts. She'd wanted to protect Lilah from her dad's influence and the pressure to be the perfect Robidoux from the moment she'd entered their family. She would have protected her own child the same way. No wonder she was having what-if thoughts.

Elaina left the rest room and went down the hall toward the front of the restaurant. India and Zoe stood at the end of the hall with their backs to her.

"Have you told Elaina yet?" Zoe said.

Elaina stopped when she would have announced herself. Told her what?

India shook her head. "No. We're trying, but it could be a year before we get pregnant. I think it'll be easier to wait until we know. She's so erratic, you know. One minute she cares, and the next she doesn't. I'd rather not deal with that right now."

Zoe lifted her shoulders. "I get it."

Elaina took two steps back. When they didn't turn around, she took several more steps back down the hallway. *Erratic?* Since when was she erratic? She pressed a hand to her chest and took a steadying breath. Was that how everyone viewed her? Too irrational and unpredictable for India to talk to about trying to get pregnant?

Their words sent shards of pain and discouragement slicing through her gut. If her own family could only see her as erratic and uncaring, then maybe that's all she really was. Anger and frustration were close on the heels of her pain, and Elaina's hands clenched into fists. Yes, she'd reacted badly when she'd first found out about Travis and India, and she hadn't invited them over for fun and games, but the situation was awkward. She'd first needed time to get used to the idea and later didn't want to make them think she was angry or jealous. All she did was try to hide her feelings so they would be more comfortable. She went out of her way to prove to everyone she was fine, yet they still thought she was erratic.

She hadn't been raised to be the warmhearted, understanding one. She'd been raised to take care of her responsibilities and do what was expected. Why was she trying to be more when they still couldn't see more? Was the effort even worth it?

The bathroom door opened, and Lilah came out. Lilah's brows crinkled when she saw Elaina. Elaina did what she knew best. She pushed back the anger, frustration, discouragement and sadness. She'd deal with all of those later when she was alone, after this, probably with at least one glass of wine. She pasted on a reassuring smile. "I wanted to make sure you came out okay."

The line between Lilah's brows disappeared. She rolled her eyes. "I'm a big girl, Auntie."

"Still, you're a baby to me." Elaina softened the words with a smile. Lilah came over and slid her arm through Elaina's. Some of Elaina's anger cooled. Lilah was why she'd agreed to the outing in the first place, but how long before Lilah, too, saw her in the same way?

They walked out together. India and Zoe stepped apart. The *Elaina is erratic* conversation was over. Her emotions still churned, but she kept the conversation going on the ride back, participated in the latest sing-along, and gave no indication of overhearing their conversation. She'd show them the opposite of erratic. Because no one wanted to see Elaina cry about hurt feelings or beg for understanding. Even if she wanted to, that's not how she was raised.

CHAPTER TWENTY-FIVE

"Do you want to have kids?"

Kids? It was too early for the kids discussion. Unless...
Alex's heart lurched in his chest.

He hadn't planned to bother her, knowing she was spending the day shopping in Charlotte. He'd said he was only texting her to make sure she was okay, but when she'd said the day was *"trying,"* he had to text and ask her if she wanted him to come over. When she'd said yes, he didn't stop to think about how his willingness to run to her side whenever she called was setting an unfair balance of power in their relationship. All he cared about was being supportive. Elaina didn't reveal much, and *trying* meant the day hadn't gone as she'd expected.

Because she'd gotten back late, he'd shown up at her house with the food from the deli packaged and warm. She'd taken one look at the food, directed him to the kitchen with it, and said food could wait. She was in his arms the second he'd put the bags on the table. Again, he didn't question the motive. He had just given her what she needed and taken her straight to her bedroom.

Now Alex shifted onto his side next to her in bed. "Kids? Not at this moment, but, I mean, I'd be okay if something happened."

Elaina frowned for a second. Then her eyes cleared, and she shook her head. "I'm not pregnant, and I'm not planning on getting pregnant. It was just a question. Not a precursor to a life-changing announcement."

She tossed the covers back and slid out of bed, then grabbed his T-shirt off the floor and put it on quickly.

Well, he hadn't handled that well. He jumped out of bed and hurried around to her. "Hold up. That didn't come out right."

"It came out just fine." She stalked out of the bedroom and into the kitchen.

He was on her heels. She got wine out of the fridge and a glass from the cabinet. Alex crossed the kitchen right after she poured some wine into her glass and placed both hands on the counter on either side of her, effectively pinning her in place. She avoided eye contact, but after several heartbeats of his steady attention, she finally met his gaze. Her dark eyes were wary and unsure. He wanted to kick himself for not thinking first.

"I'll admit I could have answered in a better way," he said, measuring his words. "Your question threw me. I haven't had a real relationship conversation."

"Well, neither have I," she snapped back.

His head drew back. He found that hard to believe because she'd been married, but there was no lie in her eye. She'd been told to get married to a guy she'd just been sleeping with. She hadn't mentioned any other long-term relationships. He felt even more like an asshole. "Before my heart attack, I never had conversations about tomorrow. Everything was superficial. There were no thoughts of kids or forever. So this is new for me, too."

Some of the frost melted in her eyes. She leaned back on the counter. "Well, do you?" She watched him as she sipped her wine.

Alex sighed and removed his hands. He shifted to lean

next to her on the counter, too. "I don't know. They're a big responsibility, and I'm still trying to make sure I take care of myself." He placed a hand over the scar on his chest. What would have happened to a kid of his if he hadn't caught the heart attack early and had bypass surgery? How would they have made it if he'd gone so young?

"In the hospital, I wondered what it would be like if I had a wife or kids around who could be there for me, but once I got better, I worried more about what would they do if that happened again and I wasn't so lucky."

Elaina placed her hand over his. "You're too stubborn to go without a fight."

He smiled and strung his fingers through hers. "You might be right. Getting married just to have someone to take care of me one day no longer appeals to me. I love my niece and nephew with all my heart. I'll do anything for them. But it's also nice to send them home with my sister and brother at the end of the night."

Elaina chuckled. "I can see the point of that."

"What about you?" he asked carefully. Though she'd mentioned the child she'd lost before, she hadn't talked about that since.

She took another sip of her wine. "I don't," she said surely. "When I got pregnant, my dad said I couldn't take over the company if I didn't clean up my image. So I agreed to marry Travis. He tried, but I was so…angry. One slip." She held up her index finger. "And the rest of my life was altered forever. I would hope and pray every day for things to be different. That I'd find a way to get back at my dad, to escape the pressure of being the perfect wife, soon-to-be mother, and career woman. I wanted to be free from everything." The longing in her voice was evident all these years later. She stared straight ahead, seeing something that wasn't in the kitchen. He squeezed her hand, letting her know he was there.

Elaina let out a shuddering breath. "Then, one afternoon, Travis came to see me at the office. He'd packed a picnic lunch and wanted to surprise me. He had flowers and chilled champagne. The women in the office swooned. I was furious. I couldn't believe he'd dare to pretend as if we were in love. We'd broken up right before finding out I was pregnant, yet there he was, acting as if our marriage wasn't a sham." Her face hardened. "When I saw the label on the champagne was my dad's favorite brand, I knew why he was there. I couldn't stop laughing. Not only was I trapped in a sham of a marriage to a man I didn't love, but my dad was still influencing everything. I kicked him out and then cursed everything. My dad, Travis, me and the damn kid." Her voice caught. "I miscarried the next day."

Alex slid closer to her. The pain on her face and in her voice was like a sword thought his gut. There was nothing he could say that would make her feel better. He placed her hand on his chest again.

"I felt terrible," she whispered. "I thought it was my fault. That I'd wanted out so bad I willed it. What was worse…" Her eyes met his and they were tortured. Unshed tears shined beneath the lights in the kitchen. "Underneath the grief was relief. I was finally free. Then I saw the devastation on Travis's face. He wanted the baby. He'd been willing to make things work and would have loved that child and maybe even me. We stayed together because it looked better for the family image. He never brought up having another kid and neither did I. Our marriage disintegrated."

He wiped away the tear that trailed down her cheek. "I'm sorry."

The edges of her lips lifted in a sad smile. "After five

years, we finally agreed that misery didn't love company and got a divorce. My dad was disappointed, but there wasn't anything else he could do. Byron and Travis were friends. They had a law firm together. I'd proven I could run the business and was well respected. The earlier potential for scandal with me getting pregnant with the guy my dad had taken under his wing was long forgotten. We moved on and played nice even through Travis eloping with my baby sister."

She brought her glass to her lips. It was empty. She frowned and put it down. She moved to refill it. Alex placed a hand on her arm.

"It wasn't your fault," he said.

She nodded. "I know that. I don't just internalize my anger. I've gone to counseling and gotten a lot of advice. Apparently, I like to deflect."

"I've noticed," he said with a half smile.

She bumped him with her shoulder. "I know I put unrealistic expectations on myself. I know a lot of pregnancies end the way mine did, and I didn't *will* it to happen. I even acknowledge that I use alcohol as a crutch." She pointed to her glass. "See, I listen to my therapist."

Alex squeezed her hand tighter to his chest. He'd noticed she relaxed more with a glass of wine in her hand. He'd also noticed she was meticulous about when, where and how much she drank. "Don't joke."

"What do you want me to do? Cry?" she said flippantly.

He didn't take the bait or let her deflect. "I just want you to do the same thing you asked of me. Be honest with me and yourself. Why did you ask me about kids?"

"Because I don't want to feel trapped again. I don't want unnecessary ties to anyone. I don't want to open myself up to being controlled by anyone, including a kid."

Alex brushed her hair behind her ear and let his fingers trail down the soft skin of her neck and shoulder. "I don't want to control you or keep you tied to me unwillingly." He pulled her close. "Just let me be with you. Just let down your guard and be with me. I'm not your dad, or Travis, or anyone else."

"What do you want from me?" She asked as if she really didn't know. As if the idea of someone just wanting her and nothing else was unheard of.

"I want you to trust me." He cupped the side of her face. His heart jacked up in his chest. "I want you to love me."

She sucked in a breath. He expected her to pull away or tease him. Instead he saw the barest flare of hope in her eyes. "I'm halfway there," she admitted.

The joy that spread through him nearly buckled his knees. He grinned so hard his cheeks hurt. Then he pulled her into his arms, but she placed a hand on his chest.

"I don't know how to do this the right way. I always mess things up. I don't know how to open up completely."

He wasn't scared off by her admission. What she'd revealed about her upbringing and marriage was enough for him to know love and trust would be just as hard for him to earn as it would be for her to accept.

"Then I'll remind you when you should be more Elaina and less Robidoux. Trust what you feel with me."

Her eyes glistened. She lifted her chin and pointed at him. "Don't you dare make me cry."

He continued to grin and lowered his head. "How about I make you cry in other ways? We'll both pretend that's the real reason." His lips covered hers.

Her body trembled and she sighed against his lips. "Deal."

CHAPTER TWENTY-SIX

ALEX SAT AT his desk, reviewing a report, when his cell phone rang. Warren, his biological father's name, displayed on the screen. Surprised, he answered.

"Warren, what's up?" Alex hadn't called Warren Mitchell Dad in decades. His parents were only married for a short time, and he hadn't hesitated to grant full custody to his mom when she'd remarried. Though he'd always been a part of Alex's life, and held no animosity toward Brenda or Thomas, he also wasn't the man who raised him. Calling him Dad felt disrespectful to Thomas.

"I'm calling with good news." Warren's deep voice was filled with enthusiasm. "I'm in Atlanta for business. I'd like to see you while I'm on this side of the country."

Alex relaxed back into his chair and smiled. He hadn't seen Warren in years. "Sounds good. How long will you be here? I'll see what I can rearrange." He pulled up the calendar app on his phone.

"How about the day after tomorrow? I'm wrapping things up today and can travel your way."

Alex put him on speaker and set his phone down. "Is there anything wrong?"

"Nothing's wrong," Warren said with deep chuckle. "I haven't seen you since you were sick and moved to North Carolina. How do you like it?"

"Seen him" was technically correct. Warren video-chatted with him after Alex got out of the hospital because he'd been in London at the time. By the time Warren returned to the States, Alex was on the mend and making plans to move to Jackson Falls with the rest of his family. "I like it."

"Are you sure? Don't ever limit your potential. You were on the fast track to great things in New York."

"I had a heart attack and I'm just over forty. I think it was time for me to slow down," he rebuffed gently. "I appreciate the concern, but I'm doing just fine here in Jackson Falls."

Warren chuckled. When he spoke, he didn't sound at all offended by Alex's subtle cue for him to mind his own business. "I know you're doing fine. You're a smart guy. You'll do fine anywhere you go. All I'm asking is if you're still enjoying the job and living a slower-paced life."

Alex stared at the report on his desk and the multicolored appointments on his calendar. Compared to his life before his heart attack, it did seem mild. Though he still felt as if he were overwhelmed. As if he were faced with challenges and concerns he no longer had the driving energy to solve. Grant was slow about naming a permanent CEO, Elaina was adamant about not coming back to work at the family company, and Alex was stuck in the meantime until something was settled.

"The pace is slower compared to my previous position," he admitted. "But it's just challenging enough to keep me busy and on my toes."

"Good. I'm glad to hear that. You've always been good at what you do. I told you years ago you're destined for greatness."

Alex smiled but rubbed his temples. That was the one thing he'd gotten from Warren. His father always tried to instill in Alex an unflappable confidence and belief he could be and do anything. Warren might not have wanted the family life, but after having Alex he'd at least done everything he could to make sure his kid wouldn't believe in the word *can't*.

What would he say if he knew Alex didn't want the CEO position? Best to leave that lecture for the day they met.

"Do you want to stay at my place?" Alex offered, knowing the answer.

"No, I'll find a hotel. Let's plan to meet up for dinner. Show me the best place in town."

"Fancy or casual?" Alex asked.

"Casual. You know I love soul food, but I can't find anything decent where I'm at."

"You're in Atlanta. I'm sure you can find decent soul food."

"I'm talking about back home. Besides, I don't want comfort food by myself. I'd at least like it with my son. It'll celebrate our reunion."

"Sounds like a plan. I'll see you in two days, Warren."

They hung up, and a reminder popped up on Alex's phone for a video conference call in fifteen minutes. He didn't have time to dwell on the reasons Warren suddenly decided to pop in and see him. A trip to the East Coast wasn't enough to make him insist on seeing Alex. He'd had a connecting flight in New York on his way to London right before Alex had been in the hospital and hadn't taken the opportunity to see Alex.

Alex loved Warren and respected him, but he was well aware of his biological father's failings. Warren was a hustler and ambitious businessman. He'd keep his guard up for any probing questions or attempts to lure Alex to work with him. Though he was happy to see Warren, Alex also wasn't interested in participating in whatever game his father was in town to play.

"YOU LOOK GOOD with a paintbrush in your hand."

Alex stopped painting a pillar that was part of the set for the debutante ball and grinned at Elaina over his shoulder. She and the rest of the committee in charge of the ball preparations were finishing up the last touches on the items needed for the rapidly approaching event.

"You're only saying that because I insisted on repainting them," he said. He turned back to adding the final coat of silver paint on the pillar.

"I came out here to check on you and the rest of the people you brainwashed into painting."

Alex glanced around the lot in the back of the clubhouse. When Elaina suggested tossing the white pillars and purchasing new ones, he'd countered they only needed a new coat of paint. He'd gotten a few you-are-ridiculous looks, but he'd also gotten a few volunteers to help him paint them.

"No brainwashing involved," he replied. "I just had a good idea and they agreed."

"I'd roll my eyes if you weren't kind of cute with those overalls on." She tugged on the splattered white overalls he'd borrowed from the building and grounds crew.

Alex wiggled his brows. "Want me to bring a pair home for later? We can play repair man and desperate housewife."

Elaina rolled her eyes, but the corners of her lips twitched. "That sounds as ridiculous as your idea to paint the pillars yourself." She looked around at the rest of the group working. "But I'll admit they do look a lot better with the silver paint. I can't do much about the theme of this year's debutante ball, but I can at least make sure it's tastefully run. I want everything to be great for Lilah's first club event."

Alex leaned over and kissed her temple. "Everything will be fine. Calm down."

She swatted at his chest, but a smile hovered on her lips. "Of course it'll be fine. I'm in charge," she said, ever confident.

"We should be done out here in another half hour or so. I spoke with George, and he said we could leave the pillars out here to dry overnight," Alex said, referring to the head of maintenance. "He'll get them moved back into the storage area tomorrow."

Elaina nodded. "Good. I think that's everything related to the setup. Now it's just waiting for the day of. That's one thing off my plate," she said, sounding relieved.

Alex ran the paintbrush over the pillar. "Nervous about tomorrow?"

She shook her head. "Why should I be? My plan is sound, our repairs are coming along, and we'll be ready to open as expected."

In the weeks since they'd made s'mores and later talked about their future, Elaina seemed to trust him more. She even talked more about the plans for her new facility. She'd had several meetings with new investors in the past few weeks, even traveling to meet them where they lived in DC, Charlotte, Columbia and Atlanta. He'd been impressed by her persistence and didn't believe Grant's efforts to thwart her plans would work.

"It's okay to be nervous. That doesn't mean you're not prepared."

She scoffed and waved a hand. "Being prepared means there's no need to be nervous."

He wrapped his arm around her waist and pulled her close to him. She pressed her lips together as if hiding a smile. Alex kissed her temple again.

"You're sounding like a Robidoux. Remember what you told me to do when you sound like that."

She rolled her eyes again. "I am a Robidoux." Her voice was light and teasing.

He whispered in her ear. "And I'm to remind you to relax and remember people plotting world domination are typically the villains in a movie." He squeezed her a little tighter. "You'll do great. I know you will."

He'd picked up that her bravado was typically a sign that she was nervous. For Elaina, showing nerves or fear was a weakness she'd been raised to hide and ignore. As long as he was beside her, he'd give her the safe space she needed to be vulnerable. He never wanted her to hide her fears or suppress her concerns in case he'd take advantage of them.

She took a deep breath. "I will. Thank you." She squeezed his arm. "Now, let me go before you get paint on my designer jeans."

"I told you we were painting today. You decided to wear designer jeans." He let her go.

She looked over at the rest of the team, then back at him. "I've got to get up early for travel to a meeting with a potential investor in the morning. Can you come over tomorrow night?"

Alex hesitated. He was having dinner with Warren the following night. He doubted Elaina would expect to meet his biological father, but he also didn't want her to think he was hiding her from him, even though that was exactly what he was doing. Warren analyzed every situation and didn't hesitate to offer his opinion. Alex didn't want Warren's opinion on Elaina. Nor did he want Elaina and his relationship subjected to his father's shrewd eye. His mom and dad would keep any concerns they had to themselves unless they thought things were too much. They hadn't said anything and liked Elaina. That's all he wanted and needed for now.

"I've got a work thing tomorrow night, but I'll call you when it's over." The explanation was vague and sounded like bullshit to his ears. He braced himself for the questioning.

"No problem. I remember those late-night meetings at Robidoux Tobacco." She squeezed his bicep. "Don't let Daddy talk too much. He always bores the partners. Call me when you're done." She gave him one last squeeze, then turned and went inside.

Alex watched her walk away. There hadn't been a hint of suspicion or doubt in her eyes. Elaina trusted him. The thought sent warmth through his chest. This was the last lie. It was a minor lie. Not even a real lie but an omission of the truth. He pushed aside the guilt. Keeping her away from Warren and off Warren's radar was a good thing. Their relationship was fragile. He wasn't about to do anything to potentially damage that.

CHAPTER TWENTY-SEVEN

ELAINA ARRIVED AT Byron and Zoe's house with a bottle of wine in one hand and a specialty baked cake in the other. She hummed quietly to herself and bounced on the heels of her feet.

Today had been a very good day.

Not only had she secured a new investor, but she'd also gotten a favorable lead with a second one. The plan to talk to people not connected with Robidoux Tobacco or any of her family's other holdings had been a good one. She was able to convince them of her merits based on the results of the work she'd done without fear her dad would see them at the next corporate function and undermine everything she done.

She was looking forward to tonight's dinner. Although she spent a lot of time with Zoe due to the work project, she hadn't spent much time with Byron since everything went down between her and her dad. She missed when Byron would stop by the estate and the two of them would talk about their day or his campaign, or just tease each other.

Zoe came to the door and led her inside. "You didn't have to bring anything," Zoe said, taking the wine and cake from Elaina.

"I never come to a dinner party empty-handed."

"This isn't a dinner party," Zoe said with a smirk.

"Don't tell her that." Byron walked over and wrapped

an arm around Elaina's shoulders. "Elaina is just like our mom. She treats any dinner invitation as a formal event."

Elaina shook her head. "That's only because you're more than happy to show up places empty-handed. I've always had to make you look better."

Byron laughed and squeezed her shoulder. "You think that." He let her go and looked in the cake box. "What type of cake is this?"

She held up the cake box so he could look through the clear top. "Lemon raspberry. I thought I'd try something new."

"That sounds delicious," Zoe said. "I take back what I said. Feel free to bring cake anytime you visit."

Elaina looked around. The rest of the spacious condo was quiet except for the soft music playing through the speakers in the ceiling. "Where's Lilah?"

"She's out with one of her friends," Zoe said. "Apparently there is a party at the skating rink, and everyone had to be there."

Elaina raised a brow. "And you let her go with no problem?"

"Wesley is also there," Byron said, referring to his driver and bodyguard.

Elaina laughed as she imagined Lilah's chagrin over having to be chaperoned. "I bet she just loved that."

"Lilah knows we're going to keep an eye on her." Byron's voice was unwavering. "After the scare with her dad, she understands the importance of security and us knowing where she is."

"That's good to hear." Elaina glanced at the stove. "What smells so good? I'm starving."

Zoe's eyes lit up. "I'm trying a new place that opened downtown. You preorder meals for the week and they prep them for you. Tonight is herb-roasted salmon with apple-apricot chutney, garlic roasted potatoes and grilled zucchini."

Elaina's mouth watered. She'd barely had lunch before the meeting, and the turkey wrap she'd picked up in between had been barely edible. "Then let's eat."

Byron hesitated. "Not just yet. We're expecting one more person."

"Who?" Elaina asked.

Zoe also looked at Byron with confusion. "I didn't know anyone else was coming over."

"I ran into Dad earlier and mentioned Elaina was coming over. He asked if he could join us. I thought it would be a good idea."

Elaina's hand tightened into a fist. If Byron had tossed her off of the roof, she might have felt less hurt. "Why would you think that was a good idea?"

"Elaina, we're still a family." His tone pleaded for understanding. "We can't keep pretending you're not a part of it."

"So you decided to ambush me with a dinner with the hope that we'll hug it out and make up?" she snapped back. "That's not how things work."

"It can work that way if you try." Impatience bled into Byron's voice. "He wants to see you. If he didn't, he wouldn't have asked to come."

"Or he just wants another chance to gloat," Elaina said. She headed toward the door. "I'm not doing this tonight."

Byron rushed to stand in front of her. "Elaina, please. Just dinner. It's my place, which is neutral territory. I won't let him say or do anything out of line."

"I'm not in the mood to fight with him tonight."

"Then don't. Trust me. I know Dad isn't perfect, but he does love us. He wants to see you. We both know how he is. Butting in tonight is, in his weird way, taking a step forward. I'm not telling you to forgive him, but I would like for us to have at least one family meal together."

The doorbell rang. She was out of time. Byron always forgave their dad faster than anyone else. Grant had even accepted Zoe and Lilah into the family, so of course Byron would see this as Grant taking a step toward reconciliation. Whether she wanted to give her dad a try or not was a moot point. Leaving before he arrived was one thing. Running away after he arrived wasn't an option. She wouldn't give him the satisfaction.

Byron went to open the door. Zoe came over to Elaina. "I didn't know about this."

"I know. Byron was always the optimistic one."

Zoe lifted a shoulder. "He wants things to get better between you two."

She knew that. Byron had his own battles with their dad. In the end, Byron still looked up to Grant. Somewhere deep down, she loved her dad, but it was buried under years of hurt and distrust.

"It'll take much more than dinner to make things better," Elaina muttered.

"Something sure smells good in here." Grant's booming voice came from the front door.

Elaina took a deep breath and squared her shoulders. A few seconds later, Grant and Byron entered the kitchen area. Grant's lips spread into a satisfied smile when he spotted Elaina.

"Elaina, it's good to see you," he said in a pleasant tone as if they hadn't gone months without speaking or seeing each other.

Elaina lifted her chin. "Hello, Daddy. I'm surprised you

decided to join us tonight." She glanced over his shoulder and back. "Where's Patricia?"

"Patricia's not feeling well. She's got that stomach bug that's going around, but she sends her love. I asked Byron at the last minute to join you." Grant walked over to her. "I hope you aren't upset that I'm here."

She thought she heard a hint of concern in his voice. Searching for hints of concern from her dad had broken her heart enough over the years. She pasted on an unbothered smile. "Why would I be upset? I know how much you like to pretend we're one big happy family."

Byron cleared his throat. "Okay, how about we eat? Everything is ready."

Elaina smiled sweetly at her dad. "I'd love to."

She turned away and helped Zoe set the table while Byron plated the food. They settled around the dining room table. Thankfully, Byron guided the conversation. He talked about his work in the mayor's office, the plans for a revitalization of one of the commercial districts, and the latest drama between the council members.

Despite that Elaina wanted to stay on alert with her dad in the room, Byron's charm as a politician eventually had everyone engaged in the conversation. Elaina was quickly drawn into Byron's discussion and giving her input on the revitalization project. Eventually the tension eased. Grant fired no shots her way, so Elaina decided to go along with her brother's wishes and didn't fire any of her own. As long as things stayed like this, she could survive the impromptu family dinner without letting her dad get under her skin.

"The problem with revitalizing that neighborhood is that none of the business owners really care about how it looks," Grant said. His lips lifted in a smile. "When I was a kid, that was a thriving part of town. I remember there was this bakery over there I used to take your mom to when I was trying to win her over. She only liked their pound cake. I'd take her there, buy a slice, and we'd sit by the window and share it." Wistfulness entered his voice.

Elaina and Byron shared a glance and sad smiles. When she was younger, she remembered her parents bringing back a slice of cake from that bakery. Those were the early days when things were still good between them. Just before the need to make their family legacy bigger and better became their sole focus. Sadly, those memories were blurred and faded like neglected photographs.

Grant cleared his throat and shifted in his seat. "That place closed down shortly after your mom died. Now everyone wants something new and trendy. They're gravitating back towards downtown, and the shop owners can't compete."

Elaina shook her head. "I disagree. The project the city is undertaking is a good thing. I think revitalization will make people start visiting and shopping in that area again."

"Painting some storefronts and putting in new street signs aren't going to bring people back to the area," Grant countered.

"That's where you're wrong," Elaina said getting drawn into the debate. There was no animosity as they spoke. That too was like the good old days when she'd first started helping her dad run Robidoux Holdings right before her mom died. "The updates will go a long way toward renewing pride in the area. The town can also hold festivals there to bring people back over. It would be a good location to consider for one of the community partnerships programs at Robidoux Holdings."

Grant nodded. "It is time to start looking at new community projects."

"That would be a big help for us," Byron said. "It'll make it a true public-private partnership and prove the entire community is interested in keeping all parts of Jackson Falls thriving."

Grant patted the table. "I'll bring the idea up to Alex tomorrow and ask him to coordinate the project with our nonprofit side."

Elaina's hand clenched. The easy flow of the night shattered like cracked glass. She'd started to get drawn in by the idea of working with Byron through Robidoux Holdings to revitalize the commercial district. Tonight had felt so much like old times, she'd forgotten she no longer worked for the family anymore.

Elaina sat up straight in her chair. Jealousy that her dad would work on this project with Alex instead of her tried to creep up. She reminded herself this was Grant's doing. Alex wasn't deliberately working with Grant to undermine her. Grant was using Alex to get back at her. Probably to even undermine their relationship. She wouldn't give him the satisfaction.

"I'm surprised you're not with him at the work thing tonight," Elaina said.

"Work thing?" Grant said with a frown. "What work thing?"

Elaina's body stilled. She searched her dad's face for signs of deception, but he appeared genuinely confused. Had Alex lied to her? She couldn't believe it. He was the one person to promise not to lie to her. Grant watched her closely, as did Byron and Zoe. They already thought she was foolish for being with Alex. Admitting he might have lied would only make things worse.

She shook her head and smiled. "Sorry, I was confused. He has a family thing tonight."

"So it's true," Grant said, sounding disappointed. "You two are dating."

She met her dad's eyes. "We are."

"Are you sure that's wise?" he asked as if she'd announced she was skydiving without a parachute.

She was taking a leap believing in her and Alex. A leap that had the capability of crushing her, but it was a leap she wanted to take. "Are you against it because you didn't choose him for me, or for some other reason, Daddy?" she asked sweetly.

Grant's jaw tightened. "I hired him because I knew what he could do and how he operated at his previous job. He's just like me. Can you trust him?"

The smug glint in his eye made her stomach clench. Unease and suspicion slithered though her veins like a den of snakes. She knew what Grant was doing. She knew it just as sure as she knew the numbers of fingers on her hand. He wanted her to doubt Alex, because if she doubted him, she'd be out there alone. Once she was alone, he'd swoop in and remind her how she could only rely on family and try to bring her back under his thumb.

Elaina leaned back and clenched her jaw. "More than I can apparently trust you."

CHAPTER TWENTY-EIGHT

ALEX AND WARREN got settled into the one of the booths at Frank's Fish and Chicken. It was one of the town's staples and family-owned, making it a perfect location for the down-home dinner Warren wanted.

Warren looked over the laminated menu and nodded. "Everything looks good. I don't know where to start."

"I'm going for the two-piece catfish basket," Alex said, not bothering to glance at the menu. He didn't do fried food a lot, but he'd been there enough with Chris to know what he liked. "It's what they're known for."

Warren frowned and shook his head. "Catfish is not my favorite. I'll go with the chicken and whiting tenders plate." He handed their menus to the waitress.

She nodded and took their menus. "I'll be right back."

Warren watched her walk off with a smile on his face. "I can see why you're okay staying in Jackson Falls for a while. There's something appealing about these Southern women."

Alex shook his head and sipped his sweet tea. "You're only in town for a night. Can you try not to get into any trouble?"

Warren's grin didn't fade as he scanned the crowd in the restaurant's dining area. "It's never any trouble, and being here for one night makes things even better." He looked at Alex and winked. "No cause for confusion."

"Considering you're here to spend time with me before traveling again, how about you focus on catching up with me instead of chasing ass?"

Alex wasn't irritated. Watching his biological father pick up women was something he'd once admired. Warren had coached him on flirting, given him frank and sometimes embarrassing advice about how to please a woman, and paid for his first lap dance when he turned twenty-one. Warren never planned to settle down and loved the freedom of being single. Alex had once believed he wanted that life, too. He saw the good example of marriage his mom and Thomas had, but when he'd been younger, Warren's fast-paced life seemed a lot more enticing than his parents' domestic bliss.

Warren chuckled and took a sip of the sweet tea he'd ordered. "What's this about? It used to be we'd enjoy the delights together. Remember that time we met up in Vegas?"

Alex thought back to that weekend. He'd been twenty-five and in Vegas for a conference. Warren had come through on his way to some business event. It was the longest time he'd spent with Warren, and Alex had tried to keep up with him. As soon as Alex finished with work, they'd hit up every club they could, drank hard, and Alex couldn't even remember the names of the women he'd hooked up with.

He rubbed his temples and shook his head. "I try to forget about Vegas."

"What? Why? We had a good time out there."

"I had the worst hangover that last day and barely caught my flight back to work," Alex said. "My boss told me he expected me to have a good time, but tone things down next time."

Warren waved a hand. "I remember your boss. He was

at the same clubs we were in. He just had to say that for appearances."

"Maybe so, but I toned it down after that." Alex patted his chest. "Now I tone it down to avoid going back in the hospital."

Warren appeared startled. He glanced away from Alex and took in the room. "Your mom said you recovered well."

"I did."

"Well, you're better now. You look good. Did they tell you why you had a heart attack? Seems like you're too young for that."

"The usual suspects. A clogged artery and too much stress on my body," Alex said.

Warren frowned. "Then we could have gone somewhere else to eat? Are you on one of those kale and water diets now?"

Alex laughed and shook his head. "This one meal won't hurt me."

Warren's shoulders relaxed. "Good. Then the two of us seeing how friendly the waitresses in here are won't hurt either."

The waitress came back then with two steaming baskets of food. She put Warren's down first. "Here you go, sir." The second plate she put in front of Alex. "And for you, Mr. Tyson. I made sure those green beans came out of the vegetarian pot just like you like them."

"Thank you, Vanessa," Alex said.

"Y'all let me know if you need anything." She smiled, showing her dimples, before nodding and walking away.

Warren's brows rose. "Oh, so that's the thing. You've already conquered."

"Not at all. The Robidoux family does a lot of business with Mr. Frank and his family. The other big difference between Jackson Falls and Vegas is that I live here. No more wild nights and hookups for me."

Warren shook his head. "You sound like an old man, and I'm older than you." He picked up the hot sauce bottle and sprinkled a heathy dose on his fish.

"I've decided to take it easy for a while. Especially after the heart attack."

"Since you don't want to talk women," Warren said begrudgingly, "tell me about work. I know I said I understand why you're happy here, but can you really be happy here forever? I don't see how the work would be half as fulfilling."

"It's challenging enough," Alex admitted. "Grant Robidoux can hold his own against anyone I've ever worked with. He put me in charge while he looks for a new CEO."

Warren's brows rose. "Yeah, I heard he gave his daughter the boot."

"How did you hear that?" Alex asked.

"Robidoux Tobacco and their other subsidiaries are a major corporate player with international reach. I pay attention to any high-level changes at companies," Warren said.

"Then you already knew that I was acting as CEO."

"I knew. Plus, your mom called me a few weeks ago."

Alex froze in the middle of taking a bite of green beans. He lowered his fork. "What for?" When he was a kid, his mom only called Warren if Alex needed something. She'd never tried to hold on to Warren in a romantic sense and had always approached their relationship like a business partnership. They got along, but Alex wouldn't have expected them to continue to talk to each other.

"She had some questions about this new venture your dad is going into." Warren spoke the words as if they were no big deal, but the way he focused on breaking off a piece of fish and putting it between slices of bread instead of meeting Alex's eyes told a different story. Had his mom asked Warren to step in?

"She called you about Dad's business plans?" Alex asked, incredulous. "She wouldn't get you into that."

Warren took a bite and chewed slowly. After he swallowed, he met Alex's eyes with a resigned expression. "She would and she has. Your mom has run business ideas by me for years."

"She's what?" Alex dropped his fork. "Why?"

"Because I'm a good businessman," Warren said, the *obviously* implied by his tone. "She knows I wouldn't lie to her."

"Neither would my dad."

"No, he wouldn't, but your dad is also idealistic. Your mom is more facts-based. It's not that big a deal."

"Why is Mom still going to you for help?"

"She only calls me occasionally for advice. Don't read anything else into it than that," Warren said. "Your mom and I haven't been more than friends in decades, and that won't change. I never wanted kids, but she had you, and I'd never take that back. I'll always respect her and your dad for raising you. I wouldn't fuck that up."

Alex sat back, stunned to know his mom still called Warren for business advice. "Why is she worried about things now? I thought the farm was doing well."

"It is. Your mom is concerned about the deal you're making with Grant Robidoux's daughter. She's worried you may be biased."

Alex's back straightened. "Biased."

"You are sleeping with her," Warren said as if that were all the evidence he needed.

He was long past the days of being embarrassed to discuss his sex life with Warren, but still he didn't like the way Warren implied Alex's relationship would compromise his decisions. "I wasn't when she approached Dad. In fact, I wasn't sure if she was the right person to go with. She got the offer on her own merits. Not because of anything I did."

"But is she still the best offer? I hear she's having trouble with investors."

"How did you hear?"

"I have my ways," Warren said casually. He took another bite of food and swallowed. "Your dad is putting all his hopes in one basket because he trusts you and your judgment. Your mom is worried you're falling for a woman you once hated and aren't thinking straight."

"I never hated Elaina," Alex countered.

Warren leaned forward and met his eyes. "Is she the best choice? I don't care about you sleeping with her. Sometimes the best sex is with a woman who gets under your skin, but you're too smart to let your dick guide business decisions. I at least know I taught you better than that."

"She is a good choice." Alex didn't doubt that at all. Elaina was working her ass off to get her facility up and running.

"That's not what I asked. I asked if she's the *best* choice? Can you guarantee her facility will be up and running in time to handle your dad's first harvest?" Warren's gaze was unwavering.

As much as Alex wanted to say she was, the practical side of him couldn't say she was the best choice. "Robidoux Holdings purchased another facility. It's already up and running and can more than handle what he offers. Grant mentioned us supplying them."

Grant had pushed the purchase through without Alex's signoff. He hadn't approached Alex again about Thomas supplying hemp since that long-ago day in his office, but Alex knew the offer still stood. Things were going so well with Elaina, he'd ignored the opportunity. She was working hard, and he wasn't going to do anything to undermine her efforts. He also didn't want to hurt her by telling her Grant was trying to undermine her. She kept fighting, and he feared that if she knew what Grant was up to, she'd focus on fighting Grant instead of her ultimate goal of getting her business open.

Warren leaned back. "So, there is a better offer on the table. One that's more stable."

Grant's offer was better. If he wasn't with Elaina and seeing how hard she worked, he would have told Thomas to take it. Another reason he couldn't tell Elaina. He couldn't bear the look in her eye knowing Grant could and would snatch away everything she'd worked for. "Grant only made the offer to sabotage his daughter."

Warren shrugged in a so-what manner. "Their family drama has nothing to do with your family business. Always remember that. Do what's best for the people who raised you."

"We already made the deal with her." Alex broke eye contact. Warren's point stabbed at another spot in his conscience. If he told Thomas about Grant's offer, then his stepdad would sign with Robidoux Holdings before Alex could get the words out. Keeping the secret from everyone was for the best, even if it tore his conscience to shreds.

"Any deal can be broken," Warren said. "Especially when there's a better deal on the table. You know this, Alex. When it comes to love and money, there's no place to be weak or softhearted. Do what's best for your dad's new venture. Worry about making Elaina happy later."

CHAPTER TWENTY-NINE

ELAINA'S NAGGING SUSPICION something wasn't right about Alex and his "work thing" wouldn't go away. She spent the rest of the night going over their conversation. Had she misunderstood what he'd said? Had he flinched or given any other indication that he wasn't telling the truth? Why would he say he had to work if he really didn't? What was worse about the nagging was remembering all the mistakes in her past and the warning signs she'd ignored before things hit the fan.

She didn't want to be the paranoid person she felt herself becoming, but the memories of the way Robert had looked at her as if she were stupid for thinking he cared about her were too fresh. That along with the humiliation when he'd texted another woman the day after they'd split. As much as she didn't want to believe Alex was seeing someone else, she also refused to be played for a fool again.

Instead of going home after dinner, she went to his place. His car was in the yard. Elaina almost relaxed, until thoughts of him being home with someone else flooded her overactive brain. Damn her dad for making her doubt him in the first place.

He'd been right about Robert.

She pushed all of that out of her mind. If there was something going on, she'd find out tonight.

She got out and walked with determined strides to the

front door. She pushed the bell and squared her shoulders. She would not react with jealousy or anger regardless of what she found on the other side of the door.

Alex answered, and his eyes widened with surprise right before he smiled and reached for her. "I was just thinking about you."

Relief nearly made her jump in his arms. Instead she hugged him stiffly after coming into the house.

"How was work?" she asked.

He turned and closed the door. She didn't go further into his home. What he said next would determine if she stayed or left quickly. When he faced her, whatever lie he'd been about to tell drifted from his eyes.

He took a long breath. "I wasn't at work tonight."

She swallowed hard. The realization that he had lied was like a punch in the throat. "I figured as much when Grant showed up for dinner at Byron's house."

She gave him credit for not flinching or looking surprised that she'd figured him out. "I had to do something."

"Something you couldn't tell me about?" She nodded stiffly. "Okay. It's good to know that we're still doing the let's-keep-secrets-from-each-other thing. Duly noted." She walked toward the door.

Alex stretched his arm out and pressed his hand against the door. "My biological father is in town. He wanted to meet for dinner."

She slowly turned to face him. He stood close enough for her to see the varying shades of brown in his dark eyes. "You couldn't tell me your dad was in town? Seriously, Alex, that's the story you're going to tell?"

"I didn't want to introduce you to him."

His words were a slap in the face. She sucked in a breath.

She worked hard to keep her expression neutral when she wanted to lash out at him. "Naturally."

She moved to turn back toward the door. Alex's other arm shot out and blocked her in. "Not naturally," he said, ever calm in the face of her anger. "It's not because I don't want you to meet him."

Elaina crossed her arms, and he leaned back. She needed distance. His embrace had always been her weakness. "That's usually the main reason behind not introducing two people."

"Not because I don't think this is serious. You've already met my parents and my siblings, but Warren is different. He's cynical and calculating. He'd dissect our relationship and poke holes in it before we've even finished figuring out what we want to do. I'm not ready to expose us to that."

"Why? Because you don't think we can handle it?" Honestly, she wasn't sure if they could. A few words from her dad and she'd rushed over here because she automatically thought the worst.

"Why undermine the foundation when you're still building it?" He lowered his hands and dropped them to her crossed arms. His fingers were firm but gentle as he spread her arms. "I'm not introducing anything negative to us when we're still figuring things out."

"Why?"

He placed her hands on his chest. His heartbeat was strong and steady beneath her palms. "Because I feel like we have the potential to be more."

Warmth spread through her midsection. Her fingers curled into the fabric of his shirt. She wasn't sure if she was going to push him away or jerk him closer. He didn't fight with her. He just systematically faced her anger and gave his explanation. Then he had to do it with such simple but heart-meltingly sincere words.

"He can't be worse than my dad," she said. "If there was an award for meddling I-know-best fathers, Grant would win every year."

Alex relaxed, and the lines around his eyes drifted away. She pulled him slightly forward. As if knowing what she wanted, he wrapped an arm around her shoulder and pulled her in for one of his comforting hugs. "Warren runs a close second. He's smart and too observant. He built his fortune reading other people, taking advantage of their weak points so he could purchase and sell their businesses. He can't help but do the same with me." He led her into the living room, and they settled on the couch.

Elaina rested her head on his shoulder. "I thought you two got along."

"We do get along. I was once just like him. I know he's not quite convinced I'm good with the changes I've made in my life, and dating my boss's daughter is another thing for him to go in on. I should have told you."

He should have, but since he admitted he was wrong, she didn't press the issue. "So...what did he have to say about me?"

"Surprisingly little. He talked more about work."

"Well, that's good then. If he didn't talk much about us then he's less likely to butt in." One intrusive parent was enough in their relationship. She toyed with the button on his shirt.

"I don't know if that's good or bad. He may call next week and say something outrageous, or he may believe we'll fizzle out and there's no need for him to give me a lecture on my dating practices."

The idea of her and Alex fizzling out made her feel

empty inside. Of course, they weren't meant for forever. She harbored no illusions that she and Alex would fall deeply in love and live happily ever after, but the idea of them not being together for a long time seemed just as unacceptable.

"I'll say it's a good thing," she said. "I've got enough on my plate without worrying about the reasons for your biological father's disinterest in our relationship."

He placed his hand over hers on his chest and nudged her head with his chin. Elaina looked up and met his gaze. "I'm sorry I didn't tell you up front," he said. "I thought you would be upset about me not inviting you to meet him."

She shook her head. "If you'd just explained why, I would be okay. There's no reason for you to protect my feelings. I'm a big girl, Alex. I can take a few hits."

His hand gently squeezed hers. "I'm not supposed to be the one providing the hits."

"The hit is a lot worse when I don't know what's going on. No lies, remember. Is there anything else?"

He watched her for a few moments, then shook his head. "Nothing else. Warren came, we talked, and he's leaving tomorrow."

"You didn't offer to let him stay here with you?"

Alex frowned. "No. He didn't want to stay with me anyway. He was busy trying to go home with one of the waitresses at Frank's Fish and Chicken. He's got his own plans."

Elaina leaned back, stunned. "Oh, so your dad is a lady's man?"

"He thinks so." Alex reached over and took her hand in his. "Enough about Warren. How was your day? Why was Grant at dinner tonight?"

She frowned, not wanting to relive the episode, but knowing Alex asked because he cared. She liked having someone to tell her true feelings to. She kicked off her shoes, pulled her feet on the couch and settled her head back on his shoulder. "Byron told him I was coming over, so he took it as another opportunity to gloat and remind me I've been exiled."

Alex stiffened. "He said that?" Anger was steel in his voice.

Elaina patted his chest. She didn't tell him about Grant's plans to participate in the neighborhood renovation project. Grant would expect her to. She was staying out of the business of Robidoux Holdings. That was the only way she and Alex would work. "Not so much, but unlike your dad, he did have something to say about our relationship."

Alex's head cocked to the side and curiosity filled his gaze. "What did he say?"

"He doesn't think I should trust you."

Alex sat up straight. "What?"

"Don't take it personally. That's his standard go-to line. He says things like that to make me doubt myself. Tonight, he almost got me." She'd been so paranoid and had let his words get under her skin. How many times had he nudged her in the direction he wanted by playing on her insecurities? She didn't believe Alex would lie to her or try to deceive her for his own gain, but one word of doubt from Grant and she'd believed he'd lied to her and was treating her the same way Robert had.

"Not telling you about Warren only made that worse."

"It didn't help, but I'm not letting my dad get to me anymore. Besides, things are starting to look up for me, finally."

"In what way?"

"I've got a new investor," she said, smiling and bringing back the good mood she'd been in before the dinner. "I confirmed it this afternoon, and I'm meeting with another potential investor later this week. If that comes through, then we'll be able to open on time."

"Wait, were you not going to be able to open on time?"

Although she'd been more forthcoming about her plans for the facility, she hadn't told him anything about the trouble she'd had with investors. Things were getting better, but she still faced more no's than yes's. One: because she hadn't wanted him to worry. Two: because she hadn't wanted him to tell his dad and lose a potential supplier.

"I lost the interest of a few people, but that was because my dad got to them and made them uncomfortable working with me. I decided to pursue some new avenues, and that's working out." She finished with a confident smile and watched him for any signs of unease. She couldn't afford for him to have any doubts in her abilities or take those doubts to his dad.

"You will open on time?" he asked. "My dad is depending on being able to supply to your facility. He hasn't looked into any backup locations."

"And he doesn't need to." She straddled his hips. "I will open on time. Your dad's investment is safe with me. I promise."

Alex stared at her for a long time. She placed her hand on his cheek and kissed him softly. She didn't like the worry that flashed in his eyes. She was going to make this work. She was going to prove everyone wrong, starting with her dad.

Her fingers went to the buttons of her shirt. "Trust me." She slowly released each button and slipped the shirt off.

Desire darkened Alex's eyes. "Are you trying to distract me?"

She lifted a brow. "Are you distracted?" She reached behind her and unhooked the bra. Her breasts fell free.

Alex bit the corner of his lip. His hands dug into her waist. "Slightly."

Smiling, she leaned forward. The hairs on his chest tickled the sensitive tips of her breasts. "I promise, Alex. I will get everything together not just for your dad but also for the employees who've waited too long for these improvements."

She pulled back enough so he could see the truth in her eyes. She didn't want him to doubt her. Not when he was the only person who seemed to believe in her.

The belief that replaced the doubt in his eyes was like sunshine after a storm. "I believe you."

Something bigger than relief went through her. She kissed him before he could see the emotions swelling inside her.

CHAPTER THIRTY

"Have you given any more thought to my offer?"

Grant asked the question seconds after Alex seated himself across from him in Grant's spacious office. Alex had requested the sit-down meeting first thing that morning. He needed to talk to him about some items related to the investors and a few other projects, but that was just a cover for what he really needed to say. The time had come for Grant to leave Elaina's business alone and stay out of her relationship with Alex.

"I have," he answered.

Grant leaned back in his chair. He eyed Alex with cool composure. "And?"

"And we're going with Elaina's company. We made the promise to supply her facility and we're going to stick with her."

Grant shook his head. Disappointment covered his face. "You know you could do better if you work with us."

"We may be able to make more money selling to you, but that's still an unknown."

"Elaina won't make it," Grant said with determination.

"Which is why I'd like to set up supplying to Robidoux Holdings as a backup if her facility doesn't open on time," Alex said evenly.

Grant's brows rose. He tented his fingers in front of him. "Oh, really. Are you starting to have doubts?"

Alex had no doubt Elaina would succeed, but he couldn't completely ignore Warren's advice. Last night the relief on Elaina's face had been palpable. He'd watched her work hard these past months. He knew she'd been struggling to get things together, but he'd figured it was the struggle that came with opening any new facility. She'd always been so calm and confident when she talked to him and his dad about opening her facility and being able to handle all of their crop. He'd believe in her despite Grant's efforts to make her lose investors.

Warren's words had nagged him, though. He couldn't put all his eggs in one basket. If Elaina fell through and his dad was left scrambling to find a place to sell to at a good profit, then his family would suffer. They trusted him to make the right business decision. He couldn't let his feelings get in the way of doing what was right.

"I have absolutely no doubts that Elaina will open her facility on time and that she'll be able to deliver everything she promised."

"But…" Grant said with a raised brow.

Alex ignored the sick feeling in his gut at the smug look on Grant's face. Doing the right thing for business didn't always mean it felt like the right thing personally. He tried to remind himself of that as he continued. "But, I'm also not going to focus all of our efforts in one place. It makes good business sense to have a backup plan."

Grant smiled as if he'd won the lottery. "In the end, you'll work with me."

"In the end, if I find out that you've done anything to make her fail, then I don't care how good a business move it'll be. We won't supply to you. There are other places we can sell to, and I'll look into those options as well."

Grant's smile broadened. "Trying to protect her. That's almost cute."

"I care about Elaina. I won't do business with someone who willingly hurts her."

Grant's face sobered. When he spoke, his voice was filled with a remorseful heaviness Alex didn't understand. "I'm not going to do anything to hurt Elaina. I'm only trying to help her. Everything I do is to try and help her. Elaina's headstrong, but she's also impulsive. She pushes back just because she can't stand to be told what to do. If I didn't use a little…encouragement to get her to do what's best, then she would have made a mess of her life."

"Is that why you pushed her into a marriage she didn't want?"

Grant's eyes snapped to his. "I see she's telling you all kinds of secrets during pillow talk."

Alex's spine stiffened. "I meant what I said. Back off her. Let her finally stand on her feet and succeed without caving to your demands."

"Elaina always does what she wants to do. She may have cried and told you she was forced into the marriage, but she knew what she was doing. When she gave me her answer, I asked her if she was sure, and she said she was. They remained married for years despite the unfortunate situation that happened afterwards, and she couldn't stand to see him date after the divorce. I just pushed her to do what she wanted to do anyway."

Alex shook his head. "You really believe that, don't you? You really think that just because she went along with it, she was happy about the situation. Or that she had other options when she didn't. I'm glad she's no longer under your control."

Grant stood and gave Alex a tight smile. "I think it's

time for you to leave now." He tugged on the front of his suit. "I'll have the lawyers draft up a contract for your dad to consider. When Elaina fails, through no intervention on my part, I'll be happy to sign it."

"When Elaina succeeds, I'll be happy to tear it up in your face." Alex got up and walked out of Grant's office.

ALEX WENT TO his parents' home later that day. He decided to find out if Warren had already convinced his mom they needed a backup plan. He didn't believe they would. Elaina could do anything she set her mind to. Considering other options wasn't a betrayal, so why did he feel so bad?

His mom was at the house, working on a dress for his niece. Alex had to do a double take when he saw his mom sitting behind a sewing machine.

"When did you start sewing?" In all his years, he'd never seen her so much as sew on a button. Now she had an entire setup with a sewing machine, various boxes of thread and needles, and a mannequin.

"I just started," she said with a bright smile. "I need something to do to fill up the time during the day. Helping Thomas grow hemp isn't as exciting as I thought it would be." She slid on a pair of glasses and looked back at the items in front of her.

"You always said you and dad would travel when you retired. You two haven't really been anywhere."

She lifted a shoulder. "Getting this place renovated and then ready to produce took time. Now that we're finally settled and may actually sell something this season, we should get a chance."

Alex watched her pin a thin paper pattern for a shirt onto a white-and-yellow-flowered cloth. The first few years of moving to Jackson Falls had been filled with getting the farm settled. His mom had always been a busy person before the move.

"Are you happy to have moved down here?"

She glanced up. "Why wouldn't I be?"

"You were always so busy before. Parties, traveling, business meetings. Now you're sewing and adopting this farmer's wife persona when all you talked about was how much more fun you'd have when you and Dad retire."

She chuckled and waved off his words. "I know what I said, but I am happy doing what I'm doing. Your heart attack wasn't just a wake-up call for you. It made me realize I should relax and enjoy instead of pushing all the time. I'm letting go of my old ways." She put another pin in the pattern. "My grandmother used to sew. I always told myself I'd pick up sewing one day. Well, now I've got the time and the inclination."

Alex grinned despite a multitude of homemade practice shirts in his future. "I saw Warren yesterday. He told me you called him. That doesn't sound like a person who's completely letting go of their old ways."

She raised a brow as she added another pin. "Why, because I want to be sure we're making the right business decision? Because I need him to remind you that business and pleasure need separation?"

"I know that already." Alex crossed the room to sit on the couch.

"I know you do, but people don't always do what they're supposed to when they fall in love."

Alex sat up straight. "I'm not in love."

"Aren't you?" his mom said in that patronizing way mothers had. She lifted a hand. "Fine, maybe you aren't, but you're defiantly feeling something for Elaina that I haven't seen you feel with other women. Before, women

were in your life, but none of them were a part of your life.
You're making her a part of your life. I'm happy for you,
but I know that if I questioned you about her, you'd get defensive and dig in deeper."

"So you called Warren."

"I did. You love and respect him, and because he wasn't
as close to you growing up, you also don't get upset when
he says the same thing either your dad or I would say."

"I didn't need you to get him to check up on me," Alex
said. "I know what I'm doing."

"Fine. You do. Now, what did you come here to tell us?"
she asked with a knowing smile.

Alex clenched his teeth. She was right, and her plan had
worked. He hadn't looked at the business decision rationally because he was falling in love with Elaina. Warren
had snapped him back. Made him pay attention more. Now
he was making contingency plans.

"I need to talk to Dad," he replied.

Her smile widened. "He's in the field, checking on the
plants. My golf cart is in the garage. You can take it out
to meet him."

"Fine." He pushed off the couch and stalked toward the
door. After forty years, his mom still knew how to get what
she wanted out of him.

"Alex," his mom called.

He stopped and looked over his shoulder. "Yes?"

"I do like her. I'm happy you're finally falling in love, but
I also need to protect the person I love. You understand?"

He did. If the roles were reversed, he would do the same
thing. He wasn't mad at his mom for stepping in and getting his head back on business. He nodded, then went out
to find the golf cart.

CHAPTER THIRTY-ONE

AFTER SECURING YET another investor for her facility, Elaina was ready to celebrate. She'd worked hard and busted her tail to stop any of Grant's efforts to block investors interested in working with her. She wasn't exactly where she wanted to be, but with the new influx of funding, she'd be able to open the facility on time.

She wanted to celebrate, and weirdly she wanted to celebrate in the place where she'd always gone to when things went well for her. It was the first field that Robidoux Tobacco had planted. The place where their company legacy began.

She flipped her cell phone in her hand. Going to the family's first field required going on the estate. Going on the estate meant dealing with her dad. She'd rather pull out her teeth with a rusty blade than deal with her dad right now. She wanted to enjoy the moment. Not spar with Grant and have him deflate her joy.

She stopped flipping the phone and opened her contacts. She found the right name and tapped on the Call icon. After four rings, Patricia answered.

"Elaina?"

Elaina couldn't blame Patricia for sounding confused. If it wasn't related to one of the parties at the estate or coordinating her father's schedule, she didn't talk to Patricia. The only reason she'd called today was that she remembered what Byron said. Patricia was on her side when it came to Grant being wrong for firing her.

"Hello, Patricia. How are you?"

"I'm good," Patricia said, still sounding confused. "Is everything okay? Your dad isn't with me. He had an important stakeholder meeting today, and I don't expect him to be home until later."

Good. She had worried Grant would be with Patricia when she called. "That's fine. I don't need him. I called to talk to you."

There was a moment of silence in which Elaina imagined Patricia looking around to see if she was being pranked. "What can I do for you?"

"I need you to get Daddy away from the estate tomorrow. For the entire day if possible, but definitely for several hours in the afternoon."

"What am I getting him away from the estate for?" Suspicion crept into Patricia's voice.

Elaina suppressed a sigh and leaned back in her office chair. "It's not for anything nefarious. Though I'm flattered that you'd consider me a threat."

"You are a threat, Elaina. More than you realize," Patricia said, sounding tired.

The idea was so ridiculous she almost laughed. "Threat? How am I threatening? Grant is the one who fired me and is working to make it harder for me to start my business."

"You are your dad's pride and joy and his biggest weakness."

"You've got the kids mixed up. India is Daddy's pride and joy, followed very closely by Byron. I am the headache."

"That is far from the truth. He loves you just as much as he loves India and Byron. It's just that you are a lot like your mother. You fight him. You challenge him. He's gotten his way for so long, he doesn't know how to get his way with you except by bringing down the hammer."

"Funny, because he likes to remind me that I'm nothing like Mom." Elaina fought to keep the bitterness out of her voice. She knew she wasn't like their mother. She tried hard to be like her mom. She tried to think of the business, guard herself from potential pain, and be strategic about every decision she made. No matter how much she tried, she always ended up in the wrong situation.

"You are like her. I think your dad forgets how hard he had to try to win your mother over to his side. In the end she knew how to work with him, and by the time he fell in love with her, he deferred to her, so they butted heads less and less."

Elaina remembered how much her dad used to concede to her mom. Her mom could calm his anger with a few words and a hand on his shoulder or change his mind with a carefully worded comment. Things Elaina didn't have the patience or the skill to do.

"I'm not Mom, and I don't want to be. If he can't work with me, then it's best that I'm stepping out on my own."

As she said the words, she realized she meant them. She'd tried so hard for so long to live up to her parents' expectations. To be the best hostess, businesswoman, and even wife the way her mom told her to be. She didn't want perfection anymore. She didn't want to host her dad's parties. She didn't want to be the type of businesswoman people thought would intentionally ruin their parents' lives. She didn't want to be considered erratic when she no longer suppressed her emotions and let her true feelings show.

"But Elaina—"

"No buts. Patricia, I appreciate what you're saying and what you're trying to do. I know that Daddy loves me, and

SYNITHIA WILLIAMS

261

in his own twisted way, he thinks he's doing what's best for me. Honestly, leaving is good. I should have moved out of the estate and started my own business a long time ago. I'm happy."

Patricia was silent for several seconds. "Are you really?"

Elaina thought about the investors she'd convinced to invest in her who weren't connected to Robidoux Tobacco or their other subsidiaries, the comfort of going to her own space and learning to be okay with the silence of her own company, the freedom of not having to solve multiple problems that came up at Robidoux Holdings. Well, she still missed solving the problems, but she'd be more than fulfilled when her facility was opened and she purchased more companies. All in all, she was becoming satisfied with her new life.

"I am," she answered. "And because I'm happy, I don't want to run into Dad and get into another argument when I visit the estate this weekend. That's why I need you to get him to go somewhere else. I just want a moment back home."

"Is that all?"

"That's all."

"Fine," Patricia said, sounding satisfied. "There's a show I wanted to see in Charlotte. I nearly have him convinced to go."

Elaina let out a relieved breath. She hadn't been sure Patricia would help her out. "Make that *nearly* a *definitely*."

"I'll do my best."

"Thank you." Elaina moved the phone away from her ear to end the call.

"Elaina," Patricia called.

She put the phone back to her ear. "Yes?"

"Think about what I said. I know you and your dad are in a rough spot, but if you talk to him—"

"The time for talking is over. I love Daddy, too, but I won't back down on this. If he continues to make things hard for me, I will fight back. Don't ask me to do anything differently. You'll just be disappointed." She ended the call without waiting for a reply.

THAT SATURDAY, Elaina drove Alex through the gates of the Robidoux estate with no trouble. When she asked Sandra if Grant and Patricia were home, she was told they'd gone to Charlotte for the day. Smiling, Elaina thanked Sandra and took Alex to the garage.

"Did you know your dad would be out today?" Alex asked as they walked to the multicar garage.

"I had a heads-up he'd be out," Elaina said. She'd thank Patricia one day for the favor.

"I wondered if that's why you decided to bring me." He glanced around at the manicured lawn. "Why are we here?"

"Because I want to show you something. I secured another investor this week, and I want to celebrate. I want to show you where I go to celebrate."

"You go somewhere on the estate?"

She nodded. "Yep. You'll see."

In the garage, she went to one of the golf carts lined up along one wall. She told Alex to hop in.

"This is what we use when we want to go out to some of the fields." She drove out of the garage and headed toward one of the paths that led from the main estate toward the outer edges.

Alex glanced around as the manicured lawn gave way to tall pine trees with azalea bushes in between. To the east was the pool house. Elaina took the southern path toward the first tobacco fields. "I thought most of your family's tobacco fields were outside the estate."

"The newer ones are," Elaina said. "The original fields are still on this property. My grandad used to take me, Byron and India out to the first fields and tell us the story about how he got started. How difficult it was to get the grants and subsidies some of the other farmers in the area received. His parents were sharecroppers on this land. He left, got a degree in agricultural science, became a professor, but worked multiple jobs to save enough money to buy the land his parents used to work. Once he turned a profit, he bought other farms. Pretty soon he owned most of the tobacco fields in Jackson Falls."

Alex spread one arm across the back of her seat. "That's pretty damn impressive."

Elaina remembered the proud grin on her grandfather's face whenever he told the story. That same pride coursed through her as she told the story. "It is. He would buy a lot of property at tax sales or offer the owners more money than they thought the land was worth, only to rework the soil and turn things around to once again produce well. When Daddy took over, he wanted to branch out into other areas. He knew agriculture wouldn't be the only thing to sustain them. Momma had the eye for what was coming, and she helped him invest in real estate, small startups and technologies. Daddy takes the credit, but Momma laid the foundation for Robidoux Holdings."

Alex rubbed her back, and she drove the golf cart off the smooth path onto a rougher path toward the first tobacco field. "She sounds like a smart woman."

"She was smart. She was calculating and never let anything stop her from getting what she wanted. Even if it meant keeping Byron from the woman he loved for years or having me so convinced love wasn't important that I agreed to get married just to protect the family name."

She stopped at the edge of the field. The original field wasn't used anymore. Grass had taken over the once perfectly plowed rows where tobacco had grown. Now the land was used for family events. Garden parties and campaign events were at the main estate, but their family reunions took place out here where it all started. A pillar with a bronze plaque stood in the middle of the field.

"Come on. I want to show you something."

Alex followed her out of the golf cart. She grabbed the bag she had tossed in the back and threw it over her shoulder. When Alex reached for her hand, she didn't pull away. They walked hand in hand toward the pillar.

When they stood in front of it, she smiled at the bronze plaque.

"'This land is dedicated to Mattie Davis and Lou Robidoux,'" Alex read. He looked at her. "Your grandfather?"

She shook her head. "My great-grandparents. When my grandad bought the land and later built the house, he said he wanted it big enough for a king because he hated the shack his parents grew up in. His dream was to build something his parents never could imagine. I don't remember my great-grandparents. They died when I was still a toddler, but my granddad said they were so happy when he bought this place and made it profitable again."

She took the bag off her shoulder and pulled out the bottle of whiskey she'd brought with her and the two paper cups. She handed the cups to Alex and opened the bottle. After she poured whiskey into the cups, she took one from him.

She turned back to the plaque and raised her cup. "Grandma Mattie, Grandpa Lou, I've done it. I'm starting a new business. It's not as big as Robidoux Holdings, but one day it will be. Not only will it be big, but I'll make it bigger. All this work is for you. I hope I continue to make you proud." She tapped the cup to the plaque, then looked at Alex and raised a brow.

"Oh." He quickly tapped his cup to the plaque.

Elaina smiled, brought the cup to her lips and downed the shot. The burn of the whiskey lit a fuse of excitement in her system. She grinned up at the sky.

"Everything is going to work out," she said, more optimistic than she'd been in a long time.

Alex downed his shot and coughed. Elaina laughed. "Sorry, it's a strong blend. My granddad always drank this."

"It'll put hair on your chest," Alex wheezed.

Elaina patted him on the back and chuckled. When his eyes cleared, she sighed and looked around the empty field. "When I was younger, my grandad would bring me out here. This field was still in use, and I'd help him check the leaves or pick the tobacco during harvest time."

"You picked tobacco?" His brows rose nearly to his hairline.

Elaina grinned and poured another shot for them both. "I learned the business from the ground up. Literally. He told me about the soil and the best way to cultivate the tobacco. Whenever we had a good year, he'd come out to this field, take a shot and talk to his parents. He'd tell them how things went during the year and his plans for the next year, and ask for their blessing. Daddy never came out here with him, and eventually Byron lost interest. Even after Granddaddy got sick and couldn't work, he'd ask me to bring him out here to talk to his parents. After he passed away, I continued the tradition. I would come out here and talk to my great-grandparents, ask them to make things go smoothly, and promise them I'd make them proud." She shot a glance at Alex to see his expression. He watched her with interest, and she relaxed. She'd never told anyone about her keeping up with Grandad's habit. Not even Travis, who'd thought she visited the old fields just to make sure they were well-kept. "When we retired the field, I convinced Dad to put in the marker and use it for family reunions instead of letting it go unused. I think Grandad would be happy about that. Plus, it's a way to remember where we started."

Alex wrapped an arm around her shoulder and pulled her close to his side. "Thank you for bringing me."

"Well, I kind of want them to meet you, too," she admitted. Her cheeks heated as Alex leaned back to stare at her. She avoided eye contact. She felt a little foolish and over-dramatic, but she was here now. Alex was a new beginning for her, too. He'd seen through her from the start. Saw her flaws and insecurities, but also admired her strength and determination. He wanted her to love and trust him, not to gain anything, but just because he wanted to love and trust her in return.

The last time she'd come to this field to talk about the guy she was with, it was because she'd been angry about being forced into a marriage. She'd never come out here to talk about Robert, and now she realized she'd never truly believed their second-chance romance was legitimate. Everything felt different with Alex. She didn't feel as if her hope for them was one-sided.

She looked back at the plaque and held on to the hope that she wasn't once again making a big mistake. "This is Alex. I like him. I don't think Daddy is good with my choice, but it is my choice. I'd like to think you all would approve and give your blessing if you could."

Alex turned her to face him. She hesitated to meet his gaze. What if he laughed at her for being silly? Even worse, he could be freaked out like he had when she'd asked about kids. Either way, this was a part of her, and she'd offered to share it with him. She straightened her shoulders and lifted her chin. When she met his gaze, her breathing caught.

Alex's eyes were filled with wonder. He gripped her hands in his. "You're asking your ancestors to bless our relationship?" He said the words with such disbelief. As if she'd given him a cart of gold or something.

The emotion in his eyes was too much. She'd brought him here, but seeing him recognize how much this meant to her was more than she'd expected. Fear that she wouldn't live up to or deserve the love in his eyes made her heart pound. "It's no big deal. You don't have to get all serious."

He brought her hands to his chest. "No, I want to take this seriously. I want you to know that I take this seriously. I love you, Elaina."

Her eyes shot up and met his. The pounding of her pulse became a rush in her ears. "You love me?" She couldn't believe the words. They hadn't been together long enough. She was still figuring out how to be open. "How?"

He laughed. "Because you say stuff like that. Because you're strong and fierce and unbelievably determined. You don't have to say it back. I know this wasn't what we agreed upon when we first got together, but I need you to know that no matter what happens, my feelings for you are real."

She opened her mouth. The words *I love you too* stuck in her throat. She cared about Alex. More than she thought she would and more than she cared about anyone else she'd been with. He deserved her love more than anyone, but fear kept the words locked inside. He knew how she felt. He saw what she was still unused to saying.

She glanced at the plaque, then back at Alex. "I think they've already started blessing us." She lifted on her toes and pressed her lips to his.

were it with you. She immediately extended a gloved
hand. She was as cute as a button beneath all that
makeup.

CHAPTER THIRTY-TWO

ALEX EXPECTED THINGS to be busy the day of the debutante
ball. He hadn't expected to be running nonstop from one
end of the country club to the other. The entire day was
nothing but emergencies that needed to be handled. There
were missing decorations, lighting that wasn't set up, not
to mention the sudden disappearance of four of the tables
needed for the dinner after the ball.

By the time everything was settled, he was exhausted
and not ready to put on a tuxedo and attend the event. Elaina
ran around just as much as he did. Not once did she com-
plain, and he didn't think he saw her break a sweat. The
woman was amazing. She insisted they both go home to
shower and change before the ball. By his calculations, he
should have enough time to catch a quick nap before heading back to the country club.

His dreams of a blissful twenty minutes of rest were interrupted when his doorbell rang as soon as he got out of
the shower. Alex slipped on a pair of sweats and a T-shirt
before going to the door. He was surprised to find his dad
standing on the stoop.

"Dad, what's up? Is everything okay?" Alex asked.

Thomas nodded and followed Alex inside. "I know
you're busy with the thing at the country club today, but I
just got a phone call and I needed to talk to you about it."

"Who called?" Alex asked. He led Thomas into his living room. Thomas didn't sit. He tapped his foot, and his brow furled as he watched Alex. Unease crept through Alex.

"I have to ask you a question, and I need you to be completely honest with me," Thomas said, sounding a lot like he did when Alex had done something wrong as a kid.

"I'm always honest with you," Alex said. Just like when he was a kid, whatever Thomas was asking, Alex figured he already knew the answer. Now he had to figure out how much trouble he was in.

"Is Elaina's facility really going to open in time? Should I be looking into other places to sell? I don't want to wait until it's too late and then I won't get the best price or try to sell to a broker and get scammed. If there are better offers out there, I need to know now."

Alex's unease transferred into irritation. "Who called you?"

"Grant Robidoux. He said he wants us to supply their new facility but that you've been holding out because of your relationship with Elaina. He also said her facility wouldn't be open on time. Why wouldn't you tell me? You know I wanted to work with Grant from the start. I only went with Elaina because you seemed to trust her. If she's not the best person to work with, then I need to know now."

Alex's stomach clenched. Damn Grant and his interference. He was furious, but not surprised Grant went straight to Thomas. Alex vowed not to work with him if he tried to ruin Elaina's plans. Him going directly to Thomas meant it would be harder for Alex to convince his dad not to work with Grant if Elaina's facility didn't open. "She's back on track."

Thomas stepped forward, his eyes wide and confused. "Back on track? Does that mean at one point she wasn't on track? Alex, come on. You know I've got a lot riding on this. I may not be bankrupt if I don't turn a profit, but that doesn't mean I want things to fail after moving here and putting all of my efforts into this."

Alex pressed a hand to his temple. "I'm not compromising your efforts," he said evenly. "I do believe Elaina's facility will be up and running on time. Yes, she did have some hiccups, but what startup doesn't? I also let Grant know that if for some reason things fell through with Elaina, we'll sell to him."

Thomas blinked, and his frown deepened. Guess Grant hadn't shared that information. "Are you sure? Maybe we should go with Grant."

Alex shook his head. "Grant has his own agenda and reasons for targeting us."

"Such as?" His dad sat on the edge of the couch.

"Such as not wanting to see Elaina succeed. Part of her problems came because he convinced investors not to work with her. She found a way around that and is still on track."

His dad scowled. "Why would he do that to his daughter? It's bad enough he fired her."

"Their relationship is complicated." That was the nicest way to say it without telling his dad about all of Elaina's personal business. "Unfortunately, I'm in the middle of it despite my efforts to stay out of things."

"But are you really trying to stay out of it?" Thomas asked, sounding unconvinced. "I understand you didn't have anything to do with her approaching me about supplying her facility, but outside of that, you are in the middle. You still work for her dad, you're dating her, and you even made a deal to work with Grant if things don't work out on her end. You're involved." His dad shook his head. "I think we should look to sell to someone completely different. I don't like being a part of this family feud."

"We're not in their family feud." He twisted his shoulders, feeling uncomfortable even saying the words.

"But you're also not trying to stay completely out of things. You need to figure out why you're standing in the middle and what you'll gain or lose from being there."

His dad's words hit on a truth he hadn't wanted to acknowledge. He stood in the middle because he wanted to see Elaina succeed. The guilt he'd carried for getting her fired had never gone away. He knew this situation was between her and her dad, but if he hadn't vented his frustrations that morning, things wouldn't have gone down the way they had.

"I owe her this much," he admitted.

Thomas leaned forward. He looked at Alex with empathy. "Is that the reason you're dating her?"

"No," he argued.

Thomas stood and crossed the room. He gave Alex the same you're-not-going-to-like-this look he'd given him before doling out punishment. Alex braced himself for whatever his dad had to say.

"Then truly get out of it. You're too involved in that family to make a clear decision. You can't see the big picture because you're so busy working to try to fix small things. If Elaina succeeds, then what's the next thing Grant's going to do to mess her up, which you'll have to stop or ignore? If you and Elaina keep dating and she does well, how long before Grant sees you as a potential threat and comes after you? You're not their referee, and you don't have to continue to be."

THE COUNTRY CLUB buzzed with activity when Alex arrived. The various teens participating were there along with their parents, stylists and makeup artists. The early arrivers for the ball mingled around the bar, discussing business and whose kid or grandkid was participating. Servers went through the growing crowd, providing appetizers and keeping drink orders filled.

Alex scanned the crowd for Elaina. He knew she would be in the middle of everything, making sure all preparations were taken care of and everyone knew exactly where to go. He spotted Lauren Holmes, the country club's fundraising director, headed in his direction.

"Have you seen Elaina?" Alex asked.

Lauren frowned and glanced around the filling room. "The last time I saw her, she was on her way to check on the debutantes. I wasn't sure she'd be able to pull things together with everything going on in her life. But she did a great job."

Alex nodded. "It wasn't easy, especially since she's also doing a lot of travel and work on her new business venture. She's an amazing woman." Alex said that intentionally, not forgetting how Lauren and some other people at the club had secretly gloated when Elaina was fired.

Lauren blushed and nodded. "Well, I need to go greet some of the other attendees."

Alex let her walk away and headed toward the stairs to the second level where the debutantes and their escorts prepped for the ball. His foot was on the first step when he spotted Grant Robidoux strolling into the ballroom. Alex stopped and changed direction.

His dad's words had forced him to take a hard look at why he continued to stay in the middle. He couldn't keep playing middleman. He had to pick a side and stick with that side. The choice was clear. He was with Elaina. He loved her and wanted her to succeed. Giving his resignation during the debutante ball wouldn't be official, but he wanted to let Grant know as soon as possible that he was no longer standing at this crossroads.

"Alex," Grant said with a big smile. "Just the guy I was hoping to see." He looked around the decorated ballroom. "Looks like you all did a good job. When I suggested you get involved at the country club, I didn't know they'd wrangle you into planning the debutante ball."

"We need to talk." He wasn't in the mood for small talk.

Grant nodded. Though the smile didn't leave his face, his eyes sharpened. "Of course. There's actually something I want to talk to you about as well."

Alex led Grant away from the ballroom, down the hall toward the stairs to the basement, to get away from the noise and avoid being overheard. He wasn't sure how Grant would take the news of him leaving, but he doubted it would be good. Once he got this over with, he'd look for Elaina and get through the ball with no more ties to Grant or feeling as if he was stuck in the middle of their fight.

"Look, Grant, I've thought a lot about what we discussed in your office the other day. I can't play both sides of the fence like this anymore."

Grant smiled and nodded. "Say no more. I understand."

"You do?" Alex didn't believe Grant expected him to resign.

Grant put a hand on his shoulder. "You've tried to do right by Elaina, and that's admirable, but in the end we both know your decision to sell to us is the best decision. Elaina won't have her facility open in time, and even if she does, it'll take longer for her to turn a decent profit. That means the next year, she'll probably close shop, and you'll be back in the same situation, needing a place to buy your dad's hemp."

"But—"

"I spoke with your dad earlier, and he's on board, too. I'll have the paperwork over to you both on Monday." He pulled Alex in closer and lowered his voice. "But we'll keep this from Elaina tonight. You can break the news to her on Monday."

The door to the storage stairway opened. Elaina stood on the other side, a box of microphones in her hands. She looked from Alex to Grant with an impassive expression. Alex's heart dropped to his feet.

"What are you doing down there? I thought you were checking on the debutantes?" Alex's voice came out more accusatory than he'd intended. Had she overheard what Grant said?

"I was but realized someone left the microphones downstairs. Once we get the sound system hooked up, we'll start lining everyone up." She glanced at Grant again. "Hello, Daddy. I see you're conspiring in corners again?"

Grant dropped his hand from Alex's shoulders and chuckled. "Just talking a little Robidoux Holdings business with Alex before we get started."

Her smile was tight and didn't reach her eyes. "I'll let you two finish plotting. I have things to do."

She turned to walk away from them. Alex reached out and took her wrist in his hands. "Elaina."

She stiffened but didn't pull away. Her face was expressionless, her eyes cool when they met his. "Yes."

"We need to talk. I have something important to tell you."

The corners of her mouth lifted slightly. "I'm sure you do." She pulled away and marched down the hall.

Alex spun back to Grant. "I quit. That's what I came to tell you. Not that I'm taking your deal. I'm no longer playing a part in this push for control over Elaina's life you insist on having."

Grant didn't appear fazed or concerned. "You quit, huh? We'll see about that come Monday."

"I'm serious, Grant. I love Elaina. I won't let you use me to hurt her."

Grant's eyes widened. He appeared genuinely surprised by Alex's words. A second later his face hardened with resolve. "I'm not trying to hurt her. No matter what you think about me, understand that when it comes to getting her way she's stubborn and willful and will cut off her nose to spite her face. Until she accepts and realizes that all I'm trying to do is help her go in the right direction she'll continue to make the wrong decisions. Don't throw away a promising future with Robidoux Tobacco because you think I'm treating her unfairly. In the end, you'll realize I was right all along."

CHAPTER THIRTY-THREE

ELAINA'S HEART BEAT heavily in her chest, and her stomach churned. She wished it was just because she'd overheard what Grant said to Alex, but she'd felt off all day. She'd considered it nerves because of the ball and ignored the feeling. Now she knew it was intuition telling her today was going to suck.

She'd gotten the call during the break she'd taken to go home and change. *"I'm sorry, Elaina, but you're too much of a risk. I've decided to invest in the new facility your father is opening."*

She'd nearly thrown up afterwards. Her dad had gotten to someone else. She had no idea how she could replace that investment. How she'd possibly open on time. With each step she took, her stomach twisted, and breathing was difficult. No matter how much she'd wanted to believe in Alex, what she'd overheard couldn't be denied. He'd plotted to work with her father all along. Anger coursed through her veins like liquid fire. She wanted to tear him to shreds, but doing so in front of her dad would have been exactly what Grant wanted. Another example of Elaina's inability to lead effectively.

She was angry at herself. Angry for believing Alex was different. Why did she keep doing this to herself? Why did she keep believing in happy endings when she wasn't suited for them? Now he wanted to talk. Oh, she bet he had a lot to say. She wouldn't give him the chance to humiliate her tonight.

"Elaina, are we ready to start?" Sade asked.

If only she'd let Alex leave with Sade all those weeks ago, her heart wouldn't be breaking like this today. Elaina nodded stiffly. "Yes. The microphones are set and we're ready to go. I'll get the kids lined up."

Elaina entered the room where the debutantes dressed. Lilah sat at one of the first tables in front of a mirror. Her eyes lit up and she bounced up from her seat when she saw Elaina. "Aunt Elaina, is it time?"

Elaina pushed aside her rage, twisting stomach and heartache. She'd deal with Alex later. Right now, she was about Lilah.

She nodded and went over to smooth back Lilah's hair. Zoe had arranged Lilah's braids in a simple twisted knot, which Elaina had adorned with a small crystal tiara. She looked beautiful.

"It's time to line up." She smiled at Lilah. Ignored the trembling in her hands and gave her niece a quick hug. "Let's get started."

The next forty minutes made it easy to avoid Alex. The fourteen debutantes and their escorts were lined up and introduced to the rest of the country club members. After the introductions, the first dance took place. Elaina intentionally remained on the opposite side of the ball room from him during the activities. Every attempt he made to catch her eye or come to her side she quickly diverted.

No matter how much she tried to take reassuring breaths, remind herself that she'd get through this, and not think about how much it hurt to know Alex had worked with her dad all along, she still felt sick. Her hands trembled, and a light sweat broke out over her forehead. A waiter passed by with champagne. Her eyes widened. Something fizzy would settle her. She took a flute and downed it quickly.

After the introductions were over and dinner was served, Elaina hugged Lilah and congratulated Zoe and Byron, who both beamed with pride, before saying she needed to check on things. She wouldn't be able to sit and eat and couldn't bear to be around the smugly married members of her family. Not when her love life was once again turning into a shit show. The champagne seemed to help, so she had two more glasses. Her trembling stopped and the pain dulled.

Every time she saw Alex, she got lost in the crowd. With an event this big, there was always something that needed to be done. She busied herself trying to be useful.

She took another glass of champagne from a passing waiter as the dinner ended and people moved to the dance floor. The DJ had switched from light background music to some of the hits of the day. It was a suggestion Elaina made after the sing-along with Lilah on dress shopping day as a way to make the ball more fun for the teenagers.

A hand rested on her arm as she brought the champagne to her mouth. She turned and scowled. Then her mouth fell open when she met Byron's concerned gaze.

"Haven't you had enough?" Byron's voice wasn't hard or accusing. Worry laced his voice.

Elaina lifted her chin. She'd only had three, or was this four? Did it matter? She pulled on her arm and Byron let her go.

"Who sent you over here to babysit me?" Elaina said coolly.

"No one sent me to babysit you. I've been watching you. What's wrong?" Byron asked.

"Nothing is wrong. I'm busy. It takes a lot to make sure things run smoothly tonight."

Byron studied her and shook his head. "No, there's something going on. You're avoiding Alex. Did he do something? Are you two fighting?"

She thought of what she'd heard, and her stomach clenched. She swallowed hard and took a shaky breath. "Stay out of it," she answered. Her pain was too new to think about sharing it with anyone. Including her brother.

"I won't stay out of it if you're going to spiral like this on Lilah's big night."

Elaina's head snapped back. She let out a caustic laugh. "Spiral? Me?" She shook her head and scoffed. "If anyone in this family has a right to spiral, it's me. But I wouldn't dare do anything to embarrass Lilah, and you should know that."

She spun on her heel. The room wavered for a second. Byron put a hand on her elbow. She jerked out of his reach, took a moment to steady herself, and marched in the opposite direction. Maybe she could eat something small. Bread or the rice they'd serve. That might help.

She glanced up and met Alex's eyes. He headed in her direction. She'd have to face him if she wanted to get to the kitchen. Scowling, she took another sip of her drink, changed directions, and went toward the bathroom. She couldn't avoid him all night, but she needed more time. Showing him how much he'd hurt her was out of the question. If he really had gone behind her back and made plans to work with her dad instead, then she couldn't show him how much she cared. She couldn't let him know she'd fallen in love with him, too.

"Don't tell Elaina, okay?"

India's insistent words to Zoe were the first things she heard as she entered the bathroom. Both women looked up and jumped as if seeing a ghost. Guilt covered both of their faces. Elaina was hot all over. Sweat trickled down her back. What now? They were talking about her, too. Expecting her to spiral.

"Don't tell me what?" Elaina asked.

India shook her head. "It's nothing."

"Obviously it's not nothing if you're whispering in bathrooms about not telling me." She glared at them both. "Just get it over with. Are you going to work for my dad, too, Zoe?"

Zoe's brows drew together. "What? Of course not. Why would you think that?"

"You wouldn't be the first person to ditch me tonight," Elaina said. "So? What is it?"

Zoe looked at India. "Just tell her. She'll be happy. I know it."

Elaina stared expectantly at her sister. "Happy about what?"

India straightened her shoulders and smiled hesitantly. "I'm pregnant. We just found out earlier this week."

Elaina's head cocked to the side. A whirlwind of emotions hit her. Excitement at being an aunt again. Happiness seeing the joy in her sister's gaze. Satisfaction knowing India and Travis would make great parents. But something else crept into her heart. Something she hated to acknowledge but was too hurt and sick to ignore. Jealousy. Everyone was getting exactly what they wanted, and she was being duped again.

"Why wouldn't you want to tell me that?" she asked in a voice sharper than she'd intended.

India flinched. "I was worried you'd be upset."

"Why would I be upset? You and Travis could barely keep your hands off each other. The second I gave my okay, you ran off and got married. Of course I'd expect you to get pregnant soon." She sniffed and lifted her chin. "I'm surprised it took this long."

"Elaina," Zoe said in an admonishing tone. "Do you have to say it like that?"

"Like what? Everyone's happy, right? Travis finally gets the family he wanted. Daddy gets a new generation of Robidoux children to take over at the company. India get to be the perfect mother, because let's face it, India, you couldn't be anything other than the world's most perfect mother."

Tears filled her sister's eyes. Frustration clouded Zoe's features. Guilt swamped Elaina. She was being out of line. She knew she shouldn't talk like this, but the words were coming before her brain could rationalize them. She turned and walked out of the bathroom. The sound of footsteps rushed after her.

India grabbed her arm and swung her around just as Elaina reached the ballroom. "Why do you have to do this? Why do you have to make things worse?" India accused.

Her sister's words hit like poison daggers. The people near them gasped and turned to look. Elaina's stomach flipped. Heat filled her neck and cheeks.

"I don't know what you're talking about," she said evenly. "You're making a scene. Calm down."

"Calm down? I just tell you the most important thing that's ever happened to me and you crap all over it. I love you, Elaina, but why do you have to be so mean?"

Elaina's jaw dropped. "Mean? Me? What the hell do you want from me, India?"

India pressed a hand to her chest. "To at least be happy for me?"

All she'd done was try to be happy for her sister. She'd gone out of her way to not make anyone feel uncomfortable, but no matter what, they still tiptoed around her. Kept secrets as if she couldn't handle their good news. She was sick and tired of being happy for everyone else when her life was in shambles.

She took a step forward and pointed. "Why? Because you're having a baby? So Daddy can flaunt that in my face along with everything else I couldn't do?"

Tears welled in India's eyes. In a flash Travis was next to her with his arm around her shoulders. "I think it's time for you to go, Elaina." His voice was rock solid.

Elaina looked around at the shocked faces of the crowd. A hand slipped into hers. "I'll take you home," Alex said.

She tried to jerk away. He held on tight. "You can't drive. Don't argue with me."

She clenched her jaw and jerked her hand again. "I'll call a driver." She spun on her heel. The room spun with her. Her stomach heaved, and she threw up on the floor.

ELAINA WAS SICK for the next three days, and it had nothing to do with the champagne. Alex stayed with her the first night, and when she was sick the next morning, he insisted on taking her to the doctor. That's where she learned she was the latest victim of the stomach flu going through Jackson Falls.

On the third day, she was finally able to eat without fearing she would vomit, and she no longer felt as if someone was tearing through her insides with razor blades. She'd sent Alex away the night before and spent most of the day in bed, testing her stamina with soup and saltine crackers. He hadn't wanted to go, but she'd figured he'd seen enough of her sick to last a lifetime. On top of that, his attentiveness was making it a lot harder to hate him. When she'd been doubled over in pain, she hadn't thought much about the reason why she'd been upset with him in the first place.

As her health returned, she could no longer ignore what she'd overheard. He'd made plans to sell to her dad. His father had even talked to Grant and was okay with the decision. While she struggled to get things up and running on time, he'd listened to the lies her dad spread about her incompetence and believed them. Not once had he come to her and talked about it.

Her anger rose as her sickness waned, but after he'd taken care of her when she was admittedly at her worst, she no longer believed his feelings for her were fake. Did that mean she could trust him, though? Would he become another person Grant would use to assert his influence on her life? The answer was yes.

She couldn't stay with Alex while he still worked for her dad, and she couldn't ask him to leave his job.

Her cell phone rang. Elaina reached to where it rested on the end table next to the couch. The name on the screen was familiar, Nathaniel Thompson, the recent investor she'd met with the day she'd taken Alex out to her family's estate and hoped their relationship would be blessed. He hadn't gotten back to her, and after she'd lost the other investor the day of the ball, she'd assumed he'd changed his mind as well.

She cleared her throat and answered. "Nathaniel, how are you?" Her voice was raspy from days of being sick, and Elaina hoped he didn't notice.

"I'm good, but I just got an interesting phone call," he said, sounding wary.

Elaina sat up and pulled the blanket around her shoulders tighter. "Oh, really? Interesting how?"

"It was from someone at Robidoux Holdings. A guy named Randy Clark called because he heard I wanted to invest in a hemp manufacturing operation and said Grant Robidoux is interested in meeting with me."

Elaina's hand clenched into fists. She'd guessed correctly. "That is interesting. Are you planning to meet with him?"

"That's why I'm calling you. I thought this venture of yours was separate from your dad's company."

"It is."

"Then do you know why he wants to meet with me?"

Because he's trying to teach me a lesson and convince me I'm nothing without him. But admitting that wouldn't help her situation. "Probably to convince you to work with him instead of me. I apologize for the confusion."

Nathaniel was silent for a second. "Hmm…does he know that I'm working with you already?"

"If he's calling you, then he knows." Elaina was too tired to muster up the amount of indignation needed to fight. For the first time, the real possibility that her dad would ruin this came to mind. "Look, Nathaniel, I meant everything I said when I met with you, but I also understand what a powerhouse Robidoux Holdings is. If you decide to meet with my dad and ultimately decide to work with him, I understand."

"I have no intention of working with your dad. I've followed your career, and I know what you did for Robidoux Tobacco and Robidoux Holdings. I don't know why you ultimately left the company, but as long as you plan to deliver what you promised when we met, then I plan to keep working with you."

Elaina smiled, and relief washed through her. "I plan to deliver all of that and more."

"Good. I look forward to working with you."

They ended the call, and Elaina's head fell back on the

chair. She needed that win. But how had her dad found out already? Only a few days had passed since she talked with Nathaniel.

Her head shot up. He'd spoken to Randy Clark. Randy, on Alex's team. She frowned. Could Alex have said something to his team? Even more worrisome, was Alex working with Grant to make her fail?

The doorbell rang before that thought could take hold. Pushing herself up from the couch, Elaina went to the door and checked the peephole. She sucked in a breath and ran a finger through her mess of hair. Then dropped her hand. He'd seen her a lot worse than this.

She opened the door and stepped back for Alex to come inside. He was calm and put together as always. His button-up shirt was still unwrinkled despite a day in the office, his chin strong and firm. His hair had the straight edges of a fresh cut.

He looked her up and down, and she fought not to tug on the edges of her pajama shirt. "I didn't expect to see you."

"I told you I'd be back to check on you today."

She frowned, then remembered him saying something like that while pulling the blanket over her before leaving. She'd been nearly asleep when he'd left and had the first night of uninterrupted sleep she'd had in days.

It wasn't lost on her that no one from her family had called and probably didn't know she'd been sick. She also remembered the horrible way she'd handled India's good news. She had no idea how she was going to make up for that.

"Well, I'm fine," she said. She turned and went back into the living area and sat on the couch. "I ate, rested, and will be back at work tomorrow."

Alex settled into the end chair. She didn't want to think

about how that little decision said a lot. He typically sat right next to her and held her. "I'm glad you're feeling better."

"Thank you for taking care of me. You didn't have to do that."

"I couldn't leave you here. Especially when I realized you were sick and not…"

The corners of her mouth lifted. "Not drunk? Don't feel bad about saying it. I'll admit I've had problems knowing when to stop before. I know how much is too much. Besides, I wouldn't do that at Lilah's debut."

"But you did make a scene," he said evenly.

She pressed her lips together and winced. "I'll apologize to everyone."

"What about talking to me? You avoided me all night. Why didn't you give me the chance to explain?" The question wasn't spoken like an accusation, but there was disappointment in his voice.

Elaina lifted her chin. She would not feel bad about what she'd overheard. What he'd done. "Explain what? That you made a deal to supply my dad instead of my company?"

Alex leaned forward. "That's not what happened."

"Did you or did you not agree to supply my dad's processing facility?"

He sighed. "I did, but only if your facility wasn't ready on time."

She nodded slowly, her heart squeezing as the truth of how little faith he had in her punched a ragged hole in her chest. "Did you really think I wouldn't be able to get the facility open?"

"You were having trouble finding investors. You said so yourself that you'd worried you wouldn't be able to meet your deadline."

Elaina clasped her hands together in her lap. "I told you that in confidence and because I thought you'd appreciate the hard work I put in. Instead, you go to my dad and make a back-door deal in case I fail. Even when you knew he was trying to undermine me."

Alex scooted forward to the edge of his seat. "I told him I wouldn't work with him if I knew he was intentionally trying to make you fail."

She crossed her arms. "Do you really believe he was going to stop because of that? That Grant Robidoux would suddenly develop a strand of empathy that would make him lay down his grudge and leave me be?"

"I'd hoped he would understand that he was hurting you."

"He doesn't think he's hurting me. He thinks he's teaching me a lesson and that I'll crawl back to him and beg for my job. That I'll be okay to comply with whatever demands he puts on me because that's what I've always done."

"I realized that when he called my dad," Alex admitted. "I knew then that he'd backed me into a corner."

Elaina let out a humorless laugh seeing the trap Grant had set. "You couldn't back out of his offer if your dad knew he had another buyer and my opening failed. Typical."

"My plan at the ball was to tell him that I couldn't work with him," Alex admitted. "I don't want to be in the middle anymore."

She wanted to believe him, but she couldn't let her emotions cloud her judgment. "If that's the case, then why is your guy calling my investors?"

Alex's brows rose. "What guy?"

"Randy called Nathaniel Thompson to schedule a meeting with Grant. Did you tell him to do that? Have you always been working with him behind my back?"

Alex's shoulders straightened. "Of course not. Why would you think that?"

"Because you're the only person outside of Zoe who knew about my meeting with Nathaniel. Not long after I tell you, a guy on your team is calling and trying to steal another investor from me. What else am I supposed to believe?"

"You're supposed to trust me," he said, his voice hard. "You're supposed to believe the man who loves you wouldn't intentionally hurt you."

Elaina scoffed and stood up. "I've been hurt by people who claimed to love me before." She turned to go into the kitchen.

Alex's footsteps followed. His hand wrapped around her elbow, and he moved to block her steps. "I'm not those people. I thought you knew that?"

"I want to believe that, but I also know I can't put my trust in other people. I can only count on myself, and I'll be played for a fool if I let emotion and sentiment guide me."

His hand dropped away. He stepped back. "You're still spouting that bullshit at me?"

Frustration was her only defense. She crossed her arms to suppress the urge to push him. "It's not bullshit. It's the only thing that's kept me from being hurt."

"But has it really kept you from being hurt, Elaina? You try to live by the advice your parents drilled into you, and all it's gotten you is hurt and disappointment."

"No, every time I go with my heart or emotions, I end up in a bad situation. I end up realizing everything they said was true. Love isn't for everyone, and even those who find it don't always keep it. I'm realistic, not romantic."

"And I've done nothing but be honest with you."

She pointed a finger at him. "No. You haven't. You worked with my dad to help me fail. Even if you didn't tell him about Nathaniel, you agreed to supply him if I failed, meaning a part of you believed he would succeed at my expense. I don't need that in my life."

"What are you saying?"

Her heart raced. The disbelief and pain in his eyes made her want to take back the words. But taking them back meant trusting he wouldn't do this again. Even if her dad had painted him into a corner, Alex listened to Grant when he'd planted the seeds of doubt in her ability to open the new facility. He said he loved her, but how long would that love last when they were on opposite ends of a battlefield? Even if he was her lover, he was still her dad's employee. The CEO of the company that tossed her out.

"I'm saying that maybe we've gone as far as we need to go," she said.

His jaw clenched. He took a step forward. "You want to break up?"

"I want to cut our losses before things get even uglier."

"What about the other day at your family's estate?"

She lifted her chin. Her throat felt tight and her stomach clenched, but from a different kind of sickness. The idea of losing what she'd hoped could be real was like a knife in her gut.

"That was me being sentimental after a good day," she said in her best I-don't-care voice. "We both knew this is where the relationship would end."

"No, we didn't both know that," he said, giving her the don't-try-to-fool-me stare she always hated. The same stare that saw through her defenses to the truth. "We both wanted more, but you're too afraid to try."

His words hit her in the chest, but she refused to back down. "And you're too sentimental. Accept it, Alex. We were never meant to be more than what we were."

CHAPTER THIRTY-FOUR

ELAINA WENT TO India and Travis's place the next day. She owed her sister an apology, and she wasn't going to procrastinate in delivering it. Her romantic life might be in shambles, but she didn't want to also completely ruin the budding closeness between her and India. She didn't call before making her way over, because she didn't want to give her sister a reason to leave or an opportunity to tell her not to come.

Travis answered the door after she rang the bell. He watched her warily for a few seconds.

"I'm here to apologize," Elaina said, knowing he wouldn't let her in if he thought she was there to make things worse.

The stiffness left his jaw, and he took a step back. "She's in our room. Give me a second and I'll go get her."

Elaina followed him inside and to the living room. He motioned for her to take a seat before disappearing down the hall. She didn't sit. She was too nervous to sit still. She walked over to the window and stared out at the street outside. The minutes ticked by. Elaina imagined India asking Travis why she was here and the two of them debating if it was worth her coming out or not. Was she really that difficult to deal with?

Well, if India refused to come out and talk to her, then she'd just go back there and make India hear her apology. She spun on her heel and took a step toward the hall. India came into the living room at the same time. Her sister was in a pair of black leggings and one of Byron's old campaign T-shirts. Her curly hair was pulled back in a messy pony-tail, and she looked as if she'd just woken up.

"I didn't mean to disturb you," Elaina said.

"You showed up unannounced. You meant to disturb me," India said coolly. She walked into the center of the living room and crossed her arms over her chest. "What do you want, Elaina?"

Elaina hadn't expected an overly warm welcome, but she also hadn't expected the chill in her sister's voice. Or the way her eyes were flat and angry as they assessed her. After days of being sick, she'd wanted to feel like her-self again and dressed in her favorite pair of beige slacks and a champagne silk top. She'd straightened her hair so it fell in a smooth sheet to her shoulders and had put on full makeup. Seeing her sister in her lounge clothes and Travis in a pair of sweatpants and a T-shirt, she realized she was overdressed for a casual visit with her sister.

"I want to apologize," Elaina said.

"For what?" India snapped back.

"For being rude when you told me about being preg-nant. I was in a bad head space and I took it out on you. I shouldn't have done that."

One of India's shoulders lifted. "So?" She shot out the word as if she expected more.

"So... I realize I was wrong. I am happy for you and Tra-vis. I'm looking forward to being an auntie again. I'll even throw you the best baby shower this town has ever seen."

India threw up her hands. "Do you think that makes everything okay?"

Elaina blinked rapidly. The anger in India's voice was

hotter than she'd anticipated. "I mean, if there's anything you or the baby need just let me know."

India put her hands on her hips and glared. "It isn't about you doing whatever the baby and I need or throwing me a baby shower. It isn't even about you coming over here giving me an apology for acting like a royal bitch when I told you about being pregnant."

"Then what is it about? I don't know what else you want from me. Do you want me to grovel or beg for your forgiveness?"

India pressed a hand to her temple. "No, Elaina." She sounded exasperated.

"Then what?"

"I want you to stop being in a bad head space and taking it out on the people who care about you. I want you to figure out why you're like this."

"Like what?" she asked defensively.

"So damn hard all the time. You're hard on your employees. Hard with your family members. Most of all you're hard on yourself. I can't think of a time when I thought you were happy. Maybe if you figured that out, then you wouldn't be so insufferable all the time."

Elaina pressed a hand to her chest. "Insufferable?"

"Yes!" India shouted back. "You're unbearable and intolerable most of the time. I love you, but you make it so hard to like you sometimes."

Pain pierced through Elaina's chest as if she'd been shot. This was not how things were supposed to go. She was supposed to come over here and apologize. She was supposed to make things up to India by being the best sister and auntie for the baby. India, who was the sweetest of all of them, was supposed to tell her it was alright, she understood, and they were okay. Elaina wasn't supposed to be attacked.

She squared her shoulders. "I'm hard and *insufferable* because that's how I have to be."

India took a slow breath as if seeking strength. When she opened her eyes and spoke again, her voice was calmer. "No, it's not. You always swore you fought against Daddy, but in the end you only did what he wanted or expected. You're trying so hard to be what you think is expected of you that you don't even know who you are or what you want."

"I know exactly what I want." To open her facility. To beat her dad at his own game. To build her own legacy.

"Do you?" India asked. "Because if you do, it seems like all you want is to push people away under the guise of being some superstar businesswoman. Well, I'm tired of tiptoeing around you. I'm tired of feeling as if I'm entering a minefield whenever we talk."

"I don't know how to be any other way," Elaina shot back. "This is me."

India stepped forward and stared Elaina in the eye. "And if this is the only version of you that you want to be, then fine, but that doesn't mean I have to deal with you. I can't let you make me feel like crap, then later apologize and pretend everything is okay. I know you're unhappy." She took Elaina's hands in hers. "I just want you to figure out what makes you happy, and I'll fight with you to get there. But if you're going to continue to take out your unhappiness on other people, then for my sake and the sake of my child, I'll have to step back."

Her fingers slid from Elaina's hands. Elaina felt as if she were losing a lifeline. She wanted to reach out and grab India's hand and pull her sister close. To admit she wasn't happy, but she didn't know where to start. How to get someplace she'd never been. The fear of letting others see her insecurities still pressed heavily against her, and she held back.

Elaina closed her hand into a fist and pressed it to her abdomen. "I'm sorry for disturbing you." She lifted her lips in a small smile before walking around her sister toward the door. She waited, but India didn't call her back or ask her to stay.

ELAINA LEFT INDIA and called Zoe. After a quick conversation, she met her sister-in-law at S&E Bar and Grill. They settled in at one of the booths. Zoe ordered a glass of wine. Still unsure about her stomach, Elaina went with a club soda with lime.

"So," Zoe said. "Where've you been the past few days?"

Elaina stared at the bubbles in her drink. "Throwing up."

Zoe sat up straight, her eyes wide. "What?"

Elaina waved a hand. "I had the stomach bug going around."

Zoe leaned forward. "Why didn't you call us? We could have brought you something."

Elaina shook her head. "I felt horrible and could barely function, much less make a phone call. Alex watched me and took me to the doctor."

"He did?" Zoe sounded surprised.

"Yes, he did."

"From the way you were avoiding him at the debutante ball, I'd assumed you'd broken up."

"I broke up with him yesterday," Elaina said.

Zoe waved her hand. "Hold up? The man watched you while you were puking all over the place for three days and you dumped him afterwards?"

"There were other reasons." She told Zoe about the deal he'd made with Grant and the call from Nathaniel.

"What else was I supposed to do?" Elaina said. "I can't trust him if he's assuming I'm going to fail. Not to mention a guy on his team calling. How else would they know if Alex didn't tell them?"

Zoe scrunched up her nose. "That could be my fault."

"How?"

"I told Byron," Zoe said in a rush. She waved her finger in the same zip-it fashion Elaina had seen her use with Lilah when Elaina would have interrupted. "I was so excited about the way things turned out. We were at the estate, and Grant came in a few minutes later. I didn't think he'd overheard, but he may have."

Elaina fell back against the seat. "You told Byron?"

"I hope you're not mad, but I keep him in the loop on what's happening. I don't think he would tell your dad."

Elaina didn't either, but she could believe Grant would overhear their conversation and use it to his advantage. She shook her head. "Doesn't matter. He still made another deal because he thought we would fail."

"Elaina, we almost did fail," Zoe said carefully. "We got lucky with your idea to approach new investors not tied to Robidoux Holdings, but they could have just as easily said no. Alex had to think of other options for his dad's first crop. You know that."

She did, but she didn't want to admit it. She didn't want to think she'd jumped the gun and accused him wrongly. Didn't want to think what India accused her of might be true.

"We were never going to be together forever," she said weakly.

Zoe's head tilted to the side. "The guy is crazy about you. He took care of you when you were sick."

"So I'm supposed to forgive him and trust him just because he helped me out for a few days?"

"No, you should do that because he loves you," Zoe said simply.

Elaina took a deep breath. "He shouldn't love me. I'm not the person to give him the type of relationship he wants."

Zoe placed her hand over hers. "How do you know what type of relationship he wants? He seemed pretty content with your prickly ass." She grinned when Elaina scowled. "I think you were the relationship he wanted. You're the only person having a hard time believing what you two had was enough. Maybe you should figure out why."

Elaina stared into the bubbles of her club soda and thought about the past few days. "India says I'm insufferable. She says if I don't figure out what makes me happy then she can't be around me."

"India still feels as if her happiness is coming at your expense."

Elaina's brows rose. "What? Why?"

"You know why? She thinks that even though you gave your okay, you're still longing for what you and Travis could have been. Maybe now she thinks staying away from you is the only way she can be happy without feeling guilty."

"She doesn't need to feel guilty."

"I know that, but let's be honest, Elaina, you can be harsh and caustic. You push people away by being a bitch." Zoe placed a hand over her heart. "All this is said with love."

Instead of getting mad, she felt heavier with the weight of guilt she'd tried to ignore. That was the third person who'd said something similar to her in the past two days. "It's how I was told I needed to be. My mom said I couldn't let my emotions guide me."

"Your mom is also the person who told me I'd ruin Byron's life if I'd married him and accepted his love years ago," Zoe said without any bitterness. "She was a strong and smart woman who loved her kids, but that doesn't mean she always knew what was best."

"I've spent my whole life trying to be like her," Elaina admitted.

"I didn't know her well, so I won't say she was right or wrong. What I will say is that our parents are human, too. They made mistakes and poor choices. All you can do as their child is figure out if the advice they give is legitimately something you should follow or if it was a bunch of bullshit."

Elaina thought back on all the advice she'd listened to from her mom and dad over the years. The decisions she'd made. The way she'd planned for her future. The person she'd tried to be was the image of her mom, but had her mom been happy? She'd married the man she loved, but in the end their love was swamped by the drive to grow the business, build a legacy and pave a path for their kids. This drive had led her to push her husband into the arms of another woman when she needed him most. Elaina tried to imagine doing the same with Alex, and her stomach knotted up. Could she really do something like that?

Elaina shook her head. "If it was bullshit, I don't know who I am."

Zoe reached over and squeezed her hand. "Then figure that out first before you make any decision about Alex or anyone else. You owe that to yourself more than anyone else."

CHAPTER THIRTY-FIVE

ALEX PULLED THE stack of envelopes from his mailbox and sifted through them as he walked up the drive to his home. He paused when he got to a thick eggshell-colored one. The return address was Elaina's. His fingers ran across her name. He hadn't seen or spoken to her since she'd broken things off twelve weeks ago. Every day since then, he'd thought about her with both frustration and regret.

A car horn beeped twice. He looked up and waved at his neighbor pulling into the driveway across the street. He hurried and went inside to open the letter instead of standing motionless in his driveway, staring at it.

He tore the paper apart as soon as he crossed the threshold. Inside was a square invitation to the grand opening tour of her new hemp processing facility.

I hope to see you there was handwritten at the bottom in her familiar neat handwriting.

He pulled his cell phone out of his back pocket and called his dad, who answered after a few rings. "Did you get an invitation?"

"I guess you mean to the tour of Elaina's facility? Yes, I got it."

"Are you going?"

"I am. I would like to see how it's set up. I think she's inviting all the growers who agreed to supply the facility along with some of the other investors. Are you going?"

Alex tapped the invitation on his hand. "I'm not sure. We haven't talked with each other in three months."

"She sent you an invitation, which makes it seem like she wants to see you."

Or she wanted to rub it in his face that she'd gotten the facility open. Too many times over the last few months, he'd thought about her. He'd considered calling her and asking to see her. He'd wondered if he could talk to her more about why he'd made the decisions he'd made, if that would make a difference. He wanted to know if she'd thought about him nearly as much as he'd spent time on her. The fact that the only contact she'd initiated was this invitation made him think otherwise.

"I helped her make the deal with you," he said, trying to think practically like Elaina would. "She's just inviting me out of professional courtesy."

"Maybe she is and maybe she isn't. What I will say is that if you still care about her and want to see her, this is a good chance to do so."

A spark of hope flashed in his heart. He killed it with a cold dose of reason. "That doesn't mean it'll change anything about what happened."

"What happened between you two happened for a reason," his dad said in a reassuring tone. "No need to go back and try to make things different or relive the past. Go for your own closure."

"Who says I need closure?"

Thomas chuckled. "Chris, who told us last night that you're still not dating despite the interest of the women at the country club and that new lady you're working with."

Alex knew he shouldn't have told Chris any of that. He shouldn't be surprised that his brother-in-law had taken it upon himself to tell his family about his lack of a dating life. What, couldn't a guy take some time to regroup after a breakup? Was that so unusual?

"Tell Chris to mind his own business." He took a heavy breath. "I'll go with you, but only because I'm curious about how the facility turned out. That's all."

"If you say so."

Alex shook his head and ended the call. He should throw the invitation in the trash. Elaina was more trouble than she was worth. She came with family drama that was fit for prime-time television. Plus, he was sure this invitation was her way to prove to all of them she'd been successful in opening the facility on time.

He went into the kitchen, tossed the rest of the mail on the table, and walked to the fridge to get a bottle of water. He attached the invitation to the front of the fridge with a magnet. He pulled out a bottle, twisted the top and took a long drink. If he were smart, he wouldn't bother showing up.

THE FOLLOWING TUESDAY, Alex drove with his dad to Raleigh for the tour of Elaina's new facility. Thankfully, his dad made no mention of rekindling anything with Elaina on the ride there. They filled the time talking about the final harvest of his dad's hemp crop and the process of getting it packaged and transmitted to the facility for processing. They arrived and parked in the large lot with the dozens of other cars also arriving.

"Looks like she's got a good crowd here," his dad said.

Alex glanced around at the multiple people parking and walking toward the front of the building. "She does."

They followed the crowd and entered through the large glass doors. Inside, the lobby area was open and filled with light. Light gray walls blended with a blue-gray floor. At the front desk, a receptionist greeted everyone by checking their names on the list and giving out nametags.

"Welcome, Mr. Tyson," the male receptionist said after Alex gave his name. "The tour will start in a few minutes. If you'll join the rest of the group in the break room to the left, there are some refreshments waiting for you."

"Thank you," Alex said to the man.

They went into the break area. In true Elaina fashion, there was a full spread laid out. Dips, fruit, vegetables, cheese, crackers and meats. Soft music played in the background while people mingled and talked. Alex recognized several of them from the country club or doing business with Robidoux Holdings.

His eyes scanned the room, and he spotted Byron talking to India and Travis. He hadn't spoken to any of them since the night of the debutante ball, and he made his way over.

Byron smiled as he greeted him and shook his hand. "Long time no see."

"You're waiting in here, too," Alex said after introducing his dad to the rest of the family. "I would have expected Zoe to give you the backstage tour already."

Byron chuckled. "No, she insisted I see it with everyone else. I'm just glad the place is open already. I have barely seen my wife in the past few months."

"I'm glad everything worked out," Alex said. "I knew Elaina would get it done."

"Once she sets her mind to something, she sticks with it."

A door opened into the break room, and Elaina walked through with Zoe. Alex's breath caught at his first glimpse of her after so much time. She wore a tasteful camel-colored suit that hugged her curves perfectly. Her hair was shorter and framed her face in a stylish bob that enhanced her beautiful features. Her eyes scanned the room. She smiled at her brother and family. When her eyes met Alex's, she stilled for a second before dipping her head in a brief nod.

She looked away before he could return the gesture. "Thank you, everyone, for coming. We are very excited about the opening of our facility next week. You are the first people to see what we've done. Hopefully, this will be the start of a prosperous future and even more successful endeavors." She motioned toward the door. "If you'll follow me, we'll start the tour."

Alex hung back with his dad as the crowd followed Elaina. He wanted to talk to her, hold her again, find out how she was doing. Instead, he behaved like the rest of the spectators. Elaina led them through the various manufacturing processes. She showed them where they would take in the hemp, and the locations where it would be broken down into oil and various fibers for multiple uses. When they didn't go upstairs because the office facilities and conference areas were still under construction, he was surprised. He'd expected her to not admit that everything wasn't completely perfect when she opened, but there was no shame or frustration in her voice as she talked about plans to expand the facility as they were able to produce more products.

The tour ended in the lobby. The food had been moved out, and many of the supervisors and other team members who would be running the facility joined the rest of the people on the tour to answer any questions they might have.

"She's done a damn good job," his dad said.

"She has." His voice was filled with pride.

"I'm going to try some of the cocktail shrimp. You can take your time talking to other people while I'm over there," his dad said, elbowing him in Elaina's direction.

"You're not very subtle," Alex replied.

"Well, you've been watching her constantly during the tour. Go ahead and say hi."

Alex took a deep breath and crossed the room to Elaina. She was talking to some of the investors he knew who'd walked away after Grant stepped in. If she noticed him coming, she didn't show it. He stood in the background until she finished her conversation and turned to him. When their eyes met, hers were warm.

"Thank you for coming," she said. Her voice was pleasant and welcoming, but no warmer than it had been with anyone else.

Alex shoved his hands in his pockets. The need to reach out and touch her was strong. He missed the freedom to hold her in his arms. He missed the way her eyes warmed whenever he was near. "Of course I came." He looked around. "You did a great job."

For a second he thought pleasure flashed in her eyes, but it was gone so quickly, he couldn't be sure. "I still have work to do," she said. "But I'm learning to accept the small things and keep on moving toward the big things."

They stared for several heartbeats. So many unspoken words swirled in his head. He still loved her. That was as clear as the sweat on his palms. "How have you been?" he finally asked. She looked great. Rested, not stressed. Was she better off without him in her life, reminding her of everything she'd lost?

She smiled and shook her head side to side. "Okay. I've been figuring out some things."

"Like what?"

She lifted her chin. "Like what I want. Who I want to be. How to let go of some of the beliefs that have held me back. Or at least that's what my therapist said."

His eyes widened. She'd mentioned seeing a therapist

once, but only in a past reference. "You're going back to therapy?"

She nodded. "Yeah. It's been a good thing. How about you? How have things been?"

"Busy," he admitted.

"With what?"

Before he could answer, Grant walked over. "I missed the tour, but the guy up front let me come in anyway. You got the place opened, I see."

Elaina's smile didn't waver. "Hello, Daddy. Yes, I got it open."

Grant looked around the lobby at all the people. There was no mistaking the pride in his eyes when they focused on Elaina. "Looks like you did a good job," he said.

"I did do a good job," Elaina said with a satisfied smile. "I'm proud of what I accomplished."

"I'm proud of you, too," Grant said. "You always were just as stubborn and hardworking as your mom."

The smile on her face fell away. "Maybe too much like her."

Grant's expression clouded for a second. He looked away from Elaina to Alex. "I see you decided to come."

Alex inclined his head. "I wouldn't miss it."

Grant's brows drew together. "You still like teaching over at the university?"

Alex nodded. "I do. I like it a lot." He'd turned in his resignation the Monday after the ball, just as planned. He didn't regret the decision then and still didn't. He couldn't stay there and continue to watch Grant try to hurt Elaina in the name of doing what was best for her.

"If you ever want to come back to Robidoux Holdings—"

"I have no intention of coming back," Alex said firmly.

Teaching was new to him. He was still getting used to the idea of being considered old by many of the students. It was definitely different from working in a corporate setting, but he enjoyed the pace.

Grant nodded. "The offer still stands." He looked at Elaina. "For you, too."

"Daddy, have you seen Byron and India yet? They're across the room," Elaina said sweetly.

Grant scoffed but smiled. "Want me to leave, huh? Fine, I'll go talk to your sister and brother." He turned and walked away.

Elaina faced Alex quickly. "You left Robidoux Holdings? When? Why?"

The surprise in her voice shocked him. Had no one told her? "I thought you knew?"

"I knew he hired a permanent CEO, but that's all. I assumed you went back to research and development, where you wanted to be."

He shook his head. "I quit after the debutante ball."

Regret filled her brown eyes. She reached over and placed her hand on his arm. "You didn't have to do that."

The warmth of her touch seeped through his shirt and into the coldest spot that missed her in his heart. "I'd made up my mind to quit before that."

Her expression didn't change, but her fingers tightened on his arm. "Why?"

Alex stepped closer to her. Her eyes widened slightly as the air charged around them. "Because I didn't want to be in the middle anymore. I couldn't do that and still be there for you." She dropped her hand quickly.

His dad would choose that moment to come over. "Alex, I hate to interrupt, but your mom called, and there is a leak at the house. I need to get back and fix it before she calls a plumber who'll charge too much."

Alex bit back a curse. Something had sparked in Elaina's eyes when he'd told her what was in his heart. Something that lit an answering spark of hope in him. As much as he wanted to tell his dad to get lost, he couldn't. "Of course. Let's go." He looked back at Elaina. "It was nice seeing you again."

Whatever emotion that had been there before was gone. She gave him a pleasant, professional smile and nodded. "Take care, Alex."

CHAPTER THIRTY-SIX

ELAINA WATCHED ALEX walk away and fought the urge to call him back. She didn't know what to say. She'd broken things off with him. Just because he'd come to her grand opening didn't mean he'd want to reconcile. She couldn't believe he'd left Robidoux Holdings. She never asked him to give up his career.

"I didn't want to be in the middle anymore. I couldn't do that and still be there for you."

The realization that her fear of being used had kept her from accepting the truth about Alex, and his feelings twisted around her heart like twine and squeezed. Taking the time to figure out what she wanted out of life and who she wanted to be also meant she was taking the time to accept a lot of harsh truths about herself.

More of the attendees of the event walked over, and Elaina tore her thoughts away from Alex. She finished the rest of the opening event. She was proud of what they'd accomplished and was grudgingly being okay with not letting everyone see the imperfections of the place. Surprisingly, no one seemed critical or skeptical about her ability to complete the upstairs office space. The manufacturing portion of the facility was state-of-the-art, and they'd soon be up and running with breaking down hemp into various components for a multitude of industries.

When it was over, Elaina and Zoe cracked open a bottle of sparkling cider and toasted the facility managers and supervisors who'd participated in the event.

"You all were very patient with us during this entire re-model," Elaina said, holding up a glass. "Now the real hard work begins. I know the success of this facility comes down to the work that you all do. If there is anything you ever need from me to continue to make things work smoothly, don't hesitate to reach out to me or Zoe."

Ralf Dickerson, the plant manager, raised his glass. "Ms. Robidoux, I think I speak for everyone when I say what you've done here is amazing. When you first approached us, we didn't think the Robidoux family cared about what happened to this place or its success. Here's to you for not giving up on us and giving us something to believe in again."

The rest of the staff raised their glasses and cheered her on. Heat filled Elaina's cheeks, and tears burned her eyes. She blinked quickly and nodded. The praise from her employees was better than any award she could have received. She hadn't wanted to let them down, and no matter what, she wouldn't let them down in the future.

Elaina and Zoe finished with more toasts and laughter before closing things down and heading home. They had driven together. Elaina dropped Zoe off at her place. Before she got out of the car, Zoe leaned over and gave Elaina a hug.

"You did it, Elaina. Be proud and celebrate," Zoe said.

Elaina laughed and hugged her back. "I'm celebrating with my bed. I'm exhausted."

Zoe pulled back and winked. "Call Alex. From the looks of things, he wouldn't mind celebrating in your bed with you."

Heat spread throughout Elaina's body. She'd remembered

too keenly how good it felt being Alex's arms when she'd touched him earlier. So much so that she'd almost launched herself into his embrace.

Elaina waved Zoe to get out of the car. "I broke up with him, remember."

"And you've regretted it from the moment you did it. Go get your man back." Zoe smiled and got out.

Elaina drove home and tried not to think about how much she wanted Alex back. She could grovel, but no matter how much self-reflection she'd gone through, she wasn't sure if she'd managed the level of self-awareness to be okay with groveling for forgiveness. There was a car in the yard as she turned onto her street. Her heart rate picked up. Was it Alex? She was able to hold back at the opening, but if he was there now, she'd be all in his arms in a matter of seconds. India's car waited for her instead of Alex's.

Her sister sat in the front seat, scrolling through her phone. Elaina parked next to India and got out. She frowned as she watched her sister get out of the car.

"Is everything okay?" Elaina asked. "What happened? What do you need?" Concern filled her voice as she looked her sister over. The barest hint of a baby belly showed beneath her sweater.

India shook her head and chuckled. "Nothing's wrong. I just wanted to talk to you away from everyone."

Elaina pressed a hand to her chest. "You scared me."

"I'm sorry. I didn't mean to do that," India said, looking unsure.

"Well, come inside and have some tea or something. It's cold out here, and you shouldn't be waiting around for me in the cold. Travis will kill me if you get sick."

A few minutes later, they sat at her kitchen table, India with a warm cup of tea and Elaina with a sparkling water.

The urge to get a glass of wine was there, but the other thing she was working on was not relying on wine to wind down at the end of the day. Wine had gone from being an easy way to decompress to her best friend. The thing she relied on no matter what her mood. That was another hard self-realization she'd had to accept. She wasn't sure if the need would ever go away, but she was at least working on getting better at acknowledging her dependence.

"What did you want to talk about?" Elaina asked.

India hesitated a second, then spoke. "I want to apologize for what I said after the debutante ball."

Elaina blinked, definitely not expecting that. "Why? Everything you said was right."

India shook her head. "I was out of line, and it's bothered me ever since. Seeing you today and what you accomplished made me realize I never should have questioned you. You're good at what you do, and turning businesses around makes you happy. I know you can't have a soft heart in the corporate world, and that may transfer over into your personal life. I don't want you to think you have to change because of me."

Elaina took a deep breath. "What you said was a wake-up call. I've always known people think I'm a bit of a bitch, but I thought that was because I have to be. I don't. Especially not with the people I care about." She reached for India's hand, hesitated, then went with the impulse and covered her sister's hand with hers. "I do care about you. I love you, India." The words were hard to force out. Other than Lilah, Elaina couldn't remember the last time she'd told anyone she loved them. Three words her mom had taught her were weights that would hold her back.

India flipped her hand over and squeezed Elaina's.

"I love you, too. I want you to be happy. I also want my sister to be softer."

"I can't promise I won't be prickly, but I am working to be softer with you and the rest of the family. I'm proud of what I did with the facility. I can't wait to see what I can do next, but…"

"But you still want Robidoux Holdings."

Elaina nodded. She pulled her hand away and took another sip of her water. "I know it's just a symbol. I know I can be successful away from the business, but I've worked my whole life to take over. I lived and breathed that company for years. I listened to Granddaddy's stories about how he started the business with one tobacco field, and then I see what we've turned it into and the way we've branched out into other areas, and I still want to be a part of that legacy."

"Then be a part of it."

She shook her head. "Not if I have to be under Daddy's thumb. Leaving has been the most freeing thing. Succeeding despite his interference has been like winning a prize I didn't know I was up for." She lifted her chin and shook her shoulders. She would let go of the past. "I'll be fine. I'll get over not being a part of Robidoux Holdings. I'm starting something new. That's good enough."

"No, it's not." India slammed her hand on the table. "You deserve the business. Byron and I both know it. Daddy knows it, but he's too stubborn to admit it. We just have to find a way to convince…" India gasped, and her eyes widened.

Worry rushed Elaina's system. She reached for her sister's hand. "What's wrong? Is it the baby? Are you okay?"

India snapped her fingers and grinned. "I've got it. I know just how to get you back at Robidoux Holdings."

THE FOLLOWING THURSDAY, Elaina drove to the Robidoux estate for a family dinner. She hadn't been in almost a year. Not since she'd quickly moved out of the estate into the home she rented. Her stomach twisted almost as much as it had the night she'd been sick. The idea India had was brilliant and would put her back in charge of Robidoux Holdings. She couldn't believe her sister was willing to go so far to help her out.

Elaina hated to admit it, but the idea of doing this was both exhilarating and frightening. Her dad wouldn't forgive her if she was successful. No matter how much she liked getting one up on him and proving she could be just as successful and shrewd as he was, she still yearned for his approval and acceptance. The ultimate mind trick that had plagued children for generations.

Sandra greeted her with a smile when she opened the door for Elaina. Surprise and satisfaction were bright in her eyes. "Ms. Robidoux, it's good to have you back."

Warmth spread through her at the housekeeper's greeting. Elaina reached over and squeezed Sandra's forearm. The woman who'd helped and covered for her while Elaina had lived at the estate was someone she would always have a soft spot for. "It's good to see you, too, Sandra. How's your family?"

Sandra blinked, and then her smile brightened. "They're great. My daughter just had a baby boy. My first grandkid. He's such a beautiful child."

"I'm sure he is. I can't wait to meet him. I'll be sure to send your daughter something."

Sandra waved a hand. "There's no need to do that."

"I want to." She squeezed her arm again. "Is everyone here?"

Sandra nodded. "They're all in the upstairs living area.

Dinner will be ready in a few minutes. Are you staying to eat?"

Elaina shrugged. "That's still up in the air."

She went up the stairs to the sitting room. The sound of conversation and laughter greeted her at the top. A wave of nostalgia hit her. She'd always taken these weekly dinners for granted and viewed them as a chore. So many months outside of the fold of her family and she hadn't known how much she'd starved for their presence until she was back here. She finally understood what Alex meant about wanting to be around family. Another pang hit her chest with her thoughts of him. She pushed that away. One problem at a time. Fix the family, then figure out what to do about Alex.

She walked into the familiar living area. Her dad and Byron stood by the minibar. India, Zoe, Patricia, and Lilah were on the leather couches. No one noticed her at first. They were all so engrossed in their conversations. Lilah looked up, and her eyes brightened.

"Auntie Elaina," she burst out. She jumped up from the couch and hurried across the room.

Elaina opened her arms and accepted the hug from her niece. At least one person was happy to see her. She glanced over Lilah's head to India, who smiled eagerly.

"Looks like I got here just in time," Elaina said.

Lilah bounced on her heels. "I'm glad you came. Momma said today was going to be a special dinner. Now I know why."

"Very special indeed," Elaina said.

They walked into the room. Lilah went back to the couch, and Elaina walked over to the bar. She met her dad's wary glance. "Hello, Daddy."

Grant eyed her for a second before nodding. "Elaina, I didn't expect you to join us."

"I've decided that it's time for me to start coming back to family dinner," she said. "I am a Robidoux."

His eyes narrowed. "You were the only one who seemed to turn their back on that fact."

She smiled sweetly. "Really? We're blaming that on me?"

India came over and stood next to Elaina. "To be honest, Daddy, it wasn't Elaina. You're the one who kicked her out."

Grant looked at India, then back at Elaina, suspicion clouding his gaze. "I didn't kick her out. Everything I did was for your own good."

"Including trying to ruin my new business venture after firing me?" Elaina asked. "How was that good for me?"

Grant shifted from one foot to the other. "You never should have tried to stray away from the family. You became a competitor. All is fair when it comes to business competition."

"You're right. All is fair," Elaina said. "Despite your efforts, I succeeded. I'm going to be profitable and successful all on my own."

Grant's jaw was tight, but there was admiration in his eyes. The spark of someone recognizing an opponent who wouldn't back down easily. "I told you I was proud of what you accomplished no matter what."

Elaina placed her hands on the bar. "I know you are. You can't help but admire perseverance. But the thing is, opening my facility isn't enough. I want more."

His head cocked to the side. "What do you want?"

She lifted her chin, called on the knowledge that this was what she deserved, and met her dad's gaze without blinking. "Robidoux Holdings."

Grant stared at her for a second, then laughed. "You can't be serious."

There was just enough worry along the edges of his laughter to make her even more determined. Grant had raised her to take over the company, to spot a weakness and take advantage. He knew more than anyone that if she wanted Robidoux Holdings, she'd find a way to get it.

"I'm completely serious," she said with a sweet smile. "The company is my legacy. I helped get it to where it is today. I'll admit I made mistakes, but I'm not the person you fired."

"You can't have it," Grant said simply. "I've hired a new CEO, and I like her. She's got a good steady head on her shoulders."

Elaina gave her dad a smug bless-your-heart smile. "You don't get it. I'm not talking about CEO. I mean full control."

"How do you plan to do that? You'd have to get majority ownership, and none of the shareholders are willing to sell to you."

India shifted closer to Elaina. "Which is why I'm giving her my shares."

Grant's eyes widened. "What?"

Byron got up from his bar stool and stood on Elaina's other side. "Along with mine."

Grant stumbled back. He looked at all three of his children as if they'd turned green and sprouted antennae. "What the hell is this about?"

Elaina couldn't keep the smug smile off her face. She, India and Byron had met and talked about the transfer. Grant owned the majority share; he'd split shares up between the children, so the family owned fifty percent and the rest was spread out among shareholders. India and Byron were proud of the company, but they'd never been as invested in it as Elaina. They'd all agreed giving their shares to Elaina, which made her share larger than Grant's, was the best way to give Elaina the company she'd given up so much for without putting her at the whims of their dad.

"It's about us working together," Elaina said smoothly.

"Working together to betray me?" Grant accused, though she was surprised there wasn't more animosity in his voice.

Byron placed his fist on the bar. "No, working together to make things right."

India placed a hand on Elaina's shoulder. "Elaina deserves the company, Daddy, and you know it. You've even said so. When you fought to keep her from opening her facility, it was because you wanted her to come back. Well, she's back."

Elaina crossed her arms. "And I don't have to return with your approval or by jumping through any new hoops you have for me."

"Your mom wouldn't approve of this," Grant said.

"I'm not Mom," Elaina said confidently. "I've tried too hard to be like her, but I don't want to be. I loved her, and I appreciate everything both of you did for me. But now, I have to live for me. No more making sacrifices just to live up to whatever image you think we should have. If you love me at all, you'd admit your attempts to help haven't. They've hurt. A lot." Elaina's voice cracked on the last word. India squeezed Elaina's shoulder. Byron placed a hand on her back. Elaina swallowed hard. She blinked away the tears in her eyes, strengthened by the support of her siblings. She never wanted to show her dad how much his actions had hurt her, but she wasn't going to hold back anymore. "Get mad all you want, but you owe me this much."

"We did what we thought was best," her dad said in a defensive voice.

"Then don't fight this. If you love me even a little, you'll let this happen and give me what you promised me the day you told me a whore wouldn't run your company."

Grant flinched. Her sister and brother gasped. Grant covered his face and shook his head. "I was upset. I didn't mean to say that."

"But you did," Elaina said evenly. "Now I'm saying this. I will run Robidoux Holdings, and I will do whatever the hell I want with my life. Your approval is not required." She hugged India and then Byron. When she looked at Travis, he nodded, and she nodded back.

Sandra knocked on the door. "Dinner is ready."

Elaina looked back at Grant and smiled with smug satisfaction. "Good. We can discuss your new role over dinner."

CHAPTER THIRTY-SEVEN

Alex was reviewing the class notes he planned to upload later that day when there was a knock on his office door. He glanced at the time in the lower right corner of his computer screen. The faculty meeting was scheduled to start in five minutes.

"I'm coming, Amber. Go ahead without me. That way we won't both be late," he said, not looking up.

Amber Geiger was another professor in the department. They'd struck up a friendship as she'd shown him the ropes of being a new faculty member. Alex had a sense she wanted their friendship to turn into something more. His brother-in-law Chris kept pushing him to ask her out for drinks. Alex had avoided saying he didn't want to get involved in another office romance after what happened with Elaina. Seeing Elaina the other week proved something he hadn't wanted to admit. He still loved her, and no one would easily fill her shoes.

"Sorry. Not Amber."

Alex's head jerked up. Elaina stood in the door of his office. He blinked several times just to make sure he wasn't seeing things. Dressed to the nines as usual, she looked radiant in a champagne silk top and dark slim-fitting slacks.

"Elaina?" He slowly turned his chair away from his computer to fully face the door.

"You're still wearing those ridiculous glasses," she said with a quirk of her full lips.

Alex unhooked the glasses and refastened them around his neck. His heart pounded. Blood rushed in his ears and to his dick with the memory of her admitting his glasses turned her on. The way she'd pull them off before straddling his lap.

He cleared his throat. He didn't know why she'd come to see him, but straddling his lap in his office was probably not the reason.

"What are you doing here?" The words came out sharper than he'd expected. He was still processing the shock of seeing her.

She stood straighter. "I wanted to see you. We didn't get to talk much at the opening the other day."

"You were busy."

"Did everything go okay at your parents' house? With the leak, I mean?"

He nodded. "Yeah. The rubber gasket in the toilet was bad. It overflowed and came through the ceiling. We got it fixed."

She smiled and nodded. "That's good. I hope no major damage."

"No damage." He shook his head. He couldn't believe they were talking about toilets. She was in front of him. In his office. Unexpectedly. "Why are you here?"

"Abrupt as usual," she said with a small smile.

"We haven't seen each other in months. We haven't talked. Now you suddenly show up."

Frustration bubbled in his midsection. Mostly frustration with himself. He was so damn happy she had popped up. He wanted to believe she was there to say she wanted him back. If those words came out of her mouth, he'd agree.

He'd jump back on the Elaina bandwagon faster than someone discovering a new fandom. Just like a new fan, he'd be all in. All Elaina all the time, and the thought scared him.

She'd broken up with him. She hadn't given him the chance to explain. She'd never even admitted she loved him after he'd said the words to her. Now he was going to take her back with just a few words? He was pathetic.

"I know it's unexpected," she said evenly. "I know I don't have a right to be here. I want to apologize."

"For what?"

"For jumping to conclusions. For being hard on you. For not trusting you." She paused and shifted from one foot to the other. "For breaking things off the way that I did."

"You said it yourself. We went in knowing things wouldn't last long." The two-minute warning for the faculty meeting popped up on his computer. Alex grabbed his notebook and stood. "I've got a meeting."

"I'm in charge of Robidoux Holdings now," she said.

That stopped him. "How?"

"India and Byron gave me their shares. I'm majority owner. Daddy was upset, but in the end, he didn't fight us. I think he knows he owes me."

So she'd found a way to outplay her dad again. Despite himself, he smiled. She deserved the company. He knew that now. "I'm glad that worked out. You've always wanted it."

She took a step into his office. "You see, that's the thing. I've got it, but I'm still not satisfied."

He met her eyes. "Why not?" He held his breath. As much as he hated how much he wanted to be the reason, he also wanted to hear it.

"Because I don't have you. I miss you, Alex." Her face

broke down, and he saw the same misery on her face he'd felt since the day they'd broken up. "I miss you so much."

He missed her so much it was a physical ache in his chest. He wanted to go around the desk and pull her into his arms. But was that enough? Could they make it? Missing him wasn't the same as loving and trusting him.

There was another knock on the door. "Alex, we're going to be late," Amber said. She smiled at him then looked to Elaina. "Sorry to interrupt." She didn't sound the least bit sorry.

Alex wanted to tell Amber to get out, but she was just the save he needed. He wanted time to process what Elaina said. He couldn't just take her back the second she said jump. "Coming." He looked at Elaina. "We can talk more about this later."

She looked ready to argue. He waited for her to argue. Waited to see if she'd insist they hammer this out now, the way she used to. "That's fair."

He swallowed the disappointment. What did he expect, for her to fight for his attention in front of Amber, a complete stranger? Elaina didn't break down or show her emotions in front of anyone. He grabbed a pen and walked around his desk.

Amber smiled and lifted a cup filled with candy. "I brought Hershey's like you like. I know it makes getting through these faculty meetings easier for both of us."

Alex walked out of the office after Elaina and Amber. "Thanks." He took the cup from Amber. He met Elaina's eyes. For a second he thought she was going to say something. Then she averted her gaze. "Goodbye, Elaina."

He turned away and headed down the hall. Amber followed, her arm brushing against his.

"I love you!"

Alex's world froze. For several heartbeats he forgot to breathe before sucking in air with a whoosh that made him feel light-headed. He spun back toward Elaina. "What?"

She cleared her throat and squared her shoulders. "I love you. I should have said it that day at the field, but I was scared. I understand if you don't love me anymore. I understand if you never want to take me back, but I had to say it at least once. That I love you, Alex. I'm sorry I hurt you." Her eyes glistened. She wiped them quickly, then turned away.

Alex didn't think. He dropped his notebook, rushed the few steps to reach her and spun her around. Her eyes widened as they met his. He pulled her into his arms and covered her mouth with his. His heart and body felt energized with the emotion coursing through his system. Elaina's arms wrapped around his neck. She pressed her body to his and kissed him back.

When he finally came up for air, tears streamed down her face. He brushed them aside and kissed her again.

"You're always so damn extra," he said with a laugh.

She let out a shaky laugh and hugged him tighter. "Does this mean you're taking me back?"

"Taking you back? Elaina, you never truly lost me." He pressed his forehead to hers. "I never stopped loving you."

The brightness of her smile made him want to shout with joy. "Then never let me go, because I promise I plan to hold on to you from now on."

He pulled her tighter against him. "I promise," he said with a kiss.

CHAPTER THIRTY-EIGHT

ELAINA WATCHED A tray of hors d'oeuvres go by and frowned. "Are those oysters?" She took a step to follow the passing waiter, but a hand grabbed her hand.

She stopped and looked back. Alex shook his head. A smile hovered on his full lips. "You're supposed to be enjoying the party. Not running it."

Elaina took a deep breath. Her dad was throwing yet another party to garner support for the neighborhood revitalization project. Since Elaina took over as majority shareholder and chair of the board, she'd made suggestions, but allowed her Aunt Elizabeth, who ran the philanthropic arm of Robidoux Holdings, handle the exact details. She'd also let her aunt oversee planning and hosting the party.

With one last glare at the oysters, she stepped back next to him. "Byron's allergic to oysters."

"And I'm sure Byron is old enough to know not to eat one." He pulled her against his side and kissed her temple. "Relax."

Despite her annoyance at the oyster sighting, she did relax into him. "I'm not used to sitting back during a family event."

"I know," Alex said. "I saw how hard you worked at that garden party a year ago. No one seemed to notice or step in to give you a break. I much prefer you by my side than watching you run around like a chicken with its head cut off."

Her eyes widened and she glared up at him. "I did not run around like that."

He lifted a shoulder. "I saw it. I know what you looked like."

Elaina rolled her eyes, but she still smiled. Stepping back from filling in as hostess for her family events had been a good thing, even if she was having a hard time letting go. She no longer wanted to be her mom or fill her mother's shoes. Letting go of the pressure to be everything her parents wanted and focusing on being what she wanted felt like she'd had a weight on her chest that was suddenly lifted away. Old habits were hard to break, but she had to admit she was much happier now that she'd let go and could breathe.

"I never realized how boring these parties were," Elaina said. She glanced around at the multiple people in the backyard. Byron and Zoe were across the lawn, talking to council members and potential campaign donors. India and Travis were gradually making their way toward the house, probably so they could sneak out and get back home to their daughter. Grant and Patricia were surrounded by a group of people who laughed at whatever story her dad told. Her eyes landed on her Aunt Elizabeth, who had been running from one end of the party to the other.

"What did you do before you were in charge of hosting?" Alex asked.

They hovered near the bar. Elaina sipped her club soda with lime and tried to remember. "I haven't not hosted a party since before my mom died." She though back to those days, and her cheeks heated. "You don't want to know."

Alex's eyes lit up. "Oh, I want to know."

She shook her head. "Back then I was testing my boundaries. Typically by sneaking off to get into trouble."

Alex moved behind her and wrapped an arm around her waist. He lowered his head and whispered in her ear. "What kind of trouble?"

She glanced around the party again. Things were under control, despite the oysters. For the first time, the freedom of not having to be in charge truly settled on her. "I'll show you."

She took his hand and led him through the crowd. They were stopped along the way. People congratulated her on the success of her facility. Others stopped Alex to mention they'd heard good things about his work at the university. It took forever, but eventually Elaina got him inside the house.

"Where are we going?" he asked.

"You wait and see." With his hand in hers, she made her way to the stairs.

Sandra's voice stopped her. "Ms. Elaina, your dad is looking for you."

Elaina's foot froze on the first step. She turned back to Sandra. "Tell Daddy to wait."

Sandra grinned and nodded. "I'll do that."

Elaina squeezed Alex's hand and hurried upstairs. Once they were behind the door of her old room, she stopped. Alex pulled her into his arms, and she let out a satisfied sigh. She loved being in his arms.

"Was this your usual place to sneak off to?"

She shook her head. "No. You're the first guy I've snuck up to my room. I've never trusted anyone else in here before."

When she was younger, half the thrill of sneaking off with Travis had been doing so in someplace exciting. Even then her room had been her personal sanctuary. She hadn't trusted anyone else in her space.

"This was where I was free to fantasize about happy endings without anyone seeing me."

She kicked off her shoes and sat on the bed. Alex sat next to her. "You don't mind me seeing you."

She threaded her hands with his. "Truth is, you've always seen me. That's why I didn't like you. You saw through my excuses and forced me to see what I didn't want to."

"I saw someone smart, strong, and infuriating at times. You drove me crazy, but mostly because I was also crazy about you."

Her brows drew together. "You can't be serious."

"I'm very serious. Even then I wanted you." He brushed a lock of hair behind her ear. "I still can't believe I'm lucky enough to be with you now."

He felt lucky to be with her. Not because of her name. Not because of her money. Not because he thought she would be anything else. "You really do love me for me. Despite my flaws."

"Not despite your flaws. Your flaws are a part of you, and Elaina, there isn't a single part of you that I want to change."

Love swelled in her chest. A year ago, she never would have guessed she would be this happy. This content with all aspects of her life. She was far from perfect, but she had more to love about herself than hate.

"I love you, too." The words were easier now. They were no longer a weakness or hindrance. Love for herself and with the right person was strength. She wished it hadn't taken so long for her to realize that.

"Nothing you'd change?" he asked with a raised brow.

"Well…there is one thing." When he frowned, she grinned. "For you to stop wearing those ridiculous glasses."

Alex laughed and reached into the pocket of his jacket. "And I just upgraded to ones that fold up nicely." He unrolled the glasses and snapped them on.

Desire sparked in Elaina's chest. Hotter than ever because love ignited the flame. She pushed him back on the bed. "That's it. Now I've got to teach you a lesson, professor," she said in the cool voice she'd used when they worked together.

Alex grinned, wrapped her in his arms, and rolled her beneath him. "Teach me."

* * * * *

Don't miss Foolish Hearts,
the next sexy and irresistible book in
Synithia Williams's Jackson Falls series
featuring the Robidoux family!

CHAPTER ONE

ASHIYA SCANNED THE numbers on her computer screen and grinned. Another profitable day for her consignment store, Piece Together. Another day that she'd kept the store she'd opened on a whim to avoid being considered a contender for best dramatic performance by a Robidoux family member. Another day she'd taken that whim and turned it from *"that little store,"* as her mom referred to it, and cemented Piece Together as *the* place to shop in Jackson Falls for quality, pre-owned designer clothes, with a healthy helping of fashion tips and perfect accessories on the side.

She shimmied her hips in the chair as she hit Enter to save the day's profit numbers in her bookkeeping software. Six years ago, when she'd decided to open her store, she hadn't believed she'd be here for this long. Honestly, she hadn't believed she would be able to make it work. She might have grown up in the mix of the Robidoux family with all their drama, fighting for control, and business acumen, but she'd never wanted any of that. She wanted to live life on her own terms with little interference from her family.

Piece Together was something she'd known her mother, cousins and uncle wouldn't care about. They'd let her "play around," and she'd get peace and quiet. Who knew she could actually run a business successfully?

A knock on the office door snapped her from her internal celebration. She glanced up from her computer to the door of her office in the back of the store. Lindsey, the store's assistant manager, stood there. She'd been one of the first people Ashiya hired to help run Piece Together when she'd opened. Lindsey, with her no-nonsense personality, straightforward style, and keen eye for fashion, had stayed by Ashiya's side through those early, lean years when Ashiya hadn't been sure the store would survive. Short, with a cute face and an upturned nose that reminded Ashiya of a pixie, Lindsey could easily pass for one of the college kids in town despite being thirty-one.

"Hey, I've finished straightening up the front of the store. How much longer will you be here?" Lindsey pulled back her normally brunette hair, which was now colored a soft pink, into a ponytail at the base of her neck.

They always tried to walk out together. Downtown Jackson Falls wasn't a dangerous town, but that didn't mean they liked to tempt fate. Their parking lot was behind the building and poorly lit, and after 8:00 p.m. served as the overflow parking for a few bars in the area. They preferred to be safe rather than sorry.

"I just finished up." Ashiya hit the Save button one more time just to be sure she cemented the success of the day. "I've got to get out of here anyway."

"Hot date?" Lindsey asked with a wiggle of her eyebrows.

Ashiya barely stopped herself from rolling her eyes. She couldn't remember the last time she'd had a hot date. Not since she finally came to her senses and told her on-again off-again boyfriend since college to get the hell out of her life. Every time she thought about the time and effort she'd wasted on that relationship, the good things she'd let pass her by, she wanted to slap herself. Whoever invented a time machine, she would pay them all six years' worth of Piece Together's profits for the chance to go back and tell twenty-two-year-old Ashiya that she should stay away from that manipulative asshole, and that good sex did not equal love.

She pushed aside thoughts of her wasted years and sighed. "No hot date. My cousin Elaina's celebrating her engagement." Ashiya powered down her computer and stood.

Lindsey crossed her arms and tilted her head to the side. "So she's really getting married, huh?"

Ashiya barely contained her chuckle at Lindsey's dubious tone. "She is, and I actually believe she's happy."

Lindsey raised her brows again. "Good for her."

"I know, right?" Ashiya said. "I'm happy for her. I hope this marriage works out better than her first one."

Lindsey crossed her heart, pressed her hands together as if in prayer, and lifted them to the sky. She wasn't overly religious, but Ashiya appreciated every bit of good vibes for a better relationship for her cousin. "I hope so, too. She can be…intense, but everyone deserves to be happy."

Ashiya crossed the small office, which was actually a former storage room that she'd converted, to the coat rack where she'd hung her purse. A black Louis Vuitton clutch she'd found at a thrift store in Charleston the year before and today had paired with a simple white T-shirt and a gauzy leopard print A-line skirt. She lived for finding deals like that.

"Now that she's engaged and happy," Ashiya said, putting the strap for the purse over one wrist, "she's also making an effort to hang out with the family more. Tonight is ladies' night to toast to her good fortune."

"Sounds like fun," Lindsey said with what sounded like forced enthusiasm.

Ashiya grinned. "It will be. I haven't gotten a chance to hang with my cousins in a while. I'm looking forward to it."

"I'm waiting for the day your family convinces you to quit running the store and start working at that huge corporation they own."

"I wouldn't abandon you like that." Ashiya flipped the lights off in her office.

"I wouldn't consider it abandonment. Just remember, if you ever decide to go and start making big deals instead of scouring thrift stores for premium goods, I'll understand and take over the store for you."

Ashiya wrapped an arm around Lindsey's shoulders as they walked toward the front of the store. "Not gonna happen, but if I ever change my mind, I know I'll be leaving this place in good hands."

They did one more check of the front before locking up the store. Ashiya knew Lindsey was teasing her, but her assistant manager also believed Ashiya should be using the skills she'd utilized make Piece Together successful toward a bigger payout working for her family's larger holding company. Ashiya appreciated her friend's support, but she wasn't about to deceive herself into thinking she was smart enough to run anything bigger than this store.

She and Lindsey said their goodbyes as they left the store and got into their cars. As always, Ashiya waited until Lindsey had driven off before easing her way out of the parking lot. She made a left out of the lot and eased into the late afternoon traffic toward the Jackson Falls country club for ladies' night.

Honestly, she wasn't sure how much fun this would be. She didn't dislike Elaina, who was remarkably more pleasant now that she'd taken over control of Robidoux Holdings and found happiness with herself and in her love life, but that didn't mean Ashiya immediately thought of Elaina when she wanted to go out and have fun. Thankfully, India, Elaina's younger sister, was going to be there as well. Ashiya refused to turn down any opportunity to hang out with her favorite cousin. Byron's wife, Zoe, would also be there. Ashiya liked Zoe well enough and believed she was the reason Elaina had agreed to the night out in the first place.

Ashiya was happy for all her cousins. They'd found love and were living their best lives. She, on the other hand, was single again for the first time since the age of twenty-two. She didn't know what to do about her relationship status. Well, she knew what and who she wanted, but she'd burned that bridge and there was no turning back.

She blasted the latest Megan Thee Stallion song on the radio to get her mind right for a night of fun, but her ringing phone interrupted the beat. A number she didn't recognize popped up on the car's console. She considered ignoring it, but once she'd ignored a call from an unknown number only for it to have been from her mom when she'd left her cell phone at home. Now Ashiya answered even if she didn't recognize the number.

Ashiya pressed the button on her steering wheel to accept the call. "Hello?"

"Hello, I'm trying to reach Ashiya Waters?" a woman's cool professional voice asked.

Ashiya rolled her eyes. Telemarketer. Hadn't she put her number on that list that told them to leave her the hell alone or something? "Sorry, I'm not interested."

"Ms. Waters, this is Brianna Simpson. I was the personal assistant for your grandmother, Gloria Waters," the woman said in a rushed voice before Ashiya could end the call.

Ashiya frowned at the screen. Her Grandmother Gloria?

Why would her grandmother's assistant call her? Ashiya hadn't had anything to do with her father's side of the family since they'd disowned him for marrying her mother. Resentment about her mother pursuing her father to gain access to his mother's then-growing beauty company went long and deep. Ashiya vividly remembered being eight or nine and overhearing her Grandmother Gloria telling Ashiya's mother that she wasn't going to get a red cent of anything that would have gone to her son.

Ashiya loved her father dearly, but knowing his family didn't want anything to do with her because of the original reason her mom had married him had hurt. She also loved her momma and couldn't see herself ever wanting to be close to someone who'd disrespected her mom like that. As she'd grown, and the animosity festering from her parents' unresolved issues infected Ashiya's life, she'd kind of understood her grandmother wanting to cut ties with something doomed to decay.

"Okay," she said slowly. "Why are you calling me?"

"Because your grandmother died two days ago." Brianna spoke in a direct manner with only the barest hint of sympathy.

Ashiya sucked in a breath. She squeezed the steering wheel. All her memories of the woman were of her telling her dad he never should have married that raggedy whore in the first place whenever they visited. Eventually the visits stopped. That didn't mean she'd wished her dead.

"I'm sorry to hear that," she said truthfully.

"I'm calling you because the reading of the will is this Friday." When Brianna spoke this time, her voice was warmer. "You'll need to be there."

"Why would I need to be there? I'm pretty sure I'm not listed."

Brianna cleared her throat. "Actually, you are."

The thought of being in her grandmother's will was so absurd, Ashiya laughed. Probably not appropriate after receiving news of a deceased relative, but she didn't believe anything her grandmother left for her required her to attend the reading of the will. "Okay, so she left me a clock, or my dad's high school clothes. Can't you just mail them to me? I don't have to show up for that."

There was a pause before Brianna spoke again. "You're getting a lot more than a clock. Ms. Waters, your grandmother left you her entire estate. You are now the majority shareholder of the Legacy Group. If you'd like to avoid having your cousins contest the will, I'd suggest you be here."

ASHIYA SAT IN her car in the Jackson Falls Country Club parking lot. She'd driven there on autopilot while listening to her late grandmother's personal assistant talk about everything she was expected to inherit. Not only the shares in the company, but a home in Hilton Head, South Carolina, multiple properties throughout the southeast, all her grandmother's money and worldly goods, and a vintage Jaguar.

The information whirled around in her head like clothes during the spin cycle of a washing machine. She didn't believe a word of it. She'd said as much while on the phone with Brianna. How could her grandmother's assistant know what Ashiya was getting if the will hadn't been read yet?

"I was with your grandmother when she made the changes with her lawyer and served as the notary. Believe me. You're getting it all."

Inheriting her grandmother's money made absolutely no sense. She hadn't seen her grandmother in years. Decades. Her grandmother hated when her dad married her mom and wanted to be sure to keep her mother from having access to even a penny of the money the company made. Ashiya always assumed her grandmother didn't want Ashiya to gain access to the company since Gloria Waters never made any attempt to reach out to Ashiya or form any type of relationship with her only grandchild. Now she was supposed to believe the company, money and property were all hers?

She had to get to the bottom of this. She couldn't go inside and celebrate with her cousins. She wouldn't be able to focus on anything. Yet she didn't want to outright snub Elaina.

Ashiya got out of the car and dialed India's number. Her cousin answered quickly. "Hey, are you here?"

"Umm…yeah, but I can't stay. Can you meet me at the front door? And don't tell Elaina."

"Sure, let me step away so I can hear you better," India said, not asking for more information. "I'll be right back," she said not quite into the phone. Ashiya assumed she spoke to Elaina and Zoe.

Ashiya arrived at the front of the clubhouse and slid through the door. India came around the corner at the same time. Her cousin slid her phone into the pocket of her pink sundress. Her curly hair was twisted into a cute puff at the top of her head, and worry clouded her brown eyes.

India immediately came over and placed a hand on Ashiya's arm. India was two years younger than Ashiya, but they were more like sisters than cousins. "What's going on?"

Ashiya let out a humorless laugh. Where would she even start? There were so many unanswered questions she was afraid to even try to begin to unravel.

"Something came up," she said. "I really need to go talk to mom and figure out what's going on."

India frowned. "Are you alright? Did my dad do something?"

Ashiya shook her head. "No. For once this doesn't have anything to do with your dad."

Ashiya paced from side to side. She wished her problem were tied to her Uncle Grant. Her mom knew how to handle him. Thankfully, because Ashiya was busy with her "little store," Grant Robidoux didn't pay her any attention. If her uncle had suddenly decided to meddle in her life, she'd know how to react. In fact, she'd rather have to deal with her overbearing uncle meddling than inheriting a fortune and the responsibility that came with it.

India reached out and took Ashiya's elbow in her hand, stopping her from pacing. A small line creased her brows. "Hey, tell me what happened."

Ashiya took a deep breath and met her cousin's worried expression. "My grandmother died."

India blinked. Her head drew back, and she frowned. "Your grandmother?" India's eyes narrowed as if the idea of Ashiya having a grandmother was unheard of before her head cocked to the side. "You mean your dad's mom?"

India's surprise by the announcement was further proof that what Brianna said on the phone made no sense. Ashiya had no ties or contact with her grandmother. There was no way the woman would leave Ashiya with all of this responsibility.

Ashiya sighed and shrugged. "The one and only."

The confusion left India's eyes, and sympathy filled them instead. "Oh, no, Ashiya, I'm sorry." India pulled Ashiya in for a hug.

Ashiya pulled back after a second in India's embrace. She didn't deserve it. Sure, she was saddened to hear about her grandmother's passing, but she wasn't devastated. She hadn't known the woman. And there came the guilt. A big, heavy weight in her chest. She didn't deserve sympathy and definitely didn't deserve money.

"Thank you, but I'm fine. Really, I am. I barely knew her, and according to my mom, she is…was evil."

India shook her head. "No one is completely evil. You told me yourself there was bad blood between her and your mom since your parents got married. There are always two sides. I'm sorry you didn't get the chance to hear her side."

Ashiya pressed a hand to her forehead. "You're right, I guess. But I got a call from her personal assistant. She wants me to come to Hilton Head for the reading of the will. She thinks my grandmother left everything to me."

India's eyes widened. "For real?"

"That's what she says, but I don't believe it. My grandmother hated Momma, and didn't like me. Why would she leave everything to me?"

"Maybe she didn't hate you and your mom as much as you think," India said in her very logical, let's-view-all-sides way.

"No, the hatred was real." She remembered the visits to her grandmother when she was young. The cold shoulder. The shouting behind closed doors. The names she'd called Ashiya's mom. Names like gold-digger, whore, two-faced witch. Names Ashiya hadn't understood the meaning of back then, but knew they couldn't be good.

She shook her head to rid her brain of the memories. "I can't believe it. I can't do it."

"Do what? Go to the funeral? I don't think it'll hurt just to pay your respects."

If only that's what she meant. She tugged on her ear and glanced around. No one was in the front of the clubhouse with them. "Take the company, the money, the estate," she said in a thin voice. "I don't know how to run anything."

India had leaned in to hear what Ashiya had to say. After Ashiya spoke, India grunted and leaned back. She gave Ashiya an are-you-kidding-me side-eye. "Ashiya, you run a business now."

"A small clothing store here in Jackson Falls. And not even new clothes. They're consignments. I can't run a corporation."

The thought of being in charge of million-dollar decisions, having to report to a board of directors, fighting for respect from people who'd spent their entire careers in the corporate world made her stomach twist in a dozen glass-encrusted knots. No, she couldn't do it. Wouldn't do it. They'd eat her alive in less than thirty seconds.

India rolled her eyes. "Girl, get out of your damn head. Before you start having a panic attack and telling yourself all the things you can't do, how about you first go find out what exactly you've inherited and what, if anything, you have to do about that?"

Ashiya took a deep breath. Her stomach still twisted. Her palms sweated, but India's words took the edge off of her anxiety. Until she knew for sure what was going on, there was no need to freak out. The freak-out could wait until she found out if Brianna was right.

Please, God, let Brianna be wrong. She sent up the quick prayer.

She met India's you've-got-this gaze. "You're right. I just never thought I'd be in this position. You know I never wanted to be a part of that world."

Understanding crossed India's features. India's desire to stay out of the running for top billing in the Robidoux family was one of the reasons she and Ashiya had been so close. That, and Ashiya, lonely and with no siblings, had mentally adopted her younger cousin as her sister from the moment India had given Ashiya her favorite teddy bear instead of laughing when she'd learned that at the age of eleven, Ashiya was still afraid of the dark and had nightmares in unfamiliar places.

"Not wanting to be a part of it and being able to survive it are two different things," India said in a supportive voice. "Regardless of what happens, I believe you can handle it."

Ashiya wished she had a tenth of her cousin's optimism. "Time will tell. Look, I need to talk to Momma about all this. See what she thinks and then make plans to go to Hilton Head. I guess I just needed to talk to someone first and get my initial freak-out over and done with. You know Momma. She'll tell me to calm down, act like a Robidoux and take everything my grandmother left and more."

At times Ashiya thought her momma forgot that Ashiya was half Waters. That even though her dad had generated his own wealth, he'd given up the wealth from his family when he'd married her. Elizabeth Robidoux Waters had not known her husband was aware that he wouldn't inherit a thing if he married her. She also hadn't forgiven him once she learned the truth. He'd only wanted to be happy, and despite her parents' strained marriage, her dad had found his own way without the help of his mom or his wife's rich family. He was why Ashiya had tried to avoid being as cutthroat as some of her Robidoux cousins.

India nodded and patted Ashiya on the shoulder. "Go. I'll tell Elaina that something came up. She'll be fine."

Ashiya reached into her purse and pulled out a card. "Give this to her, okay? I know she didn't want gifts, but I still thought I'd get her something. Tell her to enjoy it."

Ashiya had gotten Elaina a yearlong subscription to a tea-of-the-month club. Since her cousin was cutting back on alcohol, she'd focused on using tea to calm her nerves.

Ashiya hoped the gift would be welcome from the prickly Elaina.

"I will. You go. Talk to your mom and call me before you head out of town. If you need me to go with you—"

"No, I'll be fine. I may need drinks when I return."

"I've got you." This time when India opened her arms for a hug, Ashiya took it. She'd need all the emotional support she could muster if this were true.

They pulled apart, and Ashiya watched as India went back toward the dining area. With a determined sigh, she went to the door out of the clubhouse. She wasn't looking forward to this conversation with her mom, but she couldn't possibly go to the funeral and learn the contents of the will without saying something to her mom.

She pushed open the door to the clubhouse at the same time someone pulled from the other side. She lost her balance and stumbled forward on her high heels. She barely stopped herself from falling forward. A warm hand reached out and steadied her by the elbow.

"Excuse me."

"Sorry," a familiar male voice said at the same time.

Ashiya froze. The blood rushed from her face, and her lungs decided breathing wasn't necessary at that moment. Her eyes jerked up. Surprise, embarrassment and regret sent her body into a confusing tailspin. Russell seemed just as surprised to see her. Her heart squeezed while the lingering touch of his hand on her elbow turned her limbs into jelly.

Russell. The guy she should have chosen, Russell. Fine as hell, Russell. He would be the person she saw right now when she was already discombobulated.

Fine as hell was a weak string of words to describe Russell Gilchrist. Tall, broad of shoulders, thick of thighs, and sweet of heart, Russell was the perfect embodiment of good guy with just a hint of bad boy beneath to make a woman fantasize about seeing him lose control. The lights from outside the clubhouse added a silvery glow to his sandy-brown skin and brought out the gold in his hazel eyes. He'd offered her everything she'd said she'd wanted in a relationship, and in turn she'd broken his heart when the asshole came back and said all the right words with wrong intentions.

After recognition entered his gaze, he quickly snatched his hand back. "You good?" His voice had lost the concern from before he'd recognized her. Instead it was cold, clipped, as if he couldn't wait to get away from her.

"I'm fine. I was in a rush and didn't—"

"Then I'll let you get going." He stepped out of the way so she could walk away.

Ashiya sucked in a breath. Three years had passed, yet she still couldn't get used to seeing the cold look in his eye. He'd barely looked her in the eye or spoken to her in a tone warmer than an Antarctic winter in years. But she'd seen his other side. She'd seen the adoration shining in his eyes. Heard the way he whispered her name when he was deep inside of her. Knew he could be the most caring person she'd ever met. Knowing that only made this side of him hard as hell to accept.

"Russell, I…"

"I'll see you around." He walked around her and entered the clubhouse without another glance her way.

Heat spread through her cheeks. She looked to the sky and groaned. No matter what she said or did, she couldn't break his silent treatment. Not that she could blame him. She'd toyed with him. Used him to make her ex jealous, and by the time she realized she was falling for Russell, it was too late.

She wanted to rush back into the clubhouse and demand that he talk to her. That he let her explain. That he give her, *them*, another chance. Instead, she sighed and walked to her car. Getting Russell back was still on her bucket list, but she couldn't focus on that particular goal at the moment. Right now, she had to figure out how to get rid of a million-dollar inheritance.

* * * * *

Don't miss what happens next in...
Foolish Hearts
By Synithia Williams.

Available soon wherever
HQN books and ebooks are sold.
www.Harlequin.com

ACKNOWLEDGMENTS

Writing a novel never gets easier, because I want to give my readers the best story possible. Although getting words on the page is all on me, I couldn't do that without the support and encouragement of my friends, family and the awesome HQN team. Starting with my husband, who never complained when I got up at five in the morning to finish this novel. My friend Cheris Hodges, who brainstormed hemp production and all the ways Grant Robidoux is similar to Victor Newman with me. Then there are my editors, Michele and Errin, whose encouraging feedback helped me believe I'd done a good job telling Elaina's story. Each one of you supported me getting those words on the page. Finally, I want to thank my readers. You all are amazing! I appreciate you for picking up each and every book, going along for the ride, and giving the next book a try. From the bottom of my heart, thank you!

SPECIAL EXCERPT FROM

( ) **HARLEQUIN**

DESIRE

*One passionate Vegas night finds bourbon executive
Zora Abbott married to her friend Dallas Hamilton. To protect
their reputations after their tipsy vows go viral, they agree to
stay married for one year. But their fake marriage is realer
and hotter than they could've imagined!*

Read on for a sneak peek at
Waking Up Married
by Reese Ryan.

"Dallas, can I see your hand?" Zora pointed to his left han
hanging at his side.

He looked at her strangely but complied. That, apparently, w
when he first saw it, too. "Is that a—"

"Wedding band?" Zora stepped closer on wobbly legs, bar
able to get the words out of her mouth. "It is. And this—" Z
held up her hand and showed it to her friend "—appears to be
match."

Dallas's eyes widened, and he slapped a palm over his gap
mouth for a moment.

"Dallas, these aren't cheap trinkets." She pointed to his ri
"I'm almost sure those are real diamonds set in platinum."

Her friend stared at his hand again, blinking, but not sayin
word.

"My phone is charging now, but I need to check my credit cards. ll of them. I have several bags in my room from a bridal shop. I ink we honestly might've gotten—"

"Married." Dallas's voice was hoarse. He waved a piece of paper at he'd picked up off the dresser. "According to this document, e are now Mr. and Mrs. Dallas Matthew Hamilton."

Don't miss what happens next in...
Waking Up Married
by Reese Ryan,
part of the Bourbon Brothers series!

Available March 2021 wherever
Harlequin Desire books and ebooks are sold.

Harlequin.com